CHRISTMAS EVERY DAY

BETH MORAN

Boldwood

First published in Great Britain in 2019 by Boldwood Books Ltd.

A CIP catalogue record for this book is available from the British Library.

Paperback ISBN 978-1-83889-318-7

Ebook ISBN 978-1-83889-316-3

Kindle ISBN 978-1-83889-317-0

Audio CD ISBN 978-1-83889-319-4

MP3 CD ISBN 978-1-83889-360-6

Digital audio download ISBN 978-1-83889-315-6

Boldwood Books Ltd
23 Bowerdean Street
London SW6 3TN
www.boldwoodbooks.com

For Dominic, who loves to laugh

PROLOGUE

It was finally here. The highlight of the Dougal and Duff calendar. Everyone would be there, from the lowliest admin assistant to the senior partners. The oak bannisters were draped with ivy, dotted with twinkling red and white fairy lights. The doorway leading into the designated party room was framed with pine branches, a cheeky sprig of mistletoe hanging in the centre. Inside, the room looked even more spectacular than last year. Hundreds of sparkling snowflakes dangled from the wood-panelled ceiling, more fairy lights and greenery adorned every surface. The Christmas tree in the centre of the back wall stood festooned with baubles and ribbons.

Waiting staff slipped between the clusters of office cliques with trays of champagne and crumbly canapés, their black uniforms in sharp contrast to the glittering party dresses and tartan finery. A swing quartet thrummed, but it couldn't beat the buzz of festive gossip. Rumours had been flying that the newest partner, Richard Abernethy, freshly returned from yet another victory in the Paris office, had been dropping hints about an important announcement. And when a locally renowned jeweller delivered a ring-shaped box to Reception that morning, every one of the sixty-three employees knew within minutes. The only question was who. Nobody had a clue.

That was, except me.

The other PAs assumed I must have some insight to the mystery woman, given that I'd almost unlimited access to his emails and diary. They spent most of the evening trying to badger me into giving them a name. Or at least a list of suspects.

I smoothed down my ridiculously expensive dress, patted my hair, took another fake-nonchalant swig of champagne and said nothing.

Not because of loyalty to my boss. Although that would have been reason enough.

Taut with nerves, heart fluttering, resisting the urge to wash the dryness from my mouth with another drink, I not so surreptitiously watched my secret boyfriend and soon to be fiancé from across the room and wished he'd hurry up and get on with it.

I had always dreaded Christmas. Particularly these last few years when it had simply been another day alone, opening the same gift card sent by my dad and watching someone else's television. Waiting to hear from Richard, despite him telling me that he'd probably not get a moment to call.

But this year – surely I'd be spending it on his family's estate in the Highlands? I had already planned the clothes I would pack, and spent a frantic afternoon searching for the perfect 'last-minute' gifts for his parents and younger brother.

For the first time, in so long that it made my heart ache just thinking about it, I would be spending Christmas with a loving, happy family.

I took a deep breath, smothered my smile and, for the millionth time that day, silently practised my surprised, thrilled and senior-partner's wife worthy 'yes'.

1

When the house had been described as like something out of a fairy tale, I'd been picturing Snow White's cottage, or a quaint gingerbread house (minus the evil witch, whom I'd left behind in Edinburgh), not a shrunken, grottier version of Sleeping Beauty's derelict outhouse. And, in my storybook, there hadn't been an old pram, two sagging armchairs and a turquoise toilet blocking the driveway.

I peered through the taxi window, trying to kid myself it would look better once I was out of the car. Or it had stopped raining. Or if I took my glasses off. The driver pulled up in front of a rusted mangle.

'Could you get any closer to the door?' I asked, tugging the zip a bit higher on my jacket.

He swivelled his head to look at me, one eyebrow raised.

'What about parking on the lawn?'

'That ain't a lawn. It's a jungle. I ain't risking my tyres on that.'

I blew out a sigh, and unbuckled the seat belt.

'Fifty pound.

What?' My hand froze halfway to my purse. 'We agreed thirty.'

'That was before the ford, the mud pit and the overgrown branches scratching my paintwork. The car needs a full-on valet and the extra won't even cover it. I've got standards to uphold.'

I cast my eyes around the faded upholstery, scuffed trimmings and air freshener designed as a topless woman.

'You knew the address was on an unnamed road in the middle of a forest and you still said thirty.' I tried to keep the tremble out of my voice. The extra twenty pounds might not pay for a car valet but it would help me not starve for the next couple of weeks.

'I'm the only taxi-driver round 'ere who'll come out this far.' He grinned. The big bad wolf. 'I'm the only taxi full stop. If you want out of 'ere any time soon, best stay in my good books.' He tipped his head towards the house. 'And, trust me, you won't be wanting to 'ang around.

'Are you threatening me?' I did my best to channel some of the experience I'd gained working for sharks who'd sell your own baby back to you, and straightened my shoulders. After enduring a lifetime of being treated like a worthless wimp, this was supposed to be a fresh start. The new, improved, over-it, Jenny.

I opened my purse, and deliberately placed three notes on the plastic ledge between the front and back seats. 'I'm giving you the thirty pounds *you asked for*, and not a penny more.'

He curled up one side of his lip, leant towards me and growled. 'Are you sure about that?'

Letting out a squeak, I unclasped my purse again. 'And a tip! Of course. Here. I'll make it twenty.' Yanking open the door, I tumbled out into the freezing January rain, slipping and sliding round to the car boot. Hauling out my suitcase, followed by a rucksack, I stumbled out of the way just in time to avoid injury, but not a generous splattering of filthy spray from the revving wheels.

Wiping a smear of mud off my glasses with a sodden sleeve, I stared at my new home.

A semi-detached old woodsman's cottage; the grey plaster frontage streaked with grime, slumped chimney and patchy roof confirmed it hadn't worn the years well.

I squelched through the puddles, rucksack on my back, hand-me-down Mulberry suitcase dragging behind, and peered in through the ivy-smothered front window. Rummaging in my jacket pocket for the key, I gave up attempting to make out shapes in the gloom beyond.

'Right. Might as well get it over with. Get out of this rain and put the kettle on.' I wiped the worst of the dirt from the keyhole, congratulating myself for having had the foresight to have the utilities reconnected before I arrived, and forced the key in, slowly wiggling it until it unlocked.

I pushed against the door. Nothing. Not even a rattle.

Turning the key back to the original position, I tried again. As water ran in icy rivulets down my face and up my sleeves, I did everything I could to make the door budge. Pounding, shoulder-barging, kicking, taking a slippery running charge like the cops in films.

After a while, determined not to start crying, I dumped my luggage and precariously stepped along the front of the house to see if I could get around the back. No good. More bushes, the rain dripping off two-inch thorns. I glanced over at the adjoining cottage. There none of the windows were cracked and the garden didn't look as though it had been abandoned by a rag-and-bone man. Hmm. Maybe I could sleep in there instead. Just for tonight. According to my mother, the whole building had lain empty for years. There wasn't much demand for cottages in the middle of nowhere, unless done up as holiday lets, and no one wanted to holiday next door to a scrapheap.

I cautiously moved closer, trying to peek beyond the closed blinds, before looking through the letterbox, but the approaching dusk made it too dark to see. I tramped along a brick path around to the back; here things appeared much the same. A wooden picnic bench sat forlornly on a patch of weed-riddled gravel about six feet square. Beyond that, my half of the building was nearly hidden where the forest had encroached right up to the house in a twist of branches and brambles. I might be able to squeeze through to the back door. I should at least *attempt* to squeeze through to the back door.

But then again, it would probably rip my jeans, and this was the only pair that fitted. And if I scratched my face, it would be harder to find a job, and then how could I survive here? I probably didn't even have any phone reception, so I couldn't call anyone if I tripped on a stray root and impaled myself on the thorns. I quickly checked my phone (not wondering *even for a second* whether Richard had been trying to send me any grovelling messages admitting it was all a terrible mistake). See! No signal. It would be reckless and foolish to force my way into that tangle of spikes.

I shuddered. Glancing at the shadows looming around me, I imagined the kinds of animals that prowled Sherwood Forest once darkness fell. They'd find my broken body, drawn to fresh meat by the scent of blood leaking from a thousand puncture wounds. I wouldn't stand a chance.

And even if I could call that taxi bloke for help, he probably wouldn't come.

If only there were a dry, empty, nearby dwelling-place for me to take refuge in! Just to get me through the night, until the rain stopped. I stood, hesitant, and pondered whether I had the guts to go for it.

I didn't ponder for long. I was too cold, wet, muddy, hungry and bone-shatteringly tired to care about the law. If I got arrested at least I'd have a dry place to sleep and, hopefully, some breakfast.

I hurried over to the cottage, said a quick prayer and tried the door. Locked. Taking a deep breath, I grabbed a stone and bashed it through the door's frosted window.

Preparing to carefully poke my hand through the hole, I nearly severed my wrist when a pair of arms grabbed me from behind. Pulling me away from the door, the arms wrestled me over to the picnic table and pushed me down face first until my top half lay in the pool of water collecting on the surface.

'What the hell do you think you're doing?' The man held me down with a hand on each shoulder, preventing me from seeing him. Okay, so with my eyes closed and glasses fallen off I wouldn't have been able to anyway, but still. His voice sounded rough, and strong, and mad as hell.

I gasped, sucking in half a mouthful of rainwater from the tabletop, which I proceeded to choke on. As a frankly hideous retching sound emerged from my throat, the man quickly let go. 'Woah. If you're going to throw up, at least do it in the bushes, not on my bench.'

I heaved myself upright, and twisted around, one hand gripping the table, trying to stop my brain racing long enough to catch hold of a useful thought.

'*Your* bench?'

'Yes. *My* bench. *My* broken pane of glass. *My* house. So, to repeat, what are *you* doing here?'

'But nobody lives here,' I managed to rasp. 'The house is abandoned.'

'Does it *look* abandoned?' he asked, his voice getting louder.

'Can't see. Glasses.' I felt around on the table in vain until he grunted in exasperation and bent down, before thrusting the rain-smeared glasses into my hand. I clutched them for a few raggedy breaths, a little scared to put them on and see the face matching that furious voice. It looked as bad as I had feared. Thick, dark eyebrows over eyes black with anger. And behind a bristling beard, a mouth twisted in disgust.

I glanced at the house, fear shoved aside as temper sparked, my constant bodyguard these days. 'Yes. It does. No lights on. All overgrown. No car outside. And I was *told* nobody lived here.'

'And who told you that?' He folded his arms.

'My mother. The previous owner of the other house.'

'The owner died six years ago.'

'Yes. So the house went to her daughter. My mother. And, as of last week, it belongs to me. Hence I have a key.' I pulled the key out of my pocket and waved it at him.

'If you have a key, what are you doing smashing my window?'

'I couldn't get the door open.'

He raised his eyebrows, waiting for more.

'So, I came around the back. But I couldn't get to the door. And it's nearly dark, everything I'm wearing is sopping wet. And the taxi driver stole my money...' I took a long, deep breath. I would not cry in front of this man. I had vowed never to let a man think I was a pushover again. *Come on, Jenny, buck up.*

'Tezza's Taxis?'

I nodded, wiping a raindrop off my nose.

He sighed. 'The front door won't open from the outside. I'll hack a path to the back and you can at least get out of the rain. Call round in the morning and I'll give you the name of a decent taxi firm before you go.'

'Go where?'

'Back to wherever you came from.'

I gaped at him for a moment, vaguely registering that the rain had begun to ease, the background percussion replaced with the slow plop of water dripping off leaves, and the hiss of steam escaping both my ears.

'I'm not going anywhere. I live here now.'

He looked me up and down. 'Trust me. You'll be leaving in the morning. If you last that long.' He nodded towards a brick outbuilding tucked under an oak tree. 'I'll get hacking. But if the rain starts again I'm stopping to board up my window.'

'Actually, it's fine. Thank you. I can do my own hacking. I apologise about your window. Do send me the bill. Good day.'

I marched as best I could back around the house, only losing my shoe once in the mud.

'Okay, Fairy Godmother. I reckon right about now would be a perfect time for you to show up.' I scanned the woods, struggling to make out anything in the deepening gloom. After a good ten minutes pulling branches aside, stamping them out of the way and ripping my hands to shreds in the process, I found a shed.

It took only a few tries to smash the wood, encircling the

lock, to bits using a thick branch and the force of my anger. Nicely warmed up, somewhat exhilarated by my discovery, I stepped inside. Maybe a teensy bit unnerved by my neighbour's comments about only lasting a night, I decided to put off investigating the house until morning. In front of me appeared to be an excellent place to unroll my sleeping bag and seek a very welcome oblivion.

2

I awoke to the sound of scuffling. Something brushed against my cheek. Even with my eyes closed, I could sense the presence of something *other*. Fumbling for my glasses, I heard another scratching, skittering noise. Blood pounding in my skull, I carefully put my glasses on, and snapped my eyes open.

Aaaarghh!

Rat!

Rats!

MORE RATS!

It was not easy to scramble away from a swarm of giant, rabid, red-eyed rats while locked inside a Mini Cooper. Some flailing, screeching, howling and a lot of garbled gibberish accompanied my desperate attempt to find the unlock button, push past the rat on the seat next to me, fall out onto the concrete shed floor, entangle myself in a sea of cobwebs, trip over my suitcase, fling open the shed door, fight my way through the bushes that had magically sprung back during the night, rip out a sizeable chunk of hair on a branch, and collapse on the frozen earth.

Three seconds later a rat sprinted four inches past my face and disappeared into the shadows.

Thirty seconds later, I was still wheezing like broken bagpipes when my world turned dark as something loomed in front of me, blocking out the early morning sun.

And no prizes for guessing what – or who – that was, considering there were only two human beings to be found for several square miles.

I couldn't see his face, having lost my glasses once more, but could hear his irritation. 'Do you need help?'

I pulled myself upright, tugging down the three jumpers I'd worn to avoid freezing to death while sleeping in a car. Smoothing my hair off my face, I dislodged a twig, a couple of oak leaves and a massive beetle. Summoning up my last reserves of strength, I managed not to squeal again, merely gasping like a fish a few times while shaking my head to check nothing else lurked up there.

'I'm fine, thank you. I... slipped in a puddle. I couldn't see it, because I'd lost my glasses.'

As I finished speaking, he handed them to me for the second time.

Placing them firmly on my nose, I straightened my spine, daring him to disbelieve me.

'You lost your glasses walking out of a shed?'

I stared right into his eyes, which looked chocolate brown in the wintry sunlight. 'Yes.'

'You slept in *there*?'

'That's my business.'

Shaking his head slightly, he began to walk away. 'That's great. I don't want to know your business. I've got better things to do than come to your rescue every five minutes. How about next time you fall over, you do it a bit more quietly?'

'Next time, how about ignoring me? I didn't ask you to come to my rescue.'

'Fine. That's a deal. You're obviously perfectly capable of taking care of yourself.'

'Yes. I am. What made you think I wasn't? The fact I have breasts and long hair means I need taking care of?' I shouted after him.

He turned, frowning. 'I can't say I'd noticed. But you're right. People lose their glasses and slip in dry puddles while walking out of sheds all the time. *Good day.*'

I watched him stride away, non-existent retorts dissolving in my throat. Turning around to confirm that, yep, all trace of last night's puddles had dried up in the sunshine, I brushed a straggle of cobweb off my jeans and prepared to re-enter the shed to get my bags.

It was only later that I registered that the man had worn no shoes and carried a cricket bat. He really *had* been coming to save me. No, thanks. The whole reason I was here was to prove to my family, my ex-work colleagues, the slime-ball Richard, and mostly myself that I could take care of myself. Which I would start doing that very day. Once I'd found somewhere to empty my bladder and get a decent cup of coffee.

* * *

The car didn't leave much room in the shed for anything else but hung up around the walls were some gardening tools, various other pieces of worn-out clutter and an ancient-looking black bike. As I had no key for the car (thankfully I had found it unlocked, avoiding the need to break another window) I decided the bike would be the best way to reach civilisation before I died from caffeine withdrawal.

To my great relief, despite the oil, rust and flabby tyres, the bike was still rideable. I creaked along, feeling like a community nurse from the nineteen fifties, following the frosty track back towards the lane and eventually the village beyond. After a few minutes, I spied a footpath leading off the track and into the forest, with a signpost pointing to Middlebeck, two miles away.

Heaving the handlebars around, I followed the dirt path. Initially, it felt quite pleasant lumbering along between the trees. The only sounds were the cheeping of birds, or the whistle of the wind in the evergreens. The forest floor was still thick with autumn leaves – every colour from pale yellow through coppers and purples to rich mahogany. There were holly bushes laden with berries, fat and glistening in the pale sunlight. A robin hopped along the bushes beside me for a while.

I tossed my hair in defiance at my new neighbour's prediction that I'd be leaving so soon. This was great. I'd grab a coffee, wander around the village, ask in a few shops about any work... Maybe a coffee shop – or, no, a *tea room* – would need a waitress. I could sort the cottage out in my spare time, get to know some of the locals, find the key to the Mini. Everything was going to turn out splendidly.

If I could only reach Middlebeck, which was seeming more and more unlikely as the last remains of air squished out of my back tyre, and I was now bumping and wobbling along on the rims of the wheels, probably soon to be overtaken by the snail I'd passed earlier. Clambering off, I propped the bike against a large oak tree and continued on foot, sure I must have covered two miles, and the village would appear just around the next corner.

Three corners later, I saw a gate up ahead. And – was it a mirage caused by fifteen hours without caffeine, or could I smell freshly ground coffee?

Hurrying through the gate, I emerged into a large clearing. It offered space to park twenty cars or so, several picnic tables, a large noticeboard displaying a map and, to my joy and relief, a brick building with a sign that read 'The Common Café' *and* a loo.

I took a few minutes to wash my face and dab at the worst of the grot on my clothes with a paper towel. Hot water – bliss! I then scanned the chalk-board menu displayed beside a hatch designed to serve customers eating outside.

'What can I get you?' the young woman on the other side of the hatch asked.

I ordered a large Americano and a mega-breakfast cob. I wasn't sure what a cob was, but I needed the mega.

'Were you here for New Year?' The woman stepped back to throw a sausage onto a griddle.

'No. I've just moved here.'

She twisted back around to look at me, a streaky slice of bacon dangling from her fingers. 'Middlebeck? I didn't hear anyone new'd moved in.'

Wow. Mum had warned me it was a place where everybody knew everything about everybody else. How small was the village? Was *this clearing* Middlebeck?

'No. A cottage in the forest.'

She glanced over my shoulder at the footpath I'd approached from, cracking two eggs onto the griddle one-handed. 'Charlotte Meadows' place? Mack never said. But then, he wouldn't.'

I nodded vaguely, pretending to be engrossed in taking the lid off my coffee-cup and clicking it on again. Not sure whether to feel pleased, upset or embarrassed that a stranger in a café window had just told me my grandmother's name.

'You must like a challenge, taking that on.' She grabbed the biggest bread roll I'd ever seen and deftly placed the bacon, sausage and eggs inside, adding a slice of beef tomato and another of cheese, followed by a squirt of ketchup.

'Thanks.' I swapped the mega-breakfast cob for a handful of coins, and took a moment to figure out how to eat it.

'You met Mack?'

'Mmm?' I said, around a mouthful of salty bacon and a burst of sweet tomato. With a loud gurgle, my shrivelled stomach declared this a meal better than any I'd tasted in Edinburgh's fanciest restaurants.

'Bit of a mystery man, isn't he? But, hey, living so close, maybe you'll crack that rough exterior. Succeed where every single woman round here failed.' She leant on the counter, gazing off into the distance. 'You could start by borrowing his tools, asking him to steady the ladder while you paint the ceiling, or help carry out the old oven. Get to know each other a bit better, if you know what I mean.'

'Urr... I'm not looking to know anyone a bit better.'

'Oh.' She stood up again, and briskly began flicking crumbs off the counter with her cloth. 'I'll leave you to your breakfast, then.'

'No. I didn't mean you. I meant, not any men. Not like that.' She pursed her lips, still flicking. I panicked, having seemingly offended the first person I'd met beside the neighbour – Mack – with whom I wasn't exactly off to a good start. 'I'd like to get to know you better.'

She raised one eyebrow. 'Oh? Is that what you tell all the girls?'

'Yes. No! I mean, I don't know anyone here yet. It'd be nice to make some friends.'

'Really?' She stared over my shoulder, wisely dismissing me as the social freak I had revealed myself to be. *Help, Jenny! This woman seems to know everyone. Pull it back, or the whole village'll hear you're bonkers and no one will give you a job. She wants to talk about men. Give her something! Think of some girls' talk.*

'I've just come out of a bad break-up.' I spoke louder than necessary, trying to regain her attention. 'It was pretty hideous. Broken heart, betrayed by a close relative, publicly humiliated, blah blah blah. So, I'm off men for at least a decade. Including my neighbour. Mack, you said? Is that an actual name?'

She looked back at me, widening her eyes to near circles. Was it working? I was far from fluent in Girl. *Keep going, Jenny!*

'I know! I suppose he's not bad-looking, underneath the scowling, and the chauvinistic, wild-man-of-the-woods vibe. But I'm not interested in getting to know any men. Even if they do have eyes like a steamy mug of hot chocolate. So, if Mack likes to keep himself to himself, we'll be perfect neighbours.'

'Good to know.' An unmistakeable growl came from behind me.

I froze, holding up the mega-cob I'd been using to emphasise the point, like a ventriloquist's puppet. Okay, so the round eyes and strange look were Girl for 'Shut up! The man you are simultaneously complimenting and insulting, but in both cases discussing like a hunk of meat, is right behind you!'

'All right, Mack?' the woman said, cheeks flaming.

I inched around, trying to cover my face with my purchases. Keeping my eyes firmly on the ground so all I saw was a pair of tatty running shoes, I scuttled off. How much did he hear? At the edge of the trees, I glanced back to see Mack, dressed in running gear, being asked if he wanted his usual order.

'No, thanks, Sarah. I suddenly feel in the mood for hot chocolate.'

Ugh.

Breakfast eaten, perched on a tree stump, my humiliation dissolving in the glow of sunshine, I wheeled the bike back to the cottage with renewed vigour, itching to get inside and away from Mack as soon as possible. A search of my shed revealed a small hacksaw, about ten inches long and not even that rusty, so I got straight to work.

Two hours later, after I'd hacked, chopped, grappled with and stomped on a few of the thinner branches, the blade snapped. I hunted through the shed again, but the only other thing I could find that would be of the slightest use was a spade. Maybe I could *dig* a path to the door? It was only a few metres. And that would save time in the long run, as this way the bushes wouldn't grow back. *Excellent plan, Jenny! Everything is turning out awesomely.*

Two hours after that, as I wrestled a small bush out of the ground, having dug a hole big enough to bury myself in, a prospect more appealing with every aching movement, Mack's back door opened. I quickly picked up the spade again, putting all my fake attention on digging.

'Tunnelling your way in?' He stood there, in a grey hoodie and faded jeans, the trainers swapped for thick socks. I ignored how the muscles in his forearms flexed as he leant on the doorframe and crossed his arms. Not interested.

'Surprised to see me still here?' I said, trying not to grunt while attacking another root.

His beard twitched. I think that might have been a smile. 'You haven't been inside yet.'

Something burned hot in my stomach. 'I'm not a quitter.' Not any more.

'Would you like a hand?'

'Why, because the quicker I'm in, the quicker I'll be gone? No, thanks. I can manage.'

Really, Jenny, are you sure about that? Do you want all the blisters on your hand to merge together into one giant, festering sore?

'How about borrowing my saw?'

'If I dig the plants out, it'll save me having to do it later.'

Accept the saw, you stupid, stubborn goat!

'Maybe. But at this rate you'll be sleeping in the shed again.' His eyes glittered with humour.

I said nothing, an internal battle raging between my current loathing of all men and my need to get to the blasted back door before dark.

'I'm fine.' *Och, Jenny. This man is not Richard. Stop acting like a cow.* 'Thank you.'

'Your choice.' He nodded, once, and went back inside. It was only then I wondered if he was trying to laugh with, not at, me.

I thought about the rats' eyes, gleaming in the shadows, and promised myself I'd not stop digging until I was in the darn cottage. An hour later, I broke my promise. Exhausted, hungry, fingers numb with cold, feeling slightly deranged at the stress of my predicament, I walked the forty-five minutes through the woods back to the café, just in time to find Sarah closing up. She topped up my bottle of water and, after I drained it in one, refilled it. I also bought a banana and a slab of chocolate, eating them both on the way back.

I returned to find a huge, shiny saw propped up against one of the bushes, which looked decidedly less bushy than when I'd left. Glancing up at the ominous clouds now rolling in across the late afternoon sky, I swallowed the last piece of chocolate, along with my pride, and picked up the saw.

The blade snapped off on the second to last branch. But, as the first drops of sleet began to fall, I had no energy left to worry about that just then. Squeezing my way through the remaining spikes, I finally entered my new home.

3

Wheezing and gasping, I very quickly stepped out again. I could almost feel Mack laughing through the walls. Gritting my teeth, I leant back around the door and felt for a light switch. As soon as the lights clicked on, I ducked back out, waiting for the scrabbling sounds to die down as whatever lived in there scrambled for cover. I kicked and banged the door a few times, giving them all one last chance to disappear, took a deep breath of bracing forest air, and strode into the centre of what I supposed must be the kitchen.

The grandmother I'd heard nothing about until a few weeks ago – Charlotte Meadows – had passed away six years earlier. Mum only found out when the lawyers had tracked her down months later to inform her she'd inherited the cottage. Driven by guilt, shame and regret, she'd fled on a journey – both geographical, emotional and, it would seem, spiritual – with a final destination about as far from the self-serving socialite she'd been as it was possible to get.

So, I'd expected the cottage to need a clean. To have a few mice, spiders, maybe even a bat or two. I knew the roof might be missing a few tiles and was fully prepared to throw on a lick of paint. But, seriously, how bad could a house get in six years?

One look told me this house's problems had started a long time before that. The sink, table, worktops, dresser and most of the floor were covered in stuff. Pots, pans, plates, mugs and other kitchen items. Also, three metal buckets, books, radios, a guitar-case, dozens of empty bottles and piles and piles of junk. I picked my way over to the fridge, opening the door to release a blast of mouldy air that made my eyes water and throat seize up. Slamming it shut, I pulled my jacket collar up over my mouth and nose, and turned towards the oven. The hob was buried under more rubbish, but one glance inside and I had to retreat to the garden and retch a few times.

Sneaking over to the outside tap sticking out of Mack's house, I took a long drink before splashing more water over my face. I desperately needed a shower, but had a feeling that wouldn't be happening any time soon.

The rest of the house turned out to be in much the same state. Every room jam-packed with stuff, only a narrow passage through the hoard leading between the kitchen and the living room, through to what I assumed had once been a dining room, and then to a tiny cloak-room. I didn't think the toilet had been flushed since the last user, six years ago. More retching, more water, more deep breaths and wondering how on earth my life had come to this. On the upstairs landing I found three bedrooms, providing sleeping-quarters for yet more varieties of animal life in amongst the clutter. Another door revealed the boiler and shelves of sheets and blankets. I wrapped a musty pillow case around my nose and mouth before opening the final door into what had to be the bathroom.

Oh, my goodness.

My knees buckled.

There was dust, yes, stirred up into clouds of motes shimmering in the evening sunset glowing through the enormous window. A faint hint of mildew, the odd green fleck of verdigris on the copper taps. But stepping into that bathroom was like entering an alternate universe, where things were clean and spacious and white and clean and welcoming and lovely and ... just *clean*. Had I died and gone to bathroom heaven? Or was the reality of the bathroom so reeking it'd knocked me unconscious, triggering a hallucinogenic dream?

Either way, I didn't care. I crossed the wooden floor, leaving footprints in the dust, and peered into the roll-top bath. Nothing a quick swipe with a cloth wouldn't sort out. I opened the window, sat on the closed toilet seat and wept.

I slept in the bath, wrapped up in my sleeping bag. It was marginally more comfortable than the Mini. The shower that had preceded it had been the best thirty minutes of my new life. Too tired for the gnawing in my stomach to bother me, I'd locked the bathroom door to keep out my assorted housemates, and slept for twelve hours straight.

The following day, I headed back towards the village, stretching the kinks from my neck and shoulders as I walked. Bypassing the café, I carried on along a road for another quarter of a mile or so into Middlebeck. After a few big old houses, interspersed with higgledy-piggledy cottages, I arrived at the green, an area of grass circling a pond, surrounded by the village amenities. These consisted of a pub, a quaint little church and village hall, a row of shops, and Middlebeck Primary School. The shops included a general store, bakery, hairdresser, post office and a Chinese take-away. Not bursting with potential job opportunities, then, but I only needed one.

I went to the store first, loading a basket with the barest essentials of cleaning supplies, heavy-duty rubbish sacks, an electric kettle, and various food items that needed no cooking and minimal crockery: cheese slices, crackers and bread, fruit, tins of tuna and some packets of instant pasta. A box of teabags. Counting up the dwindling notes in my purse, I then added a puncture repair kit. I also chucked in a free newspaper claiming to contain over seventy job ads.

I asked in every shop about work, as well as the pub. People were polite, but firm. I'd be better off trying Mansfield or Nottingham. Wandering back to The Common Café, I wasted the last of my change on one final coffee, and sat in the crisp sunshine to search the paper with a breakfast of apple and cheese. There were one or two jobs that seemed possible, until I considered the cost of travel, and the timings, and the fact that I would rather starve to death in amongst Charlotte Meadows' hoard than ask my previous employer for a reference.

I decided the best thing to do was finish my final ever coffee while admiring the view, enjoy the birds soaring overhead and not think at all about the swanky flat where I'd use to live, the swanky law firm where I'd worked as a personal assistant, the swanky lawyer who I'd assisted a little too personally, or my swanky sister, who'd been the reason I'd moved to Scotland, and the reason I left.

While I was busy not thinking about Zara, or Richard, or

Zara *and* Richard, more to the point, a queue began to form at the café hatch. It was a Saturday, and a mix of families, ramblers with walking sticks, and dog owners were all either lining up or milling about waiting. After five minutes or so, noticing the queue hadn't moved along at all, I walked over to see what was happening.

As I approached the building, the door burst open, releasing a small child brandishing a handful of chocolate bars and an egg-whisk, closely followed by Sarah. The boy ran past me squealing, and instinctively I reached out and scooped him up. After freezing for a moment in shock, he began beating me with the whisk, screaming while his minute yet surprisingly hard feet kicked against my hip.

Sarah, wild-eyed and red-faced, pulled up in front of us. 'Edison, pack it in!' she commanded.

Edison thrashed and bucked. I adjusted my grip, ducking to avoid a whisk in my eye. 'Shall I put him down?'

Sarah blew a strand of pale pink hair off one eye, and reached out her arms. 'I'll take him. He gets like this sometimes. It's not right, a four-year-old stuck in a café with boiling oil, sharp knives and shelves full of sweets. A few minutes to calm down'll sort him.' She grimaced as he stopped struggling, his cries settling into big, jerking sobs. 'The problem is, that lot won't wait a few minutes, and neither will them burgers on the grill.'

'I can help,' I said.

Sarah lifted her head up. 'Are you sure? I can't pay you or anything.'

'How about a mug of soup and another coffee?'

She closed her eyes, shoulders dropping six inches. 'The pinnies are in the drawer by the sink.'

* * *

An hour later, I sat at a bench sipping my soup watching
Edison cavort about the Common with a group of boys. The
Common, I had picked up, was the actual name for this clearing, which explained the café's name. These new boys were
triplets, judging by the identical copper-brown hair in
various states of disarray and three pairs of slanted blue eyes.
Watching them play together felt like a designer stiletto
stomping on my bruised heart.

The triplets had arrived with a woman and a man, along
with a slightly older girl and a boy around eleven, now
building a den with fallen branches. It didn't take much
earwigging to deduce that this was all one family. I felt overwhelmed just watching them.

Once the den stood complete, the younger boys tossed
their pretend swords away and scampered inside. They called
for their mum to join them, and she persuaded the little girl
to go in as well. Once the whole family – and Edison – had
squeezed in, the man's head nearly poking out at the top,
somebody requested a photograph. The woman beckoned
me over, saying, 'Excuse me, would you mind?' and handed
me her phone.

Holding the screen up, I took a moment to focus on this
gaggle of smiling, windswept faces. The older children,
slender like their father, with the same flyaway blond hair.
The mother, beaming as she wrapped strong arms around
her wriggling triplets. Edison crouching in front of them.
Somebody made a joke at the very second I clicked,
capturing the moment the family collapsed into laughter,
knocking the den over in the process.

At that point, the oldest boy burst into angry tears,

shouting and kicking at the fallen sticks. Illusion of perfect family bliss shattered, the man bent down to speak with him while the mum hurried over to retrieve her phone.

'It's gorgeous,' I said, showing her. 'You have a wonderful family.' The stiletto stabbed me once again.

She grinned. 'Thanks. They keep me busy, but days like today make it all worth it.' She tipped her head on one side. 'Are you a friend of Sarah's?'

I made a wilful effort to slam the lid on the ugly box of memories that watching this family had opened in my brain. 'I hope so. A new friend, anyway. I moved here a couple of days ago.'

'Oh! Charlotte Meadows' old place. I heard about that. You're not afraid of hard work, then.'

I shrugged. 'No. Unfortunately I am afraid of spiders, rats, mice and bacterial poisoning. I'm just hoping that somewhere in there a lovely cottage is hiding.'

At that point, two of the triplets rushed up and threw themselves at her, one on each leg. 'Mum! Mum! Can we have a cake 'cos Dad says if you say we can then we can 'cos Dawson won't stop crying 'cos he hates the Common and wants to go home.'

'Hang on, boys. I'm talking.' She began untangling them from her skirt. 'I'd better go. Nice to meet you, though. I'm Ellen Cameron.'

'Jenny.'

'Bye, Jenny. I'm sure we'll see you around.'

* * *

Sarah gave Edison a packet of mini crackers to eat while we cleaned up.

'Thanks again. It's a nightmare having to bring him to work. I don't know what's worse, risking him running off into the woods, or cooping him up within spitting distance of a scalding chip pan.' She scrubbed harder at the griddle. 'I could *kill* Sean.'

'Who?'

'Sean. His dad. I would never say this in front of Edison, but he's a total dud. Usually my mum helps out, but she's gallivanting round the world on a cruise.'

'And Sean was supposed to watch him?'

'Yeah, but of course he cancelled last minute, like a typical dud.'

'Did he have a good reason?'

'That depends if you think hanging out at the bookies is a good reason to ditch your only child. Or going out getting bevvied. Maybe he was too busy slobbing in bed. *Waster.*'

'Are you together?'

'Do *I* look like a dud?'

We reached a deal. I would help Sarah out on Saturdays for the next three months, in return for free coffee and all the mega-cobs I could eat. I knew that probably translated as less than minimum wage, but right then having a friend and proving myself useful felt priceless. And hopefully by the time Sarah's mum returned I could eat in my kitchen without risk of catching a deadly disease.

4

I settled into something of a routine over the next few days. Sleeping in a bath was not ideal, even one as luxurious as the one that the bathroom had been endowed with. The growing crick in my neck pushed me to brave clearing out a bedroom. I picked the smallest, on the basis that it had the least stuff to get rid of, and the least foul stench, but even my plan to simply relocate most of the contents and sort them later proved pointless. The rest of the house was so chock-a-block that I soon ran out of places to move them to.

Some things I could easily bag up and put outside in the 'complete rubbish' pile. Others I was more unsure of. With no one yet phoning me up out of the blue and offering me a job – which was how I'd got my previous, and only so far, employment – I felt all too aware of my empty pockets. Anything that could be sold, would be.

Afraid of unknowingly throwing out a priceless antique – or a cheap bit of tat that might fetch a couple of quid online – I held onto most of the bedroom's treasure, squishing it between random gaps in the stacks. So far, I'd sorted: half a dozen lamps, about four million wooden coat hangers, eleven plastic bags stuffed with other plastic bags, crates of assorted glass containers, piles of mouldy linen and a complete shop mannequin.

I dressed the mannequin in a moth-eaten paisley dressing gown to preserve her modesty and found a spot for her at the end of the hallway. I called her Diana. Besides Sarah, on my twice-daily trips for coffee, and then soup or a jacket potato (it turned out my capacity for unlimited mega-cobs was pretty limited, so Sarah kindly agreed to broaden the scope of my pay), Diana was the only person I had spoken to in four days. There were plenty of mice, woodlice, spiders and moths to shriek, swear and hiss at, but they weren't *people*. Despite my self-imposed solitude, I could still tell the difference, and Diana *almost* counted.

Mack had disappeared back into his non-abandoned side of the house. Fine by me.

I received no messages from the world beyond the forest. This shouldn't have surprised me. I had always been a hanger-on, a shadow, firstly in my family, then more recently in the elite world of Dougal and Duff. And, given how things had ended, I could hardly blame my colleagues for not staying in touch.

And as for Zara and her shiny new fiancé, Richard the Richest. Well. They had made their choice. I tried not to compare what they had chosen to my current situation. Especially not when picking the mould off cheese while sitting on a toilet lid, as this was the cleanest, most hygienic seat in my new home. I didn't at all imagine them dining at the fancy restaurants he'd taken me to, sipping one-hundred-pound bottles of wine and slurping oysters. Barely crossed my mind.

Eventually, the room was empty, save for a large pine

wardrobe and a bed. I kept the iron bed-frame, but dragged the mattress through the hoard-tunnel and into the garden with the rest of the irredeemable rubbish. To my joy and amazement, one of the eight vacuum cleaners scattered throughout the house actually worked. I ripped up the carpet and took down the curtains, then vacuumed every surface before sucking all the dead insects out of the wardrobe.

After scrubbing every surface raw, I left the room to air and decided to celebrate by cycling into Middlebeck to stock up on supplies. Maybe I would happen upon a brand-new mattress discarded by the side of the road, still in its cellophane packaging. Or a washing machine. Or a fridge – oh, imagine it, a lovely, shiny, clean fridge! With a little freezer section at the top!

As lost as I was in this daydream, it took me a good quarter of a mile of pumping through the trees before I realised the bike was moving a lot faster than usual. Had my ham-fisted attempt at patching up the punctures mysteriously started working four days later? Or had all the exercise, humping furniture, carrying boxes downstairs, finally kicked in?

Stopping at the Common, I checked out the tyres. The fat, rock-solid, unworn, brand-new tyres. I wiped my glasses on my top and looked again.

Either my fairy godmother had paid a visit, or somebody, no doubt after watching me huffing and straining, red-faced and sweaty, through the forest, had taken it upon themselves to replace my tyres. I *so* wanted to be furious. This was my independent, fend-for-myself, need-no-one-and-trust-nobody new start. And who even knew about the bike? I always left it tucked behind the café. Either a stranger had been spying on me, then snuck over to the cottage and found the bike in the shed before risking the switch. Or else, someone who wasn't quite a stranger, who knew where the bike was kept, had done it.

Mack had fitted brand-new tyres on the bike.

I now owed him a window, a saw and two tyres.

I wondered if he'd take two hundred thousand coat hangers in payment. Or a lawnmower with no motor.

I let out a laugh and pedalled on, unfortunately coming across no household appliances along the way. Wondering if I should invest in a padlock now that anyone making off with the bike stood a decent chance of a getaway, I propped it beside the store entrance and hurried around the aisles, sweeping items into my basket. I had rapidly become an expert on what food a person without a kitchen should buy. No to the cheese, yes to the dehydrated soup and noodles that only needed boiling water to be transformed into, and I quote the packet, 'a delicious, heart-warming and nutritious meal'.

I thought about the juniper and burnt-butter hare I'd eaten in a private dining room overlooking the river Forth – and before I knew it, I found myself next door in the bakery, buying a cream tea.

Sitting by the window, I nursed a lukewarm cup of tea and pretended I didn't regret spending a stupid proportion of my remaining pennies on a grey scone covered in strawberry syrup that I felt too depressed to eat. As I prepared to take the plunge, the door to the bakery burst open and Ellen, who I'd met in the forest, came hurtling through, her three youngest boys swarming round her skirts.

She skidded to a stop at the counter, dumping several bulging carrier bags on the cheap carpet. 'Bread, please!' she barked, plucking one boy off the nearest table. Another one squeezed behind a display of home-made chutneys (they didn't say they were home-made, but you could tell, and I don't mean that in a good way), causing the tower of jars to rattle dangerously. The third triplet dived under his mum's skirt, lifting it up and pointing two fingers in the universally acknowledged gun shape at his brother.

'Excuse me?' the woman behind the counter asked, furrowing her brow. The boys drowned out Ellen's reply with their chorus of pows, bangs and explosions. The one she'd lifted off the table struggled as he tried to turn upside down and pull his mum's skirt up higher.

Ellen pointed to a loaf of sagging French bread, before calling out, 'CEASEFIRE!'

The boys instantly froze. A split second later they all scurried towards a table and sat down. Ellen then asked for six doughnuts to go. By the time the shop assistant had slowly picked up the items with her pastry tongs and put them on a sheet of paper, folded a box out of cardboard, lined it with a doily, carefully placed the doughnuts inside, managed to close the box and add a sticker to keep it shut, worked out six times sixty-five pence, then started the sum again including the price of the bread, the ceasefire had ended.

Ellen, flicking the curls out of her eyes, grabbed the shopping bags and ordered her children to fall in line. 'Soldiers! Qui-i-ck ... *march!*' They wouldn't have won any parade medals. As they wriggled, jostled and argued about whose turn it was to go at the front of the line, Ellen herded them towards the door. She paused by my seat, dropping one of the bags.

'Jenny! Great to see you again.'

Was it? 'Hi.'

She looked at the scone. 'Aren't you eating that?'

I pushed my glasses back up my nose. 'Um. No.'

'Brilliant. I'm having an unexpected-in-laws-for-dinner emergency and I've not eaten all day.' She grabbed the top of my scone and crammed half of it in her mouth, crumbs spraying everywhere. Grimacing, briefly, she then winked, mouth bulging, before resuming the march out of the bakery. '*Hup*, two, three, four. Come on, troops, what comes after four?'

I sat and watched her line up the boys to cross the empty road. But, as they stepped off the pavement, one of them attempted to go AWOL, his little legs powering down the road. Dropping the bags, which bounced off the edge of the kerb, Ellen snatched up the other boys' hands and raced after him.

While she shooed the absconder to the safety of the grass verge, I hurried outside to retrieve the shopping. As I scrambled after the contents, now rolling across the street, a familiar-looking taxi careened out of a side road and headed straight towards me. I scrabbled to get out of the way, but as the car veered to avoid a collision it ran right over two of the bags, the contents of which exploded in a shower of cream, eggs, passata and what smelt like vinegar. Nice.

I flicked the globules from my hair, smeared the cream off my face and wondered if it would be okay to eat it.

Tezza wound down his window. 'Are you a complete idiot? Standing in the main road, waggling yer backside at unsuspecting drivers? If it warn't fer me superior road skills I'd've hit one of them kids.'

'Excuse me?'

'If that shopping has messed up me paintwork I'll be sending you the bill,' he sneered before screeching off. Ellen bustled over. The boys, bouncing alongside, made no attempt to hide their peals of laughter.

'I'm sorry. I didn't manage to save most of it.'

'*You're* sorry?' Ellen shrieked. 'What if you'd been hit by that maniac? Dinner with Will's parents is not worth risking serious injury or death for.'

I shrugged.

She screwed up her nose and peered at me. 'Are you always this recklessly selfless?'

'I've been sat in the bakery for twenty minutes and the only traffic was a mobility scooter. It wasn't quite as fast as Tezza.'

She nodded. 'Fair point. Let's get you home and cleaned up. And you can save me from eating the remaining three doughnuts.'

I accepted her proffered packet of baby wipes and stole a glance at the triplets. Felt the bruise on my heart tremble. 'Thanks, but I'm fine. You've enough on your plate.'

I took a step back towards the bakery, to retrieve my own shopping. 'I hope your dinner goes okay.' Flicking a blob of sauce off my hand, I pulled open the door.

'Please come.'

'What?' Turning back, I saw Ellen still standing there, clutching at the ruined bags.

'I'm begging you. No. Not quite begging. *Strongly inviting* you to come and have a decent cup of tea and a doughnut with me, while I decide how I'm going to salvage my family dinner.'

I couldn't help glancing around, sure she couldn't be talking to me.

'Please?' She bit her lip, and I realised to my surprise the invitation hadn't come from pity. 'It's not going to be very nice cycling home in soggy jeans.'

I wiggled my hips, assessing the damage. 'All right.'

She beamed. 'Hurrah! I haven't had a proper conversation with an adult – other than my husband – in at least a week. I've been buried in prep for my new course.' She gestured at herself. 'Can you believe it? I'm finally going to university! *Me!* Anyway, I'm not sure I can handle any more questions about man-traps or medical mycology this afternoon.'

We began walking along the main street, the triplets hopping and climbing walls and spinning along the wide pavement.

'Sounds like an interesting university course.'

'Eh?'

'Man-traps and mycology. I'm trying to figure out what the course is. If I knew what mycology meant, that'd help.'

'Oh!' She grinned. 'No. That's the kids' questions. I'm training to be a midwife. A whole lot of different questions. Although I did have a boyfriend once who considered pregnancy a man-trap.'

We followed the boys down a gravel driveway to the Victorian house at the end.

'It's a life-long dream, and after giving birth to five kids I think I'll be a flippin' good one. But I haven't exactly worked out how we're going to manage it yet.'

After shooing the boys inside, Ellen led me through a tiled hallway full of coats and shoes into the kitchen. A battered oak table stood in the centre. An enormous oven, two solid dressers and rows of open shelving filled the walls.

'Sit down. I'll put the kettle on.' Ellen brushed a pile of crumbs off one of the chairs, and I perched on the end, trying to make sure none of the food remains on my jeans rubbed off. She kicked a path through the toys to the back door, letting the triplets into the garden, and dashed about chucking dirty pots into the Belfast sink before rummaging in an enormous freezer. She put a plastic tub in the microwave to defrost, poured the tea and offered me a doughnut.

'You have a lovely house,' I said, admiring the walls covered in children's artwork, the pots of herbs lined up on the counter-top and the brightly coloured window seat.

'It used to be. Lately it feels like the chaos is winning.'

'Chaos?' I laughed. 'You want to see my cottage. Actually, you probably don't.'

'Is it that bad?'

'Worse. Chaos and mess I can live with. Filth and animal infestations have been more of a challenge. I don't know whether to be worried or pleased about not gagging at the stench any more.'

'Are you sure it's safe to live there?'

'Right now, I don't have any other options.'

'Where were you before?'

'Living with my sister in Edinburgh.'

'So why tackle the cottage now? It's been empty for years.'

I shrugged. 'I needed to move on. When my mum offered me the cottage it seemed like the perfect answer.'

Before Ellen could ask me anything else, the door burst open and Dawson and his sister ran down the hall, Dawson elbowing his way in front as they approached.

'She's lying! I didn't do it, she pushed me first. And then she called me a brain-dead cyberwimp who doesn't even know the genetic code for E. coli. And Austin says he won't walk home with me any more if she's there, even if he is my cousin, cos she didn't shut up the *whole way* about bacteria and micro-things.'

'Not true! *He's* lying! He threw my bag over the hedge, and made me give him my crisps. He said he'd tell Austin I wet my pants in the car if I didn't.'

Dawson interrupted her. 'LIAR!' They carried on arguing at full speed, voices growing louder.

Ellen stood up, pushing back her chair, and placed one hand on each child's arm. 'Excuse me?' Her voice was quiet, but by golly it sent shivers down my spine. 'I think we'd better start again.'

* * *

After another ten minutes of he-said, she-did, Ellen wangled an insincere apology from both the children, and they stomped off to other parts of the house. She stood there, hands tugging at her hair. 'Sorry. Dawson walking Maddie home from drama club was supposed to solve one of my childcare headaches. It's a five-minute walk with no roads to cross, but Dawson is anxious about me not being around so much and he's resisting responsibility. I don't blame him. *I'm* anxious about it. In a couple of weeks the course properly kicks in, and the nanny I'd hired has taken an au pair job in California with an only child and a swimming pool instead.'

The back door crashed open and three stick-brandishing four-year-olds came hollering through, knocking over a chair, stepping on the cat's tail and leaving a trail of mud and leaves behind them.

'I can`t imagine why.' Ellen shook her head, righted the chair and glanced at her watch. 'Oh boy.' She eyeballed the mess, the uncooked dinner, the mud. 'It`s days like this I wish I had a wife. Sorry, Jenny, I don`t mean to be rude, but I really need to press on. Do you mind if we chat while I get things sorted?'

The sounds of battle wafted in from the hallway, followed by a loud thud, a high-pitched scream and a wail. Ellen closed her eyes and sucked in a juddery breath.

'I`ll see what`s happened. You carry on with dinner.' Before realising what I`d said, I was following the sobs to where Maddie stood in a bedroom doorway, clutching the broken pieces of what had once been a microscope. Her brothers were nowhere to be seen.

I pointed at one of the doors, questioningly. Maddie shook her head, extending one trembling finger to the door behind me. Opening it up, I entered an empty room. Empty apart from three pairs of muddy feet poking out from beneath the curtains.

I summoned up my best impression of Zara facing an opponent`s client. 'Which one of you broke Maddie`s microscope, and why are you hiding here instead of out there telling her how sorry you are?'

Silence.

'Believe me, it`ll be a lot nicer if you make a voluntary confession.'

'Jonno did it.' Two voices chorused from behind the curtains. 'I did it.' Another voice, raspy with emotion, echoed them.

'Right.' I pulled back the curtains to reveal three very contrite little boys, holding hands and wondering what on earth this scary lady was going to do. 'Who`s Jonno?'

I`m not quite sure how it happened, but I bundled the triplets – or as I now knew, Jonno (with the freckles), Billy (with the curls tumbling well past his ears ``cos he`s scared the scissors will chop off his head') and Hamish (with a front tooth missing from falling out of a tree) – into the shower, out again and into some clean clothes. I managed to re-connect Maddie`s microscope, and gather up the pieces of glass from the shattered specimen slides. I cheered her up with a promise of some bacteria-riddled samples of dirt from my cottage, and even coerced the four of them into tidying up some of their toys while I wiped the mud from the stairs and hallway.

It took the best part of two hours, but by the time Will returned home, Ellen had dinner in the oven, a reasonably clean kitchen, a nicely laid dining-room table and five children playing Uno with an utterly exhausted stand-in childminder.

I cycled home through the frosty evening with a tub of chicken casserole tucked into my rucksack. I'd have to eat it lukewarm, but, compared to another pot of rehydrated pasta, it'd taste like manna.

5

The following day, while I was washing my clothes in the bath, someone knocked on the back door. Quickly glancing in the mirror, I confirmed that, yes, I did have a bright red face, hair like a bottle-brush and my top – the only one not being washed – had a split shoulder seam, revealing my most ancient of bras. Shooting off a quick prayer that it wasn't Mack (for pride's sake, nothing more!) I wiped my hands on my pyjama bottoms (again, the only thing clean after yesterday's hit and run) and scrambled down the stairs before whoever it was decided to let themselves into the Hoard. An unheard-of practice in my previous life. Here, in the land where everybody knew your name, shoe size and bowel habits, I wasn't taking any chances.

And a good thing I did. The door had already begun to open by the time I grabbed hold of it, firmly placing myself between the visitor`s line of vision and the inside.

'Jenny?'

'Ellen!' I hovered in the crack, not sure how to keep her

on the doorstep without being rude. 'What are you doing here? I mean. I didn`t mean it like that. It was a genuine question. You`re my first visitor.'

'Are you free for a chat?'

'I, well, I`m cleaning. Hence the old clothes.' I laughed, awkwardly. 'Shall we sit outside, away from the mess? We can use Mack`s picnic-table. Um, would you like a drink?'

'Yes please. I have to pick the kids up in a bit, but tea would be lovely.'

'I haven`t any milk. Or sugar.'

'That`s fine.' Ellen smiled. 'I have five children. A hot drink supped undisturbed is my idea of heaven.'

'Right. Back in a minute.' I dodged through the tunnels up to the clean bedroom, where I now kept the kettle, hastily re-scrubbing out two of the mugs I`d previously sterilised, just in case something had crawled/landed/died in them since. Clattering back outside, I set them on the picnic bench.

'Marvellous.' Ellen closed her eyes and took a sip. 'Do you always wear shoes with pyjamas?'

'Until I`ve got rid of the mice, I wear shoes the whole time except for in the shower or bath. I mean bed. Well, bath or bed. Either. Both! I almost made it sound like I sleep in the bath! Hah!'

She smiled at me, unperturbed. 'I wanted to say thanks again for helping me out yesterday.'

'No problem. I enjoyed it. I hope dinner went okay.'

'It was hideous, but no amount of preparation could have altered that. Anyway, I`m glad you enjoyed it. Because I`m wondering if you`d consider looking after the kids more often. Like, four days a week. For an hour in the morning, and two or three after school. Term-time only.' She looked at me, expectantly.

'Oh! Right. Well, I am quite busy with the cottage, but I don't mind helping out I suppose, until I manage to get a job...' Was that what happened here? You did someone a favour and they expect it four days a week, term time only? I mean, Ellen was really nice. Her kids were funny, and interesting, and I genuinely liked them. But they were also mentally and physically exhausting.

Ellen sat forward, her eyes wide. 'I meant *as* a job, Jenny. What, did you think I was scrounging babysitting? I know Sarah isn't paying, but I think with my troop you'll be earning more than a chicken dinner.'

'You want to give me a job? Taking care of your kids?'

'Yes.'

'But I don't have any childcare qualifications or experience of how families work.'

Ellen frowned. 'That's not a problem. My gut tells me you're a good woman. I need someone to work for me, and you need work. No-one, apart from me or Will, has got Jonno, Hamish and Billy in the shower before. Dawson told me you played three games of Uno, without anyone throwing the cards in anyone else's face. Even I haven't managed that. And if you'll risk a hit-and-run to save my shopping, I'm guessing I can trust you with my kids.'

'They were just behaving themselves for a stranger.'

'No. They *loved* you. Maddie can't wait to tell you about the sample of *Aureobasidium* she found in a crack in the basement steps. And Billy thinks you would make an excellent general. Better than William Slim.'

I ducked my head. 'Things got kind of awkward with my last employment. They won't provide a good reference.'

'What about from an earlier job?'

'I haven't had any other jobs.'

'Okay, Jenny. If we`re being honest ... Most people find my kids too much. They find Maddie too strange, and Dawson too emotional. The triplets – well. One babysitter said it was like taking care of three piglets, only with fake swords and better aim. Children can tell if someone likes them or not. I`d rather have someone who likes them, than fancy qualifications and a great reference. If you explained why you left your job, would that help?'

I wanted to – I wanted to snatch the offer before she could see sense. I so, so wanted to be a part of this warm, crazy family. To sit in their sunny kitchen, with a coffee machine. Curl up with a story-book in the rocking-chair, children snuggled under my arm. I wanted to soak up the love, and the noise, and the life. It was everything I`d never had, and always dreamt of. But I couldn`t do it. I couldn`t take another job I didn`t deserve.

I put down my cup, straightened my glasses and tried to look Ellen in the eye. 'I really appreciate the offer. I`m amazed to even be considered. But I can`t work for you like this. I could be a child-murderer, or a confidence-trickster. A thief.'

'Are you any of those things?'

'No.'

'Well, I`m sure we can work out something sensible. Will`s a headteacher. He isn`t going to let someone loose on his precious offspring lightly.'

Ellen left a short while later, having agreed the something sensible to be two character references, what sounded like umpteen background checks and a thorough interview with Will over dinner followed by a trial period of a week.

I could find two people who weren`t relatives to provide

character references, couldn`t I? *Sheesh, Jenny, it would be a lot easier than finding two people who* were *relatives to give them.*

I meant it about having zero experience of how families work. My twin sister Zara and I are about as non-identical as it is possible to be having shared a womb. After nine months guzzling way more than her fair share of maternal nutrients, she used her three-pound weight advantage to shove her way out first and proceed to push, jostle, demand and manipulate my parents into making sure we never shared anything again, beyond a date of birth and surname. Waltzing off to boarding-school aged eight, she spent the next ten years wangling invitations to trips abroad, sponsored places on expensive summer camps and even a whole two months house-sitting in the South of France the year she finished school.

The few occasions she did end up home for more than a couple of nights in a row, she treated me with ninety percent indifference and ten percent irritation. I accepted this as exactly the way things should be. Stealing wondrous glances at the tall, blonde goddess, who flicked her glossy hair and pouted and the world bent to her will, she seemed another species altogether. A leopard and a mole. When people commented on how lovely it must be to have a special sister to share everything with, I merely shrugged and went back to reading my book. Zara didn`t have that problem. I don`t think she ever told anyone I existed.

Determined to justify her we-treat-our-daughters-completely-differently-because-they-are-individuals theory, my mum made it her mission to get me into the same university as Zara. Which happened to be Oxford. This included endless hours with a tutor, hundreds of headaches, heartaches and in the end the collapse of my parents` marriage, which disintegrated the year I turned seventeen. I lasted two terms at Queen`s College, Oxford before a nervous breakdown sent me home. The next three years were spent gathering my broken self together and wondering what on earth I was going to do, who I would be, and whether it mattered anyway. I also flunked out of yet more college courses my mother pressured me into, partly because I hated them, partly because I wasn`t yet mentally strong enough.

Then, landing in her own life-crisis, my mother sold everything she had and moved to Italy. My dad, renting a one-bedroom flat with his twenty-year-old girlfriend and seven snakes, somehow convinced the twin sister who had virtually forgotten my name to take me in (I suspect repayment of overdrafts was involved). I moved my battered suitcase up to Edinburgh, with strict instructions about never mentioning our embarrassing family to anyone, ever.

There is a reason why leopards and moles don`t live together. The odds are high that only one of them will get out alive.

And it isn`t usually the mole.

I had escaped, but it remained to be seen whether my wounds would prove fatal.

I dithered and dallied about who to call about a reference. Until, after hours of sorting crispy magazines into pointless piles, I phoned Meg, the one Dougal and Duff employee who might still consider talking to me.

'Flip, Jenny, if anyone catches me talking to you, I`ll never hear the end of it.' Her Scottish accent whispered down the phone. 'I`ll call you back.'

She did, a couple of minutes later. 'Right, we should be safe for now. I`m in the ladies`.'

'Is it really that bad?'

'Yes, Jenny. It is really that bad. When Zara heard that Elsie said you must have a good reason for what you did, you could hear the bellowing from Arthur`s Seat. Ian Dougal had to intervene before another nose got broken. Oh – hang on. Someone`s here.'

We waited in silence until they left.

'So, how`s it going?' Meg whispered.

'Um, great, thanks. But I do need a favour.'

'Ask away, my friend. Ask away. Unless it concerns my boss, in which case don`t, and you`re not my friend, and we never had this conversation.'

'No, nothing like that. I need a character reference. A truthful one.'

'A truthful one? Are you auditioning to be a cage fighter?'

'A truthful one up about my character at any point in which you`ve known me, *apart from at the party*.'

Meg laughed. 'No problem. You want me to leave out the secret fling with your boss, aye?'

'Aye.'

Enough memories for one day, I abandoned the box of papers waiting to be tackled and went for a walk instead. I chose the opposite direction to the village, abandoning the footpath to push through the trees and wild bushes. I admired the frost sparkling on the branches, transforming the spider webs draped between them into exquisite jewellery, sucked in a lungful of fresh, bright air and picked up my pace. Winding my way along rabbit paths, up embankments slippery with mulch, in between vast rhododendron bushes, walking until the ache in my thighs and feet drowned out the ache beneath my ribs. Richard had stung. A lot. But, like falling into the nettle-patch growing beside my new back door, my foolishness bothered me more than the pain. But Zara. She had been a rose, with thorns long and merciless. And where she drew blood, the wound festered.

6

Three more days of cleaning, hauling, scrubbing, eating packet soup and mega-breakfasts and dreaming of a bouncy new mattress later, I cycled through the drab grey mizzle to have dinner with the Camerons. The door was flung open before I even rang the bell.

'Hi, Superman.'

'Hi.' Superman, overcome with shyness, shuffled his feet on the welcome mat.

'Are Ellen and Will in, or are you babysitting?'

He flicked his eyes up at me, the hint of a dimple appearing in his cheek. 'I'm babysitting.'

'Are you doing a good job?'

The dimples deepened. 'Yes!' Hamish shouted, in a deep superhero voice.

'Can I come in?'

'Uuuummmmm...' He thought about it, as I flicked icy raindrops from my forehead.

'Please?'

'Uuuummmmm...'

'Ellen, have you seen my jeans?' Will came thumping down the stairs, wearing a shirt and boxer-shorts. 'What are you doing, Hamish?'

I had automatically stepped back, but as he leant past Hamish to close the door, he saw me.

'Hi.' I averted my eyes, lifting one hand in a feeble wave. 'I'm Jenny.'

'Yes. Hi. Come on in. Watch the skateboard. And the stepladder. And, well, make yourself at home. I'll be one minute. Ellen! Hamish opened the door again!' He waited for me to enter, then whipped shut the bolt at the top of the door before leaping up the stairs, two at a time, leaving Superman grinning as he hopped up the ladder.

'Is that how you opened the door?'

He nodded. Hop.

'Did Mummy and Daddy tell you not to open the door?'

He pretended to think about that. Hop, hop.

'Because it's dangerous?'

'Not dangerous for me! I'm Superman!' Hamish threw himself off the fifth rung, landing in a heap on the hall floor before scampering off into the living room.

I snuck a glance back at the door, contemplating a pre-emptive escape.

'Hi, Jenny,' Maddie said, perched at the top of the stairs.

Okay, so no escape this time. 'Hi. Where does this go?' I replied, folding up the ladder.

'Under the stairs. Daddy forgot to lock the cupboard door. You can leave it there, though. Hamish only opened the door because Jonno sounded the alarm.'

'Alarm?'

'The Jenny alarm. They've been waiting for you since swimming. They want you to play Hunt and Destroy.'

'Hunt and Destroy? Is that a computer game?'

'No.' She rolled her eyes. 'It's like hide-and-seek, only with weapons. And wrestling.'

'Sounds... painful.'

'Yep.' She stood up. 'Want to see my new sample of *Botrytis*?'

'I'd love to, but I'd better say hi to your mum first.'

'Okay. I'll not open the airing cupboard door yet, then, because they grow best at warm temperatures.' She clattered off, calling, 'She's in the kitchen trying to make it look as though we're a nice, normal family.'

I found Ellen chopping broccoli, engulfed in a haze of delicious smells.

'Jenny!' She stopped to give me a hug. I tried not to react like an ironing-board, awkwardly reaching up my arms before realising the hug was over. 'Did Will let you in?'

'Sort of.'

She tutted. 'Hamish?'

'Yep.'

'I don't know why we bothered fitting that bolt. Those boys would make a crack team of jewel thieves. Once they want something, there's no stopping them. And they haven't stopped talking about you all day.'

'Really?'

'They're four. A new woman in their life is big news.'

'Have you told them I might be their nanny?'

She chucked the broccoli into a large pan. 'I'm hoping there's no *might* about it. But, no. That would produce further excitement. And three over-excited little boys at the dinner table are not going to encourage you to accept the job.'

She handed me a jug full of knives and forks. 'Could you sort these?'

I began to lay the table, pondering whether to be honest. In this house, anything else seemed strange. 'Just to be clear, I'm absolutely certain I want this job. I presumed this evening was about Will deciding whether to hire me.'

Ellen paused. 'Jenny, Will trusts my judgement. And your character references were exceptional. I'd have considered bribery being involved if I didn't know you were broke.'

I sent out a silent thank you to Claudia, Zara's elderly housekeeper, who had adopted me as a sort of pet. And to Meg, for what she'd left out as much as what she'd said.

'Right. If you summon the troops, I'll dish up.'

I could do that – round up five children and a strange man I'd recently startled in his underwear. This was like *The Apprentice*. Only with superheroes and mould spores.

* * *

One near-impossible round of Hunt and Destroy, one micro-biology lecture and one long conversation about hobbits later, the food was only slightly cold.

Billy pushed his plate of chicken pie away. 'Yuck.

'Billy,' Will warned, with a look probably honed on thousands of school children.

'Billy hates cold pie,' Maddie told me.

'Yes,' Will agreed. 'But it wouldn't be cold if he'd come when Jenny called him. Would it, Billy?'

'I don't want cold pie. Only peg-nins eat cold food and I'm not a peg-nin, I'm a fire-robot. Cold food breaks my buttons.'

Ellen grinned. 'What do you think, Jenny? Can fire-robots eat cold food?'

'Um.' I set down my water-glass, wondering if the boardroom interrogation had commenced, and how to stop it ending with, 'You're fired.'

'Of course, I think this pie would be delicious at any temperature. And I'm sorry to hear that you aren't a Magnetron Ultra-Inferno Incinerator-Hot Robot Two Thousand, Billy. I heard they were the fastest, hottest, best fire-robot ever made. But their buttons *love* cold food. They eat it really fast, and are so hot it gets warm before it even reaches their stomach compartment.'

Hamish and Jonno watched me, eyes wide with interest. Billy gasped. 'But I *am* a Magnon Ultra-Ferno Hot Hot Hottest Robot Ever! Look!'

I caught Ellen raising her eyebrows at Will, who winked at her. *Hired?*

Shortly before I left, the doorbell rang.

"Dad?" Ellen said, sounding surprised. With one remaining shock of silver hair and a sharp suit stretched over his rounded stomach, he seemed somewhat at odds with his now flustered daughter. He shook my hand, eyeing me up and down with a shrewd eye before offering a business card.

'You're living in the Meadows' place. When you decide it's too much and want to sell, give me a call.'

I read the card: F. F. Fisher, Property Developer.

'Thanks. But I'm not planning on selling.'

He smiled. It reminded me of an overweight crocodile. 'Trust me, it's a money pit. The most sensible option is to knock it down and start again. You could save a whole lot of time and trouble, and I can promise you a decent offer. I can pop round some time next week, give you a professional opinion.'

'No, thank you.' I felt my cheeks take on the appearance

of a Magnetron Ultra-Inferno Robot. 'I'm really not interested in selling.'

I downed the rest of my coffee, trying not to think about what Fisher, or Ellen and Will – or *anyone* – would say if they saw the reality of where I was living. I would die of shame before I let F. F. Fisher poke his professional nose inside my cottage.

* * *

Easily said, when enveloped by soft cushions, sitting beside a crackling fire with a home-cooked meal in my stomach. When the storm broke, later that evening, rattling the rotten window-panes and whistling through the holes in the roof, causing a worryingly loud sound of running water somewhere behind the boxes in the biggest bedroom, the idea of handing the nightmare over to someone else seemed a lot more appealing. Lugging an armful of large bowls, I took a deep breath and ventured into the attic.

Avoiding the droppings and the worst of the manky boxes, I hunted through the freezing darkness and found four places where the rain was pouring in, the wind screaming behind it.

Positioning bowls underneath the drips, I then spent a frustrating amount of time trying to nail, then duct tape, four bin bags to the holes in the roof, while the rain lashed at my face, and my fingers became so numb they couldn't feel the tape any more.

Stumbling back out, the worst holes finally covered, I tripped over a box tucked to one side of the entrance hatch. In the light from the corridor below, I could see the box wasn't like the other plain cardboard or wooden crates.

Instead, it appeared to be a polished mahogany chest, the lid engraved with a pattern of daisies. My tiredness now over-ruled by curiosity, I carefully negotiated the steps and placed the box on the bathroom floor while I made a cup of tea.

Prolonging the anticipation, I sipped my drink, allowing the warmth to defrost my extremities while contemplating the possible contents. Jewellery? A priceless stamp collec-tion? The deeds to a secret fortune? A rotten mouse carcase?

But, no. When I managed, with some effort, to force the lid open, I found something far more valuable – I found a wodge of faded school reports, a CSE exam certificate and a thick brown envelope crammed with photographs.

I found my past.

I hastily got ready for bed and then settled down to see the faces of my history.

The pictures started somewhere in the early fifties, I guessed by the style of clothing and the furnishings. They were mostly black-and-white – a woman laughing on a beach. Dressed up in a fur-trimmed coat. Eating Christmas dinner with her parents, paper chains dangling above their heads. I grew certain the woman was my grandmother – although I had to pause and wonder how this carefree, exuberant spirit turned into the old lady dying alone in her hoarder's prison.

I reached wedding photographs – posing with a formal smile in her lace dress while the man who must be my grand-father draped one arm around her shoulder.

And then, I stopped, mouth dry, at the next photograph. It contained the same woman, but everything about her looked different. Her face drawn, bordering on gaunt. Hair scraped back, eyes hovering below the camera. And in her arms a baby, wrapped in a white blanket.

I did some rapid calculations. This must be my mother. I moved on: saw the baby growing to a girl in school uniform; wearing an Easter bonnet and seated in front of a birthday cake; standing alongside a snowman. There weren't many – three or four each year. Mostly just the girl, occasionally with her mother. But never the man. And no smiles. The pictures changed to colour, but the expressions remained grey.

I reached the last one in the stack. My mother looked about thirteen. In baggy cords and a ribbed polo-neck sweater, she squinted into the camera. Behind her, my grandmother, hair streaked with silver, skin pulled tight across sharp cheekbones.

I had learnt one thing, if nothing else: my mother did not have a happy childhood. Either that or she *really* hated having her photograph taken. And if her father had been around, he must have hated it even more.

Still, it was questions, not answers, that kept me twisting and turning in the bath that night. What happened to change my grandmother so strikingly? Did my grandfather die, or leave?

Why did we never, ever visit her?

Tomorrow's cleaning would have to be put to one side. I had answers to find.

7

After a terrible night, the sound of banging on the back door woke me. Scrambling to get out of the bath, I caught my feet in the tangled sheet, tipping me headlong onto the floor. Untwisting myself, while trying not to lose my jogging-bottoms in the process, I heard the door open and a man's voice call my name.

Oh, *pants*. Only one guess for who that could be.

Managing to pull myself up, I snatched my glasses off the window sill, straightened my clothes and sprinted out of the bathroom, hoping at the very least to prevent him mounting the stairs.

We collided in the hallway, crashing into Mannequin Diana, who thankfully broke our fall. Righting himself, Mack hauled me to my feet.

'Are you okay?' He peered at me, still holding my arms with each hand.

'What? Yes! Why wouldn't I be? And what are you doing in my house? Don't you knock and wait for an answer like normal people?'

Dropping my arms, he raised one eyebrow. 'I did knock. For five minutes.'

'So maybe I was out. Or not receiving visitors today.'

'Or suffocating beneath an avalanche of junk. Or electrocuted by the lethal wiring in this place. Or trapped by the flood of storm water that has come in via your leaky roof, and somehow made its way through your wall and into my office.'

'Say what?' I blinked, my idiot, pre-coffee brain struggling to focus beyond how cold and bare my arms felt without his hands on them any more.

'Water is leaking through the top of our adjoining wall into my office. The place in which I earn my living. Several documents are now destroyed, the floor is soaked and my laptop barely escaped with its life. If you could find it within yourself to "receive visitors", I would be very grateful,' he said pointedly.

'Are you always this rude and sarcastic?'

'While we discuss that issue, months of work will be drowning in the results of your DIY incompetence.' He folded his arms, which were bulging with tension.

'Excuse me! I've done nothing!' I folded my arms right back at him, and made a vain attempt to stretch myself up to somewhere near his height.

'If only that were true. For the past six years this house stood empty and derelict while managing to leave my side of the building undisturbed and intact. Now I have a broken window and a flood.'

'I haven't caused a flood! I actually repaired the leaks, in the middle of the night, using my own ingenuity and wits.

He sighed. 'That's what I was afraid of.'

'I worked really hard! It took ages, and I got soaked in the process.'

'Right. That would explain the hair. Now, if you're finished bristling, can I see what's causing the problem? That is, apart from you.'

I gaped. How dared he come into my house at whatever time it was in the morning and insult me like this?

'How about we start with wherever you were *fixing the leak*?'

He didn't go as far as making finger quote marks to frame those last three words, but his tone implied as much. I watched him climb the attic stairs, my simmering anger powering up the cogs of my brain.

'Fine! As long as you don't touch anything. And I didn't think you'd noticed my hair!'

* * *

So, my rescue bin-bag job hadn't quite turned out as planned. One side – the side nearest Mack's house – of one of the holes – the hole nearest Mack's house – had half peeled away, creating a sort of water slide, beginning at the hole and flowing towards – yes, Mack's house. The water had run down the bin bag, poured onto the floor at the edge of the dividing wall, found a massive crack to gather in and presumably seeped through to the rooms beneath.

Mack looked at me. '*Bin bags?*'

'I didn't know what else to use.'

'No. Not much lying around here you could use to board up a hole.'

I bit my cheek and tried to think of something to say other than sorry. I couldn't.

'I'm sorry. Has it really ruined months of work? I can try and help fix it, if you want.'

One side of his mouth twitched. 'No. I don't want.'

'I did try.' I blinked, hard.

He nodded. 'Well. I'm sorry for being a sarcastic git. I didn't get much sleep. Let's check out the damage on your side, and then I'll sort the roof before it rains again.'

He clattered down the steps, flinging open the door to the small bedroom before I could stop him. I thought I might have left my dirty wet clothes on the floor while rushing to change so I could look through the photos. If *thought* meant *knew* and *might* meant *did* and *clothes* meant *underwear,* that was.

But Mack getting an eyeful of my old knickers was nothing compared to my mortification after he then moved past me to the bathroom.

He paused in the doorway. Sidling up behind, I followed his gaze as it took in the sleeping bag, the pile of photographs and a battered novel on the wooden table I had positioned beside the bath. At least I'd moved my food supplies into the small bedroom with my clothes.

'It all looks fine,' he said, abruptly turning away, and pretending to examine the landing ceiling. 'I think the attic wall must not be flush with the walls on this level, which is why it all ended up on my side.'

'I'm really sorry.' I stared at a stuffed chipmunk, aware I sounded as wretched as I felt. 'Can I clean up your office while you fix the holes?'

His face shut down then, with a clang – making me realise how much it had previously softened. Yes, Jenny, softened with pity for the useless woman sleeping in a bath and surviving on cold baked beans and tins of tuna.

'No. It's fine.'

'Right.' I nodded. 'It's understandable you don't trust me with your stuff.'

He sighed. 'No. It isn't that. Well, not *just* that. My work is extremely... private.' He attempted a smile. 'I'd appreciate a cup of tea, though. As long as it's from the kettle in the bedroom, not the kitchen.'

* * *

'Are you a spy?' I sat the tea on one of the less manky attic boxes.

Mack glanced down, holding a sheet of wood against the roof, two nails in his mouth.

'Okay, so if you told me would you have to kill me?' I said.

He deliberately took one of the nails out of his mouth, placed it carefully in position and swung the hammer on to it so hard the roof shook.

'Because if you are a spy, I could be a threat. Like, a counter-spy sent to discover all your secrets. My bumbling incompetence would be an excellent ploy, to lure you into coming to my rescue, and then wheedle out your secrets by lulling you into a false sense of security. As demonstrated by you revealing where you keep your secret spy documents.' I took a nonchalant mouthful of tea.

'Are you trying to *lure* me?' he asked, removing the second nail from his mouth.

I choked, spluttering and coughing for a couple of minutes while he finished one repair and moved on to the next.

'Well, obviously *I'm* not a spy. It was a theory, pointing out that if you're a spy you aren't a very good one.' My voice came out rough from coughing.

'Maybe I'm a good enough spy to know you aren't a spy.'

'But what if an enemy spy takes me hostage, and tortures me to discover where you keep your information?'

He reached down for more nails. I completely disregarded how his back muscles stretched the T-shirt. 'Why wouldn't they search my house first?'

'Because kidnapping me would be more fun?'

He laughed then. A loud bark that made tea slop out of my mug when I jerked in surprise.

'Fun. Right.' He brushed off the dust from his hands, and picked up his drink. Taking a slow sip, he watched me, the smile still lingering in his eyes. 'I'm not a spy.'

'What, then? Holed up by yourself all day working on secrets. Are you an inventor? Or a computer hacker?'

'What I am is late. This'll hold for now, but you need to get a roofer to tile it properly. Thanks for the tea.' He downed the rest of the mug, and left.

Still embarrassed by Mack seeing the state of the kitchen, and my makeshift food-preparation area upstairs, I decided to forego my morning walk to the Common and spend the day working on the cupboards and counter-tops. I lugged the fridge an inch at a time outside, dumping it next to the mattress, and began sorting through the stacks of pots and crockery, deciding what to keep and what could be sold. Scouring, sorting, dumping anything that was chipped, cracked or broken and plunging the rest in scalding-hot water turned out to be a great way to scrub away some shame at the same time. I kept going until my arms couldn't lift another pan.

Had many of my thoughts drifted towards the cottage next door? Maybe. A little. Until I felt sick and tired of my mind's refusal to stop wondering about him. I had ended up here, in a home unfit for livestock, friendless and skint, through wondering about a handsome face and clever repartee. I needed to learn some DIY skills, fast, so that visits from the mystery man next door could stop.

Only the discovery of another photograph succeeded in switching my thoughts to something less frustrating. My grandmother again, an enormous baby bump stretching her cardigan as she pressed her hands against her back. She stood, grinning, several metres in front of the cottage. There was a chicken pecking at the neat gravel path by her feet, to the side a vegetable garden, runner-bean vines wrapped around a row of canes. Overflowing hanging-baskets either side of the door.

Tears pricked my eyes as I gazed at the hopes and the dreams contained in that picture. The cottage had been a home, back then. Without a single weed or crack or smear. I propped the photograph up against the kitchen window, more determined than ever to make it a home once again.

Saturday, after a morning bustling with walkers wanting to make the most of the sunshine, I helped Sarah clean up the café.

'Got any plans this evening?' Sarah asked.

'Um... a cosy night in with a book and a packet of crisps. Maybe a bath?'

I didn't add that the book, a heart-thumping bestseller by author Hillary West, was curling from damp, the crisps would be my evening meal and the bath wouldn't have any water in it.

'Fancy a girls' night?'

'I don't know. I've never been on one. What happens?' I swiped the hair out of my eyes with one arm.

'We'll have a drink and eat pizza. Crank up my girl-power playlist. Discuss why we don't need duds in our lives. Or, I dunno. Whatever you want. I've never been on one either.'

Another night away from Grime Cottage? Yes, please.

I cycled back to said cottage, hurrying past Mack's side. Going straight upstairs to look for potential girls'-night snacks, I took a moment to realise that the bedroom was different. With a start, I spun around and stared, goggle-eyed, at the bedstead.

Or, should I say, the mattress on top of the bedstead. The thick white duvet on top of the mattress. The brightly coloured patchwork quilt on top of the duvet. The massive pillows.

I touched the duvet. Smelt it. Leant over and pressed my cheek against the pillow. Turned it back and found a crisp white sheet underneath. Climbed on top, my muscles trembling, and lay staring at the ceiling, tears trickling into my ears.

This was exactly what I was talking about. A man who said nothing to my face about discovering my circumstances, but broke into my house and made me a bed with a trillion thread counts and the scent of vanilla. Who *was* this man? Did he like me, or feel sorry for me?

Right then, I was finding it very hard to care.

* * *

I sprang awake several minutes later, jumped in and out of the shower, flung on a nearly clean pair of jeans and jumper and used my rested and refreshed muscles to power myself to the Common in record time.

I sat at the breakfast bar in Sarah's little flat while we sprinkled cheese on homemade pizzas, chatting about nothing much.

Once we'd taken our glasses of wine to the squishy sofas, she got serious. 'So, what about this bloke who broke your heart, then?' Sarah counted the questions off on her fingers. 'How did you meet? Why did you fall for him? How long were you together? Why did it end?'

I took a gulp of wine. 'Do you want GCSE grades and medical history, too?'

'Not unless it's relevant. I'll go first, if you want.'

I nodded. 'I do want.'

'Edison's dad – Sean – wasn't bad-looking before he turned into a slob, but reckoned himself to be a demi-god. And, being sixteen and an idiot, I believed him.'

She went on to describe how, after a turbulent, on-off relationship, she became pregnant, ditching her college plans and moving in with Sean in the hope that they could make a go of things. That lasted until the day Edison was born when, during a flaming row in the hospital, she told him it was over. With her mum's help she just about balanced motherhood with working at her grandma's café, becoming manager after her gran retired and moving into the flat. By that time, the food was ready. We ate in comfortable silence for a while before Sarah decided it was my turn.

'Okay.' I took a deep breath, and a large bite of carrot cake. 'Richard was my boss.'

'Oh, no.' Sarah shook her head. 'That is never going to end well.'

'It certainly didn't. I'd been a PA at the law firm where my sister worked for a few years, when he joined. He was the youngest partner, and all the clichés – charismatic, arrogant, flashy. He took about four months to make a move. I couldn't believe the office hunk had kissed *me* of all people. So I didn't protest about spending the next eighteen months sneaking around, meeting up in secluded restaurants, fumbling behind locked office doors.'

'Yuck.' Sarah grimaced. *'Eighteen months?'*

I puffed out a sigh. 'I wanted to believe he really cared about me. I clung to every glimmer of hope: the expensive gifts; secret looks across the conference table; the times he called late at night because he *had* to see me; saying he couldn't manage without me.'

'But you wised up eventually.'

'Yeah.' I let out a laugh. Not a pleasant one. 'Him proposing to my sister was a pretty good hint.'

'Shut the front door!' Sarah leant forwards. 'What happened?'

I took a deep breath and told her.

A team from the office had spent two months working in Paris, on a big case. For reasons I now knew to be Zara's evil schemes, I wasn't part of the team, but Richard fabricated excuses for me to fly over a couple of times, and we were in contact most days about work. I'd never told Zara about my relationship, but we shared an apartment, so she must have at least suspected. When she decided it was time to snag herself a man, Richard was an obvious choice. I didn't know what happened in Paris. But then a ring box arrived on the day of the office Christmas party, and the gossip quickly spread. Richard was going to propose.

'And you thought... Flip, Jenny. That is *so* crap.' Sarah took hold of my arm. 'Hang on a minute, I'll just check on Ed before you tell me the rest.'

She topped up our glasses on the way back, the buzz of wine after several weeks' abstinence probably contributing to my ability to continue the story.

'It all happened as you'd expect. Me, sweating in my best dress, trying to catch his eye across the room. Champagne, a speech about how much this person meant to him, how he admired their ambition and the success they'd achieved against the odds. And, to clarify – the only odd my sister ever had to deal with was me. I stood there, a total fool, clutching my glass and grinning away, subconsciously inching closer to the front ready for my big moment. And when it finally came, and he got down on one knee...'

'Wait.' Sarah flapped her hands in disgust. 'He proposed at the *office party*?'

'It's hard to explain, but Dougal and Duff is more than a workplace. It's their whole lives. Like something out of a John Grisham novel.'

'Remind me never to read one of those. I'm more of a Hillary West fan.'

'I *love* her books. This was *nothing* like that.' I pulled a tissue from the flowery box on the coffee table and blew my nose. 'So, anyway. At first, I thought he'd got flustered, when he knelt down facing the opposite way. I even waved to get his attention. Which unfortunately meant I got a load of other people's attention instead. He had eyes for one person only.'

'You poor thing,' Sarah whispered. 'You must have been properly gutted.'

'Weirdly, no. Not at the time.' I shrugged. 'As I realised what was happening, I saw Zara flick her eyes over to me, with this look, and something inside me, like, burst, you know?'

She nodded.

'Twenty-eight years of jealousy and insecurity. That's another story, really, but pressure to keep up with Zara led to a nervous breakdown when I was nineteen. And then I'd had to accept her handout job and spare room after screwing up my future. I'd lived in her shadow my whole life. Felt grateful when she passed on her barely worn clothes, or the rare times she let me sit in on her dinner parties. Worked my butt off in that firm because I owed it to her. Tidied, ran errands, apologised, bowed and scraped. And then she took the one thing I'd managed to earn myself. And, yes, I do know how wrong it sounds that I thought I'd earned Richard's attention. So, basically, I flipped. Violence ensued, hair got yanked out, food tables toppled – *and* I broke her new plastic nose. The police were called...'

'Wow. You got arrested?'

'She decided not to press charges – for the firm's sake, not mine.'

'But you lost your job.'

'Yep. And for obvious reasons, I moved out.'

'It sounds like you're better off here.' Sarah gave my hand a squeeze. 'I know me and Ed are better off having you here.'

'Sure you don't mind a violent criminal who beat up her sister working in your café?'

'Are you kidding?' She snorted. 'You sound like a handy woman to have around.'

I wobbled back home at around half-ten, the bike's lamp casting a weak silver glow on the path in front of me. The woods around were so dark that the black seemed to have texture – like treacle. I mumbled the rap we'd composed earlier about all the reasons we were better off single, but it made a poor job of drowning out the snaps and creaks of the forest, the rustles and hoots. I felt properly spooked by the time I reached home, and grateful for the soft yellow light peeking from the edge of Mack's blind. I tramped upstairs, wondering whether, if I did manage to sleep in my lovely new bed, my dreams would be about the man who lived next door, and whether they would be dreams, or nightmares.

8

Sunday, after what had been quite possibly the best sleep of my life, my weary bones enjoying the mattress way too much to bother about where it came from, I asked Ellen if I could borrow her kitchen. She agreed, offering to provide baking ingredients if I borrowed some kids at the same time. This worked out perfectly, as my cash had dwindled to a miserably tiny amount, and I feared I might be surviving on mega-cobs and soup until my first pay day as it was.

That afternoon, ready as I'd ever be, I lined up my volunteers, wishing that sensible Dawson hadn't excused himself to do homework.

'Right, team. We have two important missions today. One big cake, not for you, and lots of little cakes, which you can keep.'

'How many little cakes?' Billy asked, 'A hundred?'

'A thousand?' Hamish asked, jumping up and down.

'A billion?' Jonno squealed. 'A billion little cakes! No! Three billion, one billion for me and one billion for Mish and one billion for Billy and one cake each for Maddie and Mummy and Daddy and Jenny and—'

'That's more than three billion already,' Maddie said. 'And don't be stupid. A billion cakes wouldn't fit in this house.'

'It would if I ate them all up really fast!' Jonno mimed shovelling cakes into his mouth.

'Well, what about cooking them? The baking trays make twelve cakes each. That's, like, millions of times we'd have to use each tray.'

'So?' Jonno frowned. 'I can do it really fast.'

'No, you can't.'

'I can!' He lowered his head, prepared to charge.

'Right!' I put one hand on his shoulder. 'We are making thirty-six fairy cakes, because that's how many the ingredients will make.'

'I don't wanna make fairy cakes,' Hamish said. 'Wanna make monster-cakes.'

'That sounds about right.' I pulled Ellen's apron strings a little tighter round my waist, wondering if a biohazard suit would be more appropriate.

Oh, boy.

* * *

Three utterly exhausting hours later, my pores clogged with icing sugar, having left behind three boys in the bath, a pile of very monstrous-looking cakes, and Maddie reading her microbiology book to calm herself down, I cycled carefully back home, balancing an old biscuit tin in the bike basket.

Reaching the cottage as twilight crept beneath the forest, I peered inside the tin, hoping somehow the effects of three rambunctious boys and their fretful sister would seem less prominent in the dusk.

No. I felt tempted to leave the squishy, lopsided, shall we say *enthusiastically* decorated lump on his doorstep and make a run for it. But that would defeat the purpose. Plucking off one of the chocolate fingers sticking haphazardly out of the top, I chomped it down, marching up to Mack's front door.

Several knocks later, he warily eyed me on the doorstep.

'Can I come in?'

'I'm in the middle of something.'

'A nap, by the looks of things.'

His eyes narrowed. 'What do you want?'

'I brought you this.' I held out the tin. 'I had some, um, help, so it isn't quite how I planned, but it should still taste good.'

He looked at me, waiting a few moments before slowly taking the tin.

'It's to say thanks. And that, well, I really appreciate you fixing my bike, and lending me the saw, and sorting the roof, not hassling me about the broken window and everything...' I was still too embarrassed to mention the bed. 'But, as I said before, I'm fine sorting myself out. I don't need help. I feel horrible that I won't be able to pay anything back for ages. So, please stop.'

'I had to fix the roof – it was damaging my office.'

'Yes, well. That won't happen again.'

He quirked one eyebrow. I ignored my pathetic fluttering heart.

'It won't! And I could have fixed it if you'd given me the chance.'

Mack leant on the doorframe, still holding the tin. I

resisted the urge to poke his bicep and see if it felt as solid as it looked.

'I could have! Look, I said I appreciate it, but I really don't need help.'

'I disagree.'

'What?' I spluttered.

'Why do you have a problem with me helping you?'

Good question. How long had he got? 'Because I want to do it myself! I don't want to owe anybody anything, any more. I can manage on my own, and would like a chance to prove it. It's weird, someone I don't know giving me bedding. Some would think it's extremely creepy. Fixing things without asking or even telling me! Sneaking into my house when I'm out. That's not just creepy, it's trespassing. How are you even getting in? How *often* are you sneaking in? Are you rummaging through my stuff? Looking for valuables to steal in the Hoard? You clearly don't like me. It's weird. I don't buy that Mystery Man stuff one bit. If I need help, I'll take it from someone honest, open and respectful of my privacy, and me. Thanks very much. But no, thanks!'

I spun on my heel and stalked away. Mack didn't follow me, *which of course I was pleased about*! But the next day, cycling back from the Common, icy puddles crunching beneath the tyres, morning coffee and banana in my basket, I found him leaning against the wall by my back door, all wrapped up in a thick jacket and beanie hat.

I watched him suspiciously. 'Hi.'

'Hi.' He pushed himself away from the wall. 'I thought you might like some cake with your coffee.'

I adjusted my glasses, trying to figure out his angle.

'I can promise you it isn't poisoned. I tested it last night, with no repercussions.'

'Did you think it might be?'

His beard twitched. 'I considered the possibility.'

My stomach, unable to face another mega-cob, rumbled loudly at the thought of that cake. I coughed, in a belated attempt to mask the sound.

'Come on. It isn't accepting charity, since you made the cake.'

I remembered the thick layer of creamy fudge icing, the smell of melted chocolate chunks, choco-balls nestling in between the chocolate fingers. 'Okay. Thanks.'

He sat down at the picnic bench a couple of minutes later, with two slices of cake and a coffee for himself.

He also had a key, which after a while he took out of his pocket and pushed across the table. 'I should have returned this earlier. But I didn't think you'd be staying.'

'A spare key?'

He nodded. 'The guy I bought the house from used to keep an eye on Mrs Meadows. After she died, he kept hold of it in case he needed to access the other side. It seemed sensible for me to do the same.'

'Okay.'

'And, for the record, if I was going to steal anything, I'd have done it long before you arrived.'

'Okay.' I nodded.

'And the mattress and bedding were from my spare room. If I'd offered them, you'd have said no. I couldn't sleep properly, knowing you were on the other side of the wall in a bath.'

'Okay.' Mack was on a roll. There was no way I was interrupting the flow.

'I didn't think of it as being creepy. I guess because, well, *I* know I'm not a creep. Although—' he cleared his throat, and looked away '—I have got used to my own company. Probably lost some social skills. So, I apologise for creeping you out.'

'How long have you lived here?'

He took a swig from the flask. 'Four years, near enough.'

'How do you get out anywhere? I haven't seen a car, or a bike.'

He shrugged. 'I walk. Run. Get the bus.'

'When?' I casually dabbed at the remaining cake crumbs.

The portcullis to Castle Mack slammed shut again. 'I've got to get back to work.' He gathered up the things on the table, but I grabbed the key as he made to move away, holding it out.

'Keep the key.'

He looked at the ground. 'I don't think so.'

'Please. I think we've established that I'm a buffoon, whose dream of being a self-sufficient, capable wonder woman is still just that. I'd appreciate it if you had a key, in case of emergencies.'

He shook his head, briefly, and glanced up at me. By golly, those eyes were as smooth and dark as the cake. 'Emergencies, by their very definition, are supposed to be rare and unexpected.'

'Yeah.' I smiled, shrugging my shoulders. 'I'm working on that.'

9

I still got that common recurring nightmare, the one where I was at school, only instead of the beyond nerdy uniform I had to wear, I was in my underwear, and instead of being invisible, a superpower I perfected during my years treading water in the ocean of academia, everybody was pointing and laughing. And I couldn't move. And the teacher was nowhere to be seen. Or they were the one laughing the loudest.

So today was sort of like that nightmare coming true. Only instead of underwear, I was wearing a milk-stained, jam-smeared hoodie and muddy jeans. One of my eyes had swollen half shut, thanks to an 'accident' with a toy aeroplane. And my hair? Best not think about my hair.

The task list had looked straightforward. Breakfast for the younger three, as Maddie and Dawson could make their own. Two plates of toast – butter and jam on one, honey on another, and a bowl of cornflakes. A three-minute job. Only the list forgot to mention the butter-and-jam toast needed to be cut into triangles, or it didn't taste 'properly'. And evidently small triangles didn't taste properly, either. The honey toast was 'burnted'. Apparently. Making toast to Hamish's exact shade of brownness should be a new skills test on *MasterChef*.

And cornflakes – how could you go wrong with shaking cereal into a bowl, and pouring milk on the top?

How indeed?

Did most children have an exact specification for flake-to-milk ratio? Decide the milk was too cold, and needed warming up in the microwave, which made the cereal too floppy, like 'yuck flakes', as demonstrated by catapulting them into their sister's hair?

And breakfast was only the start. The ragtag, mismatched, inside-out and back-to-front outfits the younger boys wore were in blatant rebellion against the neat piles of clothing laid out ready to be scrumpled up and stamped on.

Brushing teeth? Wasn't that supposed to take two minutes?

Packing bags? Not a problem. *Un*-packing the toys, stones, snail and mould specimens nearly finished me off. Like some insanity-inducing torture, every time I had one child suited and booted, coat on, bag ready, I turned around to find another running around the garden in nothing but a batman cape and armbands.

Dawson refused to go on without us, even as the clock ticked towards morning registration, instead lingering by the door and yelling increasingly frustrated orders at his brothers. At the school gate, however, he ran to his classroom, face pinched with worry. Maddie, still weeping over the cereal blobs I'd painstakingly combed out of her hair, refused to acknowledge me. She sloped off, head down, scuffing her shoes across the empty playground.

I heaved Jonno down from a wall, dodged between Billy

and Hamish's branch battle, and spent so long trying to herd them round to the reception building that the site manager had to come and help me.

When I eventually returned to find the gate locked, I gave up restraining myself, clinging to the railings while I snivelled. I had led a lonely life for a long time. But in that moment, trapped in a strange school, my black eye throbbing along with my weary head, facing a two-and-a-half-mile cycle back to Grime Cottage, where I would spend five hours silently scrubbing filth, with no one to laugh with about the morning's palaver, before cycling back to spend another two hours failing at my work probation, currently my only option of surviving...

I had never felt so alone.

'Excuse me?' A voice interrupted my pity party. 'Can you let us in, please?'

I opened my working eye to see an Asian woman with two girls, and a baby on one hip, peering through the bars. Sniffing in a most unladylike fashion, I made a pathetic gesture to indicate I didn't know how.

'The code is seven two three three. It spells "safe" on a phone.'

Attempting to hoist myself back together, I opened the gate. The children followed her in, waiting politely while she handed them their bags and kissed them both goodbye.

'Goodbye, Okaasan,' they chorused, beaming angelically before skipping off, holding hands. 'Have a lovely day! Miss you!'

Have a lovely day? I felt a fresh, hot rush behind my eyes. My farewell that morning: *I'm going to be in loads of trouble and it's all your fault... I wish Mummy was here she's nicer and funner and better at plaits... I'm going to shoot you with my poisonous arrows if you make me go... Billy said you're a stupid-glasses-head... I'm telling Mummy you pulled my arm and shouted and now it's brokened and I don't like you, Jenny...*

The woman shuffled awkwardly. 'I don't remember seeing you here before...'

I sniffed again, fumbling through my pockets for a tissue before remembering they'd all been used on Maddie's tears, Billy's scraped knees and everybody's noses.

'Here.'

I accepted the offered tissue and blew my nose, wincing as it sent shooting pains up to my eye. 'I'm the Camerons' new nanny,' I croaked. 'It's my first day.'

'Oh!' The woman nodded vigorously, enough said. 'Well, I need to let Reception know the girls are finished at the dentist. But if you can wait, you'd be welcome to come to mine for a cup of tea.' She ducked her head. 'I mean, if you like. You're probably busy. Or would rather be by yourself. Forget it, forget I asked...'

'I'd love to,' I blurted out. 'I'm not busy. And I've spent more than enough time by myself.'

She blinked at me, cheeks turning pink. 'Great. Well, I'm Kiko. And this is Hannah.' She patted her baby's back. 'I'll see you in a minute.'

She hurried off, leaving me a precious few moments to take some calming breaths. I thought about the Hoard, waiting for me, and felt the beginnings of a smile.

* * *

Kiko's house was a modern detached squeezed into a patch of land between two cottages. Inside, I perched on the pristine sofa and scanned the wall of family photographs while Kiko fetched our drinks. We chatted about how I'd started working for Ellen, and a bit about her children, while Hannah played on a mat on the floor. Kiko seemed nice, if a little tense. She asked about my plans for the rest of the week.

I glossed over the fact that my current plan started and ended with 'survive'.

'Only, I go to a book club once a month, and it's meeting this Friday. Ellen founded it, and sort of made me deputy leader now she's at university.'

'How does it work?'

'Um, we chat for a bit, then discuss the book we've just read, oh, and there's drinks and nibbles. At least, that's the theory.'

'Oh? What really happens?'

She began to bounce Hannah up and down on her knee. 'Um, no, that *is* what happens. Mostly. It's just, well. Sometimes the discussion gets a bit... lively.'

I wondered what she meant by lively. The question must have shown on my face, because Kiko hastily added, 'But mostly it's great. The club are lovely. Most of them. Most of the time. I'm just a bit nervous in case Ellen won't be there, and I'm in charge. The fights aren't that bad.'

'Fights?'

'No!' She pulled a slightly manic smile. 'Not real fights. Hardly ever real fights. It's just this one woman, Lucille, she can get a bit overheated. And then, well, Ashley gets upset if Lucille makes a comment about Hillary West, with her being a local author and everything.'

'Hillary West is a local author?' Ooh, now I loved her even more. Being able to dive into her latest book had been helping keep me sane. The way she wrote about life, and love, and all the crappy things that happened, but somehow left you full of hope... I wanted my life to be a Hillary West story.

'Yes.' Kiko stopped bouncing and looked at me. 'Ashley is her biggest fan. She keeps inviting her to the book club, but never gets a reply.'

'Sounds... interesting.'

'It beats Yellow Mickey's bingo in the village hall.'

'I see.' I saw that I probably should never go to this book club...

'You'll come, then?'

'Um. I guess so.' I shouldn't be one to judge a brawling woman, after all.

'Great! We meet in The Common Café. Do you know it?'

'I work there on Saturdays.'

'Oh! You're Sarah's new friend! I can't believe I didn't make the connection. Well, you'll be fine, then. She said you're a strong woman who won't take any—' she paused here to cover Hannah's ears, which was slightly pointless as she only mouthed the next word '—*crap,* excuse my language.' She beamed, and I couldn't help smiling back. I liked how this new Jenny was shaping up. I could back up my friend Kiko and deal with a few rowdy women at a book club.

Dawson and Maddie greeted me in the playground that afternoon with resignation. The triplets were too busy fighting invisible alien koalas to take much notice of who'd picked them up. I shooed them home and set about clearing up the mess from the morning, wincing at the thuds and crashes above my head. After one ceiling-shaking thump, I went to investigate.

The bedroom door wouldn't open. I gave it a shove, and a rattle, and called through the wooden barrier. 'Boys? Let me in, please.'

Silence. I gave a good loud knock on the door.

'Why won't the door open? What made that massive bang?'

I heard a quick scuffling noise, followed by more silence.

'I can hear you in there. Open the door.'

I knocked again, hard enough to bruise my knuckles.

'There's an alien koala in the kitchen and he's eating all the biscuits! Quick – you need to come and blast him for me!' I tried.

More rustles and thuds.

'Aren't you guys going to help me? I'm rubbish at blasting aliens. At least come and tell me what to do.'

'You need the blastabits,' Hamish called from the other side of the door. 'I think I left one in the shoe cupboard.'

'I can't hear you through the door. You need to open it.'

'It's in the shoe cupboard,' he shouted, his brothers joining in. I could hear they were close to the door, and felt a twitch of trepidation. After more failed attempts at finding out what was going on, rapidly descending into bribery, threats and, worst of all, the promise to tell their mother, Dawson came out of his room.

'When's dinner?'

'Your mum said you eat at six. It's only just after five.'

'When's she coming home?'

'She'll be home in time for dinner.'

'When, though?'

A muffled shriek from behind the closed door.

'I don't know, Dawson. Within an hour. Do you need something? Can I help?'

'Why are you talking to them through the door?'

'It won't open. Does it have a bolt or something on the inside?'

Dawson rolled his eyes. 'As if.'

'Have they done this before? Do you know why the door won't open?'

He shrugged. 'Mum would get them out.'

'I'm sure she would. In the meantime, how about you help me try?'

Dawson gave me a flat stare before going up to the door. 'Open the door. Jenny can't cook tea while she's standing here yelling at you idiots.'

'Dawson! Don't call them names.'

'Don't want any tea,' Jonno yelled back.

Dawson stomped back into his room. I tried Maddie, instead, who was watching television downstairs.

'You could look through Mummy and Daddy's window.'

I ran back upstairs, and found that Ellen and Will's bedroom stuck out from the back of the house, with a window on the side. If I pressed my face against the glass, it provided a good view into the boys' room. Maddie followed me, handing over a telescope.

'Oh, no.'

'What?' She tugged on my jumper.

'The wardrobe is on its side, in front of the door.'

I instructed the boys to empty the wardrobe, and then see if together they could push it away. No good. Time ticked on. I hadn't started cooking dinner. Shoes, coats, bags and other mess lay strewn about downstairs, and I began to genuinely panic about getting the boys out of the bedroom.

'Are you going to call the fire brigade?' Dawson asked, loitering in his doorway.

'No!' I took a deep breath. 'Well, not yet.'

'What are you going to do?' Maddie wiped a tear away. 'They'll be stuck in there forever!'

'I'm going to come up with a plan.' I walked back into Ellen's bedroom, and made a few mental calculations before going back to the kids. 'Is that ladder Hamish had out the other day the longest one you have?'

'I think so.' Dawson perked up a bit, sensing that perhaps I did, indeed, have a plan brewing. One that might be quite interesting.

'Do you think it'll reach the window?'

We found the key to the cupboard on the extensive bunch Ellen had entrusted me with. But even before dragging the ladder outside, I knew it would be far too short. Looking up at the windows in the deepening dusk, however, did lead to a new plan. A more stupid, desperate and dangerous one, but a plan all the same.

Against the side of the house was a trellis. Faded, splintered, the remains of a spindly clematis clinging to one side, it hung half-heartedly from the old bricks. We reckoned I could reach the boys' window from the top.

We poked a window key through a crack at the top of the boys' door, and with me shouting instructions, Billy managed to open the window. The next challenge was convincing them not to try escaping down the trellis themselves.

Heart pumping in my ears, head spinning, I started to climb.

Maddie had made a pile of sofa cushions underneath me 'just in case'. I wouldn't die, would I, falling a couple of metres? Maybe break a bone or two, have a mild concussion. At least in hospital I'd get free food.

'You can do it, Jenny!' Maddie cheered from below. 'Keep going, you're nearly there.'

I ignored the creaks and wobbles from the trellis, the rotten section that snapped beneath my foot, repositioned my hand and edged higher. Three wide-eyed faces stared at me, mouths open, arms dangling out of the window above my head.

'Okay, boys,' I gasped. 'Do not move. Or touch the trellis. My laser eyes are freezing you for ten minutes.'

My first hand managed to grip the window frame. Now the second. As I scrabbled upwards, leaning my shoulders onto the sill, the trellis broke away from the wall with a long, anguished shriek, followed by a solid thwack onto the cushions below.

Legs swinging against the wall of the house, I tried to screw my head around to see Dawson and Maddie. 'Are you all right?'

'Don't fall, Jenny!' Maddie cried. 'Jonno, Hamish, Billy, help Jenny!'

'We can't!' Hamish answered, while I dangled in front of him. 'We're frozen for ten minutes.'

'Three, two, one, ten minutes is up!' I garbled, breathless, as I desperately tried to haul myself in. 'Come on, show me what you can do.'

Those marvellous boys each grabbed a bit of me: a hand, a shoulder, an ear, and as my feet pushed against the wall, I kicked and scrambled inside. Collapsing in a heap amidst the total destruction inside their bedroom, I heard a voice floating through the open window. 'What on earth is happening?'

Ellen or Will's voice would have been bad enough. But as the angry tones continued demanding answers, Hamish looked at me. 'Uh-oh, Jenny. That's Grandpa Fisher. You're in big trouble now.'

Ya think?

My heart still hadn't recovered when Ellen returned, twenty minutes later. Seeming not to notice the mess, she greeted the children and leant in to give me a hug. 'So sorry I'm late. I had a load of forms to fill in. Have you already eaten?'

'I'm starving!' Jonno declared, swinging off his mum's skirt. 'What's for dinner?'

Ellen swept him up. 'Why don't you ask Jenny?'

'Jenny hasn't made any dinner 'cos she had to go up the plant ladder to rescue us, and then it fell down and Maddie and Dawson were at the bottom.'

'But they didn't die 'cos they jumped out of the way like this!' Hamish dived across the kitchen floor.

'And Jenny was hanging out of the window like this.' Billy demonstrated by dangling off the edge of the counter-top.

'And she nearly fell 'cos we were laser-frozen and she was slipping off, but the alien koalas were coming but then she unfroze us and we pulled her in like this and Maddie cried but we didn't cry we saved her and then we destroyed the barricade and Grandpa Fisher was really cross. But he went home 'cos he didn't have time to deal with it now.'

'And Jenny was like a superhero! And we were too,' Jonno squealed, waving his hands in glee.

'Grandpa Fisher was here, again?' Ellen frowned thoughtfully for a brief moment before shaking it off and glancing playfully at me. 'Sounds like you've had an exciting day. Jenny can fill me in on how much of that actually happened while we sort out dinner.'

'All of it happened,' Dawson said. 'Apart from Jenny being

like a superhero. Also, we were late for school, and she gave me the wrong lunch. This whole thing is a complete disaster. Ask Maddie.' He thumped out of the room, leaving a horrible silence. A trickle of sweat ran down my back.

'I can explain.' *Really, Jenny? Does your explanation include being both incompetent, and a danger to yourself and these kids?*

'I know.' Ellen smiled, her eyes dancing. Somehow that made me feel worse.

10

No more death-defying rescues were needed that week, which was the only discernible improvement. Chaos, lateness, clinging onto a whisper of control. Countless more mistakes. Spending a few precious hours sifting fruitlessly through documents and clearing out junk before bracing myself to pick the children up again. Each evening, Ellen and Will came home to a house upside down, a list of Dawson's complaints and a very frazzled nanny pretending she was just starting dinner. They insisted I ate with them, which was a mixed blessing as the kids revealed more of my bad decision-making, poor time-management and general failures through the hilarious (or so Ellen and Will thought) stories of their day.

I felt utterly useless and miserable. Being out of my depth was not good for me. It brought back black, oppressive memories: the constant gnaw of anxiety, the mind-numbing exhaustion, feeling trapped in a situation I was too pathetic to handle, but too hopeless to leave. My previous breakdown, floundering to live up to pressure and demands, had nearly destroyed me. After that I had held back the shadow of that bleak time by carefully living within my capabilities. Sticking to work I found easy, safe, manageable. By staying in Zara's apartment, refusing promotion, avoiding a social life, choosing a relationship where I had no power, I abdicated any sort of meaningful responsibility in order to prevent the trauma of being overwhelmed, and the horror that came with it.

Now – *now* – as if taking on the responsibility of a derelict house weren't enough, I'd added five helpless, vulnerable, impossible children to the mix.

It was pretty clear I was messing this up. Why on earth didn't Ellen fire me?

Friday, I slept until late, then lay in my lovely, warm bed for another couple of hours just because I could, ignoring the Hoard on the other side of the door. Too physically wiped out to face yet more cleaning, too emotionally wiped to go through more paperwork, I read for the rest of the afternoon, which seemed appropriate considering I had the book club later that evening. At seven, I dressed in my most Friday-night-ish clothes (a bottle-green wrap dress Zara had worn once before deciding it was too last season and a denim jacket), slung a silver pendant round my neck and slipped into a pair of shoes that had been so expensive that I really ought to get around to selling them. I felt too bone-weary to be nervous, but I did feel a buzz of anticipation while waiting for Kiko's friend Frances to pick me up.

Frances had none of Tezza's qualms, veering between the piles of junk and skidding right up to the front door before repeatedly tooting the horn on her pick-up truck until I hurried around the side of the house. She leant over and opened the door, offering a hand to help me up.

With cropped white hair and tiny blue eyes peeking out from a road-map of wrinkles, she looked so frail as she stretched across the seat that I feared she might snap in two inside her tweed suit. I hesitated, briefly, and she yanked on my wrist so firmly that I scraped an inch of skin off my shin while hoisting myself up.

'Frances,' she said, in between reversing out onto the road and zooming forwards. 'And behind you is Florence.'

Florence was a brown Labrador, sitting up on the back seat as straight as her mistress, tongue dangling.

'Thanks for the lift.' I pushed my glasses more firmly up my nose and gripped the door handle with my other hand.

'No problem. Only a minute or two out of my way,' she barked, deftly speeding around the corner.

'I'm eighty-four,' she went on. 'Did you guess?'

'About ten years too young.' I smiled.

She knotted her wispy eyebrows at the road ahead. 'I hope that wasn't an attempt at flattery. I'm not ashamed of looking, or acting, my age.' We screeched into the Common car park and pulled up right outside the café, on the grass. Opening her door, she climbed out. 'I gave up worrying about what anybody thought about me years ago.'

'Come on now, Frances.' A man near the café entrance stopped, reaching into the truck to take out a beautiful walking-stick and handing it to her. 'You *never* worried about that.'

'Ha! Well. If we all stopped fretting about other people's opinions, we might actually get something done around here.' She waited for Florence to join her before striding forwards at a fine clip for a woman with a walking stick.

'And no, this isn't to steady my old bones.' She twirled the stick. 'It's to prevent bushes, nettles, wild animals or nincompoops from getting in my way.'

* * *

The rest of the club was already inside. The man made sure Frances had a seat before introducing himself as Jamie. He coughed twice, tried in vain to smooth a fluffy clump of hair sticking out on one side of his head and said hello to Sarah, before helping her load glasses onto a tray.

Everyone else sat down around two tables pushed together, covered in a red cloth with a dinky vase of flowers in the centre, Florence curled up underneath. Kiko and Ellen waved and grinned 'hello' before burying their heads back in their notebooks.

'Hi. I'm Jenny,' I said to the person next to me.

She glanced up from her phone long enough to look me up and down. 'I know. Ellen's hired help.'

I vaguely recognised her from the school playground. 'Are you Lucille?' I guessed.

'Yes.' She slipped her phone into her bag. 'I hope Kiko made it clear that this is a serious club. We hold serious, informed, educated and intelligent discussions. For *serious* lovers of literacy.'

'Um. Do you mean literature?' Usually I would have ignored this slip, but the way her thin nostrils flared when she said the name *Kiko* meant I felt it my duty as a fellow lover of literacy, *and* literature, to correct her for the sake of future discussions. If she was going to be, like, *serious* about it.

A splotch of pink managed to push its way through her impressive layer of foundation. 'Just be warned, this isn't an excuse to drink wine and gossip. If you want a laugh or some *fun times*, try the bingo.'

No wine, gossip or laughter. I had been warned!

'Glass of wine, Jenny?' Sarah held up a bottle.

'Yes, please.'

'And don't scarper without me telling you what happened in the café today between that bloke with the smelly dog and Kylie Jones: Hot. Gossip. With a capital H.' She fanned her face, and winked at me. 'Have some crisps.'

I laughed. I couldn't help it. I blamed it on being overtired. I was especially overtired of people treating me as beneath them. I held my glass up to Lucille in a toast and laughed again. 'Cheers! Isn't this fun?'

She tutted. One tut, from between her disconcertingly white teeth.

'Almost as fun as the Oxford debating society.' I grinned.

'Oxford University?' she asked, stiffly.

'Yes. Did you go to university, Lucille?' I asked, burying my face in my glass. I knew she had gone to a nearby establishment currently facing closure due to their habit of pumping out sub-standard qualifications locally derided as equal to a Cub Scout badge. I didn't judge her for that – for goodness' sake, I'd flunked out of enough college courses. But I couldn't stand intellectual snobs. And fake intellectual snobs were possibly even worse.

Lucille narrowed her eyes, ignoring me and calling to Ellen, 'Can we get started? This book can't be adequately discussed in half an hour.'

This book, in my opinion, couldn't be discussed adequately no matter how much time we had. But we had a jolly good go.

The book was Lucille's choice, a novel entitled *The Wheel of Woman*. I had quickly scanned Kiko's copy earlier, which had left me none the wiser about the plot. Or the characters. Or the setting. I did know it was something to do with a woman. And some sort of wheel. Which might have been metaphorical. Or real. Or both.

It didn't appear to be my kind of book.

Or anyone else's, for that matter.

Sarah sat back in her chair and took a big bite of Bakewell tart. 'I didn't get it.'

Lucille rolled her eyes. 'No surprise there. Did you even finish it?'

'I read the last couple of pages. Does that count?'

'Honestly!' Lucille bristled. 'How are you possibly going to appreciate the—?'

'What did you think, Kiko?' Sarah interrupted.

'Well. Yes.' Kiko shuffled about on her cushion. 'I thought some of the description was very... thought-provoking. And the lack of dialogue – an interesting technique. I'm not sure about the sexual violence. Seven pages seemed excessive to describe one incident.'

'It was the most significant moment of the book,' Lucille snapped. 'Ripe with meaning. The broken lamp being a metaphor for the wolf. Genius!'

'So, was it an actual wheel, or an imaginary one?' This was from Ashley, the one person I hadn't met yet. A plump woman around forty, she wore a pale purple dress with a peach Alice band and frilly yellow cardigan. She reminded me of a bag of sweets. 'I might have liked it more if I'd understood the bit about the wheel.'

'The bit about the wheel?' Lucille flung out her hands in disgust. 'The wheel was the *whole point* of the book!'

'I thought it was about the woman.'

'*The Wheel of Woman*! The clue is in the title! Surely even you can understand that much.'

'And why didn't the woman have a name? I mean, just "woman". It made her a much less likeable character.'

'Argh!' Lucille stood up. 'She wasn't *meant* to be likeable! This isn't some book-by-numbers, guess-the-ending-before-you've-read-the-first-sentence, nausea-inducing, thought-rotting, auto-tune slush-fest *saga*. You might have to rummage around in your brain for the on button to read this one.' She kicked a chair with her wedge-heel.

'Sit down, Lucille,' Jamie said.

'Yes, sit down,' Frances chipped in. 'And stop kicking the furniture. You're a grown woman, not a teenage boy who can't control his hormones.' She bent down and patted Florence, who'd come out to see what was going on.

Lucille sat down.

'Anyone else?' Ellen asked. 'Jamie, what about a man's perspective?'

Jamie looked thoughtful. 'It made me want to rinse my eyes out with bleach.'

'Typical,' Lucille muttered.

'Excuse me?' Sarah asked. 'Typical what? Jamie's liked all the other books we've done.'

'He said my last choice perpetuated concepts regarding manhood that were offensive and ludicrous, and completely refused to engage in the discussion.'

'It *was* called *Winning the War Against the Y Chromosome*,' Kiko said, apologetically.

'Why do all your books begin with a W, Lucille?' Frances asked. 'What is this peculiar obsession you have with that particular letter? Have you reached W in your list of books for dominating brainless ignoramuses at book clubs?'

'Let's keep it nice, people.' Ellen held out her hands pleadingly. 'And keep it about the book, please. No personal comments. Remember, everyone's viewpoint is valid and respected here.'

'Don't be absurd!' Frances said, huffing. 'Quite clearly some viewpoints should not be respected. Especially if they aren't respect*ful*.'

Lucille's mouth dropped open.

'Any other thoughts about the book?' Ellen gabbled, before that comment could be responded to.

No, no one had any thoughts. That was, except for Lucille, but she wasn't sharing them after being so insulted.

'Well. That means we've plenty of time to choose a book for next month.' Ellen smiled. 'Jamie, I believe it's your turn?'

'Yes. Right.' Jamie sat forwards, his eyes flicking towards Sarah before settling on a stray crisp lying on the tablecloth. 'I've chosen the new book by Madelaine Smith. I've heard it's really good.'

'Flippin' 'eck!' Sarah shrieked. 'I flippin' love her books! Mum was getting me that for my birthday. She'll have to give it me early, now.' She beamed at us. 'Good choice, Jamie!'

If Jamie had turned any redder he'd have blended into the tablecloth. 'Thanks,' he mumbled.

There was a rumble of assent from around the table.

'Great.' Ellen picked up her pen quickly, her words brisk. 'That's settled, then, we're all agreed—'

'Actually,' Ashley interrupted.

'Here we go...' Frances rolled her eyes. Kiko, Sarah and Jamie all simultaneously downed their glasses. Not for the reason I initially thought.

'Last month we said we'd consider a local author next. You all agreed we've neglected local authors long enough. It's about time we supported local, bestselling author Hillary West. And, honestly, couldn't we try reading something uplifting? Something we can all understand!' She paused, chest heaving beneath the ruffles, eyes moist.

'I don't think that's quite what we agreed,' Ellen said.

'When's the last time we did a Hillary West?' Kiko asked Ellen, who flipped through the book.

'Well, let's think... could it be the last time Ashley had a book choice?' Lucille said.

'That was nearly six months ago!' Ashley cried.

'Which means it's your turn next month,' Frances said. 'No need to push in.'

'I'm not pushing in!' Ashley stood up now. 'I'm making a suggestion. All views are valid here, and I have strong views on reading local authors at the local book club.'

'Jamie's made his choice, Ash,' Sarah said. 'There's only one Hillary West book left – save it for next time.'

'Shut up!' Ashley pointed a finger at Sarah. 'We all know the reason Jamie picked Madelaine Smith, and that's favouritism.'

'Eh?' Sarah blinked. Jamie stood up, opposite Ashley. 'I told you why I picked that book, Ashley. I don't have to defend it. If we can put up with tripe about women and their wheels we can cope with Madelaine Smith.'

'Tripe?' Lucille slammed her wine glass onto the table, sloshing the recently topped-up contents onto the cloth. Florence poked her head out and barked.

'Hillary will never reply to my invitation if we don't do her book.' Ashley brushed a tear from one eye. 'Every month I ask and you always shout me down.'

'That's because it isn't your turn!' Frances shouted. 'And when are you going to take the hint, woman? She's never coming to the club! Are you dim-witted as well as unbalanced?'

'Frances!' Ellen shouted back. 'Behave!' Florence barked a couple more times in defence of her mistress.

Lucille smirked. 'And, seriously, it's women like Hillary West and her fans, teeming about the place in flouncy skirts and oversized jewellery, clogging up the roads on their bicycles and cutting their own hair – it's these women who keep the gender pay gap at 20 per cent. How can you possibly earn the same as a man when you're steeping your brain in this emotional vomit?'

'Emotional vomit?' Ashley squealed. And then she picked up her Coke glass and tossed the contents in Lucille's face.

Lucille gasped, shook her head like a wet dog, stood up and returned the gesture. Ashley ignored the drips running down her cheek and grabbed the nearest glass to hers, which was empty. As was every glass on the table, except for mine, which I hastily picked up. She swiped the crisp bowl a second before Kiko managed to grab it, and launched it at her adversary.

'If you've messed up this sixty-quid haircut I'll kill you!' Lucille screamed, as everyone not involved in the fight grabbed the remaining contents of the tabletop and backed away.

'Well, perhaps you should try cutting your hair yourself!' Ashley replied.

Ellen and Jamie scooted round and placed a hand on each woman's arm. 'Enough,' Ellen said. 'That is *enough*. We can't end every month covered in wine.'

'Not when I'm clearing it up, we can't,' Sarah muttered.

'Too much energy!' Frances pointed her stick at first Lucille, then Ashley. 'Bored and restless children misbehave, and get irritable, rude and silly. The pair of you are bored witless. You need to stop talking about other people's stories and start living your own. And that goes for all of you!' She glared at the rest of us. 'Except for Ellen, who has finally emerged from the swamp of pre-school parenting and is now making something of herself.'

'I'm not bored!' Lucille protested. 'I have a very high-powered and pressurised job, where I'm highly valued and—'

'A boring job!' Frances retorted. 'No fun and no point, just money going round and round and round. If you're not bored and dissatisfied with your boring life then why are you such a bitch?'

'Frances!' everyone but Lucille said.

'Well,' she muttered back. 'It's for her own good I'm saying it. And Ashley's. Why is she so obsessed with this author, who clearly doesn't give a hoot, if she's not bored with her own life?'

At Ellen's request, Sarah put the kettle on while the rest of us cleaned up the mess. Once reconvened with hot drinks and caramel shortbread, Ellen asked for our attention.

'Frances has a point about living our own stories instead of just discussing other people's made-up ones. So, I've a proposal. Seeing as things aren't working very well at the moment, why don't we try something different for this year? Instead of discussing books, we'll start bringing our own stories. Not made-up ones, not a writing group, but the stories of our lives. It took me twelve years to start seeing my dream become a reality. I can't wait to tell you what it's like studying midwifery. But it's crazy hard, trying to remember how to write an essay and keep up with all these eighteen-year-olds. I could use some encouragement. Why don't we all set ourselves a goal – something exciting and challenging – and over the year we can share how it's going? We can set a target to finish our goals by the Christmas party.'

We sat there for a moment, thinking about that.

'I like it,' Frances said. 'Sometimes at eighty-four you need an excuse to get up and at 'em in the morning. To beat the aches and the wobbles and the tiredness and still have a go at life.'

'I'm not sure...' Ashley picked at a loose thread on her cardigan. 'I can't think of a goal.'

'I say we go for it,' Sarah said. 'We could call it the Get Yourself a Life Worth Telling Stories About by Christmas Book Club Challenge.'

'The Christmas Book Club Challenge, for short,' Jamie added.

'Well, let's give it a month and see how it goes,' Ellen said. 'And if it can avoid wine being spilled. Or blood. Votes?'

Everyone voted yes, we could give it a go.

And I'd say this: the Christmas Book Club Challenge was anything but boring.

11

Before going home, Sarah asked if I fancied another girls' night the following Friday. 'Sean's supposed to be having Edison for the evening.' She shook her head in disgust. 'Although I've not told Edison yet. Last time he "forgot" to turn up. Apparently I should have reminded him. We'd only sorted it that afternoon.'

'I sometimes think Adam would forget he had kids if I didn't remind him,' Kiko said. 'And he lives in the same house as them.'

'Still working all hours?' Sarah asked.

Kiko nodded. 'But how can I complain when he's saving the world?' She grimaced at me. 'He manages a charity that rescues people from trafficking. Young women, kids, people working as slaves. It's horrific. I understand why he finds it hard to stop. And you can't just clock off in the middle of saving someone. Our life is very dull and safe in comparison. I'm very dull in comparison. And I feel shallow and selfish complaining about any of it. So I don't.'

Sarah huffed. 'He chose to get married and have kids. He's got a responsibility to you, too.'

Kiko looked at us nervously, her face pinched with tension. 'I'm starting to wonder if it would be best if we weren't together. The kids would probably see him more if we had custody visits like Edison and Sean. And I wouldn't spend my life feeling a disappointing second best.'

'Do you still love each other?' I asked, after a moment's silence.

She shrugged. 'I don't think we even know each other any more. I want to stay married. I never, ever thought I'd consider breaking up my family. And my parents would be devastated – they still consider divorce to be shameful, and that a man must work hard to provide for his family. But I can't keep going by myself. I can't keep having my heart stomped on every single day.' She gulped back a sob, and Sarah and I both put an arm around her.

'Come next Friday.' Sarah said.

Kiko nodded, a tiny smile flickering at the corner of her mouth. 'I'll ask Adam if he will watch the kids.'

'No, you won't!' Sarah snapped. 'You're not asking, you're telling him. Phone right now.'

Kiko paled. 'No, his mum's babysitting. Adam's working late tonight. I can't call unless it's an emergency.'

'His marriage *is* an emergency. Call him.'

She called, eyes widening in surprise when he answered. In a hesitant voice, she told him she was going out the following Friday, too. After some humming and haa-ing, Adam agreed to be home. Kiko wiped the sweat off her forehead and let out a shaky laugh. 'Right. I'll see you then.'

'Too right,' Sarah said, slamming a cupboard door shut. 'We've got a lot of work to do.'

* * *

I muddled through the weekend, working at the café and filling more bags with rubbish. I had a vague plan about borrowing someone's laptop (and Internet connection) to get some of the less-abysmal Hoard up for sale online, to supplement the tiny pile of wages I'd brought home the previous Thursday. In the meantime, I carried on sorting and cleaning, constantly on the lookout for further titbits about my family.

It was soon Monday morning. The kids and I slowly grew more used to each other through the week, spending most afternoons in a blanket fort we built (and continually rebuilt, extended, redesigned and smashed to bits), while I revealed my appalling lack of knowledge about military matters. On Wednesday Maddie had a meltdown about a specimen being knocked over during the battle of Bannockburn, but we soothed her grief with a burial ceremony for the mould, 'a worthy comrade, who fell valiantly upon the battlefield, and whose sacrifice shall not be forgotten'.

Thursday dinner-time, when nobody'd even asked me to stay, simply laying an extra place at the table as if I'd always been there, Dawson announced his pleasure that tomorrow was Friday, and, '*She* won't be here, messing everything up and making us late.'

'Dawson!' Will put down his fork. 'That was unacceptable. Jenny is doing a great job for her second week.'

No, Jenny isn't.

'It's fine,' I said. 'Of course, you want your mum there, instead of me.'

'No. I just don't want you there. I don't care who else does it.'

'That's enough,' Will said. 'You'd better think very carefully about what to say to Jenny now.'

'Sorry,' Dawson muttered. 'I'm not hungry. Can I go?' He dumped his plate, still half-full, on the counter-top above the dishwasher and stomped upstairs.

The rest of the kids, plates emptied, soon followed him.

'I am so sorry about Dawson,' Ellen said, frowning. 'I think something's going on, but I can't get him to talk about it. Please don't take it personally.'

I took a large gulp of water, and carefully set the glass down on my coaster. 'The thing is, he's right.' I forced myself to look up at my employers. 'We've been late to school every day this week. A couple of days by a lot. Today, I was late picking up from drama club because Billy hid after I told him off for chopping up a library book, and it took twenty minutes before Jonno – not me – found him. Things feel chaotic and messy. They *are* chaotic and messy. I'm making a lot of mistakes, and I'm finding coping with all five of them really challenging. I think maybe you need a professional to do this job.'

Ellen grinned. 'Was he in the wood-box?'

I nodded.

'He always goes there. Next time you'll find him straight away. I probably should have put it on the list.'

'But I'm saying I don't think there *should* be a next time. Your house is being destroyed one broken picture frame and smashed toy at a time. I'm worried I'm not good for your kids.'

'You've been here two weeks, and this was the first time Billy's hidden from you. That's impressive. I was late getting to school after the triplets were born every day for three months. And that was with a huge amount of help. This is a chaotic family. It is a messy house. If you want to quit because you hate it that's one thing – although I'd still beg you to stay. Literally, on my knees and begging. If it's because you aren't a perfect caregiver for these kids, you don't know what you're doing and you feel like they may just drive you round the bend, join the club. No one is good enough for my kids, especially not me. But together, with the grace of God and a mighty load of prayers, we can be enough. Now, are you having some ice cream? I'm off tomorrow so the weekend starts here.'

I nodded yes.

Will reached over and picked up my plate. 'You're one of us now, Jenny. For better or worse. Part of the crazy Camerons. We won't let you go without a fight.' He winked at me, and I had to pretend I needed the loo to go and pull myself together.

The thought that I might have somehow stumbled upon a place to belong, to call home, overwhelmed and bewildered me. How long would it be before these wonderful people found out what my family, Oxford University, Dougal and Duff – Richard – had all realised? I wasn't worth fighting for – quite the opposite. *Wasn't I?*

Friday morning, I woke to the blissful knowledge of a whole ten days without squabbling, nagging or wiping anybody's nose other than my own. Next week it was the half-term holidays, so Will was taking care of the kids. I thought about the latest batch of clean, crisp twenty-pound notes in my purse and hummed with glee. Today I would go food shopping. Every scream, scratch and second of stress from the previous week would be worth it. And then tonight I was heading over to Sarah's for another dose of girl-power ballads and more tortilla chips than was medically advisable.

First, I went to the shed, retrieving the car key I'd found hiding in a toolbox a couple of days earlier. Propping the shed door open, unsure of the possibilities regarding dangerous car fumes, I adjusted myself in the driver's seat. I hadn't driven since Mum gave her car to a prostitute.

I inserted the key, which to my great delight actually fitted, held my breath and turned. Nothing but a faint clicking sound. I tried again. Shook the steering wheel about a few times. Pumped randomly on the pedals while twisting the key and ordering it to start. Counted to twenty and tried it all again. Opened the bonnet, blew on everything and went over the whole palaver one more time. Went to have another look at the engine, in case a helpful arrow had a sign saying 'press this' or 'problem here'.

'It's the battery,' a voice said, causing me to bang my head hard on the bonnet.

'Really?' I asked, irritated, rubbing the sore spot. 'Are you a car expert?'

'It doesn't take an expert to know a car left undriven for years will have a dead battery,' Mack replied.

Mack leant in next to me and poked about a bit. I didn't notice that he smelled of cinnamon and vanilla, at all, as he stood beside me. Neither did I attempt to look down the neckline of his running top.

My flustered state was purely due to having bumped my head.

'So, what, it needs a jump-start?' I asked, revealing that I wasn't a total mechanical dimwit.

'No point,' Mack said. 'You need a new one.'

'Right.' My heart sank, for two reasons. One, I had been looking forward to having a car, but finding money for petrol, sorting tax, insurance and everything else was impossible enough. Repair costs would leave my dream as flat as the battery. Two, because Mack was here. Which meant that by next week I would doubtless come home to find the car purring like a tiger, equipped with a shiny new battery and a tank full of petrol. 'If I look hard enough I can probably find one in the Hoard somewhere.'

'The Hoard?' I turned to see him grinning. 'That's one word for it. It's a shame you don't want my help. Otherwise, if you found one I could show you how to swap them over, in a polite, neighbourly fashion.'

'Yes, I guess all good spies need basic car skills. The truth is, I don't even know who it officially belongs to.'

'Shame. I could help with that, too.' Mack rocked back on his heels. I said nothing.

'Well, let me know if you change your mind.' He strolled off, whistling.

I closed the bonnet, climbed on the bike and sped towards the village. Whistling. Louder.

* * *

With my groceries unpacked in clean kitchen cupboards, I spent the rest of the day hunting through the living room for car-related paperwork. (I used the term 'living room' in the loosest possible sense, since currently the only things living in there were not the intended inhabitants.) I found forty years' worth of telephone directories interspersed with junk mail. And if I could have invented a way to power a car with dust and mouse droppings I wouldn't have had to bother with a battery.

I arrived at Sarah's to find Kiko perched on the edge of the sofa, holding a glass of lemonade as if it contained cyanide.

'Don't worry about her.' Sarah offered me a bowl of popcorn. 'She's feeling guilty about being out two Friday nights on the trot.'

'I'm feeling guilty about telling you I'm considering leaving my husband!' Kiko squeaked as we plopped onto the other chairs. 'I'm happily married!'

'No, you aren't.' Sarah snorted. 'But maybe if you stopped thinking so little of yourself, remembered that you aren't put on this earth – or in that marriage – to be his unpaid servant – which, coincidentally, is otherwise known as slavery, which, coincidentally, he runs a charity to eradicate – if you could remember that, you might be able to make your marriage half decent.'

Kiko's mouth fell open. 'He doesn't treat me like a slave!'

We looked at her.

'Okay, but he doesn't mean to. He got home on time tonight so I could go out.'

'Wow.' Sarah nodded her head, fake-impressed. 'He got home on time, *once*, so you could go out. When was the last time you went on a date?'

Kiko's reply was so quiet we had to bend our heads closer to hear it. 'We went to a fundraising dinner a couple of months ago.'

'How romantic!' Sarah clutched her chest. 'I bet he didn't leave you alone and invisible in the corner for one second while he schmoozed all the guests.'

I intervened by handing Kiko the box of chocolates I'd

brought. 'Instead of making her feel even crappier, why don't we do something constructive while we wait for the food?' We had ordered take-away from a restaurant located on a campsite a few miles into the forest. 'If this is about trying to boost our self-esteem, maybe we should concentrate on something positive.'

Sarah screwed up her nose. 'Fair point, Jen. Soz, Kiko.'

We sat for a minute trying to think of something positive.

'What about the Christmas Book Club Challenge?' Sarah asked, perking up. 'Have you decided what to do yet?'

Kiko shook her head.

'I'm hoping to find something interesting in my grandma's stuff,' I said.

'Like what?' Kiko asked.

'I don't know. I never met her, and my mum never talked about her childhood, so I've no idea what I might find. Hopefully something to explain why they never spoke.' And why Grandma looked so miserable in the photos as soon as my mum appeared on the scene.

'But isn't that still someone else's story?' Sarah asked.

'It's my story too.' I shrugged. 'And, honestly, fighting my way through all that junk is enough of an adventure for now.'

The food arrived – mozzarella and chorizo pasta, steaming in the cartons. We dolloped huge portions onto plates and zoomed in on Kiko.

'What did Ellen say?' I recapped. 'Exciting, challenging. Scary. What do you want to do that's exciting and scary?'

None of us mentioned the scariest thing Kiko was thinking about doing: scooping up her kids and getting the heck out of her marriage.

'I've never really liked that kind of thing.' She gently blew on a chunk of pasta bake, oh-so-carefully.

'There must be something,' Sarah prodded. 'Some secret

dream where you think, maybe if I was an adventurous, feisty, couldn't-give-a-monkey's type woman with tons of cash and a couple of years to spare I might fancy having a go at that.'

Kiko thought about it. We helped by lobbing random suggestions at her: 'Abseiling. Burlesque dancing. Opera singing. Medieval re-enactments. Bee-keeping. Netball. Rally driving...'

When Sarah and I simultaneously paused for breath, she said, 'Well, actually...'

'Yes?' We leaned forward.

'I wouldn't mind climbing Mount Everest.'

'Right.' Sarah sat back. 'Ice cream, anyone?'

We spent a while discussing both the figurative and actual mountains that Kiko now contemplated climbing, deciding that she might as well have a look and see if it was even a possibility.

'I'm only looking for fun!' she repeated, every two minutes. 'I'm not serious about doing this!'

'That's what you reckon,' Sarah muttered, winking at me over her coffee.

'So, what about you?' I asked, hoping it was something that lay between scaling a pile of rubbish and scaling the world's highest mountain. 'What's your story going to be about?'

She put her cup down and spread out her arms like a circus ringmaster. 'I, ladies, am going to join a dating agency and find myself a fella.'

'Oooh!' Kiko said.

'Well, I'm going to have a cracking good go and hopefully a few laughs while I'm at it,' Sarah conceded. She looked at me. 'Care to join me on this tall, dark and handsome adventure?'

'Not in a million years. Let's get you signed up.'

So we did. And if Kiko laughed so hard she had a slight accident ('Honestly, I think I must be doing those pelvic-floor exercises all wrong...') it was totally worth it.

Sarah's protests that she wanted 'classy options only' soon became the catchphrase of the night. It also became apparent that any website with the word 'classy' in the description meant: 'Totally non-classy. Trashy, in fact. Trashy, slimy and quite probably perverted.'

In the end, we went for the bog-standard, mainstream site Lovelife! Then came the tussling over the profile pictures.

'No, Sarah, looking like a prison guard from Guantanamo Bay is not going to help you find a man who will suit you.'

'But doesn't that one make me look clever?'

'If clever is another word for terrifying. Or ill.'

'Please don't use that one. Please, please, please. I look like a total airhead.'

'Fun and beautiful does not mean you're an airhead!' I scolded. 'What made you think being attractive and smiley means stupid?'

'Says her with her too-big glasses and shabby jeans,' Sarah said. 'You couldn't say it more clearly if you had a sign round your neck: "Men beware– I'm not interested and deffo not interesting."'

'What?' I goggled at her.

'It's true.' Kiko giggled. 'You do look like the style you've gone for is "please don't notice me."'

'Well, how about you stop noticing me and get back to Sarah?' I huffed. Too late – my new friends launched themselves across the sofa, ripped out my bun, stole my glasses and would have forcibly removed my jeans if I hadn't loudly pointed out that this was about *Sarah* being attractive, not me.

'It's weird, though.' Kiko looked me up and down. 'You wear nice clothes but they just don't really suit you. No offence.'

'Personality-wise or your figure.' Sarah nodded wisely.

'No offence, but saying no offence at the start or end of a sentence doesn't mean it isn't offensive,' I pointed out. 'And the reason they don't suit me is because I didn't buy them.'

'Eh?' Sarah said, adding the picture I'd picked onto her profile.

'Pretty much all my clothes are Zara's rejects.' I took another swig of wine.

'Who's Zara?' Kiko asked. And that started a whole other conversation, so by the time we'd done that, and sent Sarah's details shooting off into the worldwide web, it was way too late for me to walk home. This time, when enduring another taxi ride with Tezza, I paid in advance.

12

The Monday after the holidays, I spent the morning at Ellen's, baking another cake. As I swung back out of the garden gate, Fisher slunk up in his car, eyebrows bristling through the open window.

'Still here?'

'Yes. And yes, Ellen knows I'm here, too.'

'I meant still in Middlebeck.'

I started pushing the bike along the pavement, but he simply crawled along beside me.

Glancing over, I saw the crocodile smile again. 'Can't be pleasant, living without basic appliances.'

What would new Jenny say to an arrogant crocodile? I decided new Jenny wouldn't bother.

'Top-of-the-range kitchens in the flats behind the church. Dishwashers. Induction hobs.'

I clambered on the bike, pedals spinning as I raced along the empty pavement, while Fisher called after me. 'I'll do you a very nice deal on a part-exchange. But they won't be available for long.'

Why was Fisher so keen to buy my cottage? And how did he know I had no appliances? Did Ellen know? Had she asked him to make me an offer? Didn't she know I couldn't begin to think about letting go of the only link to my family that didn't involve me having to actually speak or otherwise interact with them?

* * *

I arrived home with the cake unharmed despite the angry and anxious thoughts sloshing around in my brain and disturbing my balance. Then I sucked in a big lungful of crisp forest air and knocked on Mack's back door. Then, of course, knocked twice more before he answered it.

'Hi.'

'Hi.' His frown lessened slightly when he spied the tub in my outstretched hands.

'Peace offering?'

Ooh, that made me bristle. 'Why do I need to make a peace offering?'

He shrugged. 'A month of your prickly attitude, constant banging and the gradual encroachment of your trash-heap onto my charming garden?'

'My orderly stack is not encroaching on your raggedy, charmless garden.'

He raised his eyebrows.

'Fine,' I snapped. 'I'll move it.'

'No need.' He looked at me thoughtfully, and I'm sure a smile lurked somewhere behind those dark eyes. 'Another cake'll be more than adequate recompense. For now.'

I fidgeted on one foot, every inch of trampled pride

urging me to hand over the cake and scarper. It had nearly won, when Mack suddenly narrowed his eyes.

'Oh, no. What have you done now?'

'What? Nothing! I've made you a cake. That's all I've done!'

'But if it's not a peace offering, then why?' He pulled his head back. 'Are you trying to make this a thing, us sharing cake?'

I scrabbled for something to say that didn't make me come off worse, yet again. Mack said nothing, no doubt happy to watch me dig myself in deeper.

'I know I've not always been as nice as I could have been, and now my grandma's hideous stuff is spilling across your land because I can't afford a skip or a car, but, well, I'm working on it. And, um, in the meantime, it would be really helpful if, well, I was hoping you might...'

Mack leant on the doorframe, as if settling in for the night.

I stomped down the irksome, idiot part of me that wanted to join him, both of us leaning on the doorframe and staring at each other until morning.

'Can I have your broadband code?'

'You want to poach my broadband?' That was definitely a smile! Right there, hiding in his beard. 'Wait here.'

Before I could find the pluck to ask for favour number two, considerably larger than favour number one, he disappeared, returning a minute later with the code written on a scrap of paper.

'If you go over my limit I'll want more baked goods as recompense.'

'Actually...'

He took the paper back.

'Could I borrow your computer?'

There was a horrible silence while Mack stared at me. I held my breath and bit my lip to prevent jabbering. He had to know this was important, or I wouldn't have asked. And the only reason I asked him, and not Ellen, or Sarah or Kiko, was because he was the only one who knew about my dire living conditions. Nobody under retirement age existed without Internet access. Or a smartphone. Nobody except losers with nothing of their own, who got fired, had to return their work phone and buy the world's cheapest non-smart phone, for non-smart people who had made a total mess of things.

I think Mack must have seen something despairing in my eyes, because instead of laughing and slamming the door in my face, or joking about how I'd probably destroy his computer, he didn't even roll his eyes. 'When?'

'Pardon?'

'When would you like to borrow my computer?'

'Um... now?'

He shook his head. 'I'm working now.'

'Then, um, whenever you *aren't* working?' Ugh. I hated this. Old Jenny, relying on favours and handouts.

'I'm going for a run in a couple of hours. I'll drop it round then.'

'I could just use it here...' *I could just come in and explore the secret innards of your mysterious house...* I was dying to know what kind of furniture and paint colour and photographs Mack had. Or whatever else it was that meant he never let me across the threshold.

'What, and leave you loose in my fully functioning, disaster-free home?' He shook his head. 'I'll bring it round.'

I resisted the urge to argue. 'Thank you for trusting me with your computer. I promise I'll be exceptionally careful.'

I started to walk away, when he called my name. 'Jenny.'

'Yes?'

He held out his hands. What? Did he want a hug? Did I want to hug him back? I looked at those big, lightly tanned, toned arms and found out I did.

'Oof.' The tub I'd somehow managed to forget I was holding slammed into Mack's chest. I'm not sure who said 'oof'. I think it was both of us.

He blinked, reaching up to grab the tub. 'You forgot to leave the cake.'

Yes. Of course. Um. 'Enjoy!' I trilled, and practically sprinted across to my open door and dived inside.

A mouse was sitting on the kitchen table, laughing at me. I threw a dishcloth and it ran back into the mess. I swear I could hear it still laughing from behind the skirting board.

* * *

Two hours later, as promised, Mack knocked on my door. Without waiting for an invitation, he stepped inside, forcing me to back towards the table. I made a mental note to copy his tactics when I returned the computer. Mack scanned the room, ignoring me.

'I know. It's still a shambles.'

He tipped his head to one side. 'Are you keeping food down here now?'

'I've bleached everything! And it's all in plastic boxes to keep the mice out.'

'Are they a big problem?'

'No.' I grimaced. 'Just lots and lots of little ones.'

He kept looking around. 'I don't know whether to be impressed or appalled.'

'Try neither. Try minding your own business!' *Here we go again...* 'Look, the table's clean. Your computer will be fine.'

He nodded, placing it on the table. 'How long do you need it for?'

'Not long. An hour?'

'See you in an hour, then.' He winced. 'Please be careful.'

I waited for him to leave, then settled myself at the table. A bad thought had crossed my mind. This was Mack's computer. What if I accidentally stumbled across some personal information? A file? An Internet history? Glancing at the window, I clicked on the mouse pad and tried not to look at the icons coming up on the home screen, while sort of looking at them at the same time out the corner of my eye.

My attempt to resist temptation was futile. I had been set up as a guest user, with access to no files, no history, nothing.

Slightly peeved at the missed opportunity to do the right – and, let's be honest, maybe the teeniest chance of perhaps the wrong – thing, I set about discovering who the car belonged to.

And then I searched Dougal and Duff.

That result hit me like a swift kick in the guts. Dougal and Duff were pleased to announce that Zara Birkenshaw was now a partner. Even more splendid and wonderful was her upcoming wedding to Richard Abernethy.

The big day would be 20 July, five months away. Would my sister invite me to her wedding?

If she did, would I go?

If I did, would I end up breaking her nose for a second time?

I guess I couldn't blame them for not inviting me.

I'd stick to blaming her for stealing my boyfriend, getting

me fired and kicking me out of her flat three days before Christmas instead.

A few minutes later, Mack staggered in, panting. I quickly shut the computer down. Taking a long swig from a water-bottle, he threw himself into a chair. 'Did you get what you needed done?'

'Yeah, but I can't submit the form without a bill proving my address.'

'Right.' He picked up the laptop and left, denying me the satisfaction of telling him it was confidential when he asked what the form was for. I picked up the car maintenance manual I'd borrowed from the library, and pretended to read it. Having to wait a few more weeks before submitting the DVLA form to find out who owned the car simply gave me more time to learn about changing car batteries. Or, even better, I might have found the paperwork by then, saving the DVLA charge of two pounds fifty plus the price of a stamp. That could probably buy enough petrol to reach the village, which was nothing to be sniffed at.

I put the book down, heaved myself into the living room and opened another box.

The next Monday, I had a major work-related breakthrough.
Which led to a second, far more revealing breakthrough.
That breakthrough just about broke my heart.

The first thing was I got all five kids to school on time.
With fifty spare seconds, to boot. That morning, I had been a
machine. Toast, cereal, bags, outfits, lunchboxes, untangling
myself from sea-monster net-trap, locating runaway caterpil-
lar. Nailed 'em all.

I strode into the playground like a warrior. Head high,
arms swinging, breath only slightly more puffed than usual. I
shooed the triplets over to where their teacher stood waiting
with a big thumbs-up, hugged Maddie goodbye, and then
realised I'd forgotten to hand Dawson his PE bag.

Hurrying round to his classroom door, I found him not
yet inside.

My heart stopped, right before it cracked.

A group of boys were clustered in a circle, girls dotted
around them. That strange mix of ten-and-eleven-year olds,

some looking almost like adults, others still childlike in comparison, round-cheeked with innocent eyes.

And Dawson, huddled by the wall. Eyes on the ground, clutching his rucksack strap for dear life. The kind of utterly alone you could only be when surrounded by laughing, noisy others. Desperate to be invisible, so no one would realise what a nobody you were. Desperate to be noticed, for just one person to acknowledge you existed.

The bell rang, and the children started pushing and jostling their way inside. A particularly tall girl slammed into Dawson, causing his head to smack, hard, into the brick wall. The girl shouted in annoyance, charging after the boy who'd knocked her. But not before she paused to throw a look of such contempt and irritation at Dawson that I cringed.

Dawson held back, clutching his head, face screwed up in pain.

He hadn't uttered a sound.

I hurried down the path, but he jerked away, straightening his jacket.

'You forgot your bag.' I held it out, trying to stop my hand trembling.

He stared at the ground, face a rigid mask. 'Thanks.'

'Dawson, are you having problems with the other kids?'

'No.' He tried to sneer, but his voice shook worse than my hands.

'Have you talked to your mum or dad about it?'

'About what?' He looked at me now, and I saw fear in his eyes, despite the defiant voice. 'A kid bumped into me. It's hardly a big deal.'

I nodded. Now wasn't the time – or the place – to talk about it.

'Okay. Well. You'd best get inside. It would be a shame to

be late the one day we've made it on time.' My smile was about as convincing as his denial.

He trudged to the door, turning back as he grabbed the handle. 'You can't tell them about this. They'll only worry and fuss and end up making it worse. Promise you won't tell them.'

'Tell them what?'

'Exactly! There's nothing to tell.'

Oh, boy. What to do now? I looked at him trying so hard not to care, and knew exactly how he felt. I would have died rather than have my parents, or babysitters, or teachers, or anyone else full stop, know I had no friends. If I acted out of the upset charging through my bloodstream, I ran the risk of causing a load more trouble for a lonely, unhappy boy.

I took a deep breath. 'I won't say anything yet, if we can talk about it later.'

'Please.' His voice was a whisper. A fragment of heart snapped off and splintered my chest.

'I won't say anything without your permission.' I wanted to hug him, press him tight against my middle and absorb some of that anguish, but I knew he'd crumble. 'Go on. Shoulders back, chin up. Ignore them as best you can.'

Head down, shoulders slumped, he limped through the door.

It killed me inside because I had *been* that kid. Still felt I *was* that woman. I had scuttled through most of my life, every action an apology for inflicting my existence on the world. And during those dark nights after Oxford, when my broken soul had seemed to be plummeting down a bottomless pit of despair and hopelessness, I had at times considered that not existing was perhaps the better option.

And to see Dawson – clever, interesting, thoughtful Dawson, with a family who loved and cherished him, a home that was warm and bright and healthy – to see him cowed and hurting tore me up more than I could have imagined. I wanted to storm into that classroom, fists flying, to fight his corner.

By mid-morning I was wound up so tight I could barely think, so I decided some constructive destruction of rubbish was called for. It took an hour to build a decent-sized bonfire, piling up reams of ancient paperwork and then applying what seemed like dozens of matches to get things burning.

It was a perfect day for a bonfire – the late February air carrying a faint whiff of springtime, the gentle breeze whooshing smoke up into the blue sky, far above the treetops. I pulled my jacket hood up, perching on Mack's picnic bench while I sipped tea and wished I could send all of life's trashy bits up and away into the atmosphere as easily as old magazines.

Early afternoon, Mack joined me, carrying two mugs of coffee. We watched in silence for a while, taking it in turns to throw another armful of paper on the fire every now and then.

'Not working today?' I asked eventually, in an attempt to stop freaking out about Dawson for at least a minute.

'I *am* working.'

I swivelled to look at him.

'I'm thinking. Sorting out some problems. Fires are a great focus for pondering, I find.'

'I presumed you were making sure I don't burn the forest down.'

'That too.'

After another silence he asked, 'Have you eaten lunch?'

'I'm not hungry.'

He looked at me, face blank. 'I'm getting a sandwich. If I make two that's not me suggesting you can't provide your own lunch. It just seems... neighbourly to not sit here scoffing my face alone.'

'Thanks.' Wow. How had we reached this place where a sandwich could be so complicated? 'But I'm fine.'

Mack looked at me, face still inscrutable, for a beat before going inside. After pacing about the fire for far longer than it took to make a sandwich, watching it dwindle to glowing embers, I decided to survey the fire through the kitchen window instead.

Later, Ellen called. 'Dawson's been throwing up, so I've skived off my afternoon lectures.' There was a loud crash followed by a wail in the background. 'I have to go. I'll call tomorrow and let you know what's happening.'

'Um, well...' I groped about for something to say, how to say it.

Ellen misunderstood me completely. 'I'll still pay you, of course!'

'No, you don't have to do that, it's not that, I...'

A much louder shriek. 'Sorry, I really have to go, 'bye!'

I laced and unlaced my boots three times, certain the right thing was to tell Ellen face to face what I'd seen that morning. Yes, Dawson might not forgive me, but he was a *child*. He couldn't see what was best for himself, could he?

In the end, I decided to finish the Hillary West book in bed, with a packet of cheap chocolates. I would speak to Dawson when he'd recovered, then decide what to do next.

* * *

For many years I'd been a woman without dreams. Hobbling from one day to the next, clutching the fragments of my mental health to my chest. My only dream was that one day I might dare to have real dreams again.

And then, slowly, over the past few years I'd begun to imagine. To hope. To think about having the guts to get a job that didn't make my eyes bleed from boredom. To picture a scenario where Richard would hold my hand in public, where Zara would invite me to her parties. And I would feel so secure, so confident, I would decline, busy with a fulfilling life of my own instead. I'd begun to plan the home I would one day live in, full of colour and squishy furnishings and hundreds of books...

And now. Now at least half those things had come true. I owned a house, some potential friends, a fledgling social life, and a job that was anything but boring. And the rest of those dreams – the ones involving Richard and Zara – seemed more like nightmares.

Now, I dreamed about three things, over and over again: washing machine; oven; fridge.

Pulling an envelope out from the drawer by my bed and counting the money I'd squirrelled away inside, I wondered which one I wanted most. But soon I'd have bills to pay. I needed a cheap computer so I could start selling some things. To hire a skip. And who knew what other problems were hiding in the Hoard? I might have to give in and hire pest control if the scrabblings above my head got any worse.

I put the envelope back, shut my dreams away in the drawer and tried to be happy for those which had, so unexpectedly, come true.

14

Back working on Wednesday, I was still rushing about trying to sort coats and find enough pairs of shoes for the right feet when Dawson announced he would walk by himself, slamming the front door before I could reply. At school, I toyed with peeping around the corner to see where he was, but knew it would do nothing towards earning his trust.

Instead, I waited until that afternoon, finding him in his bedroom.

'I'm busy.' He clearly was, bent over his desk, concentrating on a sheet of paper.

'I know, but I'm worried.'

No reply.

I had thought long and hard about this, but still felt a hot, painful lump in my throat as I moved to sit on his bed. 'How long have you had no friends?'

Head buried in the paper, he froze.

'This talk is two-way; did I forget to mention that?' I added, trying to ignore my heart bashing against my ribs.

The only sounds were the clock ticking and the scratch of

his pencil against the paper. I began to think he wasn't going to answer, which left me sort of stuck for what to do next.

'I *do* have friends. They don't go to the same school as me, that's all. They live in Hatherstone.'

'Oh, okay. What are they called?'

'Lucas and Erik.' It was clear from his flat tone that he was hating every second of this conversation and had only answered, with the minimum of information, so I'd go away and stop bugging him. 'They go to our church. Happy?'

'Happier.' I took another deep breath. 'Has something happened, or has school always been like this?'

'I used to be friends with Daniel, but he moved. And then Harry and Porter started playing football with the rest.' He shrugged his slim shoulders. It made me want to cry. 'If you don't play football, no one's friends with you. It's just how it is.'

'Don't you like football?'

He carried on drawing. 'What do *you* think? And even if I did, I'm so bad no one would let me play.'

'What about your cousin, the one you walk home with?'

He shook his head. 'Austin hates me the most. And he walks with his stupid girlfriend now anyway. Which I'm glad about. I like walking by myself.'

'I really think your mum could help with this. And your dad – he must be an expert. Most kids have times when friendships change, and they need to find new people to hang about with.'

'Next year I'll be at Redway with Lucas. I don't want to be friends with anyone in my class. They're idiots.'

I thought about him shrinking into that wall on Monday. Remembered how long five months of lunchtimes, break times and group work could feel when you were ten.

'Maybe we could invite Lucas and Erik for tea sometimes?'

'I used to go there. They live in Hatherstone Hall – it's way bigger than this house so it's more fun. But you don't have a car, and they can't get here because their mum and dad work at the hall.'

'Right.' I crossed a big red line through the dream fridge and replaced it with a car battery. 'This might not mean anything, but I didn't really have any friends at school either. Or right up to when I moved here, to be honest.'

'Why not?'

'Lots of reasons. I didn't like myself, so I tried to hide away so people didn't get to know me and find out what a loser I was. And after I left school I was ill. For a long time. I didn't really get a chance to make any friends. All I'm saying is, I know that hearing other kids talking about parties and clubs and stuff like that and not being a part of it hurts, even when they're idiots. So, if ever you want to let off steam, or need a few rules bent to make things easier, I'm here.'

'I'm okay.' He went back to the picture. 'I don't need friends.'

'Maybe not. You're a strong, resourceful young man, with a family who love you. But most people find friends make life even better. I wish I'd had some sooner now I've found out for myself. If you want help with that, let me know.'

I left the room, my heart a little lighter at having connected with Dawson at last.

As I closed the door behind me he muttered, 'You could leave, so we can have a nanny with a car. *That* would help.'

I didn't leave. Instead I got back to cleaning up, chasing, buttoning, laughing and winging it for three hours, four days a week. It remained utterly exhausting, but not in a way I was used to – this was a satisfied, happy, job-well-done sort of tired.

I had decided the best way to take care of the Cameron kids was to emulate their parents, and do the exact opposite of the way my own had done it. So I loved them. I loved them with my time and attention, my praise and encouragement, my care and my boundaries. It turned out I'd been storing up a lot of love over the years. Letting some of it out was easier than I thought.

And if sloppy kisses and muddy hugs, diagrams of futuristic weaponry and fun facts about lichen were anything to go by, I was mostly loved in return. And, hey, four out of five ain't bad.

In between, I spent long hours hacking at and digging up the brambles and undergrowth round the back of the house. I uncovered a chicken-coop buried in the undergrowth, and pondered a half-hearted idea about a vegetable patch. Maybe a beehive. After a couple of days I found the remains of the boundary fence to my land. The garden wasn't huge, but I didn't need it to be – I had the whole forest on my doorstep.

In the evenings, still chilly as March blew in, I continued working inside the house. Although in desperate need of some fresh paint, the kitchen was more or less straight now. At the back of the pantry, I found my first real treasure, hidden behind a broken ironing board and covered in dead woodlice: a slow cooker. I bleached, scrubbed and rinsed it several times, then raced to the shop to buy the ingredients for a chicken casserole.

The fragrance of that casserole wafting through the house, as I searched through the pockets of thirteen hand-bags, was the best darn smell in the world: thyme, leeks, fresh protein and hope.

I declined dinner at the Camerons' that evening, whizzing home to eat my own home-cooked food. I ate so much I had to un-pop two buttons on my jeans.

Then I had to strain them closed again when I looked at the remaining food and realised I had nowhere to store it, so had better find an alternative location.

Mack opened the door looking like a lumberjack in a thick checked shirt. He wrinkled his brow, which I translated as, 'Hi, Jenny, great to see you! Come on in!'

So I did. At least I tried, until he shifted to block my entrance. That pushing-your-way-into-someone-else's-house manoeuvre was trickier than it looked.

'I made some casserole, and had loads left over. I thought you might want it.'

He looked at the slow-cooker pot, wrapped in a tea towel. 'Did you find that in the Hoard?'

'It's been rigorously cleaned. Multiple times.'

'Have you eaten from it?' He peered at me.

'Yes! It's clean!'

'Why are you bringing me leftovers?'

'What, apart from it being a nice thing to do?'

'You don't have enough to be giving food away,' he said.

I took a deep breath, wishing I had a hand free to push my glasses back up. 'I'm not giving it away, I'm repaying a minute morsel of the debt I owe you.'

'What debt? I lent you that stuff.'

'I smashed your window on purpose.'

'If I take this food can we call it even?' He sounded exasperated.

'Why are you getting mad at me when I'm giving you something?'

'Because I don't enjoy keeping score. Life isn't a tennis

match. It can't be measured in meals, or tools, or favours done. I would like to just get on with being me, behaving in a manner that means I sleep at night, without having every little thing noted down in your book of neighbourly transactions.'

'I haven't got a fridge,' I blurted out, interrupting. 'And really don't want to cycle through the dark with a massive hotpot to find someone else to give it to. Okay? So, will you please take the damn casserole before my hands start blistering?'

Mack looked at me in surprise, allowing me to seize the moment and squeeze past him into the kitchen. 'And the least you can do is finally invite me in!' I crowed, dumping the pot on the worktop and waltzing into the living room beyond.

Then I looked – properly – at the living room. My crowing fizzled to a weak chirrup.

'Wow. Your side is the exact opposite of my side.'

Mack's living room contained an ugly black leather armchair and a side table with a laptop and a dirty mug on it. That was it.

'Where's all your stuff?'

More to the point, *what do you do in here all day, with a laptop and nothing else?*

Mack, standing in the doorway between the kitchen and living room, shifted onto the other foot. 'I keep most things upstairs. Stops me getting distracted when I'm working.'

'Must be an important job you have. Either that or a really boring one.'

'Thanks for the casserole.' He coughed. 'I'll drop any left-over leftovers round tomorrow.'

I looked at him, wondering. Remembered his office was

supposedly upstairs. Remembered how he'd poked his nose all round my house before I could stop him.

I made it to the landing before he caught up with me, but I wriggled under his arm and threw myself through the nearest door, landing on my stomach in what was quite clearly Mack's bedroom.

A bed, a wardrobe. A book on the floor beside an empty glass.

I pulled myself up. 'Well, that wasn't a lie. You do keep *most things* up here, in the strictest sense of the word.'

He glared at me. 'I don't like clutter.' 'Are you undercover?'

'No. I'm not undercover. I currently don't have many possessions. And I prefer it that way. Thanks again for the food. Now, will you please get out of my bedroom?'

'What if a friend drops by? Do they sit on the floor?' I headed back downstairs. 'Do you have two mugs, or do you share?'

'We manage,' he said, voice tight, herding me onto his doorstep.

'Right. Okay. Well, enjoy the chicken,' I said, turning round to see the door already closed.

Later that night, I listened to the water gurgling through next door's pipes and replaced my smug grin with questions: why was Mack living in a ramshackle cottage in the middle of nowhere, supposedly working all the time at this mystery job? And if he 'currently' had no possessions, where had they all gone?

He seemed to be a kind man underneath his grumpiness

and need to keep a distance. He noticed things; he was thoughtful and generous.

I wondered if I'd ever be able to ask Mack the question I had asked Dawson: how long have you had no friends?

* * *

That Friday, I washed my bedding in the bath, feeling a little like my grandmother must have done in the days before washing machines, pounding and pummelling, not sure where the steam ended and my sweat began.

Someone knocked on the front door. A quick dash to the bedroom window revealed a sleek, shiny car parked a safe distance from the junk. An identical car to that driven by a local crocodile-slash-property-developer. I waited, holding my breath (because crocodiles had an acute sense of hearing). Another knock, louder this time. Was I being cowardly? Maybe. But I'd decided not to waste any more of my life in the company of people who made me feel inferior. Especially on my afternoon off.

Eventually, the letterbox rattled, quickly followed by an expensive engine purring away into the distance.

I counted to ten, ran down the stairs and then spent an age clearing the stack of old paint pots, deckchairs, plastic tubs full of nails and boxes bulging with Betamax videos before I could squeeze my arm round to reach the note pushed through the letterbox. F. F. Fisher (headed paper) asked me to call, again offering to buy the house for well above market value.

Why was he so interested in Charlotte Meadows' old cottage?

I ripped up the note and got back to my washing.

Forty minutes of wringing and squeezing later, I picked the bits of note out of the bin and pieced them back together, copying Fisher's number onto a scrap of paper. One day the house would be finished. If I was still living without basic appliances then, I might just consider Fisher's offer. After all, I'd never even met Charlotte Meadows. Staying here out of sentimentality would be stupid and pointless, right? Perhaps I would feel more sentimental about a decent kitchen and living closer to civilisation.

I blew my nose, wiped the tears – now mysteriously falling – and got back to work.

15

That evening, we convened the first meeting for the *Christmas Book Club Challenge*. Once everyone had a slice of warm apple cake, Ellen called us to order.

'Good to see you all here. I hope you've been enjoying your challenge and have some stories to share. Who's going first?'

Sarah volunteered. She'd been dying to tell us all about her first Lovelife! date.

'So, my challenge is to find a man who's not a lazy, selfish, untrustworthy waster,' she announced.

'That shouldn't be too hard!' Ellen said.

'Yeah, but he also has to be interesting, kind, love kids, properly like me and be single.'

I snuck a glance at Jamie. He looked like a stunned bear.

'Apart from that I'm keeping an open mind. But, I thought, why not kick off with the best-looking bloke on the app? He didn't seem a total deadbeat, so we arranged to meet at Scarlett's for a drink. I spruced myself up, dropped Edison at the Dud's and sat in the car park until I was ten minutes late, so's not to seem too keen.

'First impressions: miraculously, Tom looked even better in real life. Bought me a drink, didn't ogle my boobs or anything. It was a cracking start. My heart was *racing*, ladies and gentleman. It ain't thumped like that in a while.'

The gentleman opposite me looked as though he might need CPR.

'And?' Ashley leant forward, her necklaces tapping on the table, voice slightly breathless.

'And then he started talking.' She paused, looking round at us all. 'And talking. And then a load more talking. I bought us another drink, and he talked some more. It became pretty obvious what his favourite topic of conversation was: Tom. Main hobby? Tom. Primary interest? Tom. What was he looking for in a relationship? My guess, a mirror. Not a real-life woman with a brain and a mouth of her own. I don't know if a woman exists who'd enjoy listening to him r-a-a-amble on about how awesome and fit and brilliant he is. But I'm not that woman. In my opinion, nobody should spend an hour describing their daily fitness routine. Let alone on a date. I could tell you what this man had for breakfast. He probably couldn't tell you my name.

'So, lesson learnt: unnaturally good-looking, may equal, unnaturally self-centred and boring. I'm going to try a boy-next-door type next.'

Jamie, now seeming a little less shell-shocked, looked thoughtful. Perhaps he was figuring out how to move next door, given that Sarah's only neighbours were squirrels and foxes.

'Thanks, Sarah,' Ellen said. 'We'll look forward to hearing future instalments. Who's next? Lucille?'

Lucille tucked a strand of glossy hair behind her ear. 'My challenge is to run a marathon. But I wouldn't want to bore you by going on about my fitness regime.' She tossed Sarah a sour glance.

'Well, why not tell us something else, instead?' Jamie said. 'Why pick this challenge? What's training been like?'

Lucille talked for a few minutes about how she spent most of her time at work, or with her kids and husband, and rarely any time alone, just by and for herself. So, she now got up every morning at six and ran. Sometimes she used the time to think, sometimes just to *be*. She had made it up to five K in the first month, her feet were sore, her shins ached and she'd lost three pounds. The sound of her kids whining 'Mu-u-u-u-mm-e-e-e' no longer made her feel like sticking her face in the blender. She was addicted.

Jamie then brought out a large plastic tub. 'I have quite a... physical job, as you know.' He wiped one hand across his brow. After leaving the army, Jamie had started a 'problem resolution' company specialising in resolving the kind of problems he couldn't talk about, for security reasons. Reasons such as those 'problems' might come and kick the crap out of him. Or blow up his car.

He was on first-name terms with police superintendents, politicians and leading figures in industry. Ellen told me that last year he'd spent New Year's Eve with the National Security Advisor. He often worked with Kiko's husband, Adam, when things at the charity got sticky, which was how he'd heard about the book club. He frequently disappeared for days at a time at very short notice. Yet, in the past two years, he'd only missed two book-club nights. A third time he turned up late, with black paint smeared across his face and a three-inch gash along his forearm held together with duct tape. He calmly discussed the historical crime novel, drank coffee, ate chilli popcorn and patted Florence before disappearing back into the night.

But just get that sneaky, badass, fearless warrior who vacuum-packed villains for breakfast in the same room as Sarah, and see his muscles tremble. He swallowed, picked up the tub, put it down again.

'My job can be quite stressful. And violent. Leaving it behind, to switch back to being, well, human again, can be hard. So, for my challenge I thought I'd do something homely. The opposite of kicking a vicious psychopath in the windpipe. I made these.'

He opened the box with his battle-scarred hands, and tipped it up to show rows of cupcakes, half iced pink and covered in white roses, the rest blue and topped with miniature rainbows.

'They're gorgeous!' Ashley cooed. 'How did you manage those teeny flowers?'

'It took me a few goes.' He shrugged.

I could imagine the mounds of rejected cupcakes Jamie had been living on for the past month.

He offered them round, and we all spent the next few minutes ooh-ing and mmm-ing at how light and delicious they were.

'You should sell these,' I said to Sarah, who was currently licking the icing off her fingers.

'Too right.' She groaned in delight. Jamie pulled at his T-shirt as though the collar was suddenly way too tight. 'But there are food hygiene laws and stuff. You have to register your premises and get them inspected and all that.'

'Jamie could make them here,' Ellen said.

'I hardly think Jamie wants to be confronted with my first-thing-in-the-morning face and make cakes when he's got his own massively successful business to run.'

'I wouldn't mind,' he said, eyes flicking over to Sarah and back. 'That is, of course, if you like them. I mean, we could try it, see how it goes.'

Please say yes! Everyone else beamed telepathic messages over to Sarah's side of the table.

She shook her head in befuddlement. 'You're like Batman. Why would you want to do *this*?'

We all held our breaths, waiting for Jamie to tell Sarah even a hint of the reason why he wanted to bake cakes at the crack of dawn in her cramped café.

'It makes a nice change,' he said to a blob on the table-cloth. 'And I've been considering a new career. One that doesn't involve smashing people's heads against concrete pillars or wriggling through drainage pipes with a ferret's teeth embedded in my ankle-bone.'

'Oh, go on, then.' Sarah took a huge bite out of another cake. 'Come along next time you're free and we'll give it a go.'

Ashley's challenge was to get Hillary West along to the book club. This was greeted with a barrage of groans, but she dug her heels in. 'I'm not writing to her publishers any more. I'm going to find out where she lives and go straight to the woman herself! That will involve all manner of new skills, and you can't say it isn't a challenge.'

'Okay,' Ellen agreed. 'If you can come up with some adventures along the way, we'll allow it for now.'

My turn. I took a big gulp of water and sat up straighter. 'My challenge is finding out about my family. As you know, a few weeks ago I moved into my grandmother's cottage. What I haven't told you is that I never met her. I know nothing about her or my grandfather. And I don't know why. It's weird to live in a place where strangers know more about my own family than I do. But for today, I'll start by telling you why even moving here has been a challenge. And, believe me, just talking about this is a challenge in itself.'

I told them that I'd left my job suddenly, but not why. About my sister's extravagant living arrangements – the luxury apartment and the housekeeper, Claudia. The thousand-pound shoes she'd passed on to me. The super-expensive restaurants Richard had taken me to. The relentless and mindless waste.

And that I'd gladly left with one suitcase and a rucksack, and less than a hundred pounds in cash.

I described my first night sleeping in the car, and those that had followed in the bath. I didn't think people knew whether to laugh or feel horrified as I talked about the bugs, the smell, the dirt, the Hoard. Washing clothes by hand and living off cold food that I had no way to keep cold. I told them about Mannequin Diana and the squillions of mice I'd called the Borrowers.

That the only thing tethering me to earth seemed to be the cottage. The hope that I had a past, a family, a *point*. And my dreams of making the cottage into a home again, and finally achieving something.

'You have a home here, Jenny,' Ellen said. Her voice was strong but her eyes were brimming. 'Home is more than four walls.'

'I know that.' I nodded. 'And you make me feel at home in a way my parents and sister never did. But if I left next month, you wouldn't miss me, not really.'

She opened her mouth to protest, but I carried on. 'I'm honestly not looking for sympathy. I'm just explaining that my challenge was to, well, find a home. But it's changed. It's now to *make* a home. To make the most of where I've ended up, even with all the mess and the broken stuff and the questions and the mistakes. To make a story of my life I can be proud of. It's tough, but it's making me stronger. And I've never, not once, felt strong before. So, I'm enjoying it. I'm glad to be here. Glad I got fired for punching my sister in the face.'

'You did WHAT?' Ashley squealed.

'That's another month's chapter.' I rolled my eyes in a devil-may-care manner. 'Who's next?'

Frances was next.

Oh, my goodness.

She was also last.

How could Kiko possibly talk about her dreams of mountain-climbing and Ellen tell us funny stories about her midwifery course after that?

'Following some thorough and most unpleasant investigations into my bowels, some doctor with sweaty hands and a twitchy face has decided I've got cancer. I don't know why. I feel fine. Or as fine as I can hope to feel sixteen years shy of a century. Now, please don't interrupt with your murmurs of condolence and sobs and sniffles. It's hardly big news to be told I'm going to die in a year or so.'

'Can they do anything?' Kiko asked, face ashen.

'They offered me chemo, commencing next week.'

'Well, we'll help with that, of course,' Kiko said. 'Drive you to the hospital, and make sure you have whatever you need.'

'That's awfully kind of you, but won't be necessary.' Frances pounded her stick on the floor a couple of times. Florence chuffed in response. 'I do not intend to waste precious weeks being carted back and forth to hospital, vomiting into a cardboard basin and trembling with exhaustion, full of drips and wires and unnatural holes.

'I'm not afraid of going to heaven. Big Mike has been waiting for me long enough, and quite frankly I'm getting tired of it down here. Why would I pump myself full of poison to try and delay that by a few months? I don't have children to miss me. No chemotherapy. I will accept medication to ease unpleasant symptoms if and when it becomes necessary.'

'But...'

'For goodness' sake!' Frances barked. 'No buts! I've made my decision.'

'You think you're immortal!' Ashley wailed.

'I am!' Frances said. 'But this body isn't. And I'm more than ready for the new body that the Good Lord promised in the next life.'

What could we say? Frances had nursed her husband, Big Mike, through lung cancer. She knew what saying yes – or no – to treatment might mean.

'I wish I'd not found out so I could avoid the sympathy and the appointments and the whispering. But there's no point trying to keep a secret round here. And I might be needing a few favours later on, depending on how things pan out.

'In the meantime, I plan to wear this body out completely before I go. To squeeze what life out of it I can. So, that is my challenge. Wearing it out before the cancer does. Next week I've signed up to go open-water swimming for starters.'

'You could climb Mount Everest with me!' Kiko blurted.

The rest of us nodded our agreement. Nobody in that room believed for one second that Kiko was going to climb Mount Everest.

'Well, whatever you need. Just ask,' Sarah said, tipping her head back in a pointless attempt to stop the tears spilling out. 'And we're really sorry, Frances. What shitty news.'

'Yes.' Frances nodded briskly. 'Shitty. Literally and metaphorically, as Lucille would say.'

Lucille said nothing. Like the rest of us, any words were blocked by the lump of sadness and frustration and love clogging up her throat.

That was not the last time we would cry with Frances. But, boy, in the weeks to come we would laugh with her a whole lot more.

16

'Stop it!' I hummed with irritation, anger, humiliation and a smidgen of joy.

'Excuse me?' Mack's face appeared, dark and foreboding in the forest shadows.

'How many times do I have to tell you to stop this?' I was flapping my arms around like a crazy woman. The kind of person who named the mice infesting her home.

'I don't particularly appreciate people hammering on my door in the evening and yelling at me.' Mack looked past me into the night beyond and huffed out a long sigh. 'I don't like being ordered about, and I don't know what the hell you're talking about. So... bye.' He started to shut the door.

'The fridge!' I squawked. 'I've seen your house now so you can't pretend you have random spare household items lying around. I insist you take it back.'

Mack opened the door again, his brow wrinkled. I pointed at the tiny fridge, which I'd dragged over balanced on one of those ancient shopping trolleys on wheels.

'You *insist*?' he asked.

'Yes! I'm not going to listen to your explanation about how this is somehow doing you a favour, blah blah blah. So, don't even go there.'

'Okay.'

'I'm earning now. I can pay for the things I need myself. In my own good time. Perhaps I want to choose my own fridge.'

'Good point.'

'You'll have to take it back.' I started trying to push the fridge over his front step, but it was too heavy. Plus, Mack was standing in the way.

'Are you going to help?' I asked, glasses askew, hair stuck to my forehead, aware I might have been slightly pungent after a full-on day of gardening, cycling and manhandling a fridge onto a shopping trolley (seriously, much harder than I expected).

'No.'

I looked at him, baffled. 'Why not?'

'I suggest you take another look at the fridge.' He went to close the door, only pausing to say, 'And next time, try opening with "Hi, Mack, how are you?"'

The door slammed shut. Muttering and fuming, I had another look at the fridge. White. Shiny. A door... A fridge was a fridge, right? Some shelves inside. A note in the butter compartment... Oh. A note.

Jenny,
This has been sitting in my garage since we got a new kitchen. I've checked it still works. Hope it helps you feel at home,
Love
Kiko xx

I pulled the fridge back across the yard. In half the time,

due to the powerful propulsion of my mortifying humiliation.

The next day, as soon as I'd dropped the kids off, I used a stash of ten-pound notes from my kitchen appliance envelope to buy milk, cheddar cheese, fresh juice, bacon, a packet of mince, salad and the second cheapest bottle of white wine in the shop.

This time the slow-cooker leftovers went in the fridge. I think a few grateful tears might have dripped in there, too, so I didn't bother adding any salt. I did, however, lug across the yard a brown leather armchair I'd spent the previous weekend cleaning and polishing.

Mack answered first knock again. I think he was getting used to my interruptions. I hoped he didn't hate them. A five-minute chat with an annoying neighbour must be better than no chat with anyone, ever.

'I brought you a chair.'

His beard frowned.

'By way of an apology.' I gestured at the chair.

He glanced down and went back to looking at me – as if waiting for something.

'Oh, right!' I assumed a friendly grin. 'Hi, Mack, and how are you?' I then realised the grin was way too big and grinny, so I reduced it to what I hoped was a sprightly, neighbourly smile.

He closed his eyes in an extra-long blink. 'Are you going to start bringing me your Hoard now? Transfer it here one piece at a time?'

'Everything that isn't burnable. That's the plan.' I wheeled the chair forwards until it bumped against his knees. 'You have one chair. I have many, many chairs. I thought you would like this one. I promise I won't bring any – many – more.'

He rolled the chair into the kitchen, stopping to crouch down and wipe the muddy wheels with a cloth. 'I don't need two chairs. I don't exactly have many visitors.'

'I'm a visitor. Look – ta-da! You need it already.' I plonked myself in the seat, accidentally brushing his hair with my knee in the process.

Mack looked up, brow only inches from my thigh, and his eyes locked with mine. We'd been in close contact before. This was different. A spark of something – chemistry, electricity, *attraction?* – zapped like fire racing up a fuse. Oh, my, his eyes were mesmerising. For a long second my heart seemed to hover between beats. Then an owl hooted outside, breaking the moment. Mack scooted away so fast he nearly fell backwards. Still in a crouching position, he blinked at the slate tiles. Was it my imagination or was he breathing harder than normal?

Ah, no. The heavy breathing appeared to be me. I slowly sucked in a lungful of air, as quietly as possible. Tried to control letting it out again. Stuck on a bright smile he couldn't see anyway, adjusted my already perfectly centred glasses and stood up.

'Anyway, I'll let you get back to work.' I slunk to the door. 'Enjoy the chair!'

'Yeah, thanks.' He kept his eyes on the floor, hands wringing the cloth in his hand. I continued my slink right on home.

* * *

'Why was I slinking anyway?' I asked Diana, one small(ish) glass of wine later. 'I accidentally bumped his head, a 100 per cent non-erotic part of the body, with my knee. Which is, like, a 30 per cent erotic body part at most. And even if there'd been something more in the moment, I'm young and single. He's not-too-old and single. I'm a not entirely hideous woman. He's a pleasingly toned (all right, Diana, completely gorgeous) man with meltingly dreamy eyes and quite possibly a nice face hiding under the bushiness. I'm lonely... he's lonely... what's the harm in a little frisson?'

'*This* is the harm,' was my interpretation of Diana's reply. 'A brief millisecond of bodily contact with the nearest available male and you're in imaginational hyperdrive. This is what got you into trouble last time, grasping at the first man who showed you any interest.'

'Excuse me!' I brandished the wine in indignation. '*Richard* was the one doing all the grasping!'

'Even so,' Diana continued, nodding sagely (or, at least, she would have been if she had possessed a flexible neck), 'you promised to stay away from romantic interactions with men. At least until you're all straight and sorted. And isn't there a saying about men and your own doorstep?'

'I am staying away! I'm just being friendly. I'm not exactly swamped with friends. Or neighbours. I'm sat here talking to a mannequin!'

Diana got in a huff then and refused to talk any more. I finished my wine, read a few chapters of an appalling novel I'd unearthed about a grumpy, solitary cowboy falling in love with a feisty saloon owner, and went to bed. Of course, I barely thought about Mack. *Didn't* dream about him, or listen out for the odd creak through the walls. *Didn't* imagine what he'd look like in a cowboy hat. Didn't *at all* wonder if he lay, only a couple of feet away, thinking about me (and possibly not even in a bad way). Urgh! Tomorrow night I was going to read a detective story.

* * *

As it turned out, the next night I had something completely different on my mind...

That morning an invitation plopped through my letterbox.

Initially, the green and red design appeared to be a very late or even earlier Christmas card. And then I looked inside.

I had been cordially invited to a Christmas wedding. In July. Because, the card explained, 'Our love makes us feel like it's Christmas every day!'

Bleugh. As far as I was concerned Christmas once a year was one day too many. And now my twin and ex-lover had decided to extend it to July, and throw in their wedding just to add the icing on the fake-Christmas cake.

Acceptances and the name of my plus one needed to be sent to Richard's PA by the end of April. No mention of declining. Which was one more reason to decline.

I put the invitation into a kitchen drawer and went to dig up some more brambles. Arrogant, selfish, man-stealing sisters and slimy, sneaky, double-crossing exes were like brambles. Even when you thought you'd dug them all out of your life, moved away, stopped searching for them on Google, given up hoping they'd contact you, they popped back up again with a presumptuous, sickening invitation.

The thought of going to that wedding made Old Jenny poke her head up out of her grave and scream in horror.

But maybe the way it caused my lungs to cramp meant I *should* go.

New Jenny isn't a wimpy quitter! I shouted at Old Jenny, and got back to yanking up the weeds.

While huddled in my coat that evening, watching the blaze of burning brambles flickering orange and black, I heard a car pull up outside. A millisecond later, a huge, dark shadow appeared at the side of my deckchair.

I screamed, jumping so hard I would have toppled over if the shadow hadn't grabbed the chair.

'Sorry!' Jamie stepped into the light of the bonfire, dressed head to toe in black. 'I didn't mean to startle you.'

'Try not creeping up on me, then.' I gasped, clutching my pounding chest.

Mack's back door whipped open and he stuck his head out. 'Everything okay?'

'Yes. Fine.'

His eyes narrowed. 'Do you know this guy?'

I understood his suspicion. Jamie looked beyond fierce in his black cap and military-style boots. I was impressed that Mack stepped out into the garden, rather than taking me at my word and disappearing back inside.

'Jamie, this is Mack. Mack, Jamie.' I waved my hand in a sort of introductory manner.

'Do you want a drink?' I asked this near-stranger who could probably snap my neck with his little toenail, while my neighbour hovered in the gloom.

'Oh, no, I'm on my way to work.' Ah, a perfectly reasonable explanation for the get-up. 'But I brought you something.'

He picked up a large box and walked over to my back door. 'Is this your kitchen?'

I jumped up and opened the door, leading him inside. 'You can put it on the side.'

He opened the box, lifting out a mini electric oven, with two rings for pans on the top. 'I bought this when the business first got going and I lived in a caravan for a while. Anyway. Sarah thought you might find it useful until you get a proper one fitted.'

I looked at the oven, trying to figure out if the caravan story was a fib. There were a couple of scratches on one corner, but I wouldn't put it past him to have roughed it up a bit to corroborate his story.

'Thanks. I don't really know what to say.'

Jamie shrugged. 'Neither do I. Let's pretend it never happened.'

'Pretend what didn't happen?'

He winked at me. 'See you around.'

Before I could reply, he'd vanished into the night.

I still stood there, gazing at the oven – *with a mini hob! Two rings!* – when Mack stomped into the kitchen.

'Who the hell was that?' He glowered.

'I thought everyone in this village knew everybody else.' I crossed my arms, feigning nonchalance.

'I don't live in the village. He doesn't look like a typical resident. More like he'd come to burgle it.'

'He goes to my book club. And he runs a security company.' I concentrated hard on keeping my mouth from turning up at the corners.

'And he gave you an oven.'

'Yes.' I turned to look at it, hiding my failed attempt not to smile. 'You don't have the monopoly on giving me unwanted stuff.'

'Did he give you the fridge too?'

'No.' I was being deliberately obtuse. Something was starting to crackle and pop across the kitchen. And it wasn't the chilli in my slow cooker.

'I hope you know him well enough to be accepting gifts. Those cookers are pricy. Be careful you aren't sending the wrong message.'

I struggled to find a reply, too discombobulated at this surreal Mack, and the feelings he was stirring up. 'Are you saying if a man gives me gifts there's a hidden motive?' Translate: *did you mean something by the stuff you gave me after all?*

'There could be. You'd be stupid not to consider it.'

'And that if I accept them I'm sending a message?' Translate: *do you think I've sent you a message?*

'Some guys would see it that way.'

I stood gaping like a fish, ricocheting between being offended, flattered and utterly confused, when my mouth opened and got the question out there:

'Are you talking about Jamie or is this about us? Because Jamie's in love with Sarah. *I'm* not the woman he's trying to impress. Was all that help, the bedding, the bike tyres... *something*? Because what happened with the chair, that wasn't really anything but felt like something. I wasn't sending a message. And the cakes, the chicken. All of it. The only message was "Hi, neighbour. Thanks for your help. Let's maybe hang out some time seeing as neither of us seem to have many friends. Cheers, bye." That was the message. Did you think it was something different? Was all this like flirting to you?'

'What?' Mack reeled back, shaking his head. Vigorously. He looked horrified. Insultingly so, if I'm honest. 'I meant Rambo out there. I was clear about those... I'm being a friend, Jenny. Trying to look out for you. It's understandable I'd be concerned, given your ability to attract disaster. Bloody hell. No. I didn't mean me. I'm... I was only... Jenny, I'm *married*.'

Now that, I was not expecting.

Neither was Mack, judging by how white, then red, his face turned in the time it took me to start breathing again. 'Anyway, I was just checking you were okay,' he mumbled, before disappearing a lot less gracefully than Jamie had done.

Married? *Married?* Then where the heck was his wife?

I tossed, turned and twisted all night, thinking angry and conflicting thoughts about marriages. My sister's. Mack's. The one I'd probably never have.

I'd thought it bad enough having a secret boyfriend. Keeping your spouse secret was a whole other level of not-right.

17

I decided to take my mind off my current family by renewing the hunt for information on my past one, focussing my attention on a dresser at the back of the dining room.

The top half was rammed with china cups and saucers, matching teapots, milk jugs and sugar bowls. As they were too chipped to bother cleaning up for resale, I left them where they were and braved the bottom cupboards.

In amongst tins of buttons, thread, needles and a huge pair of rusty scissors, I found a pattern book, stuffed with dozens of knitting and dressmaking patterns. Most torn out of magazines, they featured hilarious pictures of models sporting atrocious hair and even worse outfits. Others were handwritten. Diagrams with notes scribbled underneath. Deciding this warranted some proper attention, I lugged it into the kitchen, jiggling with anticipation while I waited for the kettle to boil.

Oh, what treasure!

I scooped up those clues and tucked them into the derelict space in my heart reserved for family. The patterns were filed in reverse order, starting with older girls' school dresses and jumpers, a horribly plain party dress that surely even by 1980s standards was something no teenager would want to wear. There were adult patterns – but only for women, all of them practical, hardwearing and ugly. Overalls, housedresses, thick cardigans and frumpy blouses. Not a pleat, a frill, a bow or unnecessary stitch anywhere.

If this was what my mother wore as a child, it might go some way to explaining her past obsession with designer fashion. I took my time, deciphering the little notes in faded pencil: *Use spare blue wool from jumper. Replace with corduroy or won't last a week! Easter dress?*

As I continued flicking back, the smocked dresses growing smaller and the gloves turning to mittens, I finally reached the baby clothes. Knitted romper suits and blankets, a whole magazine pull-out on christening gowns.

And a dozen different patterns featuring coordinated outfits for twins. Girl twins, boy twins, mixed sex. Annotations like *Different coloured ribbon for each? Use booties from back page. Will only work if both boys. Remember extra wool if making two hats. Will I have time for this applique before June?? So sweet – I have to make these!*

I knew that it might not mean anything. *But...* a bit of a coincidence, given that the date of the magazine was 1964, and my mother was born that June.

Had my mother been a twin too? Did I have an aunt or uncle I knew nothing about?

Except of course I already knew I didn't – the twin patterns never made it past the baby clothes. And in the photographs I'd found, there'd been only one child, my mother. Could the midwife have made a mistake? Did they have baby scans in those days? Or, what seemed far more likely, my grandmother had lost a baby. My mother's sister or brother. I remembered the drastic change in the photos taken after my mother's birth. Was it more than new parent exhaustion? Had grief stripped the joy from her face?

It felt as if a piece of the puzzle clicked into place as I ran my fingers across those beautiful designs for baby clothes, the hope and the delight in the scrawled messages. Had this affected my family so deeply, it ended up splitting them apart? And if so, how? Did my mother know she'd been a twin? Would it help explain some of her own issues, including the way she'd raised her daughters, if she did?

My skin itched with questions. I fidgeted with my phone, debating whether the cost of a call to Italy was worth it, given the likelihood of it generating anything useful.

The next morning, I rang the landline number, knowing it would only be answered between ten and twelve.

I waited two gut-clenchingly long minutes until someone picked up.

Not my mother, but the office administrator. She left me waiting for another seven minutes before informing me that Mum was unable to talk that day. Perhaps I'd like to try another time?

Perhaps I wouldn't like to waste another zillion pounds on a conversation that, on the slim chance it did happen, might simply throw up yet more questions instead of answers, and might set her off and running again. I had no idea if the change in Mum was genuine or not. And we hadn't exactly had a close relationship before she'd decided to sell my home. Apparently, I was welcome to visit whenever I wanted. Even if I could have afforded it, I didn't want.

The chances were high she'd be at the wedding. Zara would have weighed up the inevitable gossip from her mother not being there, with the equally inevitable gossip her presence would cause.

That chance might just be enough to get me to Scotland's wedding of the year.

* * *

'Why doesn't Jamie ask Sarah out?' I asked Ellen the following Monday, as we prepared tacos.

'I've asked him the same question. Apart from being so completely in awe of her, and thinking he's far too old and grizzled for Sarah to find him attractive, it's really his job.' She sampled the salsa she'd been making, frowned and added a squeeze of lime juice. 'And all that about finding it tough readjusting to normal life somewhat glossed over things.'

'So, he won't even give it a chance, keep things casual.'

'He's not interested in casual. And that has implications for his work. You think twice about taking risks with a family waiting for you at home.'

'He's choosing his work over her?' I stopped grating the cheese, thinking back to Dougal and Duff where no one in their right mind would put a relationship over their career.

'You've met Jamie enough times to know he's the type of man who needs to be able to support himself. I think the plan is to sell the business one day. But that's a pretty drastic move when he doesn't even know if she's interested.'

'But he won't ask her.'

'Not until he can follow it through.' Ellen paused to shout upstairs that dinner was ready. 'But in the meantime, he's simply getting older. And more grizzled.'

I took my place at the table, plates and bowls rattling as

the house shook with the thundering feet of five hungry children. 'Maybe we should convince *her* to ask *him* out.'

Ellen grinned at me. 'Believe me, I've tried. Please, knock yourself out.'

The last Wednesday of term, I helped Maddie learn her spellings, set up a track for the boys' animal-versus-alien Olympics, and knocked on Dawson's door. Choosing to interpret the faint grunt as an invitation, I went in, moving his giant beanbag to beside the desk where he sat, pencil in hand, and plopping myself down.

'How was your day?' I asked, for want of anything better to say.

He shrugged.

'Things still the same?'

'Why wouldn't they be?'

'Have you said anything to your mum or dad yet?'

'No.' He scribbled furiously at the paper.

I sat there, mentally treading water while Dawson went back to his picture. 'I'm working on getting a car so we can go to Hatherstone sometimes after school. But it's going to be a few weeks, yet.'

'Whatever.'

'Can I see your drawing?'

After rolling his eyes so hard I was surprised they came back again, he sat back and folded his arms. I heaved myself up off the beanbag and positioned myself close enough to see while still giving Dawson space. One glance, and I had to step closer.

'Dawson.' I goggled at the paper. 'This is incredible.'

'They're not like what you can buy.'

I turned it over, read the double-page spread pencilled in on the other side.

'They're different,' I said. They were. I didn't know much about comics, but these were like a novel and a work of art all in one. The characters – a genius schoolboy inventor, a clueless teacher, a gang of bullies, a quiet girl who was kind, brave, funny – were perfect.

'Did you create these yourself?'

He nodded. 'That's only a few of them. And I'm still working on Foul Face. His hair isn't right yet.'

I laughed. 'Dawson, these are *funny*. Not ha-ha how cute, a ten-year-old boy made a joke. More like, this sums up my whole school life in one hilarious, genius-speech-bubble funny. I would buy this comic based on this one page.' I looked at him. 'And send it to everyone I went to school with.'

He stared back, uncertainty mixed with a shred of hope and pride in his eyes.

'You know these are awesome, don't you?'

He looked away. 'Well, Lucas and Erik like them.'

'How many do you have?'

He pulled open a drawer. Crammed full of finished, coloured-in comics. *Squash Harris.*

'Can I read one?'

'Promise you won't laugh?' His voice cracked.

'I promise I *will* laugh, if it's as funny as this page.' I held out one hand, gravely. 'But I promise I won't mock.'

We shook on it. I didn't know whose hand was sweatier, but Dawson insisted I wipe mine on his duvet before touching his artwork.

I read all of episode one before Ellen came home, Dawson agreeing to lend me another if I kept his secret. I could understand why. The first edition made me want to weep. How he summed up the loneliness, the casual cruelty. The pain and the fear before the schoolboy became Squash Harris the genius.

If only Dawson could stumble upon a real top-secret lab while fleeing his tormentors and become infected by a biological weapon, mutating his DNA and giving him super-human intelligence and reflexes.

Either that, or I was going to have to come up with another way to turn this ordinary schoolboy into a hero.

Or, even better, help him figure out how to do that for himself.

18

The Friday after Easter was April's *Christmas Book Club Challenge* meeting. This time, Ashley went first.

'Well,' she began, twirling the strings of multicoloured beads draped round her neck. 'I've searched the electoral roll for Hillary West and tried some other online searches but the woman is like a ghost! No social media page or anything. I can't even find a photograph.'

'Maybe you should take the hint?' Frances said, slurping a huge gin-and-tonic. 'Respect the poor woman's privacy.'

Ashley ignored this. 'So, anyway, I decided to do some old-fashioned detective work, and read everything I could that's been written about her, searching for clues.'

'And?' Kiko asked. 'What did you find?'

Ashley opened the enormous carrier bag she'd brought and tugged out a cork notice board. She proudly held it up for us all to see. There was a map of Nottinghamshire in the centre, and several typed cuttings surrounding it, each with a ribbon pinned from the cutting to a part of the map.

'Put it down, then, so we can have a proper look!' Frances said, now interested.

We gathered round. It was somewhat less impressive up close.

'So, you've got articles saying she's lived the past few years in Sherwood Forest. We already knew that.' Lucille sniffed.

'Yes, but this confirms it,' Ashley replied, undeterred. 'And, this one here says she's in her thirties. And this one says she returned to country life. So, she used to live in the country, then didn't, then did again.'

'Well, that narrows it down!' Frances said.

'It's a start,' Ellen said pointedly. 'What are your next steps?'

'I'm going to visit her publishers and pretend to be a reporter. And if that fails I'll break into her agent's office and see what I can find there.'

'Oh!' Kiko said. 'I don't think—'

'Or I could run her agent over, break his leg and then stake out the hospital waiting for Hillary to visit.'

'You can't...'

'Or I could pretend to be another author, sue her for plagiarism and wait for her to turn up at court.'

'*Ashley!*' Ellen yelled.

'I could get a job as a postwoman, find letters with her name on them...'

'You need help,' Frances and Lucille muttered at the same time.

'I bet you could help, Jamie, couldn't you? You do this sort of thing in your sleep.'

'That's not the help I had in mind,' Lucille said.

'Failing that, I'll just knock on doors until I find her. There aren't that many people living in Sherwood Forest. And I might meet some interesting people along the way. I could start a blog or something, "the Great Hillary West Hunt".'

Sarah had her phone out, searching Google. 'Ashley, there are over a hundred thousand people living in the Newark and Sherwood area. That's a lot of doors.'

'There are ways to narrow it down,' Jamie said, grinning in Lucille's direction.

'Exactly!' Ashley said. 'Like, um, I won't knock on any of *your* doors. And, um...'

'She's probably living somewhere isolated,' Jamie added. 'She values her privacy highly. Start with houses that don't have any close neighbours. And she's a bestselling author, so can afford an expensive house, with top security. Look for gates, cameras, that sort of thing. A lot of that type of homes have older people living in them, so knowing her general age will also help.'

Ellen gave Jamie a hard stare. 'Are you seriously suggesting Ashley starts scoping out every big house in the area looking for a reclusive author?'

He shrugged. 'It can't do any harm.'

'Sending an obsessed fan snooping around local houses with top security?' Ellen replied. 'What could possibly go wrong?'

We heard updates from Lucille next, who had entered a five-K race. Kiko showed us the holiday she'd found – not quite climbing Mount Everest, but hiking as far as the base camp.

'I mean, I'm never going to actually go. I couldn't just up and leave, could I? For three whole weeks? It'd be impossible for Adam, managing the kids and the house and cooking and shopping and everything—'

'And everything that you do, every day?' Sarah said. 'It's three weeks. Adam and the kids'll survive.'

'Ooh, no.' Kiko let out a giggle. 'I mean, I'm just having fun looking. I wouldn't be able to enjoy myself knowing I'd left them to struggle. And what about his work?' She paused, looking at our faces.

Nobody spoke.

'That would be ridiculous! Wouldn't it? I mean, I'm me. I don't do things like that.'

It was up to Kiko whether she went or not. She was right – there was no point going if she spent the whole time writhing in guilt and worry about the family she'd left behind. But I had to wonder if, once she got there, and stepped off that plane into the mountains, she'd suddenly find it a lot easier to leave her guilt behind.

'Twenty-one days, Kiko.' Sarah held up three fingers to represent the three weeks. 'They'll survive.'

'And have a better mother at the end of it,' Frances said. 'What kind of a role model are you to those girls? Do you want them to be women who get out there and live their dreams, or not?'

'Well, yes, of course I do, but I was thinking maybe a weekend in Snowdonia instead,' Kiko whimpered. 'It's still a mountain.'

We moved on...

Jamie had made white chocolate and ginger ice cream. It was outrageous. There was nearly another fight over the last scoop. He'd not yet baked with Sarah at the café due to a work situation he couldn't tell us about.

'Don't you just love a man who makes a good dessert?' Ashley asked Sarah, licking her spoon. 'What more could you want?'

'Quite a lot.' Sarah frowned, seemingly oblivious to Jamie's crestfallen face. 'And after the dates I've had this month the list has grown even longer.'

'Well? Don't make us beg for details.' Lucille smirked in Jamie's direction. 'Tell us *everything*.'

'Not much to tell.' Sarah shrugged. 'The first bloke was at least twenty years older than his profile picture. Not that I'm averse to an older man. Even if he did look as though he's spent every minute of those twenty years eating deep-fried food, swilling beer and slobbing. But I'm not interested in men who don't own up to who they really are.' She glanced at Jamie, who was taking a long drink from his beer bottle and staring at the ceiling.

'Unless it's for work purposes, of course. Like Jamie.'

Jamie choked on his beer.

'So I told him that. I marched straight up to him and said, "Lying to catch criminals is fine. I could be interested in a man who does that."'

Kiko ran to fetch Jamie a glass of water. Sarah ploughed on regardless. '"Lying to catch women is not. It makes me think you view women as something to be caught. You, sir, are a dud." And I marched straight out again. All right, Jamie?'

Jamie continued wheezing, waving his hand in a 'carry on' gesture.

'Date two?' Sarah grimaced. 'Date two should have been *christened* Dud.' She paused for dramatic effect.

'Date two, otherwise known as Nottinghamshire's greatest dud, was not alone.'

'He didn't bring his mother?' Ellen gasped.

'His ex-wife.'

We *all* gasped.

'It's messed up on so many levels I didn't know where to start. I told them both that, actually: "How dare you even sign up to a dating website under these circumstances? What kind of woman would be okay with this? You" – and here I pointed at his supposedly ex-wife – "need professional help. Sharpish. This man will never find a girlfriend you approve of – that's not the problem here. Get some counselling right away and save shelling out for your kids to have it later." And then I scarpered before she launched her fork at my eye.'

Ashley leaned over to pat Sarah's arm. 'Never mind. Keep looking. Love can turn up in the funniest places.'

Somehow, we all managed to resist pointing at Jamie. Sarah took another order for drinks while we squeezed in one more update. Frances.

'How was the wild swimming, Frances?' I asked.

She showed us a picture, of her in a swimsuit with a towel wrapped around her shoulders and goggles pushed up on her head, surrounded by a crowd of young men in wetsuits. 'Cold. Muddy. Tiring. Invigorating. Marvellous. But once was enough. It took three days to get the grit out of my crevices.'

'What's next?'

'I tried to book a sky-dive but they wouldn't cover me on the insurance because I'm dying. Aren't we all? I told them, surely that's the best time to do it? If I crash-land it'll save the NHS a whole lot of money it can't afford. But they wouldn't budge. So my next challenge is the Big Zipper.'

'Do you mean the big dipper?' Ellen asked. 'The roller coaster?'

'I do not.' Frances snorted. 'The Big Zipper, I said, and that's what I meant. The fastest zip-wire in the world. Over a mile long and reaching speeds of one hundred miles per hour!'

'Sounds fantastic,' Kiko said.

It did. It sounded fantastic. I hoped I wouldn't be eighty-four years old before I grew the guts and the gumption to get out there and take some risks. I made a mental note to start badgering Kiko to book that trek. To persuade Sarah to ask Jamie out.

* * *

The next morning brought with it more bad weather, leaving The Common Café empty of customers. I pottered about behind the counter while Sarah played KerPlunk with Edison. This gave me plenty of time to practise my opening line in my head:

So, Sarah, have you ever thought there might be someone worth dating at book club?

Sarah, you must have noticed that Jamie is completely nuts about you...

Look, Sarah, you're a lovely woman, he's a lovely man when he isn't kicking people's butts...

'Why don't you ask Jamie out?' I blurted, when Edison went upstairs to fetch his jumper.

'What?' Sarah squinted at me. 'Where did that come from?'

'Well, you're looking for a man. And you could do a lot worse.'

'I'm aiming a bit higher than "could do a lot worse". Recent events have revealed I could do a lot worse than just about every bloke in Middlebeck. Including Yellow Mickey.'

'Well, yeah, but Jamie's good-looking. And decent. He's got a good business. And his desserts are amazing. He's categorically not a dud.' I came out from behind the counter and sat at her table.

'Sounds like you should ask him out.'

'I'm not looking for a relationship. And even if I did like Jamie – which I don't, in that way, if I did we wouldn't be having this conversation – he clearly isn't interested in me.'

'Why not?' Sarah grinned at me. 'You're good-looking. And decent, when you aren't beating people up...'

Before I could answer, Edison scampered back in demanding a KerPlunk rematch. But that was fine – I'd planted the idea in her head. Surely next time Sarah saw Jamie she would see why he wasn't interested in me.

The rain intensified throughout Sunday night, hammering on the windows and doors while I lay in bed imagining rivers running through the roof. I could have got up to look, but I wasn't up for that information at three in the morning.

Ellen had the names of a few local roofers waiting for me on Monday. 'Ignore what my dad says. Don't let him pressure you into anything. He can be a nasty bully. It's the main reason we don't see him often, and when we do it's in small doses. Especially since Mum left. Stick at it and you'll have that house a home again in no time.'

After seeing the kids safely into school, I called the first one on the list. Three hours later he came round and quoted a figure that made me snort tea out of my nose. Deeply offended, he stalked back to his van and revved off before I could apologise.

A second guy could fit me in some time next September. Another deemed the whole house a health and safety disaster, refusing to work without a hefty 'contingency fee' to cover the additional risk.

The other two never returned my call.

I started to grow a little suspicious.

And when Fisher turned up uninvited for dinner at the Camerons' on Thursday, asking how things were going with my 'nightmare renovation', my suspicions swivelled over in his direction.

'I heard you've not found a roofer. I expect most reputable tradesmen consider it more hassle than it's worth.' He stuffed a roast potato in his mouth. 'Let's be honest, those piles of rubbish are probably the only thing keeping it upright.' He broke out into enormous guffaws.

'Grandpa Fisher, it's not allowed showing chewed-up food. Mum says its disgustering,' Billy pronounced.

Fisher was laughing too loud to hear him.

But he wasn't laughing when he followed me out into the hallway after the meal. Instead, he leant in close and murmured, 'It's a good offer I've made. But I'm a business-man. The market's dropping and my offer will reflect that. You could hand over all the worry and hassle and be in a brand-new luxury apartment by June. Think about it.'

I backed away out of the door, droplets of his greasy breath lingering on the back of my neck all the way home.

19

Friday, I popped into the café and asked Sarah if she could search for roofers on her phone. By that evening I had a decent quote from a family firm in Nottingham, a cheerful assurance that the job was straightforward and a promise that it would be done by the end of the following week.

Did Fisher think I was a fool?

Or did he want me to know he was making things difficult?

I called round to Mack's to let him know about the roofer. He welcomed me in as far as his kitchen. 'Did you use the builders in the village? Parsons?'

'Parsons wouldn't do it.'

'Why not?'

'I think Fisher convinced them, and every other tradesman round here, not to.'

'Why would he do that? Don't you work for his daughter?'

'He wants to buy the house. I can't guess why. Maybe there's some buried treasure hidden in there somewhere,' I said.

Mack looked thoughtful. 'He was sniffing around this one a few months back, wouldn't let it go. Tried swinging his weight around. But I made it clear I wasn't interested. I thought he'd got the message but then he pushed a card through my door a few weeks ago. Even if I *was* selling I wouldn't let him have it on principle. Not until I knew what he was up to, anyway.'

'Perhaps he wants to convert them into a holiday let.'

'But there's plenty of other places he could buy that need a lot less work. Why *here*?'

I shrugged. 'Hopefully he'll give up when he realises I'm here to stay.'

Mack raised his eyebrows. 'You're staying?'

'Yes, neighbour, I am. So you'd better get used to me.'

'Now, that, *neighbour,* will not be an easy thing to do.'

He caught my eye. The smile there sent a roll of delicious warmth through my insides. Was that smile flirting, or friendly? And how could someone like me, friendless (and flirtless) for so long, tell the difference?

How about the fact that he's married? I scolded myself later, when his comment pushed its way back into my head for the third time that minute.

* * *

Sunday morning, Sarah pulled up just before six in her rickety old MPV. After jamming everything we could into the boot and back seat, we headed off to a local car boot sale and spent the rest of the morning trying to look as if we were seasoned hagglers who couldn't be taken for a ride.

'Remember,' Sarah said, 'these people are vultures. They'll try every trick in the book. Everyone will coincidentally have a few quid less than we want for the item. Hold the line. And some of these guys are like Yoda. Don't look 'em in the eye.'

'Have you done this before?'

'I've watched *Bargain Hunt*. Same difference.'

We had a reasonably successful morning, although Sarah was the only one of us managing to hold the line. Once custom had trickled off towards lunchtime, we sold a nearby trader all the leftover items for a round fifty quid. I returned home with enough to cover the roofer's bill, with a reasonable amount left over. Snuggling into my duvet that night, I imagined all the ways I would spend my spare cash. A new pair of jeans, a slap-up meal, a skip...

In the end, I caught the bus into Mansfield to buy a smartphone. Which I did, eventually, once I'd wandered around reacclimatising to concrete, constant noise, strip lighting and people pushing past. Was it only four months ago I'd been pounding pavements, stressed and lonely, always rushing, never quite getting anywhere? I caught my reflection in a window, and had to double-check that this woman with a healthy glow was really me.

Today, I could see New Jenny – go for it, independent, can-do Jenny – emerging from behind the outgrown hairstyle and hand-me-down coat. And New Jenny required a decent phone. New Jenny had numbers to add to her phone contacts that weren't that of her sister's housekeeper.

New Jenny blew the rest of the money on a pair of silver shoes with the highest heels she'd ever seen.

And now she was going to have to go to that darn wedding or she'd just spent her last penny on shoes she'd never wear.

That evening, still high on adrenaline, the thrill of new

possibilities and town-centre car fumes, I fired off a wedding acceptance email to Richard's secretary. Ta-da! New Jenny and her plus one would be deee-lighted to celebrate the wedding of her evil twin and ex-secret-boyfriend.

Half an hour later my new phone rang. By the time I'd figured out how to answer it, gulping down a mouthful of scalding jacket potato, I felt a little flustered.

'Jenny Birkenshaw?' a clipped voice asked. Before I had a chance to say 'yes', despite it being about the shortest word possible, the voice continued: 'Martha Marsh. Richard Abernethy's personal assistant. I'm calling regarding your wedding acceptance. I believe you neglected to include the name of your guest.'

'Urrrr... yes. You believe correctly.'

'I need the name of your guest, Ms Birkenshaw.'

'Right. Okay.' New Jenny waved toodle-oo and left Old Jenny to get on with it.

'So?'

'So?'

'Can I have the name?'

'Yes.'

I held my breath. *Think. Think. Think. Think of a name... you can always say they got ill at the last minute and couldn't come.*

'Now, please?'

For goodness' sake, Jenny, just say the first name that comes into your head!

'Mack.'

'Pardon me?'

'My plus one's name is Mack.' Could she hear me cringing?

'And is Mack his or her full name?' Martha Marsh asked, dripping with sarcasm.

'Mack... Macintyre,' I blurted.

'Mack Macintyre,' she repeated, slowly.

'Yes, Martha Marsh,' I replied, even slower. 'His name is Mack Macintyre. Highly appropriate for the Scottish wedding of the year, wouldn't you agree?'

'Yes,' she replied. 'What an interesting coincidence. I'm sure the bride and groom will look forward to meeting Mr Mack Macintyre.'

'And so they should.' I hung up, before I could say anything even stupider.

Rats.

Where did I put the rest of that potato?

And really, it wasn't a problem, I'd simply call them the day before and say he couldn't make it. Who knew? By 20 July I might have an actual, real-life plus one to bring. Which would be massively preferable to going to what must surely be Most Awkward Wedding Ever alone. If I was going to spend it trying to somehow reconnect with my mother, I could do with some back-up.

For a brief second, an image popped into my head of me in my gorgeous new shoes, nodding graciously to Zara while hanging off Mack's arm. Her eyes bulging at how devastatingly handsome he looked in his suit. Richard speechless with envy and regret. Mum helpless to resist Mack's MI6 interrogation techniques, revealing the whole of her family history before we get to dessert.

My phone beeped with a message:

You terminated the call before I informed you that all guests must provide a photograph for the guest book. Black and white, head

and shoulders portrait, minimum resolution 300ppi. By 6
June. MM.

Great. Now all I needed to do was find a black and white,
high resolution, portrait photograph of an imaginary man. I
could ask the actual Mack... but I'd be willing to bet no such
photograph even existed.

I found out later I would have lost that bet.

20

Later that week, I found Maddie's head buried in a kitchen cupboard.

'Maddie?'

She spun around, cheeks flaming, whipping her hands behind her back.

'What's going on?'

'Nothing.' Her eyes darted in every direction but mine.

'Come on, what are you hiding?' I stepped closer, and she bristled briefly before letting her shoulders sag in defeat. Slowly opening her hand, she revealed a cherry muffin, a banana and two chocolate biscuits.

'You're sneaking food?'

She nodded, miserably.

'Why?'

'I don't want to say,' she whispered, tears balancing on her eyelashes.

'If you're hungry, why didn't you tell me? Sometimes when children are growing fast, they get hungry all the time. It isn't naughty.'

'Okay.'

'But we need to make sure it's good food that will fill you up and keep you healthy. Let's put these biscuits back. If you're still hungry after the banana and the muffin let me know.'

Peeling the paper case off the muffin, Maddie looked too miserable to eat it.

I gently propelled her to the window seat and curled up next to her before asking, 'What's going on?'

She shook her head, a teardrop tumbling down her cheek. 'I don't want to be a snitch.'

'Okay.' I thought about that. 'Well, what if I guessed? That wouldn't be snitching.'

'Wouldn't it?'

'Definitely not.'

She nodded, picking crumbs off the muffin.

'Was the food for you?'

'Yes.'

'Did you eat your lunch?'

A shake, no...

And we carried on the yes/no game until I reached the last question, a bowling-ball of dread sitting heavy in my stomach.

'Do you know why Dawson is eating your lunch?'

She shrugged.

'I have to talk to him.'

Maddie looked at me, face aghast.

'I'm not going to tell him off. But he might be in trouble. And even if he's cross, it's still the right thing to do. He'll understand.'

Her mouth opened and closed in panic.

'Trust me. It'll be okay.'

I ignored Dawson's long, irritated sigh when I came in his room and pulled up the beanbag again.

'Who's stealing your lunch, Dawson?' I hoped he'd appreciate my direct approach.

'Nobody.' He scribbled furiously on the picture he was working on.

'I'm going to sit here annoying you until we talk about it. The sooner you do, the sooner you can get back to Squash Harris.'

'I can't believe Maddie.' He spoke through gritted teeth. I was surprised the pencil didn't snap.

'I caught her taking food. She's nine. I'm a great interrogator. And it wasn't hard to guess what's happening.'

'Yeah, but still. She's broken the Cameron code.'

'That may be. But what matters is why you've been doing it, not how I found out.'

'You *know* why.' He looked at me now, eyes blazing. 'I shared her lunch because I'm starving. Because I don't want to eat food that's been spat on. Or kicked about. Or dunked in the toilet.'

'Oh, Dawson. Why didn't you say?'

He didn't blink. He knew I knew why.

'Is it one kid, or a few of them?'

'It doesn't matter. I'll tell Maddie I'm sorry and I'll stop eating her lunch. So you can forget about it. I'll have a bigger breakfast or something instead.'

But his entreaties were half-hearted. I suspected Dawson had reached his limit.

'Dawson, there is a difference between not having friends, and people being actively mean to you. If this was Maddie, would you think it was okay for me to do nothing?'

'I've only got three months left. If you tell Mum and Dad they'll talk to school. Everyone will know.'

'I can't not tell them about this.'

'They'll be really upset.' He pulled at his cheeks in distress.

'That's not for you to worry about. It's part of being a parent. Families work together, share their problems, help each other.'

Well, families like the Camerons did, anyway. I couldn't recall that being part of the Birkenshaw code.

We talked a little more about what had been happening, when it had started. The least worst way for us to tell Ellen. Apologising to Maddie.

It was a long, tough, heartache of an evening. I sat down with Ellen, Will and Dawson straight after dinner, almost drowning in the guilt of not having spoken up earlier. And by the time I'd put the other children to bed, they were still talking, weeping, hugging, listening. Will insisted I stay. I witnessed a masterclass in family life that night. Marvelled at how Will and Ellen spoke hope and encouragement to their son, even as they wiped their own tears away. Reminded him of who he really was – loved, precious, amazing. Told him how proud they were. That they would find a way through. That he could do it, he was strong and brave. Shared stories to help him know he wasn't alone in going through this. Reassured him that good teachers knew how to handle bullying.

Eventually Dawson leant into his daddy's chest and agreed they would speak to his teacher.

Ellen drove me home.

'I'm so sorry,' I said as soon as we pulled away. 'I really messed up.'

'Yes,' Ellen said. 'And right now my heart's very sore, so I'm pretty angry about that. It was stupid, and wrong, to keep this from us.'

'I thought if I betrayed his trust on this... I thought he needed an ally. Someone impartial to talk to...'

'He needed his parents to know what was going on so they could help him,' Ellen replied, her voice sharp. 'You knew we were worried sick.'

'I know. I'm sorry. It won't happen again.'

'Honestly, Jenny. What were you doing, trying to be his friend, not the responsible adult?'

I sucked in some air, had to force my words past the lump wedged in the back of my throat. 'I guess it was because I knew how he felt. And the worst thing I could have done was tell my parents. I don't know if it's my family that's weird, but we never had a conversation like that. My whole childhood could be summed up as "pull yourself together, get over it and try harder".'

'And you genuinely thought that's how *we* would deal with this? After being with us for this long?'

'I wasn't thinking at all. I was feeling – sad and scared and wretched. I was remembering.'

Ellen was silent for a while.

'You got bullied at school?'

'*And* at home.'

We pulled up outside the house. 'I'm sorry. That's awful.'

I unbuckled my seat belt, gathered my things. 'Ask Dawson about Squash Harris.'

'Squash what?'

'Just ask him. And thanks for the lift. And I am so, so sorry. Sorry this happened and sorry I made it worse. I'll understand if you want to find a different nanny. Anyway. I hope it goes well with school tomorrow.'

As I skulked away, Ellen climbed out of the car and ran after me. I turned to her, half braced for a slap round the face, but instead Ellen wrapped her arms around me tightly, pressing her head against mine. 'Forgiven. Forgotten. I'm sorry it took me this long.' She squeezed me even tighter. 'Thank you for loving my kids.'

I've never believed in angels. But if they did exist, they'd surely look a lot like Ellen Cameron.

* * *

Things chugged along fairly uneventfully for the next week or so. The roofers came and roofed. Dawson's teacher started paying attention, so at the very least he got to eat his lunch in peace. I fumbled my way along, sorted and priced another load for the car boot sale. Played KerPlunk a hundred and twenty-two times with Edison. Lost a hundred and twenty-one times. Saw fleeting glimpses of my neighbour as he ran through the woods. Ignored the excellent excuses I thought up to knock on his door.

'Urgh! How low the mighty New Jenny hath fallen!' I railed at Mannequin Diana, resident relationship expert. 'That is the worst, worst, WORST type of terrible thing to do. I might as well chain myself barefoot to the kitchen sink for the rest of my life if I'm going to play the helpless, hapless female to get a man's attention. A *married* man.'

I seized another load of yellowing nighties from the chest of drawers and stuffed them into a bin bag. 'Well, yes, I could just go and ask him if he wants to come over for a cup of tea. But we both know that time alone with Mack is not a good idea. No. The best thing to do is keep busy and concentrate on my real friends.'

Before I knew it, May had arrived, drab and grey compared to the earlier spring sunshine. But the lighter evenings meant cycling home in the daylight, and every day the forest seemed to burst with new life amongst the bluebells and cow parsley. Pheasants, squawking in the bracken, grey squirrels darting up the branches. One evening a fawn sprang across the path and vanished into the trees up ahead of me. Why had I ever thought chugging to work in a car, spewing out carbon emissions, would be preferable to all this?

I would soon find out.

21

I had an idea. It might turn out to be a completely rubbish one, but might just be better than doing nothing. While Will had been coming home early once a week to take Dawson to see his friends, I couldn't bear watching Dawson drag himself to school every morning, eyes on the ground, his spirit drooping behind him. If he walked into his new school like that in September, things were only going to get worse. Dawson desperately needed a boost.

I had a boost-tastic idea.

I hoped.

But, for my plan to work, I needed a decent computer. Preferably one I could have regular access to that belonged to someone who didn't know the Camerons.

For my plan to *really* work, I needed someone with hard-core, and quite possibly illegal, computer skills. The kind of skills a spy might possess.

I ended my three-week Mack-fast and knocked on his door.

Another two knocks later, he finally flung it open. His

dark eyes were rimmed with red, hair standing up in every direction, beard bristling; he was wearing a sagging jumper and the most unflattering pair of tracksuit bottoms I'd ever seen.

My heart lit up like a firework, whooshing around my ribcage for a few seconds in a flurry of happy sparks.

'Yes?' he croaked out eventually, sounding as though he'd not said a word in those whole three weeks.

'Can I come in?'

Mack frowned.

'Or you could come to mine?' I blurted. 'I wanted to ask a favour, not for me, but for a ten-year-old boy who really needs a break.'

'I'm in the middle of something. I have a deadline coming up and...'

'Can I at least explain what it is and then you can say no? No pressure, I promise.'

That got me a cynical look.

'Okay. Not much pressure. And you're perfectly capable of resisting me.' Whoops. That came out wrong. The warmth flooding my cheeks could save a fortune on heating bills. All I'd need was to keep remembering how Mack had straightened to attention, jaw locked, and I could keep the radiators off all year.

'It's not that big a deal,' I gabbled. 'And I don't know who else to ask. No, scrap that. It's a big favour and a big deal. Too big. It's a stupid idea and I should never have thought of it. It's just so damn hard not being able to help him. Sorry to have bothered you. I know you're busy. Just pretend I was never here. Thanks. Bye.'

I scuttled away before humiliating myself any further. What on earth had compelled me to ask Mack for help?

Forty minutes later, while I was lying on the only available space on the living-room floor, making shapes out of the stains on the ceiling, Mack poked his head in through the doorway.

'Wow. You've made progress.' He nodded in approval. I scrambled to a sitting position, as dignified as I could manage in the limited space.

'Or... not?' he questioned. 'Jenny?'

'I'm trying to work out if you're being sarcastic.' I pushed my glasses up.

He grimaced. 'I was trying to be friendly. Or, at least polite. And to answer your question.'

I waited. This was interesting. Mack's hair was damp. He wore a clean sweatshirt and decent jeans. I was pretty sure he'd trimmed his beard. Looking at him, filling up half the room, I couldn't actually remember what the question was.

'Because I haven't spoken to anyone apart from Sarah all week. Because you remind me that's not a good way to live. Because your hare-brained schemes are the most interesting thing that's happened to me all year. Because, contrary to what you have, quite justifiably, concluded, I don't hate helping you out.'

Ah, yes, I remembered the question now.

He coughed. 'And sitting there wondering what crazy idea you've come up with is preventing me from getting any decent work done.'

We let that hover in the air between us for half a minute.

'Do you want a cup of tea?' I eventually said, way too fast and too loud.

'Um, yes?' He crossed his arms, uncrossed them again. Scratched his beard.

'I can tell you all about it,' I said, trying to squeeze past without touching him, then, realising this was impossible, backing off and gesturing to indicate he should go first.

Relocating to the kitchen helped, a bit. Mack didn't seem to be sucking quite *all* the oxygen out of the air in there, and I could stand at a nice, safe distance while he leant against the worktop.

'I did mean it about the house. It's loads better.'

'It doesn't feel like it. It's over three months and there's still so much to do. And the more I clear out, the more I can see how much work needs doing. It wants gutting from top to bottom.'

Mack shrugged, accepting the mug I offered. 'You'll figure it out.'

'Either that or I'll snap one day while sorting through the millionth box of hideous tat and call Fisher. I mean, why feel loyalty or obligation to a house that belonged to a woman I never knew? Loyalty does not exactly run strong in my family. Mum couldn't even be bothered to come and look at it.'

'Because family is important. So is sticking to a commitment. Even one you made to yourself. Even when it's tough.'

'Is your family important to you?' I asked, over the rim of my tea.

Mack cleared his throat. 'So, what's this favour you need, then?'

I took another slow sip.

'Yes. My family is important to me,' he huffed. 'The favour?'

I told him about Dawson. And then I offered him Squash Harris, Episode One.

I dug out a packet of biscuits while he carefully turned the pages, eyes scanning every detail.

'I thought you said he was ten.'

'He is. Eleven in July.'

'Are you sure he made this?' He flicked back to the beginning, started again.

'I've watched him draw it.'

'Yes, but he could have got the idea from somewhere else, copied the characters, the storylines. Are you sure it's all his own original ideas?'

I clicked through my phone onto the Middlebeck Primary School website. 'This is his headmaster. And his class teacher.' I scrolled down through the photographs. 'That boy there, with the red hair, is Austin. Dawson's cousin.'

'He's a genius,' Mack muttered. Then he looked up at me, eyes sharp. 'But what do you want from me?'

'I want to put them on a blog. I think if I can get some people reading this, when Dawson sees the positive comments, it's going to really help. And he can start secondary school with his head a little higher. But I need a proper computer with the right software. And I'll have to regularly add on new editions, filter the comments and things.'

'Why don't you use the Camerons' computer? Do it with them?'

'Because I'm scared it might backfire horribly. And because there's no point having a blog if no one knows about it. I have less than ten contacts in my phone. I've never done social media. But if we can get the comic where people can see it, I'm trusting it's good enough that word will spread.'

'I don't know what you've heard about me, Jenny, but I can't help you with this. I don't have the kind of contacts you think.' Mack's face was on lock-down again.

'I want to hack into the school website and post a copy there. I figured your secret spy-type skills could do that?'

He blinked at me for a minute, before his eyes crinkled at the edges and he full-on smiled. 'Jenny, I'm not a spy. Or a cop. Or a hacker. I have a boring job requiring minimal IT skills.'

'Okay. But what if you had to tell me that, but really it was a cover? What if, you helped me set the blog up, and then an *unknown, anonymous* person left a rogue copy on the school website?'

'If that happened, it wouldn't be me. I'm sorry. And I can't keep letting you have access to my computer. I do have confidential work on there of an utterly tedious nature.'

I clutched the mug tighter, trying to swallow down my disappointment.

'That's fine.' I kept my voice steady. 'It was a stupid idea anyway. Sorry for wasting your time.' I was growing tired of Mysterious Mack. Whoever decided enigmatic men were attractive hadn't lived next door to one.

He sighed. 'Look, I do have some contacts who might help. Not hacking the school website, but proper marketing. If you let me have a copy I'll see what they say.'

'Who are your contacts?' I asked, my words flat.

'I can't tell you.' He paused, thinking. 'But I can tell you I'm self-employed. I work primarily for a large company with a huge marketing department, producing customer-driven solutions to generate sales and maximise brand awareness through providing significant input into innovative products designed for worldwide distribution.'

'Stop!' I yelled. 'I get it. You have a completely boring job. I'll get a photocopy done at the library. And, thanks.'

22

It was the book club's spring bank holiday barbeque. We were sampling Jamie's homemade sourdough when Sarah's phone buzzed.

'Kiko's not coming.' Sarah shook her head. 'Adam's working. If he bothered to give her a bit of notice she could sort a babysitter.'

'That's such a shame.'

'Yeah. Like it was a shame she missed the Christmas party, and the book festival. And hasn't managed a trip to visit her parents once, since they moved back to Japan.' Sarah tapped out a reply before scooping up the plate and gliding towards the café door. 'I've suggested she spend the evening booking herself that trek. He can find out what it's like to have to drop everything because the other parent's suddenly unavailable.'

'Surely that can't end well.'

'It'll end with her coming home to a husband ready to hear what she's got to say. That's better than the alternative ending, when she doesn't come home at all.'

'Are we ready to start?' Frances asked, once everyone had loaded up their plates and got comfortable on the patio sofas. 'I need an early night tonight and don't want to miss any updates.'

'Why don't you kick us off?' Ellen asked. We sat back to hear about the Big Zipper.

'It was simply marvellous!' Frances told us, eyes sparkling. 'Like flying. I'd forgotten what it felt like to move without creaking and groaning. I enjoyed it so immensely, they let me have another go free of charge.'

She paused, looking down, and, for the first time, seeming every one of her eighty-four years. 'It's crept up on me. This old body. Sometimes I go to stand up, or bend down, and I forget how bloody *slow* I am. It won't do what I tell it to any more. Especially the cancer parts. They are the most misbehaved of all. I knew this must happen, but I somehow wasn't expecting it. To be so tired.'

She looked round at us all, trying to discreetly hide our sniffs behind gingham napkins. It didn't take long for the steely glint to return.

'What's next?' Ellen asked, dabbing at her eyes.

'A camel trek.'

Of course it is!

Lucille showed us a leaflet entitled 'Tough Muck'. The picture on the front was of a man, crying, neck-deep in swampy water, blood smeared across his forehead. She tugged at the lapel of her designer jacket while we read about the ten kilometres of mud, near-impossible obstacles, pain and torture. She twiddled a Tiffany bracelet with her manicured fingers and patted her coiffed hairstyle.

'I don't understand,' Ashley said, peering at the photo of a woman, T-shirt hanging off one shoulder, clinging to a rope halfway up a rock-face, a tyre on her back. With her teeth bared like a rabid wolf, beneath the filth her face looked like a purple skittle.

Lucille shrugged. 'If Frances is wild-swimming and camel-trekking, a straightforward race didn't seem enough. It's not until September, I've got time to train.'

'It looks awesome,' Jamie said. 'I quite fancy it myself.'

'Pshaw.' Sarah rolled her eyes. 'You do stuff like that all the time, only with maniacs shooting at you and bombs going off in the background. That's why your Christmas Book Club Challenge is perfecting a pie-crust.'

Jamie cleared his throat. 'Actually... a lot of my job is just sitting around. Watching and waiting, gathering information. Meeting with clients. I'm starting to leave the running around to the younger guys.'

'Ooh, you're still young,' Ashley said, looking pointedly at Sarah.

Jamie's face was starting to resemble the purple woman on the leaflet. 'Maybe. But you reach a point when risking your life day in, day out starts getting old. When you get, um, ready to settle down a bit.'

Everyone in the room held their breath. Except for Sarah, who leant forwards and grabbed another handful of sweet-potato crisps.

Ashley lightened the mood for us with her detective's board, pointing out progress made in narrowing down the Hillary hunt. It was more a list of assumptions than anything approaching an accurate investigation, but at least she'd kept it legal for now. And when Lucille started to question her methods ('Just because most of her books feature rivers, it doesn't mean she lives near one'), Sarah said, 'Oh, put a sock in it, Lucille.' Normal relations were resumed.

I updated everyone on progress with the cottage, and lack of progress in finding anything out about my family.

Ellen told us about her midwifery lecturer, who couldn't mention any female body parts without breaking out into a sweat and stuttering. 'He gave the whole session on anatomy facing the projector screen, and the remote kept slipping out of his hands. Some of the students are merciless. They keep asking him to repeat himself, and pretending they can't read the labels on the diagrams. One asked if the plural of vagina was vagini. It took him three minutes to get the answer out.'

By the time she'd finished her second glass of wine, Sarah was ready to tell us about her latest dud date.

'Was he terrible?' Ashley asked. 'I can't imagine anything worse than last time.'

'Nah.' Sarah shrugged. 'He wasn't terrible. He seemed all right. Was nice-looking, and we had an interesting conversation, found some things in common.'

'Sounds like a right dud!' Lucille snarked.

'No. This time the dud was me.'

The sausage from Jamie's hotdog shot across the patio and landed in a plant pot, leaving him gripping an empty bread roll. 'He thought you were a dud?'

'No. He asked to meet up again.'

I asked, 'So, what then?'

'I just... felt nothing.' She tore a strip off her napkin. 'He was a nice bloke. I had a fun evening. But the thought of going through all that palaver again, shaving and plucking and straightening my hair. Dressing up. Asking all these questions, waiting to spot the clues that he's a wimp, or a scumbag, or a member of UKIP. I can't be bothered. I suddenly realised I could take it or leave it. So, I left it.'

'Fair enough,' Ellen said. 'But love's not always lightning bolts.'

'I know.' Sarah pulled a wry face. 'Which made me decide I'm not up for dating right now. When the right man doesn't feel right, perhaps the right thing is to forget men altogether.'

'Maybe you just didn't fancy him?' Ashley blurted. 'Maybe because your heart already belongs to someone else. It seems a little early to give up on romance altogether.'

I kept my eyes firmly on Sarah and off Jamie. I couldn't bear to look.

'Nah. Life isn't a Hillary West novel, Ash. I dunno what I was thinking, really. I'm happy with just me and Ed. I'm relieved it's over.'

'Quite right,' Lucille, miraculously, agreed. 'You don't need a man to complete your life, Sarah. Most men are more hassle than they're worth – I said *most* men, before you bite my head off. They distract you from who you are until, before you know it, you're living your life, making decisions, choosing an outfit to please them, not you.'

'There's nothing wrong with making decisions to please someone else. That's called compromise,' Ellen interrupted. 'It's how marriages succeed.'

'There is when it's at the cost of your own self! Look at Kiko! Except you can't, because she's missing our barbeque, sacrificing her needs to please a man. Again.'

'Then again, thinking about it, I've changed my mind.' Sarah waved her glass at Lucille. 'Maybe I will try a few more dates. Find a nice man to take care of me, pay off my credit card and squish spiders. Put up shelves and change the oil in the car. Tell me who to vote for.'

'Anyone fancy a top-up?' I said, before things got out of hand. There was a lot more food to chuck around and drinks to hurl than usual. And I was wearing my new slippery shoes. Which reminded me...

I managed to corner Jamie in the kitchen when we were clearing up.

'I have a strange request.'

'Okaaay?'

'Do you have a photo I could borrow?' I explained what it needed to be like.

'I'm finding it hard to work out why you need a high-res image of me.'

'I'm finding it hard to work out a good explanation.' I sighed. 'My twin sister is marrying my ex and they want photos of me and my plus one for the reception.'

Jamie glanced behind him. 'Jenny, is this a roundabout way of asking me to be your date? Because, well—'

'No! No. Not at all. I gave a fake name, thinking I could tell them he's sick, but then they asked for a picture. I need it by June.'

'You're going to your twin sister's wedding. To your ex. Alone. With a picture of a poor, sick, fake boyfriend. Is there a worse way to spend a day?'

'Sitting at home cursing yourself for still not plucking up the courage to ask out the woman you're in love with?'

Jamie gave me a sharp look. I shrugged. 'You're right. The wedding is worse.'

He scrolled through some pictures on his phone. 'I have a few from my army days. But nowadays I keep a low profile. I deliberately don't have any images on the website.'

'Maybe if you had one without a weapon in your hand? Or a can of beer? And your clothes on?'

'I doubt it.'

'Right. Well, I think I'd better pass. But thanks for that interesting glimpse into your previous life.'

His eyes darted over my shoulder. 'It was a long time ago. And not as bad as it looks. Stuff happens in the military that, well. It's hard to explain.'

'Don't worry.' I winked before turning to join the others. 'I won't tell Sarah.'

'What?'

'You should tell her about it yourself some time. Take her out for a drink. Or a bite to eat at Scarlett's. She loves it there.'

I whirled away, bumping into Sarah in the doorway.

'What are you grinning about?' she asked.

'Ask Jamie. He'll tell you everything.' Then I remembered the first part of the conversation about the non-existent plus one and the photo. 'Actually, don't bother. It really wasn't that funny. I think I ate too much cheese.'

* * *

I asked Will about a picture one evening when I'd ended up staying until after the kids had gone to bed. Embarrassed about the real reason, I made something up about a Father's Day present. Will turned on the laptop and we spent an amusing hour going through the photo albums. It soon became apparent that there wasn't a single picture of him this century without his wife or a child in tow. And I was not sending Martha Marsh a photo of a man with a curtains hairstyle. Or wearing a baseball cap back to front.

'I have a work headshot.' Will clicked onto his school's website.

'Yeah, I was thinking of a more casual look. One where you're smiling.'

'I *am* smiling!'

'No, Will.' Ellen lifted her head out of a textbook. 'It's the same face you pull when your parents come for dinner. Or when someone tells you triplets must be a nightmare.'

'I'm *trying* to smile.'

'I know.'

'Don't worry.' I got up to go. 'It was only an idea. Thanks for letting me look.'

I declined a lift home. It was a clear night, and those old photos had conjured a twinkle in Will's and Ellen's eyes that made me figure they wanted some alone time.

I needed some alone time myself, to think about Fake Photo Plan C. Mack.

Maybe I should just ask him if I could take one? I reckoned that confidential laptop of his could take a decent picture. I considered the likelihood of Mack adopting a cheerful, attractive pose while I snapped away.

And then I heard it.

A noise in the trees to my right.

I cycled this path several times a week. Had been here countless times in the dark.

The sounds of the forest had become as natural to me as the hum of traffic used to be.

This sound was not a natural one. Crackles. Crunches. Something big was moving in the darkness of the trees.

I took a deep breath, tried to keep listening over the frantic hammering of my heart and restarted the bike. Went through all the possible things it could be: a deer? Horse? A large dog? Would a badger make that much noise?

But as I cycled on, fighting to keep the handlebars steady, the crunches continued alongside me.

Not crunches. Footsteps. Running, several metres to the side.

I sped up, almost dizzy with panic. The fence separating the footpath from the forest suddenly seemed like the flimsiest, tiniest, most pointless barrier possible.

My ragged breaths echoed off the tree trunks. The headlamp penetrated about three metres in front of me. To the side, beyond the fence, there was only blackness. And footsteps crunching through the undergrowth.

It must be an animal, I repeated in my head. *It's following the light.*

And then it coughed.

Deep.

Either a man, or the kind of woman you didn't want chasing after you in the middle of a forest in the pitch black.

23

Six minutes from home. I bumped and rattled, careened and skidded over branches and loose stones. I was fast these days, and could have followed the path without the lamp, I knew it so well. But I was also petrified and the thought of crashing, or falling, kept my fingers on the brake, legs restrained.

Another couple of minutes. The path curved. I braced myself, kept the bike as close to the left as I could. Thought about turning back. Or abandoning the bike and legging it into the forest on the other side, finding a tree to hide behind and calling for help.

Calling who, Jenny? I screamed in my head. *And telling them what? That I can hear footsteps? That there's something moving about in the forest?*

I held my breath, gritted my teeth and kept on going. And, as I whizzed past the bend, nothing leapt out. I listened hard but couldn't hear the footsteps any more. The only sounds were the whirr of pedals spinning at about two hundred miles per hour and my heart trying to escape out of my chest.

Until the path straightened out again, when a burst of laughter exploded into the night. Deep, raspy, gleeful. It sounded like sticky, black slime would if it could cackle. Like the menace that had roamed the labyrinth in my head for three long years after my breakdown.

I couldn't even remember the last half-mile. I must have dumped the bike beside the door because that was where I found it in the morning. Throwing myself inside, hands shaking so hard it took three horrible attempts to get the key in the lock, I slammed the door, locked it, and hurtled straight up the stairs before throwing up the whole of my guts, my newfound confidence, my can-do attitude and any peace I'd managed to garner through finally owning a home, in one ugly splatter.

Pride abandoned, I tried banging on the wall between the two cottages, but there was no response. I didn't have Mack's number, of course, so couldn't call him. I felt too scared to go back downstairs, let alone outside to knock on his door. Should I phone the police? To report that a man in the woods laughed?

Head whirling, I couldn't form a coherent thought. The ebbing adrenaline left me trembling and exhausted.

I wedged a chair under the bedroom door, crawled into bed and pulled the duvet over my head. Some hours later I drifted off to sleep, the distant echo of cackles reverberating through my nightmares.

* * *

After unconsciously pressing the snooze button a few times, I finally dragged myself out of bed in time to pour half a gallon of coffee down my throat and swap the clothes I'd slept in for something that didn't reek of cycling for my life. I felt desperate for a shower, to scrub off the terror and the bad dreams, wash that laugh out of my eardrums, but it would have to wait. Shaking off the temptation to call Tezza, I decided the best way to deal with my churning stomach and frazzled nerves was to get right back in the saddle. Literally.

Stepping out into the spring sunshine, seeing the butterflies dancing past, I sucked in a lungful of fresh, bright air and took a good look around. A little brown bird hopped across Mack's picnic table. I spied a rabbit disappearing into the bushes. It seemed more likely I'd encounter Snow White skipping through the woods than a freaky, creepy cackler. With no time left to work myself into a state, I picked my bike up and creaked off, managing to look behind me no more than every ten metres or so.

And if I arrived at work a little dishevelled, and somewhat clammy, hey, at least I was on time.

For reasons I hadn't yet made up, once the kids were in school I cycled back home along the main roads. What a lovely change, I trilled, ambling alongside houses and hedgerows. Ooh, look, some sheep. And a middle-aged couple on a ramble. All these sights I've had missed if I went the normal, boring, quicker, lunatic-riddled route.

After stashing the bike away, I knocked on Mack's door. Or possibly pounded, continuously, for the six minutes it took him to open it.

'What have you done now?' he rumbled. 'I've not had breakfast yet so it had better be good. Or should I say bad?' He peered at me through bleary eyes. 'You're dry. And clean. That's a hopeful start.'

'Can I come in?'

'There's no emergency?'

'No. Yes. I don't know.' To my horror, a glob of panic started working its way up my oesophagus. I blinked, hard, and did my utmost to swallow it back down. 'Were you out running late last night, in the woods near the Common? Because if you thought it was funny, to race beside me when I couldn't even see it was you, it wasn't. And I *really* didn't appreciate being laughed at, when I was quite clearly scared out of my wits, because whoever that was was definitely laughing *at* me, not *with* me.'

'What the hell are you talking about?' Mack stepped back, hustled me inside and sat me down, his face waking up.

Oh. Not him, then.

Quietly, fighting to keep my voice steady, I told him what had happened.

'Have you spoken to the police?'

'I was kind of hoping I wouldn't have to.'

He shook his head. 'I'm choosing not to get offended by that, appreciating that me being the creep is slightly less horrific than it not being me, and that you're clutching at straws here.'

'I thought it might be some bizarre countryside custom.'

'Running about the woods scaring the pants off women?' He handed me his phone. 'Call the police. It'll make their day, something more interesting than a missing cat to investigate.'

'But it's not really a crime, is it? I wasn't hurt. I didn't even see them.'

'No, but they can keep an eye out.'

I hesitated.

'You might prevent something awful happening.'

I called the nearest police station, and a straight-to-the-point policewoman who instructed me to call her Brenda promised to visit later that day. Mack's gaze was steady. 'You should have knocked on my door last night.'

'I was too busy panicking to think.' I tried to smile. 'I did bang on the wall a few times.'

'That was you?' He looked apologetic. 'I thought it was the boiler playing up.'

'Maybe I should have your phone number?'

Not the circumstances in which I'd imagined uttering that sentence.

We swapped numbers, and I stood up. 'Right. I'd best get back, then. Don't want to miss PC Brenda.' I put my phone in my jeans pocket, took it out again and looked at the screen for no reason, slid it back in. Nodded my head a few times. 'Thanks for listening. And for your phone number. Good to know you can call me if you need rescuing.'

I shuffled over to the door, opened it, turned back to face Mack but couldn't think of a single other excuse to delay going back to the empty, lonely, rustly side of the building.

He'd gone. Without even saying goodbye.

'Sorry.' He hurried back into the kitchen. 'I was getting my laptop. Oh, and I need my shoes. Hold on.' He vanished into the hall again, popping back in a few seconds later. 'Right. Ready. Let's go.'

'Um. Go where?'

'To your house. To wait for the police.'

'You're coming with me?' I asked, momentarily confused.

'Would you rather I didn't?' Mack said. 'Because from the way you were dithering by the door I assumed you were nervous about being home alone.'

'I wasn't dithering. Sheesh, Mack. Every time you do something kind you have to open your mouth and ruin it.'

'Yeah. So I've been told.' His face darkened, and it didn't

take a genius to figure out that the telling had probably been done by the invisible was-she-real-or-invented-to-keep-me-away wife.

'I don't need you to babysit me. I'll lock my door and keep my phone close by. I'll be fine,' New Jenny said.

Please delete that comment, Old Jenny shouted in my head.

'I'll only be sat here worrying about you,' he grunted.

'You think I should be worrying?' A shiver scampered up my back at the thought that Mack considered it a possibility that whoever it was might come to my house. Followed by a traitorous thrill right on its heels at the thought *he'd* be worrying about me. The shiver slunk back down with the realisation he would probably only be worrying about getting dragged into facing a madman. Or that after a few days my mutilated corpse would start to smell. Or that the house would get burnt to the ground, taking Mack's side with it...

'I think there's zero chance of that moron making an appearance.' He shifted his laptop from one arm to the other. 'But it'd be abnormal not to be freaking out a bit. It's only neighbourly to provide you with some company.'

I smiled at him. 'I think you're scared to be alone in your cottage. And, in that case, you may come and reassure yourself with my presence while I sort through the filing cabinet I managed to pry open yesterday.'

'Thanks.' He nodded, sombrely. 'I owe you one.'

'Ooh, I think we've stopped counting who owes who what, haven't we, neighbour?'

'Get out of here,' he growled. 'I've work to do.'

* * *

'Wipe that look off your face!' I hissed at Mannequin Diana

as I caught her smirking at me through the open master-bedroom door. There was no way she could tell whether I'd been spinning an elaborate, detailed daydream about me pottering about upstairs while my lovely husband worked at the kitchen table, him calling up to offer me a cup of tea, leaning in for a kiss as he handed it to me, then getting caught up in the moment, putting the tea on the dressing table before he lowered me manfully yet tenderly to the bed...

'Jenny, do you want tea?' Mack called up the stairs. My face: virtually bubbling with molten embarrassment. Diana's face: smug and suggestive at the same time. I spent about two minutes sticking my head out of the window to cool down before he appeared.

'It's a bit stuffy in here.' Mack offered the tea. I backed away so far he had to lean forwards and stretch his arm out. 'You must be boiling – your cheeks are pink.'

'Yes,' I mumbled. 'My cheeks are pink because it's stuffy.'

He turned around, leaning on the sill. 'How's it going?'

'Tediously. How about you?' I asked.

He shrugged. 'So-so.'

'I'm sorry I've distracted you.'

'No.' He sighed. 'It's not you.' He opened his mouth as if to say more, but was interrupted by a knock at the door.

'That must be her,' I said, while the tone of my voice said, *Eek!*

Mack led the way, swiping a golfing umbrella from the hallway as he did.

Brenda was way better than I expected. I decided then and there I flippin' loved the police. She listened, carefully, wrote everything down, asked questions, nodded sympathetically and promised to keep me informed.

'We'll have a look for evidence of anyone hanging about in the forest. I'll make some calls, see if any of the usual suspects aren't where they're supposed to be, and follow it up if I smell anything suspicious. We'll have a patrol officer make themselves known the next few nights. That's usually enough to deter any more funny business. My gut instinct? Kids messing about. I really don't think you need to worry.' She nodded. 'I'll be in touch.'

I expected Mack to make a move once she'd left, but instead I found him rummaging in the fridge.

'Do help yourself.'

He pulled back out, a pot of soup in his hand. 'Do you mind? I didn't have breakfast. Or lunch.'

'Crap! Neither did I. Why didn't you say something?'

'I figured you didn't have much of an appetite.'

My stomach, suddenly realising that, yes, today of all days it deserved a darn good lunch, made itself known. 'I'll heat the whole pot.'

A few minutes later, as we sat eating together, *not at all* like a married couple, and I wasn't thinking *at all* about Mack's wife, he put his spoon down and took a deep breath.

'Do you think you'd be better off using an alternative form of transport, just for now?'

'Like what?' I took a moment for my brain to catch up with my ears. 'The Mini?'

I sighed. 'I've not heard back from the DVLA yet. And even if it *is* mine, I still need to get the battery and whatever else might be wrong with it sorted. Never mind insurance and tax.'

'It's taxed and insured as of this morning. The battery can be swapped over in a day. Borrow it for as long as you need.'

I stopped eating before I dribbled soup on my chest. 'It's *your* car?'

He scratched his chin. 'It's, well, complicated. I bought it as a gift for, um, someone. But it's not practical for them to use it right now. I didn't think it would do any harm to keep it in Charlotte Meadows' shed temporarily.'

'Why didn't you tell me earlier?'

'I did offer.'

'You're sure it's okay if I drive it? Just until this gets sorted? The owner won't mind?' *The owner – or for the purposes of this conversation shall we refer to her as* Mrs Mack?

He nodded. 'It'll do it good to get a run out. And you can use it in exchange for storing it in your shed. I'll pick up a new battery and give it a once-over. The last thing you need is to break down in the middle of nowhere.'

'I'll pay for the battery.'

Mack frowned, about to say no. Then he paused. Looked at me. Looked down at his bowl. 'Thanks. I'll let you know how much it is.'

He glanced at his watch during the awkward silence that followed. 'Don't you have to leave soon?'

I checked the clock. 'Damn. Yes. And I don't have time to cycle the long way now.'

'I'll come with you.' He got up. 'Give me two minutes to get changed.'

'You have a bike?' I called after him, already out of the back door.

'I don't need one,' he retorted. 'I've got legs.'

'Really?' I huffed. 'And you think your legs can keep up with my wheels? We'll see about that.'

Which was probably the whole point, I realised, pumping my way along the path, Mack a blur alongside me. Even bearing in mind the bumps slowing me down, he could at least have had the decency to be gasping for breath by the time we reached the Common.

I hopped off and wheeled the bike towards the village exit, waving at Sarah through the café window. She wiggled her eyebrows and smirked when she spotted Mack, mouthing 'call me later' while holding an imaginary phone to her ear.

'I'm fine from here,' I said, indicating towards the dog-walkers milling about up ahead. 'Thanks for keeping me company.'

'What time do you finish?'

'Oh, I'm staying late again this evening. Ellen and Will are going out for their anniversary and won't be back until ten. I'll—'

'I'll be there at ten.' Before I could reply he had sprinted off into the trees.

'Traitor,' New Jenny jeered at the smile that refused to stop curling up the side of my mouth all the way to school.

24

The rest of the evening was, to put it mildly, freakin' exhausting. Hamish and Jonno were playing a new game about an invisible snake that slid up their trousers and into any holes it could find there, causing Billy to wet himself, too afraid to pull down his underwear when required.

Maddie was trying to learn 'Baby Shark' on the recorder, taking seriously her teacher's comment that practice makes perfect while simultaneously proving it to be false.

Dawson was having a bad day. His class had been on a museum trip. Although he refused to talk about it, he spent a long time drawing Squash Harris getting trapped by the bad guys in a museum storeroom with no windows or lights, teeming with monster spiders and rats, their beady eyes glowing in the darkness.

'I woke up trapped in a car with some rats not so long ago,' I casually mentioned, when I came in to check if he had any homework.

'And I care about that because...?' he said in a monotone.

'Because it's an interesting story ending in my total humiliation in front of another person. I thought you might want to hear it.'

He swapped his pencil for an eraser and dabbed at the corner of the page. 'I'm busy.'

'Okay. Let me know if you change your mind.'

'I won't,' he replied in a sing-song voice as I shut the door behind me. I closed my eyes and wished very, very hard that whatever Mack was doing with the sample comic-book, he would get some good news soon.

Then a scream broke out from the other side of the house: 'I HATE YOU AND I HATE INVIBISLE SNAKES I'll CHOP OFF ALL YOUR HEADS AND TAILS WITH THIS AXE!'

I opened my eyes and hurried downstairs to avert the slaughter.

By the time Ellen and Will arrived home, the only person who seemed remotely tired was me. The boys were pretending to be asleep, but while I was running through the events of the evening in the living room, Hamish burst in. 'There's a pirate in the garden and when I opened the door to ask him where his boat was he waved at me and said he's waiting for Jenny. Jenny are you being a pirate and can I come too? I know how to hoist a mainsail and rip out guts with a cutlass and follow a treasure map and all those things like pirates do.'

'You opened the front door again?' Ellen scolded. 'And more to the point, why aren't you in bed?'

I squeezed past her, having handled enough mischievous four-year-old for one day.

'I'll lock it on my way out,' I called, slipping my boots on.

'I promise to tell you all about my adventures on the high seas tomorrow, Hamish, if you promise to go straight back to bed and not open the door again.'

'Can I be your cabin boy?' Hamish shouted, over the top of his mother's telling-off.

'Maybe another time.'

'You really didn't have to do this,' I said to the pirate as he handed me the bike I'd left leaning on the wall. We started walking back towards the village green.

'Yeah, well, I'm curious.'

'Curious about what?' I glanced at him. 'Are we going monster-hunting?'

'If there's a monster in my woods, I'd like to know about it.'

'Too scared to look alone?'

'What do you think I've been doing since I dropped you off?' He paused, waiting for a car to pass before we crossed the street. 'Are you getting on that rust-bucket or not?'

I did, pedalling slowly along the now empty road while Mack jogged beside me on the pavement.

'Did you find anything?'

He shook his head. 'No.'

We turned onto the footpath, the yellow of Sarah's apartment lights glowing through the gaps in the trees. By the time we reached the Common, my heart was scrabbling to get out of my chest again, via my lungs.

Mack looked across at me. 'Maybe you should get a taxi.'

'I'm fine,' I wheezed, ignoring my hands jerking about on the handlebars.

'You don't need to do this. You've got nothing to prove.'

Oho! New Jenny cried. *I think you'll find I have.*

But the only thing my stupid, stubborn self proved was that I was too stupid and stubborn for my own good. As we reached the tree line my semi-paralysed limbs could no longer pedal fast enough to stay upright, causing me to slowly topple into a pile of nettles. Nettles I hadn't seen because my eyes, wiser than my idiot brain, refused to remain open and watch the impending spectacle unfold.

Mack heaved me to my feet. The front light on the bike had gone out, reminding me the rear light wasn't working to begin with as we plunged into darkness. Guiding my huddled form back to a bench, he lowered us down and pushed my head between my knees.

'Glasses?' I rasped.

'I've got them.' He took his hand off the back of my neck. 'I'll get Sarah.'

My arm shot out, fingers clutching his hoodie with surprising strength for someone dangerously low on oxygen. 'No,' I gasped. 'I'm fine. Just need to catch. My breath.' *And you are not leaving me here alone, in the dark, while I'm unable to breathe, let alone defend myself from an evil lunatic.*

'Okay.' He shifted a little closer, turning his body slightly so I almost leant on him. 'No rush.'

Darn it. The solid weight of Mack's chest, entirely still save for the steady rise and fall as he breathed against my back, did not help my struggle for composure. I scrabbled for a conversation topic to lighten the atmosphere, tense for a lot of dangerous reasons now that barely included the Beast of Middlebeck.

'Why did you replace my bike tyres?'

Mack said nothing for a few moments. Which, in the darkness, felt more like several hours.

'It was painful watching you hobble about on the old

ones. And it would've wrecked the bike if you'd done it much longer.'

'Why didn't you tell me? Hey, neighbour, I noticed you needed new tyres, thought I'd make it my random act of kindness for the week.' *He'd been watching me.*

'Something gave me the impression you wouldn't take kindly to my help. Oh, yeah, it might have been you hollering that you didn't want my help.'

'You were pretty rude to me when I first arrived.'

'Right back at you, woman.'

'Well. I was dealing with some issues.'

'As I said...'

'Is there someone out there?' Sarah's voice drifted across the Common. Mack went rigid.

'Don't move,' he muttered against the top of my head. 'She's leaning out of the upstairs window. If we keep still she can't see us.'

There was no point in retorting that we weren't doing anything wrong, or that minutes before Mack had been going to knock on her door with the express purpose of telling Sarah we were here. Me, huddled on a bench, in the complete dark, my glasses off, jacket skew-whiff, with a married man. It was all I could do not to spring up and gallop home.

'The police have been round,' Sarah shouted. 'They're patrolling all night. I can have them here in seconds. With dogs.'

Mack's arm began to quake where it gripped the bench next to me. He let out a tiny snort of laughter.

'You are *so* not a spy,' I murmured. He sucked in a deep breath, and tried to hold it, his whole body vibrating.

'Jamie?' Sarah asked, with a trace of hope. 'Is that you? You can just come and knock on the bloody door, you know.'

Mack and I willed each other not to release the bubbling volcano of mirth as Sarah continued to call out small talk to the non-existent Jamie. After a minute or so Edison asked, 'Who are you talking to, Mummy? Is it Spider-Man?'

'Nah, Jamie,' she replied. 'But come to think of it, I have never seen Jamie and Spider-Man in the same room. Have you?'

'Jamie, are you Spider-Man?' Edison yelled across the clearing. 'Will you come in and show us your web shooters? Mummy wants to see your Spidey sense. Do you want to see his Spidey sense, Mummy?'

'Please stop,' I whispered through clenched jaws. 'I can't take much more of this.'

'Jamie!' Edison yelled. 'Why won't you say anything?'

'Try thinking about the Hoard,' Mack breathed. 'Tax returns. Fisher. Whether or not it's about to start raining.'

'The reason we're out here in the first place,' I muttered. And suddenly nothing was funny any more. Not even when Edison offered Jamie/Spider-Man his teddy to cuddle.

'She's gone.' Mack spoke quietly, handing me my glasses. He stretched the stiffness from his limbs and strode over to retrieve the bike, nodding to a pile of dock leaves. 'Rub it on the nettle stings.'

'I'm fine.' I ignored the leaves, taking hold of the bike.

'So you keep saying.' Mack didn't let go of the handlebars.

'We'd better get a move on. I wouldn't be surprised if Sarah does call the police.'

'We can walk back to the village and get a taxi.'

'After all that shouting, no one will still be hanging around.'

'I'm more concerned with whether you'll be terrified into another panic attack,' he whispered.

'I said. I'm okay.' I tugged on the bike until he let go, and started wheeling it across to the exit. Mack soon caught up with me. 'Do you want to hold my hand or something?'

'Why, are you feeling nervous?' I shot back. 'I'll go with the or something, thanks.' Right then, feeling queasy at how lovely it had felt to have him touching me – albeit between two layers of clothing – I couldn't have meant it more.

'Just trying to be a good friend,' he muttered. 'But I guess that moment's over.'

But it wasn't, though. Far from it. And that was a much bigger problem than being chased through the woods by phantom cacklers.

We kept silent for the rest of the way, Mack alert and watchful, me wondering when my tongue grew so big I couldn't swallow properly, while trying – and consistently failing – not to flinch at every rustle from the other side of the fence. I was suitably distracted from my inappropriate Mack-related feelings enough to thank him, politely, as he waited patiently for me to unlock my door.

'I told you,' he huffed. 'It's in my own interest to hunt down monsters running about in these woods.'

'And you thought they might be hiding in the Camerons' front garden? I thought we were past all that pretending not to be nice to each other.'

He grinned, his eyes glinting in the moonlight.

'Do you want me to come in and do a quick search for beasties?'

I opened my mouth, working hard to make sure the right words came out...

'Let me guess. You're fine, right?'

I nodded.

'Night, then. Try not to have nightmares.'

Mack waited while I went inside and shut the door. I dragged my confused, shattered body to bed and fell asleep before I could worry about nightmares.

25

PC Brenda popped round the next day to tell me they'd not found anything to be concerned about, and while they'd keep checking in on the woods she was certain it was kids messing about. She did suggest I rethought travelling alone at night all the same. 'You could break your neck on a branch. Or skid on a patch of mud and go head over heels, impale yourself on a fence post. Believe me, Jenny. These things do happen.'

Nice.

I messaged Mack to say Ellen would drop me home.

He replied the next day: Car ready. Key in ignition. Petrol tank full. Be careful.

And when I replied by asking how much I owed him for the battery, I got the longwinded reply of: £45.

I tested the Mini out on Friday morning by driving to a large supermarket, seven miles away, almost reaching the speed limit on the quieter roads. I danced up and down the aisles (which seemingly stretched on forever in endless rows of wondrous variety) splurging on items never to be found in Middlebeck (luxuries like avocados, cinnamon bagels and winged sanitary towels), feeling deliriously wild and carefree enough to toss a bottle of wine and a chocolate cheesecake into the trolley.

I drove home, brushed my hair, practised my casual, *but of course we're just friends* smile and knocked on Mack's door. Phoned him, still standing on his doorstep. Knocked again. Went home, sorted out a suitcase full of tatty old maps into the 'useless rubbish for recycling' pile and called round again. This time he answered.

'Oh! Are you ill?'

Mack eyed me. His beard, which had reached the point where it could be classified as a separate life-form, eyed me too. Pale-faced, hair like a toilet-brush, smelling nearly as bad, in a T-shirt I had almost certainly seen in the women's section of French Connection: Ouch.

'I brought wine, and cheesecake. To say how grateful I am for the loan of the car. Oh, and the money I owe you.' I adjusted the bag on my shoulder and offered an envelope.

He took it. 'Thanks.'

'But perhaps now's not a good time?' I let the question die away...

'Not really.'

'Do you, um, want the wine and the cake anyway?' There was probably a law about not offering alcohol to a man in that state, but I didn't know what else to say. Mack rubbed a hand through his hair, looked as though he was trying to remember how to speak in full sentences. 'Maybe another day.'

'Are you okay?' I considered whether this time I could force my way inside, and offer some sort of intervention. Intervention against what, exactly, I wasn't sure...

'Yes. No. The car... brought back memories. I'll be fine in a few days.'

'Mack, if the owner of the car has, um, passed away, you should have said. I'd never have accepted it if I thought it would upset you this much.'

He shook his head, irritated. 'I'm not *that* upset.' Then his eyes widened, and a look of utter dejection and misery fell across his face. 'And they haven't died.'

So. Wife: alive. Location: still unknown. Mack: still in love with her.

I tried not to feel too weirded out at driving Mack's missing wife's car. Or at how his dealing with the car had resulted in seriously bad personal hygiene and women's clothing. Instead I kept my head down and tried not to rev the engine too much every time I bounced down the unpaved road.

* * *

School, and therefore my work, had a week's break at the end of May. The Saturday, 2 June, was my birthday. Way back in January, Will and Ellen had required my date of birth as part of their background check, and, being two of the kindest, most optimistic people ever, they had noted it on their calendar even back then.

'The kids are throwing you a party,' Ellen had told me. 'It's not going to be the height of sophistication. Balloon animals, a bouncy castle and rainbow jelly are involved. Oh, and Dawson is preparing a magic show. But hopefully a firepit, summer cocktails and Kiko's karaoke machine later in the evening will bring us back from the brink of full-on kids' party hell.'

'It sounds perfect.' I cleared my throat, blew my nose and tried very hard to pretend I wasn't crying about being thrown a children's birthday party.

When I was very young, every birthday had been shared with Zara. Unsurprisingly, the attention, choice of activity, number of friends (and therefore number of presents) had not been an equal split. Later on, they had been spent visiting Zara at boarding school, where I'd tried to appease her irritation at having to share her special day by remaining as insignificant as possible. Birthdays as an adult had been worst of all, sitting alone in the apartment while Zara had gone off celebrating. I had pretended I wasn't bothered about birthdays, but the truth was I had managed to convince myself that nothing about me or my life was worth celebrating.

For the first time, that was starting to change.

And then, three days before my party, it started to rain. And rain. And then it rained even more – a power-shower of rain, hammering on my repaired roof and racing down the window panes, filling the yard with puddles. By Friday the puddles had merged into a lake. Several inches of water lay between me and the Mini, hidden away from Mack's memories in the shed. I could only hope it kept the water out better than it had the rats. Pulling on boots, I sploshed to the road, and then round to the footpath. I was up a creek without a canoe, let alone a paddle.

Head down against the downpour, arms tightly folded to keep out the chill, I smacked straight into Mack as I turned back towards the house.

'*Oomf.*'

I bounced off him, managing to stay upright, and just stood there, too miserable to do anything else.

'Hey,' he said, holding his umbrella out so it covered both our heads.

'Hi.' I tried to smile. My mouth wobbled.

He peered closer at me. 'Are you crying?'

I shrugged.

'The roads aren't safe. We'll have to wait it out.'

I nodded. He frowned. 'The rain will have stopped by morning. It'll be clear a day or so after.'

'Mm-hmm.'

'Do you have something you need to do? Because, really, it isn't safe to try to leave.'

'Yes, I have something to do.' I sniffed. 'For the first time ever I was going to spend my birthday with other people. People who I think might like me. Love me, even.' My voice cracked. 'The kids have baked a birthday cake. Maddie has made pass the parcel, and Dawson has been practising his tricks. There's pancakes with bacon and maple syrup for my birthday breakfast, and I've made a giant chocolate trifle.' *Okay, Jenny, bring it down an octave...* 'And without meaning to sound presumptuous there might have been a present and some cards and singing happy birthday and fun and happiness.' I gulped in a huge, honking sob. 'There would be happiness.'

Mack looked slightly alarmed.

'And now, once again, I'm spending my birthday with a bowl of soup and my own sodding company. I can't even get to the Common to buy a decent coffee. What *is* this place? Why would anyone *choose* to live here?'

I took a deep breath. Mack carefully stretched out one hand, took off my glasses, wiped them on a tissue and handed them back to me. I breathed in again, tried to suck in some of his calm.

'What are you doing out here, anyway?'

'I saw you leave. Thought you might try to swim it.' He blinked. 'Ellen invited me, but I had plans this weekend, too.'

I sighed. Pulled my thoughts back into line. 'I'm sorry I called you a hermit.'

'Don't be. I have been living a hermit-like existence the past few months.'

'And I'm sorry for ranting on like a madwoman. It's a bit of a thing for me, birthdays. Though not quite as bad as Christmas. At least on my birthday the rest of the world aren't celebrating while I'm feeling crap. Now Christmas, I really hate.' I gave a small shudder.

'You hate Christmas?'

'I don't hate Christmas in principle. I just happen to have hated every Christmas so far.'

'Now that is really sad.'

'I need to get into some dry clothes.' We waded back towards the house, where I trudged inside, had a long hot bath and, in blatant disregard to it being eleven in the morning, crawled into my softest pyjamas and pulled the duvet over my head. For the rest of the day I wallowed in self-pity, left a fake-cheerful message for Ellen, cried, giggled, gasped and oohed at the Hillary West book I'd bought myself as a birthday present, and ate over half the trifle. The rain died to a drizzle as dusk fell, and I went to sleep praying for a birth-day, road-clearing, miracle.

On reflection, I'm rather grateful God said no to that prayer.

26

I woke up to the sun streaming through my window, accompanied by the sound of music. Rubbing the sleep from my face, I listened harder and realised it was the Shakin' Stevens' Christmas classic, 'Merry Christmas Everyone'.

I fumbled to put my glasses on and leapt out of bed, for one glorious moment sure a miracle had indeed occurred, or simply that Mack had been wrong about how long it would take for the water to recede, and the Camerons had come to collect me for the best birthday in the history of the universe, ever. Who else would choose to play Christmas music in June but those crazy Cameron kids? Flinging on a T-shirt, feeling like Noah after his millions of days in the ark, I ran to the window, expecting to see a row of little faces beaming up at me.

Water. A bird huddled on the shed roof. More water. No Camerons.

The music got louder. And could I smell coffee?

Tentatively, thinking rattled thoughts about chocolate-trifle-induced delirium, I opened the bedroom door.

The music grew louder, the coffee smell stronger.

Mannequin Diana was wearing a Santa hat.

I crept down the stairs, selecting a walking stick from the stand by the front door. Somebody was in my kitchen. Whistling.

I pushed open the door. 'Happy birthday, Jenny.'

Mack, too, wore a Santa hat. And a jumper with a reindeer on it. The table was set for two, with red and white snowflake napkins. Fairy lights adorned the window frame, and a jug stuffed with holly and ivy sat on the dresser. His coffee machine gurgled merrily on the worktop.

'I'm a bit confused.'

'Nobody should hate Christmas, so this is your birthday present.'

'Eh?'

'I'm giving you a happy Christmas. It won't make up for all the terrible ones, but it might help you feel better about the next one.'

I stood there, speechless.

'Sit down then.' Mack waved a spatula at the nearest chair.

I sat. Then stood up again, walked over to where he stood by the mini oven, and, before I could chicken out, kissed him on the cheek. 'Thank you.'

He nodded, a smile peeking out from his whiskers. 'You'd better eat a lot of pancakes, because dinner isn't going to be a feast.'

We both ate a lot of pancakes. And bacon, and a sticky old drizzle of syrup from the back of Mack's cupboard.

And then we took our drinks into the living room.

I nearly dropped mine on the floor.

'How did you do this?' I gaped at the tree, standing in a

pot of earth, the old baubles and tinsel I'd discovered weeks earlier dangling from its branches, the magical scent of fresh pine-needles wafting over everything. There were more fairy lights, more decorations I didn't recognise. But what got me most was that half the contents of the room had disappeared. The piles of stuff and ugly, scratched furniture were gone. The boxes still waiting for disposal. The dusty ornaments and dingy, faded pictures of farm animals. One sofa now sat against a wall, a throw covering the threadbare cushions, a chair that didn't completely clash with it to the side. There were a few end tables, a larger coffee table and a couple of bookcases. And that was it. Apart from the fireplace.

Previously hidden behind all the junk, the (hideous) electric fire tucked inside now bathed the room in the most delicious orangey glow.

'I can't believe you did this.' I was agog. Utterly blindsided.

'Neither can I. But once I'd started I sort of had to finish. Else it would have been really weird.' He went over and turned the fire off. 'Sorry, that was for effect, but until it's been tested I don't want to risk burning the house down.'

'What time did you start?'

'About three. I woke up when the rain stopped.'

'I'm not crying.'

'You'd better not be.'

'I think my sinuses are having trouble adjusting to the dust-free environment.' I laughed. 'No. I *am* crying. Mack, you have no idea. Nobody, ever, has ever... Nothing like this.'

'Well, I've never done anything like this before. I was half expecting you to freak out because I'd let myself into your house again and messed about with your stuff. But, well, it's Christmas. Sort of.'

I flapped one hand at him. 'Oh, I'm so over getting annoyed at that.'

We collapsed onto each end of the sofa and simultaneously took big sips from our coffee mugs.

'What were Christmases like, when you were a kid?' I asked. And, to my surprise, Mack told me. Nothing special – parents, two older sisters, grandparents, a dog, arguments over food, films, presents.

'What about once you got married?' I asked.

The Mack portcullis clanged shut.

I sat there, watching him stare very hard at the switched-off fire.

'This might sound pathetic, but I've never had a proper friend before,' I started, my voice hesitant. 'Until I moved here. I have no clue about boundaries, or hanging out, or even what friends talk about. You've met Sarah – she told me all her dirty secrets the first time I went for dinner. And Ellen shares about anything. So, if I ask a question that's too probing, or personal, please bear with me, just tell me and don't get all, y'know, inside yourself.'

I coughed, and adjusted my position on the sofa. 'Having said that, I don't think it's beyond the realms of acceptable conversation to ask why your friend's wife is never there.'

Mack slowly put his mug on an end table. 'My wife is currently in London.' He went quiet again.

'Was that your other plans? Were you hoping to see her?'

'I was hoping to bring her home with me.'

'Ah.'

'I need to start dinner.' He stood up.

'Can we cook and talk?'

'Yes, but it's your turn. I need some meat, and at least half that trifle, before sharing the mess that is my marriage.'

'Okay. But you might have to settle for a third of the trifle. Quarter.'

So we cooked – a chicken breast and one roast potato each, a hotchpotch of vegetables cobbled together, instant gravy and a disastrous attempt at home-made stuffing. And I told Mack about my family, including Zara, right up until the day I moved to Edinburgh.

'Why did you leave?' he asked. 'What happened?'

'Nah-ah.' I shook my head. 'Food is ready. We eat, open this bottle of wine, you tell me about your messy marriage. *Then* I'll tell you about Edinburgh.'

I had to consciously slow down and not scoff my dinner like a warthog, I was so intrigued and excited to finally hear more about the mystery wife – but not in a gossip-hungry way, just a looking-forward-to-getting-to-know-you-better way. I think. And definitely not in a tell-me-all-about-your-awful-marriage-so-I-can-feel-less-guilty way either. I hope.

It turned out to be significantly less exciting, and far more depressing, than I'd anticipated.

'We got married four years ago, six months after meeting at a conference. Both in the same industry, both sharing this dream of working from home, in a cottage in the woods. She chose Sherwood Forest. Had this Robin Hood thing going on since that old film.'

'Prince of Thieves or the Disney fox?'

Mack looked at me sternly.

'Sorry. Not important. Carry on.' I took a sip of wine.

'We bought the house straight away. I liked it here. She didn't. My career took off. Hers didn't. She got resentful, bored and finally went back to London.'

'I find it hard to believe you didn't follow her.'

He grimaced. 'Oh, I did. Stalked might be a more appropriate description. But she wasn't having any of it. And neither was her boyfriend.'

'Ouch. So, you came back?'

'I did.'

'So why had you planned to see her this weekend?'

He topped up our glasses. 'She emailed me. The day after we met Brenda.'

'Ah.' I tried not to let what I was thinking show on my face. What I was thinking was not very nice. Particularly considering it was pretend-Christmas.

'And, given my career's currently in the crapper, that solves the jealous and bitter issue.'

'Your wife was jealous of you?'

'Yeah.' He sighed. 'She wasn't perfect. But it was a tough time, moving up here. We barely knew each other, really. No social life, no career. She's not exactly the Yellow Mickey's bingo type.'

'Still though—'

'No. No still. The only still is that she's still my wife. We're still married. I take that seriously. I take the vows I made seriously. If there's a chance we can make it work, I have to try. This is bigger than my ego or where we live or the mistakes we've made. Better or worse. As long as we both shall live. I meant it.'

'I don't know a lot about marriage.' I pulled a face. 'But for it to work don't *both* parties have to mean it?'

Mack was quiet for a few moments. A wave of grief passed over his face, so raw and desolate my heart ached. 'She invited me to visit her.'

'Well.' I sucked in a deep breath, stuck on a big, cheery fake-Christmas smile and lifted my glass in a toast. 'To your marriage. Sorry you had to spend today stuck here with me. I really wish you all the best.'

We clinked glasses. 'Why don't you give her a call while I clear up?'

And with that, I swiftly scuttled back into the friend zone. And I was not complaining. I didn't have a lot to compare him to, but Mack was turning out to be an awesome friend.

That evening, having drunk probably more Baileys than was wise, following several hours of films and a nap on the sofa, and Mack's brief conversation with his wife, my Baileys-soaked brain decided to show Mack the wedding invitation.

It was worth it just to see the haunted creases on his face lift. When he reached the section on guest etiquette, he even laughed. 'Who *are* these people? Please tell me you aren't going to this spectacle.'

'That—' I pointed to one of the photos of Zara '—is my twin sister. And *that—*' pointing at another photo '—is my ex-secret-boyfriend, who was also my boss. So, yeah, I'm going.' I took another slurp of Baileys. 'And I told them you're my plus one.'

'What?' Mack gave me a sharp look.

'Not that I was really going to ask you to come! But Martha Marsh needed a name and I panicked. Because, really, was I going to admit that I didn't have a date? Particularly given that I'm hardly going to pass by unnoticed, thanks to the whole breaking-the-bride's-nose-at-the-engagement-party incident. And, like I mentioned before, no friends. So I told her my plus one was Mack Macintyre.'

'Hang on, let me get this straight. You were in a relationship with your boss, who is now marrying your twin sister?'

'Yes.'

'And you broke her nose.'

'It was plastic. Less robust than bone.'

'Anything else?'

'I need a black-and-white, high-res photo of Mack Macintyre by Wednesday. My plan was to send a random photo off the Internet and then have him suddenly get a horrific stomach bug on the day. But Martha Marsh is already suspicious. I bet she'll do a search and find out I've made the whole thing up.'

'You *did* make the whole thing up.' Mack frowned. Then he looked at me, and his eyes glinted silver. 'I think Mack Macintyre needs to come with you to this wedding, Jenny.'

'Yes, I'll send him a text, shall I? Join Sarah's dating agency and hunt down all the Mack Macintyres until I find one who'll be my plus one? I can't bring just anyone. It has to be someone... reasonable.'

He waited for me to get it.

'You aren't coming with me.'

'Why not?'

'Because as soon as the road's clear you're driving your wife's Mini to London. I don't think she'd take kindly to you hopping off to Scotland with me a few weeks later to be my wedding date.'

'Well, I appreciate the vote of confidence, but—'

'However, if you have any photos, that would be great. Then I can tell them you're sick, and if everyone spends the whole day thinking I made up a boyfriend, well, I've spent more humiliating days.' I flopped back onto the sofa cushion.

'Really?' He looked at me, eyes wide. 'I'll swap you a photo for hearing about one of those even more humiliating days.'

'Okay, deal. But if you really want to hear stories about a woman at her most pathetic, that says more about you than it does about me.' I rolled my eyes, then elbowed him in what I hoped was a friendly manner. 'But thanks for offering. That was incredibly kind of you.'

'Why are you going? Wouldn't it be easier to stay away?'

'Yes. But I'm trying to stop taking the easy way out. And I want to talk to my mum about something. Believe me, this will be less torturous than visiting her. Even if I could afford it. Which I can't.'

'This something must be important. Can you tell me about it?'

And that took us on to a whole other topic of conversation. Which made us hungry, so we ate cheese on toast and made hot chocolate. And before I knew it, it was one in the morning, my pretend Christmas birthday had finished and Mack now knew my whole life story.

It was only after he'd dragged himself home, and I'd tumbled into bed, I realised I still didn't even know his last name.

Presuming it wasn't Macintyre, of course.

27

The only contact I had with Mack over the next week was an emailed picture on my phone. I clicked open the attachment and every nerve in my body sprang to attention. He looked like Mack, but not Mack. Healthy and happy and fun and alive. As if this were the real Mack, and the man I'd met was just the old exoskeleton floating about. A professional shot: he looked slightly off-camera, eyes crinkling as if someone had caught him about to burst out laughing. His beard a faint shadow. Posture relaxed, chin up. This was either a very ancient photo or I was looking at Mack pre-broken heart.

Wowzers.

I wanted to kiss him and slap his stupid, selfish, ungrateful wife round the face.

A message accompanied the attachment:

Thanks for Christmas Day. Your stories were a perfect distraction. Still smiling every time I think about you wrestling your sister onto the buffet table.

Mack Macintyre.

I made that sad, solitary, lovely man smile.

He had been thinking about me.

Yes, Jenny. He said it himself: you are a distraction.

I walked to the Camerons' house that Friday for a significantly scaled-down, late birthday celebration. I would have driven the Mini, but it had gone.

No bouncy castle or pass the parcel, and Dawson was sleeping over at Lucas and Erik's, so the magic show would have to wait, but a barbeque with my new friends, sitting out under the stars with a glass of Prosecco and a fudge cake topped with birthday sparklers, a choreographed alien koala fight as entertainment and smashing a bacterium-shaped pinata to smithereens was by far my second-best birthday celebration ever.

I didn't even wonder for too long how my twin had celebrated our birthday. Or felt too sad that she would not have been wondering about me.

Inevitably, word had spread about the Beast of Middlebeck. Everyone at the party wanted to know if it was true, I'd been attacked. Chased? Fought off a would-be abductor?

At one point in the evening, Fisher slithered up. 'The Beast of Middlebeck, eh?' He winked. I managed not to vomit up one of Kiko's delicious sushi rolls. 'But, of course, an intelligent young woman like yourself wouldn't be bothered about nonsense like that, would she?'

A prickle ran up my spine. I felt a lot more bothered by Fisher turning up uninvited to my party and breathing alcohol fumes in my face.

'You don't seem the type to get spooked when in the woods alone, wondering what's hiding behind every tree. Who or what is following you home.'

'Excuse me.' I took a step away. 'I'm going to talk to someone else now.'

He snickered.

I turned around. 'You underestimate me if you think kids mucking about could drive me away from my grandmother's home.'

Fisher's eyes narrowed. Flabby lips still curled in a smirk. 'Kids? Are you sure about that? My offer's dropped by five grand, by the way.'

I left him and his slimy grin to it.

The next day, despite being so knackered I felt full of sand right up to my eyeballs; as soon as I got up I headed to the attic.

Rummaging around in a sweltering hot, filthy attic, the only light an old camping lamp, was not a pleasant way to spend a day.

Disintegrating bin bags full of mildewed clothes and bedding, boxes rotten and mouldy, the contents a black, stinking mush. Animal droppings, a bird skeleton, spiders running for their lives every time I moved anything. It was all heading straight to the skip pile. Until I found a metal box, about one by two feet, rusted and bent with age. When I brought it into the light for closer inspection, I could see what appeared to be a hardback notebook through a corroded crack.

The box was locked, of course. But I had about a thousand hairgrips. However, after spending thirty minutes scanning videos on amateur lock-picking, I discovered the keyhole was so full of rust I couldn't get the pin in properly.

I tried banging, stamping, throwing the box down the stairs and prising it open with a screwdriver. Nothing was going to get that box open save a blowtorch – which would destroy the contents – or perhaps a tiny saw, one of the only objects on planet earth not found in the Hoard so far.

I left it on the kitchen worktop, making a mental note to ask either Jamie or Mack if they could help, whichever one of them I saw first. It might well be nothing, anyway. A book of accounts, or my mum's maths homework.

In the meantime, I had leftover party food to eat and my good deed for the day to complete. The Camerons had given me a laptop as a birthday present. And no matter how many times Ellen tsked that it was only small, cheap, and nothing worth crying about, I felt as though they'd given me a window to the world.

Fortified with a plate of mini-quiches and a huge dollop of dip on one side, I fired it up, clicking impatiently through to the Internet.

Four hours, one accidental snooze with my face plastered on the keyboard, a dangerous number of canapés for any one woman to consume and a million hits of the delete key later, I had finished.

Without a scanner it looked disappointingly rough – the laptop camera was okay but the comic pages were obviously photographs – however, the Squash Harris website was up and running.

I started the publicity campaign by emailing Kiko and Sarah a link, with a note saying I thought their kids might like it, and why not leave a comment if they did. And then I couldn't think of anything else, so, too tired to bother climbing the stairs, I rolled up in a blanket on the sofa and conked out before I could worry about where all those attic spiders had run to.

* * *

The first thing I did when I woke up, after trying to get blood back into my right leg, was to check the website. No comments. None at lunchtime, or that evening after a day of hauling decomposing bags and boxes of gunk down two flights of stairs into the garden. I spent the rest of the evening researching how to get traffic onto websites until my eyes were too blurry to read the screen any more.

By Monday morning there were *still* no comments.

I barrelled up to Kiko in the playground, giving the tiniest nod to 'hello' before launching straight into it: 'Did you read the comic?'

'Pardon?'

'The link I sent you. Squash Harris.'

'Squash what?'

Hannah threw her stuffed rabbit out of the pushchair and into a puddle. I waited for Kiko to retrieve it, shoving it into a carrier bag while Hannah wailed in protest.

'Never mind.' I turned and started to trudge away.

'Wait!' Kiko skidded up next to me with the pushchair. 'I'm sorry, I've been sort of distracted.'

'You seemed a little twitchy at the barbeque. I thought it was because Adam was there.'

Adam had managed a whole two hours of the party. Having built him up in my head as a thoughtless, neglectful dud who took his wife and kids for granted, I had been surprised by his open face, easy nature and the way one hand had stayed glued to Kiko's back the whole time.

Kiko's face dropped. 'Yeah. He was really nice. He even let me have a lie-in.'

'That's a good thing, isn't it?'

She flicked her silky fringe out of her eyes. 'He's been working nearly every hour since. I think the only thing he's said to me is, "Sorry, something came up." And, "Where are my keys?"' We left the playground and started across the green. 'I have better conversations with Hannah, and she can only say five words. I'm so lonely, Jenny. It's lonelier with him there than when he's away.'

'Oh, I'm sorry.' I wrapped one arm round her as we walked. 'Let me buy you a doughnut.'

'That sounds awesome, but I can't.' She straightened up, tilted her chin. 'I've got packing to do. Preparations to make. Flights to check in.'

'Are you kidding me?'

She sucked in a huge breath, eyes boggling. 'I've booked the base-camp trek. I leave on Friday.'

'What did Adam say?' I asked, when I'd picked my jaw back up off the muddy pavement.

She looked at me worriedly, biting her lip.

'You haven't told him!'

'He hasn't asked.'

'Not a normal question to ask, is it? "Oh, by the way, are you planning any trips to the Himalayas in the next week or so?"'

'No, but, "How are you?", "What have you been up to this year?", "Why are there piles of outdoor gear in the utility room and a suitcase on the bedroom floor?" are.'

'You have to tell him.'

'I will. It's all in the instruction manual I'm putting together. Which he'll find in the freezer, on top of all the meals I'm leaving him. It's three weeks. His parents will be around to help out so he can get some work done. What's the worst that can happen?' At that, she let out a huge hybrid snort-sob, gripping onto the pushchair so tightly I thought the handle would snap.

I gave her a squeeze. 'They'll be fine. Me and Sarah'll keep an eye out.'

'Keep an eye out on what?' Sarah asked, back to doing the school run now her mum was around to open up the café.

'Give me one of Jamie's caramel doughnuts and I'll tell you. Kiko's got packing to do.'

'You are *kidding* me.' Sarah's face broke into an enormous grin.

'That's what I said.' I steered her towards the Common. 'And afterwards you can leave a lovely comment on the comic-book website I told you about and which you so rudely ignored.'

28

The Christmas Book Club Challenge met that Friday. Kiko wasn't there, having phoned Adam from the airport to say, 'Please pick up the kids from school, and by the way I'm not coming back for three weeks.'

I decided to cycle, daring myself to face the journey home in the dark. Brenda had confirmed there'd been no further signs of anyone making mischief. With the word spread that the police were keeping an eye out, the Beast of Middlebeck was sure to have gone to ground. Or back to harassing imaginary people on his Xbox, according to Brenda's professional opinion. Given that the Mini was still gone, and for all I knew it was never coming back, or if it did then its rightful owner might well come back with it, I felt determined to get back out there alone without the need for a chaperone.

I arrived just as Ashley drove up, Frances in the passenger seat. Frances wasn't driving as, she said, 'The medication those meddling doctors have put me on is clogging up the messages from my head to the rest of me.' The way she jerkily climbed out of the car and leant on her cane as she plodded inside made my heart weep.

We knew it wasn't the pills making Frances tired, or slow. She had been slender when I met her back in January, but the hollows in her cheeks and the wrist-bones jutting out of the end of her jacket sleeves revealed what brave words and a spunky attitude tried to conceal.

'Did you go on the camel-trek?' Ellen asked, avoiding the obvious.

'I did.' A hint of a twinkle returned to Frances' bleary eyes. 'It was quite possibly the most uncomfortable, ridiculous thing I've ever done. I almost met my match with that ugly great brute they put me on.' She showed us a photograph. 'Reminded me of my Great-Aunt Jocelyn.'

She described to us what it had been like, bumping along the trail. 'I will tell you this, though, I felt rather like a queen. Which was some consolation for all the bottom bruises.'

'So, is that the end of your adventures?' Ashley asked, unable to keep the hope out of her voice.

Frances glowered. 'I'm not dead yet!' She broke out into a fit of violent coughing, leaving the rest of us exchanging worried glances.

She took a drink of water and wiped her eyes. 'I'm going on a sunset hot-air-balloon ride. Not much chance of it wearing me out, but my body seems to be managing that by itself.'

'Oh, how lovely!' Ashley said.

'If I deteriorate much further, I might just throw myself out of the basket once we're high enough.'

'Frances!' Ellen scolded. 'How would that make the other passengers feel? Let alone the owners of the balloon.'

'Yes, yes,' she grumbled. 'It was only a thought.'

I had been in a place where life had seemed so black, so bleak, I could understand the appeal of throwing yourself out of a hot-air balloon. But my brokenness had all been in my head. To watch Frances, so proud, so *alive,* slip away before our eyes, knowing each day would be worse than the last, I couldn't just sit there saying nothing.

'How can we help you?' I asked, fully expecting her to reject my offer.

Instead she hesitated, and when our eyes met there was an openness there, a connection, one human being to another.

'We could drop some meals off, make sure your freezer's stocked up. I get sick of eating all the café leftovers myself,' Sarah said quickly.

'And we can do cleaning, or washing,' I added.

'You have enough cleaning to do with that scrapheap of yours,' Frances said, but it was a half-hearted response.

'To be honest, I'd appreciate the company,' I replied. 'We can just have a cup of tea.'

'I'm not an invalid.'

'Neither am I, but I enjoy a drink with a friend. Especially one as fascinating as you.'

Frances shook her head, refusing to meet our eyes. 'I'll think about it. Now, who's next? This whole ruddy meeting isn't about my slide into enfeeblement.'

Ashley excitedly showed us a press clipping from a literary magazine featuring Hillary West.

'"An unnamed source at her publishers, Hickleton Press, confirmed that the deadline for the next book was in February. 'There's not been a peep out of her, even a title. The editors are in full panic mode,' our source reports. The word on the street is that the elusive writer is suffering from a serious case of writer's block!'"

'You seem weirdly happy about that, for the world's biggest Hillary West fan,' Sarah said.

'But don't you see?' Ashley cried, twirling her shell necklace. 'This is it! This is my challenge – to SAVE her!'

Lucille looked as though Florence had farted under the table. 'Give me strength.' She shook her head. 'How exactly are you going to do that?'

'Once I've tracked her down, I can help her figure out all the issues with the current storyline. Who knows what makes a Hillary West story work better than me?'

'Um, Hillary West?' Jamie muttered. 'Her publisher, editors, agent...'

'Are you any closer to finding her?' I asked.

Ashley's brow furrowed. 'I started a list of possible houses. But then this article happened and I spent the rest of the time planning how to unblock the block. And I have sent a few emails to her agent offering my services.'

'Please, no.' Lucille groaned. 'I dread to think how many "a few" means in Ashley world.'

'No more than eight. Or twelve,' she bristled.

'And did the agent reply?' Lucille asked, her smile sweet as vinegar.

'They're very busy people.' Ashley's face was turning blotchy.

'Shall we move on?' Ellen said. 'Jamie?'

Jamie brought out a cardboard box containing a selection of doughnuts iced with a variety of funny animal faces – frogs, cats, pandas. The penguins were my favourite.

'These are brilliant!' Ellen took an elephant. 'My kids would love them.'

'They've sold out both mornings Jamie's made them for the café,' Sarah said, her mouth stuffed with a ladybird. 'He could make a proper business out of it if he could bear to give up saving the universe.'

'I *could* bear to,' Jamie mumbled. 'It just takes time sorting all the paperwork.'

Sarah hadn't been on any more dates, but she'd been chatting to one guy for the past month who had managed to keep her interest.

'He's funny. And he calls me on my BS. And he's, I dunno, sweet isn't the right word. Kind? Honourable? Anyway, I'm thinking I might be up for meeting with him. We'll see how it goes.'

I glanced at Jamie. His eyes, fixed on the table, as always when Sarah was describing her romantic life, flickered up for a second and back down again. Was he banking on this new interest being as hopeless as previous dates?

We waited for Ashley to take a drowsy Frances home before I finished off the evening by bringing out the box.

'Anybody got any ideas about how to get into this? Jamie? I thought you might know a trick or two.'

Jamie picked up the box and walked into the kitchen. By the time Sarah and I had got up to follow him, he had come back out.

'Here.' He put the box on the table.

'Thanks.' I slid it over to where I was sitting. Everyone looked at me expectantly.

'You can open it now,' Jamie said.

The problem was, I didn't want to any more. Not here, with all of them looking.

I cracked open the top of the box until I could make out the hardback notebook on the top. The faded blue cover had wrinkles in the places where water had managed to seep in. There was writing in the centre, too smudged and worn to decipher.

'Well?' Lucille asked.

'It's a pile of notebooks. But they're really damaged and if I take them out they'll probably fall to pieces. The pages look stuck together.'

'You could try tweezers,' Jamie suggested.

'Good idea. I'll try when I get home, then.'

There was a general groan of disappointment.

'Sorry, guys. You'll have to wait for next month's instalment.'

As soon as I arrived back at the cottage, after taking a moment to breathe a sigh of relief that I made it home intact, I carefully extricated the four notebooks from the box and placed them in the airing cupboard to dry out. Unable to resist, I did try opening the first one, but when the soggy page started to tear I hastily laid it back down again and left them to it.

'Probably maths homework,' I muttered on repeat as I thrashed about in bed that night. Because everyone locked up old homework in a metal tin and stored it in the attic. I didn't think even my oddball grandmother would do that.

The next morning, Saturday, the air was sweet and mild, the sky a startling blue. Having been relieved of my café job by Sarah's mum, now back from her cruise, I decided to take a walk to Frances' farm. After a brisk two miles through the woods, I arrived pleasantly worn out, tangly-haired and warm-cheeked.

The modest white farmhouse stood at the end of a concrete drive surrounded by outbuildings, not a discarded plant pot or scruffy weed in sight. A willowy figure I assumed to be Frances' farm manager was plodding up the edge of a field that rose steeply behind the house. I rapped the red front door's brass knocker. Frances opened it the instant I took my hand away.

'Jenny. Saw you out of the window and thought you must be heading this way.' She was a little breathless, stooped over slightly, with deep purple shadows under her eyes, but her shirt was ironed and her hair neatly combed.

'I couldn't face another day sorting out the Hoard alone. Do you have time to share some lunch?' I swung the rucksack containing sandwiches and a carton of soup off my back.

She looked down her nose at me. 'Don't pretend this visit is for your benefit. I'm old and ill, not yet senile.'

'Which is why you're great company. Please don't make me go back to scrubbing mouldy window frames.'

'The house isn't very tidy.'

I burst out laughing at that until Frances, realising who she was talking to, had to crack a smile.

We settled in her conservatory, the French doors flung open to allow the summery air in, although Frances still huddled under a thick woollen blanket. We talked about this and that while we ate, I asked if she had known my grandmother, but she said she had only moved to the forest ten years ago, and Charlotte Meadows had already been something of a recluse by then.

She told me stories about Big Mike, the years they'd spent travelling the world. Her job as a teacher, all the way from private schools in Hong Kong through to mud-shacks in Uganda. I told her about my own failed attempts to further my education, which she dismissed as simply not having found the right path yet.

'What are you going to do once the house is finished?'

'I don't think I can see that far into the future.' I shrugged.

She sniffed. 'You can't keep running forever.'

'Running from what?' I put my plate down on the side table.

'Your true self. It's worth a little thought, isn't it? What do you love? Where do your passions lie? What are you good at? Who are you, Jenny, and why are you here?'

'Wow.' I rubbed my face. 'Are you trying to put me off coming over again? Truthfully, I have no idea who I am. That's why I'm living in a derelict germ-pit in the middle of nowhere, hoping that as I sort through the mess and the muddle, I might find myself in the process.'

She sat back, nodding. 'Well, keep looking. You'll get there.'

Not long after that, she sent me off to make coffee, and when I returned she had fallen asleep, which was what I'd been waiting for. I spent the next two hours cleaning up Frances' kitchen, scrubbing her bathroom and changing her bed. I swept the wooden floors and hung sheets to blow on the washing line, making a fresh pot of coffee just as she woke up.

'Ah, thank you, Jenny. I fear I may have dozed off for a moment there.'

'I took the liberty of giving things a quick once-over while you rested. I hope that's okay.'

She scowled at me. 'No. It is not okay. But if you happen to be adrift next Saturday, you may share your lunch with me again.'

'I'll look forward to it.'

Although Frances couldn't look forward to Ellen, Sarah, Ashley, Lucille and Jamie calling in the rest of the week, because I wasn't going to tell her. She'd figure it out soon enough.

* * *

Sunday afternoon, I helped a young couple who'd responded to my Freecycle ad carry out several small pieces of furniture to their car. I nearly dropped the glass side table when I saw the Mini had returned. Almost dying from curiosity, I hastily loaded the table into the couple's boot and tiptoed back past Mack's kitchen window, feigning a casual glance inside.

Two mugs sat on the draining board.

Heart pounding, I scanned the room. A red and green handbag hung off the back of a chair.

For a brief moment, I hated that handbag.

Then I remembered that Mack loved his wife, 'til death did them part, and as Mack's friend I was, of course, supposed to be happy for him.

Still, it *was* an ugly bag. Pretentious. Too small to be of any genuine use. Hardly designed for forest life. I stomped on past and kept on stomping until I reached the Common. Then, realising I hadn't brought my own sensible weather-proof bag, which also happened to contain my purse, I stomped back. After spending a while pricing up lamps for the car boot sale, while pretending not to be straining my ears towards next door, I turned some music up, loud, and logged into the Squash Harris website.

There were three comments.

One, from Sarah, quoting how much Edison loved it.

She'd also shared the link on Facebook and a couple of people had responded.

They loved the comic. One of them asked when the next edition would be posted.

I nearly forgot all about the blood-red, bile-green handbag.

A few more messages and it would be ready to show Dawson.

I had another go at carefully unpeeling the notebooks, still crisping in the airing cupboard. The outer two thirds were dry, but I wasn't going to risk opening them until they were completely ready.

So when Ashley phoned, asking if I wanted to go Hillary West hunting with her, I was in my black jeans and hoodie before she'd pulled into the driveway.

29

It was fully dark by the time we pulled up alongside the wall of a vast property three miles from Middlebeck.

'What now, boss?' I asked, as we sat in the car with the lights out, about thirty yards from the gate.

Ashley fiddled with her jacket zip. 'I'm not sure. I thought we could look through some windows, or knock on the door and pretend to be lost, but I don't think that's going to work here.'

'You could go for the bold approach, try buzzing the intercom and ask for Ms West.'

'I couldn't do that!' Ashley gasped. 'What if she invites me in? I can't have her meeting me like this. I'm not even wearing lipstick.'

'I don't think she's going to notice the lack of lipstick.' I squinted at her. 'But she'll probably call the police if you keep that ski mask on.'

'We should have worn civilian clothes, pretended to be dog-walkers or something.'

'With no dogs? At ten at night?'

'We could have borrowed Florence.'

'I bet you could climb one of those trees and see into the grounds.'

'Ooh! I did bring binoculars, like Jamie said.'

'Why isn't Jamie here?' I whispered, as we tiptoed towards a particularly sturdy-looking willow tree, not too far from the wall.

'I didn't ask him,' Ashely replied, the whites of her eyes round in the moonlight. 'He's far too scary. And this is *my* challenge. Can you imagine me stumbling along behind while he slips through the shadows like an assassin? I'd only go and get him caught, and he's got a reputation to maintain.'

'So, you're going to get me caught instead?' I smiled.

'Well, I thought, being a civilian like me, you'd be more likely to... well, you might not...'

'It's fine.' I giggled. 'I don't have any reputation worth maintaining. And I'm glad you asked me. Come on. Have a go at reaching for that branch.'

I gave Ashley a clumsy boost, and she heaved herself up to where she could peer over the top of the wall. Afraid to take pictures using a flash, she instead hissed down a description for me to jot into a folder.

'Three windows with lights on, two of them covered in blinds... the third appears to be a dining room...'

She dictated two pages of notes about the house and what she could see of the garden, before sucking in a huge breath.

'Another light has gone on. Behind a door. The door is opening. Something's coming out!'

'A woman?'

'A dog. Two HUGE dogs. They're running, sniffing. Oh. Heading this way. And they don't look happy.'

She didn't have to tell me any more. Ferocious snarls

rapidly approached the other side of the wall, punctuated by a duet of deafening barks.

The whole area suddenly lit up with at least a dozen perimeter floodlights, one of them directly above Ashley's head.

'Crapcakes!' She froze, swivelling her eyes down to where I stood, caught between laughing, squealing and peeing my pants. 'What do I do?'

'I don't know. What would Jamie do?' I wheezed. Whatever we did, there was a very high chance we were both ending up dog food.

A woman's voice erupted into the night, bellowing threats. Most of which involved an avocado peeler, whatever that was. Ashley let out a squeak, dropped her binoculars and toppled right out of the tree, landing in a crumpled heap on a pile of rotting leaves. I hurried over, trying to keep hold of the folder while heaving her up. She grappled for purchase on the wet leaves, slipping and sliding, flinging one arm around my chest as I leant down.

'Ow!' she yelled, tipping over again as she snatched her foot off the ground and bringing me with her. 'My dodgy ankle.'

As we scrabbled back onto our feet, a mechanical whirring sound started up from the direction of the gates. The woman ordered her beasts to do something that would make the avocado peeler threat redundant.

'If they find we don't possess those body parts, maybe they'll leave us alone,' Ashley huffed, as I dragged her hopping, flopping body towards the car.

Flinging open the passenger door, I gave her an almighty shove towards the direction of the seat, before sprinting round the back towards the driver's side.

If it hadn't been a teeny-tiny car, I didn't think I'd have made it. The dogs, who looked more like tigers crossed with hyenas crossed with velociraptors, launched themselves in a growling, baying whirlwind of fur and teeth and spittle at the door the second I slammed it shut.

'KEYS!' I screamed at Ashley, who pulled and flapped at her jacket pocket, her whimpers lost in the thuds of animals flinging themselves against the car.

Several minutes, or what was probably more like five seconds later, she hurled them in my direction, where they sailed past my quivering legs into the foot well. Another panicked fumble and I had the keys in the ignition, engine on and foot firmly on the accelerator. We revved away, the dogs racing alongside us until we picked up enough power to pull ahead.

'I don't have my seat belt on!' Ashley wailed, hands braced against the seat. 'Slow down!'

'I don't want to give her time to record the number plate,' I said, still trying to catch my breath.

'Did she have a phone out? She could have taken a picture.'

'I wasn't looking at her!'

'Jamie would have covered the plates. Or used a stolen car,' Ashley jabbered.

'Jamie would have karate-chopped those freaks in the neck, rendering them momentarily stunned but unharmed. Maybe next time we should bring a pork chop as a distraction.'

'Next time!' she squawked. 'There will *be* no next time.'

'But what if that was her?' The adrenaline rush might have rendered me temporarily insane.

Ashley turned to glare at me, wincing as she jarred her ankle. 'That... person was not Hillary West!'

'It might have been.'

She stuttered, failing to get out a reply.

'Just because she writes beautiful books about love, doesn't mean she has to believe it. Maybe we caught her on a bad day. Maybe that was her housekeeper. Or cook, judging by her fondness for obscure kitchen utensils.'

'Hillary West would never employ someone like that. And besides, she's allergic to avocados.'

'You don't know that for sure.'

'THAT WAS NOT HILLARY WEST OR HILLARY WEST'S HOUSE!'

I slowed down to turn onto the main road. 'Okay. It's your challenge.'

'Do you WANT to go back?' Ashley cried. 'Look at me! I'm bruised and filthy and, as well as a sprained ankle, I think I may have a serious concussion because for a moment there it sounded like you wanted to go back to the house with a couple of pork chops and face those Hounds of the Baskervilles for a rematch while that hideous woman sharpens her apple-corer!'

I thought about it. 'You're right. A pork chop would only hold them off for a couple of seconds. I'm sorry. I haven't had so much fun in ages.'

I thought a bit more. 'I haven't *ever* had so much fun.'

I glanced across at my partner in crime, her eyes bulging through her ski mask, a large rip down the sleeve of her jacket, a bloody tissue pressed against her ripped nail.

'Next house, you do the climbing, I'll make notes,' she said.

'Deal.'

We drove for a few more minutes in silence. 'Maybe we should ask Jamie for a job,' I said, pondering my conversation with Frances about what made me feel alive.

We laughed the whole way home.

* * *

I was squelching around the side of the cottages towards my back door when Mack's opened, and a woman stepped out. She glanced at me briefly, then took another sharp look, eyebrows raised in alarm.

I froze, Old Jenny painfully aware of the leaves in her hair, mud streaking her clothes and wonky glasses hanging off one hinge. Mack's wife wore a mint-green sundress and red heels. Expensive-looking sunglasses held toffee-coloured hair off her round face. Honestly? I had been expecting Mack's wife to look like a snobby bitch. She was more like a pretty, shiny apple. Under the fitted dress she was soft and curvy and... luscious.

I swallowed, hard, and tried to force my limbs towards my own door, aware I must appear like a demented puppet.

Before I reached her, she disappeared, slamming the door shut. I jerked my way inside and scurried upstairs. It had only been a few days. We hadn't even been that close, yet. But I missed my friend all the same.

I stripped off my filthy clothes and took a long shower. Cried some lonely tears, ate a packet of chocolate biscuits, then decided that was enough wallowing. If Mrs Mack was here to stay, why couldn't that mean two neighbours to be friends with – double the best friends? If Mack loved her she had to be a nice person.

Of course, anyone with half a brain knew why the lonesome neighbour couldn't be hanging out gooseberrying with the recently reconciled couple next door.

I flopped into bed, briefly wondering if Mrs Mack would want her duvet back, a thought swiftly followed by the image of her cuddled up in bed on the other side of the wall, and realising that, no, she'd probably be fine without it.

30

I hustled into the playground with five very late children. Irritable and distracted, I felt as if I'd slipped back two months in my childcare capabilities. I'd given Dawson a perfect excuse to moan and snipe at his sister all the way to school, while she fussed about rushed plaits, thrown-together lunch and the upcoming spelling test I had failed to find the time to test her on.

I hoped no one would notice the triplets' wrinkled shirts, mismatched (or, in Billy's case, lack of) socks and unwashed faces.

Then I spotted Adam running across the street towards the playground with his three daughters and I knew that absolutely no one was going to notice Jonno's felt-tip tattoo.

He tumbled through the gate, getting Hannah's pushchair stuck on the railings for a frantic couple of minutes, while the older girls hopped with agitation at their increasing lateness.

The eldest, Lily, was wearing what must have been her younger sister's school trousers, revealing three inches of ankle and a pair of jelly sandals. She clearly hadn't been near a hairbrush since her mum left on Friday, and, instead of her usual Pokemon rucksack, was clutching a plastic carrier bag.

Her little sister had apparently dressed herself, foregoing the regulation school uniform for that worn by princess fairy ballerina mermaids everywhere, including a huge matted blonde wig and a pink flashing sword.

She stamped her rainbow wellies like the star of Riverdance. 'Come ON, Daddy! You have to tell Miss Howe about the washing machine so I don't get in trouble.'

'I know, hang on.' Adam pulled and twisted the pushchair to no avail, as Hannah wailed.

'I'll sort this,' I said, hurrying over. 'Go and get the girls signed in.'

He gave me such a look of relief I almost felt a teensy bit sorry for him.

'Um, I'd take Abbie's wig off, though.'

'NO!' Abbie screamed, grabbing both sides.

'There was an... incident with a pair of scissors,' Adam mumbled.

I remembered my promise to Kiko, and beckoned to Abbie. 'Come here, let me see what I can do.'

A few minutes later, I bounced Hannah about on my hip while Adam took the girls inside, Abbie's real hair now twisted to cunningly conceal the missing chunks, Lily's neatly brushed.

It was only when he jogged back out that I noticed Adam was wearing pyjama bottoms. He clearly hadn't shaved, and, judging by the reek as he took Hannah out of my arms, hadn't showered either.

I pushed my glasses up. 'Going well so far?'

He wrestled a squirming Hannah into the pushchair, and straightened up to face me. 'About as well as it would if I landed Kiko with the job of running the charity out of the blue.'

'This isn't a job, it's your children.'

'No. My job is nothing compared to this.' He shook his head. 'I have no clue what I'm doing.'

'Didn't you find the manual?' We started to walk back towards Kiko's house.

'The manual doesn't include what to do when Abbie refuses to eat dinner because one of her noodles wriggled like a worm, or how to stop them arguing over every single, little, infinitesimal thing. Or why Hannah won't stop trying to climb out of the pushchair. Or a reminder to check the washing machine for foreign objects before you put the kids' clothes in there and rip them to shreds.'

'Hannah wants her rabbit.'

'What?'

'She's crying for her rabbit. Well, she probably wants her mum, but Rabbit is better than nothing.'

Adam, having reached his front path, stopped and looked at me. 'I am a terrible father.'

'Yep.'

'I can't believe you knew that, and I didn't.'

I didn't ask if he meant Rabbit, or being a rubbish dad.

'It's not hard to believe, considering how little time you spend with your family.'

'I thought Kiko enjoyed it. She *wanted* three kids. She *chose* not to work...'

'Are *you* managing to get much work done *and* look after them, with absolutely no help from a partner? Can you imagine what her life would be like if she tried to work on top of this? Do you think she would enjoy it then?'

He rocked the pushchair, face drooping.

'There are women who do it – and men – spend all the time they've got, wearing themselves to the bone working and looking after kids, being there for them, providing love and affection and time as well as hot dinners and clean clothes and all the other ten million practical things it takes to raise a family. Always, always putting themselves last, with hardly a thanks or a well done. Let alone a hot cup of tea or a foot-rub. Those people are called single parents. When was the last time you made Kiko feel cherished, precious? Beautiful? Didn't you make a vow about that once?'

He ran a hand over his stricken face. 'It's just, my job, it's so important and...'

'And your family isn't?' I pointed at him, just about shaking with rage. 'You can train people to do your job, give them some of your hours. Presumably the charity hasn't ground to a halt now you're taking some time off? You are the only husband and father they have. Well. At the moment you are.'

His face crumpled. 'What do I do? How can I make this right?'

'Number one, man up.' I looked at him for a long moment. Did he really expect me to give him the answers? 'That's it. Just be a bloody man and make the right decision.'

I spun on the heels of my trainers and strode off, straight to Sarah's for a koala doughnut and a smoothie. Adam was an idiot. He'd made some giant mistakes, but I didn't think *he* was a mistake. He'd lost his way, but for all their sakes I prayed he could find his way back. I texted the number Kiko had left us and offered to have a look through Maddie's old uniform and see what I could find to fit his girls.

He replied five minutes later: Thanks, but I think they deserve something new.

* * *

The notebooks were dry. I had planned to get started on them straight away, but now, feeling twitchy and stressed, I instead logged onto SquashHarris.com. Seven new comments. Six of them made me smile. The seventh made me screw up my nose and hit delete. After another couple of hours figuring out how to get a spam filter on the website, I felt so stressed I was ready to look at the notebooks just to change the subject.

I gingerly placed one on a clean tea towel. Taking a deep breath, I opened the first page:

1 January 1962

Charlotte Meadows' diary.

My hand shook so hard as I turned the next page, it ripped right down the middle.

Charlotte Meadows was a woman in love with the minutiae of everyday housewifery. Her diary, far from consisting of amusing anecdotes, an outpouring of her deepest feelings or the antics of a young newly-wed, was 90 per cent lists, 10 per cent footnotes about the lists.

Shopping, meals, housework, money spent, people she'd seen, snails on the cabbages, hours and minutes spent each day doing nothing of any interest whatsoever. And yet to her, all of it was wonderful. Some pages were unreadable, the ink having run into a giant smudge, others torn to shreds when I tried to open them. I didn't feel as if I was missing out on much.

But I kept going. This was the kind of boring, ordinary stuff that other people got to find out about their grandparents just through seeing them from time to time. I learnt her favourite recipes, that she'd knitted her husband a cap for his birthday, had once enjoyed a social life:

Harvest Supper. Brought two apple and raspberry crumbles.

A life emerged from the pages as I pressed on – a woman, with little time and not a spare ha'penny, but determined to enjoy what she did have. Strong, hardworking, competent.

That evening, after hastily packaging up a broken transistor radio that I'd auctioned off for a bewildering amount online, I continued into the second notebook. I read of her delight in becoming pregnant, caught a whiff of worry once the midwife told her to prepare for twins. The list of jobs done shrank as days became consumed with getting ready for her babies: knitting, decorating, scrimping and saving. She sewed nappies and sheets, sold her mother's jewellery to buy a cot large enough for two, drank each night the half-pint of stout the doctor recommended.

Slept, ate, slept even more.

And then, Isobel:

Isobel Anne Meadows born at home. S. at the Red Lion so no time for hospital.
5lb 1oz. She is healthy.
The boy died. I called him Thomas.

In three lines, everything changed.

I shut the notebook and spent the rest of the evening watching stupid videos of pets online.

They failed to shift the boulder of granite sitting in my

chest, but at least helped muffle the sound of my weeping heart.

* * *

When I arrived back from school the following day to find a car in front of the house, I initially assumed it was more Freecyclers. However, as I walked closer, a man stepped out from behind a broken wardrobe, wearing a hard hat and holding a clipboard.

'Ah. Are you the owner of the property?'

'Yes.'

'Darren Smith. Environmental Health.' He held out a hand. I shook it for the shortest length of time possible.

'Oh.'

'Want to know why I'm here?' he asked, with a cheery grin.

'I'm not sure.'

'Well, legally I have to tell you.' He rolled his eyes, as if to say, '*Silly old laws!*'

I waited until he'd cleared his throat, tapping his pen on the clipboard a few times. 'A concerned citizen contacted us about the waste accumulation, pest hazard and general disrepair of your property. Somebody is worried you're going to do yourself a mischief.'

'Who?'

'Well, me, for starters.' He chuckled.

'Who contacted you?'

'I'm not at liberty to say. But...' he screwed up his face as if talking to a small child '... they do have a point.'

'I'm clearing out my grandmother's house. She had a lot of stuff. I'm selling what I can, and either recycling the rest or offering it up on Freecycle, but that takes time. Once I'm down to just the rubbish no one wants I'll hire a skip and move it all out in one go.'

'Yes, I completely understand and that's no problem at all, as long as it's all gone in the next seven days.'

'*What?*'

'You have seven days to clear the outside of the property and restore it to what I deem to be an acceptable standard. Now, if you don't mind. Well, whether you mind or not, I need to inspect internally.'

'Why?' I tried to summon up New, Kickass Jenny from where she'd hidden behind my pale, lily-coloured liver. 'Do you have a warrant?'

'I have all the required documentation.' He flipped over the top sheet on the clipboard and waved it under my nose.

'Why do you need to inspect it internally? It's not affecting anyone else.'

'Rat infestations don't respect property boundaries. Neither does substandard plumbing. Damp. Dry rot. Poorly repaired roof. Electrical issues posing a fire hazard.'

'Did next door call you?' My voice wobbled weakly.

'As I stated clearly before, I'm not at liberty to confirm or deny that. Shall we proceed?' He strode up to the front door.

'I don't use that one. You need to come round the back.'

He frowned at me, all pretence of jollity gone. 'Do you have documentation to confirm you are the owner?'

'Not in my pocket, no.'

He narrowed his eyes. 'If you're being obstructive then I'm within my rights to call the police to obtain forced entry.'

'I'm not being obstructive! The front door is obstructive, so I use the back.'

'Please watch your attitude. Environmental Health

employees have a no-tolerance policy regarding physical or
verbal abuse.'

Not trusting myself to reply, I stalked off, assuming the
power-crazed inspector would follow. As I marched past
Mack's kitchen, the blind twitched back into place.

That gave my mind pause. I knew Mack hadn't tipped off
the council. But was there a chance his big-city wife had?
And if so, why?

Nearly an hour later, I had trailed Darren Smith around
every inch of my house. He'd scrawled pages and pages of
notes, accompanied by those teeth-sucking noises builders
made and lots of head shaking.

I followed him right to his car, ensuring he couldn't do
anything sneaky like plant a rat's nest in the cracked sink on
my drive.

'So, what's the verdict?' I asked, aiming for confident,
breezy, on-it. Sounding more like a woman who'd only just
realised the green and brown speckles on her dining-room
wallpaper weren't part of the original design.

'I will be sending a full report.' He pursed his thin lips.
'To summarise, however, as well as needing to clear the exterior of the property, there is extensive work required internally in order to render the dwelling fit for human
habitation. This includes a full rewire, multiple plumbing
works, damp-proofing, mould treatment and control of the
rodent infestation. To start with.'

'How long do I have?'

'We try to be reasonable, Ms Birkenshaw. The grounds
need to be cleared within the week. As does the infestation.
I'll give you a month for the rest.'

'I can't get all that done in a month.'

'Well, that's no problem. We can do it for you.' The grin

was back. 'Only it will cost significantly more if we have to arrange for the works to be carried out. No good reason why decent, honest taxpayers should be forking out for us to clear up your mess, now, is there?'

'I'm clearing up my own mess – it just takes time. You can't expect...'

I was arguing with the wind. Darren Smith, Environmental Health Officer and all-round twazzock had driven off.

Five seconds later I was hammering my fist against Mack's kitchen door.

'Oh, hi, Jenny.' He wore a spotty shirt and jeans that were, in my opinion, way too skinny for a man over the age of twenty-five. 'Is everything okay?'

'I just had a visit from the council.' I barged into the kitchen, resisting the urge to sweep two breakfast bowls off the table and onto the floor.

'What did they want?'

'They wanted,' I snapped, 'to carry out an inspection in response to an anonymous tip-off from someone concerned about the effect of my house on the neighbouring property.'

'Ah.' Mack crossed his arms and leant against the worktop.

'Did you call Environmental Health about me?' I blinked hard to stop any tears leaking out.

'Of course not.'

'You don't sound too sure. Did your wife call them?'

'I don't think so.' He frowned. 'No. I'm sure she didn't. But she's on the train back to London right now.'

'Then what? What aren't you telling me?'

He sighed, scratching his even trimmer beard. 'She *has* been in touch with a couple of estate agents.'

'You're selling the cottage?' The sense of betrayal – stupid, irrational, but there nonetheless – was a punch in my guts. 'But you *love* living here.'

'Maybe so, but it's not just about me. And I've told them I won't accept an offer from Fisher on principle. I can't imagine there'll be many other people queuing up to pay the asking price.'

'Things don't work out with her boyfriend, she comes running back and suddenly you're giving up everything for her? Are you moving back to London? You hated living there.'

'I know you're angry, but that was way out of line.' Mack spoke through a clenched jaw.

'I have nothing, Mack, but this wreck of a house. Nowhere else to go. This is the first place I've ever felt like I could build a home and a life. And now I have this great big list of impossible stuff I have to do, *by the end of the month*, on a part-time salary and the few quid I get for flogging the least horrendous parts of the mounds of horrendous crap I have a week to get rid of. Right now, I can't even afford to mend my glasses! Your wife has forced me out. She's the one who crossed the line. So, forgive me if I don't know where the hell it is any more.'

I managed to keep all my angry, rejected, terrified, hopeless tears in check until I'd made it back into what was, for now, my home.

31

Once the flow from my tear ducts had dribbled to a stop, I decided to look for an answer in the June sunshine. Leaving the bike in the shed, I paced through the trees, letting my feet carry me wherever they felt like, roaming deeper through the dusty trails, overgrown with prickly branches and bracken. For the first time in weeks I was able to push on without even a whisper of fear. The mood I was in, I was ready to face the Beast of Middlebeck head-on. Nothing could be worse than what I'd already faced that morning. Bring it on.

By the time I'd reached the village, hungry, thirsty and about ready for a long nap on the Camerons' sofa, I had narrowed it down to the same two options I'd started with.

One. Spend a week salvaging what I could from the Hoard and then swap my house, my history and my dreams for one of Fisher's soulless flats. Two: I could fight.

I was plumping for option two.

I just needed some sleep first.

Mack came round that evening, letting himself in before I'd had time to take my shoes off.

'Seriously? After what's happened we aren't back to knocking?'

'Nope.' He slid onto a kitchen chair.

I busied myself making two cups of tea, ignoring how glossy and glowy and (ugh) *happy* he looked.

'She's gone back to London?'

'Yes.'

Ooh – maybe he was happy because she'd gone?

'She'll be back next weekend.'

'Lovely. You'll have to introduce us properly.'

Mack leaned back on two legs of the chair. 'Not until you've lost that manic glint in your eyes.'

'Why are you here again?' I took the chair opposite.

'To help. I don't know if the estate agent contacted Environmental Health, but it was nothing to do with us.'

Mack was an *us* again. Good for him.

'I can take a few days off work, help you get through the last of the Hoard, sort a skip, find storage for the stuff you want to sell and start work on some of the other problems.'

'I don't want your help.' If I gripped my mug any harder the handle would snap off.

'Maybe not, but you need it.'

'How does your wife feel about you taking time off to rescue the woman next door?'

He looked away, rubbing one hand across the back of his neck. Then I realised.

'You're doing this so you can sell the house! Did she send you round?'

'No.' He swallowed, uncrossed his arms, took a sip of tea and put it down again. 'Yes, it will help sell the house if the garden's cleared. But that's not the only reason. Not even the main reason. I would hope, after the past few months, you wouldn't find it too hard to believe that.'

'Thanks for the offer. I'll think about it.'

I didn't want Mack's help. I didn't want him scrubbing mould or catching mice or replacing rusty pipes. I didn't want him here, using his rumpled T-shirt to wipe the sweat off his brow. Flexing and fixing and making things beautiful. Being generous and capable and kind.

I didn't want to need Mack.

New Jenny didn't need anyone.

New Jenny was an idiot.

* * *

Feeling overwhelmed by the day's events, lost and more than a little forlorn, instead of getting stuck into sorting or tidying or photographing for eBay, spurning the idea of investigating skip hire, I chose a mug of hot chocolate and my grandmother's diary.

Picking up where I'd left off, a few pages into the third journal, I continued to read the stark notes that followed the birth of my mother, and the loss of her brother.

Feeding – how often, how long for. Nappies. Sleeps. A few acquaintances brought round meals, or helped with laundry. On one date the simple line:

Funeral, 2 p.m.

But within days the entries became sparser, the hand-writing more erratic, and the tone entirely different.

The girl won't sleep. Cries. What can I do to make her sleep?

*Mary Robson came today, pretending to drop off a meat pie. I
know what she really wanted. She's not taking the girl.
The girl wouldn't stop crying and I know they're listening and
waiting for their chance. I won't let them take my girl.
He's at work again. Never here when they call. Does he want them
to take her? Is he sending them?
I see him plotting with the doctor. I hear them whispering. I won't
let them take you.*

Whew. It carried on. In amongst haphazard lists about
eggs and washing and trips to market, my grandmother's
sickness and paranoia staggered through the pages. Her rants
about her husband grew fiercer and more explicit. It sent
chills down my spine.

And then, about eight months after her daughter was
born:

He's gone. It's just me and the girl now. Good riddance to him.

As I read the remainder of the journals, it felt as
though some of the fuzzy edges surrounding my mother
came into focus. Remarks about how difficult things were
without a husband's income, the shame of being abandoned, combined with the continual struggle to keep their
hardship secret, drove Charlotte into an increasingly
isolated and obsessive existence. I couldn't discern whether
her belief that the villagers were judging, mocking and
seeking her ruin was true, but either way her bitter
response to it could not have made life easy for her
daughter.

For the first time I began to feel sympathy for my mother,
to understand something of why she'd left and couldn't face

going back. The journals were depressing enough to read, let alone actually living through it.

As I wrestled with the ghost of the little girl I now pictured in every room, as my imagination lingered on the woman she'd become, my own resentment began to waver. It didn't undo the damage she'd inflicted. I still felt angry as I dwelt on how her strange childhood had affected mine. On the pain caused and love lost and how it was all so wretchedly unfair. But it made me realise that running away was not the answer. Not for her, and not for me.

And weirdly, this feeling began to grow that I'd not had in a long time. An ache inside that confused and scared me. I didn't want to see or speak to her. I was anxious and filled with dread about what she might say. Yet, despite all this, I just really wanted to give my mum a hug.

Friday night, as I stuffed some very depressed soft toys into a bin bag, someone knocked on the door. Wiping my hands on my jeans, I opened it to find Ashley, wearing walking boots and carrying a dog lead.

'No,' I said, as firmly as I could, removing a piece of fake fur from my mouth.

'Come on!' Ashley pleaded. 'You promised you'd help. We can't give up after one go.'

'I think one go was enough to demonstrate that, yes, we can and most definitely should give up.'

'Rubbish! We just need to learn from it, so we don't make the same mistakes again.'

'No, this time we would only make new ones. We don't know what we're doing, Ashley.'

'Wrong!' She pulled out a piece of paper from her pocket. 'I know *exactly* what we're doing. This time I have a cover story all planned out and everything.'

'An innocent dog-walker, by any chance?'

'Who's lost her dog, and thinks her poor Labrador has strayed onto the property of Birch House!'

'Birch House?' Birch was the name of the hero in Hillary West's latest book.

Ashley looked smug. 'Precisely! Plus, it is bordered by two streams, each heading in different directions.'

Birch's childhood home had also been bordered by two streams. The book was called *The Space Between the Waters*.

'It sounds a real contender. I don't think you need me,' I replied. 'Which is good, because I'm in the middle of something.'

'Well, that's not a problem. I'll help you finish it off and then we'll go.'

There was the sudden sound of high-pitched laughter, and Mack and his wife appeared around the corner of the building. She was hanging onto his arm, a straw hat perching merrily on her apple head.

I jumped back out of view. 'Fine, I'll come. I just need to get changed and brush the worst of the grime out of my hair.'

Five minutes later, I scurried past Mack's kitchen window, tugging Ashley behind me, and set off on another Hillary hunt.

* * *

Birch House was just a few miles away. At the end of a long, unpaved track. It was clear nobody in their right mind would walk a dog in that direction.

'We'll say she spotted a rabbit and was off before we could stop her.' Ashley started marching up the track.

We arrived at another high wall, this one brick, with a broad pair of iron gates sporting a perfectly dog-sized gap at the bottom. 'Florence!' Ashley started shouting. 'Come here, girl! FLORENCE!'

She leant close to whisper at me, 'The best lie is the one closest to the truth. If anyone asks, we're walking the dog for our poorly friend.'

We yelled a couple more times, before I got bored and tried the gate. To my surprise, and dismay, it creaked open.

'Let's knock on the door and ask if they've seen Florence,' Ashley said, way too loud. 'Frances will be devastated if we've lost her.'

We made our way across the large, circular driveway, making a slightly ridiculous show of looking for the dog, no doubt currently curled contentedly at her owner's feet.

With no street lights or other illumination the garden was already a mass of jumbled shadows. Ashley took a fortifying breath, stepped up onto the porch and banged the brass knocker on the large black door.

'Oh, no!' She gasped, horrified. I clutched her elbow, spinning around in alarm.

'What?'

'I forgot to touch up my lipstick!'

My clutch turned into a shove. 'For goodness' sake. I thought you'd spotted something awful.'

'It *is* awful!' She pouted. 'I'm about to meet my heroine. She's not going to invite us in if we look like riffraff.'

I looked pointedly at Ashley. 'She is not going to invite us in, full stop.'

Ashley ignored me, swiping a bright pink slash of lipstick

across her face, about half of which she managed to get on her lips.

At that point, the door flew open. Ashley jolted in surprise, stumbled and took a backwards dive off the porch.

A man hurried out of the door and joined me in helping Ashley to her feet.

'Are you all right?' he asked, brushing her chest down a little more thoroughly than strictly necessary, given that she'd landed on her bottom. He looked to be somewhere in his forties, his thick black hair and white T-shirt vaguely reminding me of someone.

'I landed on my dodgy ankle,' she groaned. I tried to manoeuvre myself in between her and the man, who, despite being shorter than me, and considerably flabbier, was remarkably strong.

I looked down when he trod on my foot, and, spotting his pointy blue shoes, I realised the person he reminded me of was Elvis.

'Come on, then,' he said in a reedy voice. 'Let's get inside and sort you out.'

Ah, Elvis in looks only, it would seem.

'I think we can manage,' I said, as the Elvis took hold of one arm, leaving me pulling on the other in a human tug-of-war. 'Our car isn't parked too far away.'

'Don't be ridiculous.' He smiled, teeth glowing. 'You shouldn't be roaming about anyway, two young women, this time of night. If you were my wives I wouldn't allow it.'

Ashley made a not so subtle attempt to wrangle her arm back. 'I'm fine, honestly. Sorry to bother you. This ankle thing happens all the time. Thanks for your help!'

She gave another yank and the Elvis let go. 'Why did you

knock on the door, anyway?' he asked, raising one unnaturally smooth eyebrow.

'We were looking for our dog,' I gabbled.

While at the same time Ashley said, 'Does Hillary live here?'

He curled his mouth in what I feared was meant to be a sexy, enticing smile. 'Yes!' Elvis opened his arms wide. 'Forgive my rudeness. You know how Hillary values her privacy and she hadn't mentioned visitors. But come in, come in, we're about to mix martinis.'

And before I could ask 'Hillary who?' my partner in crime hobbled up the step with weird Elvis.

Ashley's obsession had blinded her to the fact we were willingly entering the house of a complete – and seriously unnerving – stranger. I pulled out my phone as I followed Ashley, who was limping down a wide corridor with zebra-print walls. Unsurprisingly, out here in the wilds of Sherwood, I had no signal. As we entered a large room, I scanned the plush interior for potential weapons before taking a seat as close as possible to the crystal bowl on the coffee table.

Elvis hustled over to a bar in the corner. In the light of the chandelier dangling from the ceiling, his face was startling. Like a doll left too close to the fire.

Ashley gaped at me, her face as white as that famous jumpsuit. 'Hillary abhors plastic surgery,' she hissed. While I knew she really meant unnecessary cosmetic surgery wasn't generally portrayed in a positive light *in Hillary West's novels*, I wasn't about to argue with her.

'Here we go, lay-deeeeze.' Melted Elvis placed two very large, very full glasses on the table. 'Now, how about we get a little more comfortable?' He snapped his fingers, and the lights dimmed at the same moment as 'The Wonder of You' began tinkling out of invisible speakers.

'I thought Hillary was here?' I asked as he squeezed up beside Ashley on the sofa. 'You only got three glasses out.'

'Oh, she'll be here soon. She's probably freshening up somewhere. You know Hillary. But I'm much more interested in you two lovely lay-deeeze.' He put one hand on Ashley's thigh, making her flinch.

'Shhh,' he whispered, picking a drink up off the table and handing it to her. 'Relax.'

'Which of her books is your favourite?' I asked.

'Oh, how could I choose?' Melted Elvis purred into Ashley's neck. 'That's like asking me to pick between the two of you. Why narrow it down when you can enjoy them all?'

'Right, we're going. Thanks for the drinks.' I stood up and moved to grab Ashley's hand. Melted Elvis leant one arm on her leg, preventing her from getting up. 'I thought you were here to see Hillary? She'll be down any second. *HILLARY?*'

There ensued a brief tussle while I tried to dislodge Ashley, forcibly inserting myself under his arm and creating enough space for her to wriggle out. He then pulled me into his lap, and stuck what felt like a warm slug in my ear. As I fought against his clamped arms, my heart galloping, a mounting scream wedged in my throat, I wondered for a brief, horrible second if something utterly hideous was going to happen. Then, a dull thunk and Melted Elvis went limp. I scrabbled off, yanking his arms off me as I would a poisonous snake, and sprang back to catch sight of Ashley, face stricken, holding the crystal bowl.

'Shuttlecocks!' she squeaked. 'I've killed him!'

He let out a long, shrill whimper and a considerably manlier fart.

'Go, go, *GO!*' I yelped.

We went.

Following our second Hillary West hunt, we did not laugh all the way home.

* * *

SquashHarris.com slowly began to gain more likes. Dawson lent me the next episode, with several insistent requests for me to guard it with my life: 'I mean, don't look after it like you do us.' People liked it even more than the first one. They asked for a hard copy. Merchandise. Someone had, in fact, made a Squash Harris T-shirt. I needed to find out about copyright, trademarks, intellectual property. My reluctance to do this might have been due to me potentially breaching all three.

Maybe one more episode? A few more followers?

Dawson seemed to be doing better. He saw Lucas and Erik at least once a week. His teacher had set up a lunchtime art group. Lily, Kiko's eldest, had started going. Dawson casually mentioned, about forty-seven times, that she 'doesn't think I'm a total loser'.

In the latest episode of Squash Harris, the hero met a girl with shiny black hair.

I was aware that Lily might find out about the website herself, now more kids at school were looking at it. Given Adam's shambolic state, I felt pretty sure her mind would be on more important things than a comic. Like, whether she had any clean clothes to wear or three meals a day. Or if her mum would be on next Thursday's flight from Nepal, as promised.

Which gave me a bit of stalling time before I confessed. Soon. I would tell him soon.

* * *

The last Friday in June, despite having had no return visit from that charming Environmental Health inspector Darren Smith, I bit the bullet and hired a skip. The pile in front of the house had grown to a towering, festering mess. I'd sold, given away and recycled what I could. That still left a lot of junk that had nowhere to go but landfill.

Sarah's mum agreed to manage the café for the morning, and by some strange coincidence Jamie had the day off. Ellen, having ditched her essay on something to do with snipping during labour, which caused my ears to fold in on themselves long before she'd finished explaining, brought Frances to oversee proceedings. Lucille had stopped me at school the day before to say she would have helped, had she not been indispensable at her very important, astronomically successful, marvellously well-paid and teeth-grindingly tedious job.

I *had* wondered if Mack might join us, but there was no sign of life from behind the windows. For a brief millisecond I imagined sending them all home and struggling on alone, until I got myself into an idiotic jam like falling in the skip or being crushed beneath an avalanche of toppling rubbish and needing to be rescued by the only person within a two-mile radius.

Then I remembered I was New Jenny, and Mrs Apple Mack was returning this weekend. I stuck my Sellotaped-together glasses back up my nose and gave my brilliant friends a big grin.

Working together meant that only a couple of hours later we were sitting in the sunshine toasting the shabby relics of a lifetime poking out from the top of the skip. I hid my sadness as the others mused on Charlotte Meadows and the disbanding of her Hoard.

Then Jamie remembered he'd brought a box of pastries, and the shadow of the past dissipated in a delicious cloud of icing sugar and flaked almonds.

'You'd better have the last pastry, Jamie. You did more than the rest of us put together,' Sarah said. 'No wonder you're so buff.'

Jamie sloshed half his tea down his jeans. When Sarah jumped up and started brushing at the wet patch with a cloth, I honestly thought for a moment he was having a stroke.

'I'm fine,' he garbled, eyes darting everywhere.

'Oh, of course you are, tough guy.' Sarah draped the cloth over his head and sat back down in her garden chair. Jamie left it there, obscuring his face.

I pointed at Sarah, trusting he couldn't see through the cloth. 'You're flirting!' I mouthed, and she shrugged.

'What's going on?' I mouthed again.

'Nothing!' she mouthed back, rolling her eyes. 'Grow up!'

I wondered if Jamie had made any progress with handing over the operation of his business. I wondered about Sarah's conversations with the guy online. I wouldn't have to wonder for long, I hoped.

The weekend was spent working on the now much emptier house. To my amazement and delight, the skeleton of a home was emerging from the chaos. I was falling in love. Good solid walls, original fireplaces. The staircase would be beautiful once I'd replaced the broken bannister and stained it. I pictured the kitchen with new cabinets, the dining-room dresser painted duck-egg blue. A real oven. Flowers in a cheery jug on the windowsill.

And I knew, with absolute conviction, that if Fisher, the Environmental Health Officers or anyone else, were going to take my home they'd have to starve me out first. I had enough furniture to construct a solid barricade, after all. And I'd got used to being hungry in recent months.

Monday lunchtime, an envelope with the DVLA logo plopped through my door. A reply to the form I'd completed – and long forgotten – about the Mini's registration. A waste of time and money, since I now knew it was Mrs Mack's.

Only now I got to discover her name. Which meant I could spend the rest of the afternoon looking her up on the Internet.

Which would be a stupid, pathetic and humiliating waste of time.

I put the envelope in the bin.

But if Mack shared her surname, I could Internet stalk *him*. Find out his job. Get some background information in case anyone asked at the wedding. As Ashley so very rightly said – the best lie was one closest to the truth.

I picked it out of the bin. Tossed it in again. Then took it out, scrumpled it up as hard as I could and shoved it underneath a heap of teabags and an empty tin of tomatoes. I went back into the dining-room and picked up some sandpaper. Gave the table three half-hearted strokes, threw the paper down, ran back into the kitchen and yanked the envelope out of the bin like an addict.

'I've paid good money for this information,' I called up to Mannequin Diana, who was, as usual, judging me from the top of the stairs. 'I might as well read it. You never know when it might come in useful. What if Mack has a heart attack and I need to give the paramedics his details?'

Ripping it open, I scanned the form for information.

Blinked. Shook my head in case adjusting my brain would make the letters rearrange themselves.

Sat back down at the table.

Shook my head again, this time in wry acknowledgement at the twists and turns life brought, and the smallness of this crazy world.

I had only gone and found Hillary West.

And it looked as though she (sort of) lived next door.

32

There was nothing for it. As soon as I was home that evening, I showered, changed, attempted to dry my hair in some sort of style, redid the Sellotape on my glasses, plastered on my cheeriest smile, scooped up the most expensive bottle of wine they'd had at the village shop (nine pounds fifty) and went to say howdy to my new neighbour.

Hillary West, bestselling author, recluse, enigma, opened the door.

'HI!' I cried. Coughed. Tried again. 'Hi.'

'Hello.' Cool as an apple ice-pop, she looked at me from beneath her fringe.

'I'm Jenny. From next door. I just wanted to say welcome back, and it's so nice to meet you. Um, here.' I held out the bottle. 'Just a little, well, welcome to the neighbourhood, neighbour!'

After a brief hesitation, she took the bottle. 'Right. Thanks. I'm relieved to see the front's cleared.'

'Yes. I hired a skip.'

'That should help with the sale.'

'Yes. I hope so. I mean, I don't hope you move, like I want rid of you or anything. Not at all! I just, well, hope it for your sake because you hope it.'

'Well.' She glanced over her shoulder. 'I'd invite you in for a glass of this, um, wine.'

'Thanks! That'd be lovely.' I pulled what I hoped was a fun, funny face. 'Kind of why I brought it, after all!'

Hillary continued talking over me. 'BUT I'm snowed under with a deadline. You know how it is. Well, you probably don't. Hard to imagine the kind of pressure this level of success brings.'

'Oh. Yes. And I completely understand.' I completely understood that I was now completely humiliated. 'I did hear your deadline has proven, well...'

Hillary narrowed her eyes. *Let's go with* not *mentioning the writer's block issue upon first meeting bestselling author Hillary West, shall we, Jenny?*

'Deadlines! Pah! Who needs 'em? Getting in the way of valuable drinking time!'

'I need them. So, goodbye?'

'I'm a huge fan!' I yelped as the door closed in my face.

I spent the rest of the week torn. Entangled in the moral dilemma of this revelation. By Friday's Christmas Book Club Challenge meeting I felt no closer to making a decision. I had found Hillary West. Would I tell Ashley? Would I tell anyone else? Reasons for keeping quiet were:

One: Hillary didn't want to be found.

Two: Even if she did, no one would want Ashley pestering them.

Three: Ashley would inevitably drag me into it.

Four: This would put Hillary in even more of a hurry to move, taking Mack with her.

Five: Mack would consider it mean and petty for me to blab his wife's secret. I really, really didn't want him thinking me mean and petty.

The reasons for spilling were:

One: Ashley was my friend.

Two: No more Hillary hunts.

Three: Meeting Hillary might help reduce Ashley's infatuation, given that she seemed a bit of a rude, patronising cow.

'All right, Jenny?' Sarah asked as she brought a tray of drinks over. 'You seem a bit ruffled this evening.'

Understatement. 'I'm fine. Just tired.'

'Whatever. You can tell me later.' She winked, handing out the rhubarb gin and tonics without even looking at them.

Jamie kicked us off, carefully lifting a selection of cake boxes out of a large paper bag. 'See what you think. Sarah'll put any that are good enough on the menu as a July special.'

'These are *all* good enough,' Ellen gushed.

'You haven't tasted them yet,' Lucille said.

'OW!' She glared at us all, scooting away from the table and clutching her shin. 'Someone kicked me!'

After an awkward silence, Frances muttered, 'Well, you shouldn't have been rude. It was only a nudge.'

'I'm going to have a bruise there tomorrow. If you've affected my training, then—'

'Then what?' Frances crowed. 'Are you going to kick me back?'

'Ladies, stop acting like children and try Jamie's cakes!' Ellen said, in her no-nonsense-mum voice.

In the end, for research purposes, we all had one of each save Lucille, on a strict training diet, and Frances, who only managed a nibble: dainty pink macaroons, gooey chocolate truffle tarts topped with strawberries, crisp spice cookies iced like smiling suns.

The vote was unanimous, of course. Jamie had better get baking.

Frances showed us pictures of her balloon ride. 'It was glorious. As the sun rose I could almost have stepped out of the basket and straight into heaven. But I'm not quite ready yet, so I shouted up some instructions to Big Mike instead.'

I tried not to sound too apprehensive. 'Instructions?'

'Well, I told him to put the kettle on. And to let the family know. I've been waiting a long time to see them. I'm particularly curious as to whether my sister, Susan, is still so enormously fat.'

'What did the other people in the balloon think about that?' Ashley asked, eyes wide.

'Well, I don't know, I didn't ask them,' Frances huffed. 'I'm hardly in a position to waste time worrying what people think.'

'It looks amazing,' Jamie said. 'What's next?'

'Next month, I'm going with Lucille to Tough Muck,' Frances said. 'If I can't race, I can cheer from the sidelines. Have you all sponsored her yet?'

It turned out Lucille was running for Cancer Research. Frances insisted we all donate before moving on, and somehow in doing that we ended up promising to come and watch. Thank goodness race entries had closed, or who knew what would have happened?

Ashley went next, recounting the Hillary hunt as I squirmed, a heated debate going back and forth inside my head. She brought out the updated detective's board, and listed the next prime contenders. I concentrated hard on my sunshine cookie, and said nothing.

Sarah hadn't been on any more dates. 'Not for want of trying. I dunno what to make of it, to be honest. This guy is dead lovely. He's a trainee chef, so we've loads in common, and when he asks me questions he even listens to the answers. He doesn't make me feel like a stupid girl who had a kid with a dud, works in her nan's greasy café and spends her evenings watching crap telly.'

'How *does* he make you feel?' Ashley breathed.

'He said I was a talented businesswoman.' Sarah's eyes filled with tears. 'And a good mum. So, he makes me feel bloody fantastic.'

'Why are you not dating this man in person?' Ellen asked.

'Because he won't meet me. Keeps putting me off. Says he's working away a lot, and he's shy.' Sarah ripped her yellow spotty paper napkin in half. 'I reckon he might be married.'

'Perhaps he's...' Jamie started to say, when his phone started beeping. He looked at the screen, and swore under his breath. 'Sorry. I have to take this.' He stood up, throwing a long, despairing look at Sarah, unable to wrench himself away until the phone beeped again. 'Ah, damn it.' He sprinted out of the room, phone pressed to his ear.

All eyes turned back to Sarah.

'What are you going to do?' I asked.

'I dunno.' She kept ripping the napkin. 'Maybe it's time I told him, it's now or never. I'm not messing about here. I've got enough friends and I'm not wasting much more time chasing a man who can't – or won't – see me face to face. For all I know it's a bunch of twelve-year-old girls having a laugh.'

Jamie appeared in the doorway. 'Sorry, guys, something's come up. I need to have a chat with a very bad man.'

'Bye, Jamie,' we all chorused. 'Be careful.'

'Oh, and, Sarah. About that, um, well. Yes. I'll see you when this job is finished.' He left, only to poke his head back around the door again five seconds later. 'I'm glad this guy makes you happy.' And with that, he disappeared.

'Well, that's disappointing!' Frances said.

'Yeah, but at least he got to share his baking first,' Sarah said.

'That wasn't what I was referring to,' Frances said.

'Jenny?' Ellen asked, giving Frances a meaningful stare.

'I think you all know how my challenge is going.' I managed a smile. 'I've restored a couple of tables, and have started planting seeds in the vegetable patch. Not much else to say yet.'

'But what about the box?' Lucille asked. 'What was in it?'

'Oh, just some of Charlotte's journals.' Flushed cheeks betrayed my dismissive tone. I hoped the last squeeze of Zara's fifty-quid concealer was doing its job. 'And not interesting ones. Shopping lists and housework mostly.'

'Oh, that's a shame,' Ashley said. 'After all that!'

'Yes. A real shame. Ellen? How's things in the world of midwifery training?'

Ellen kindly took the hint. 'Wet and sticky, thanks to a labouring woman's waters breaking all over me. My shoes were squelching the rest of the shift...'

* * *

I cycled to the Common the next morning to pick up a quiche for my lunch with Frances. When I got back, Hillary was staring up at the house.

I didn't have to ask why.

Speechless, I climbed off the bike and wheeled it over, gazing at the ugly spray paint scrawled across the brickwork.

'I can't believe it,' Hillary said, voice shrill. 'This is a disaster.'

I struggled for a few seconds to find the right words. Nope, still couldn't find 'em.

'I mean, why?' Hillary said, turning to me. 'Why *do* this?'

'I don't know.'

'Why would you do this to us *today*?' she shrieked. 'We have a house viewing in forty minutes! We might as well cancel it! It looked better with the scrapheap outside than... *this*.'

Okay, words found... maybe not the best ones, but they were flying out anyway. 'I didn't do this!' I shook my head in disgust. 'Do you think *I* spray-painted that I'm a bitch *on my own house*?'

'You want to keep the famous author living next door. Wangle your way in and see what you can get out of it. And if Mack goes you'll have no one to spy on, will you?' She screwed up her nose. 'I've seen the way you look at him. What's your plan, seduce him and sell your story to some sleazy magazine?'

'What on earth are you talking about? I know authors need a good imagination but let's try to keep a grip on reality, shall we?' My head was starting to fizz. I put my hands on my hips to stop them accidentally punching a nearby nose. 'Someone has graffitied our houses with horrible, slanderous things about me, and somehow this becomes all about *you*? I think the fame's gone to your head.'

'Well, if you're so bothered then why aren't you up a ladder cleaning it off?'

'I only just saw it!'

'What, you didn't see it when you left this morning?' she spat. 'A likely story!'

'I'd say it's pretty likely that I didn't ride my bike backwards as I left, yes.'

'Well, you've seen it now so what are you going to do? You've got thirty minutes to sort it or I'm going to sue.'

I laughed then. 'You can try.'

Before she could slap me, and her hand was twitching angrily, Mack drove up. He climbed out of the Mini and proceeded to lift a pressure washer out of the boot.

'Hi, Jenny. I'm really sorry.' He walked over to give Hillary a kiss, but she reeled back. Just as well, because I thought I saw froth bubbling out of the corners of her mouth.

'I can't believe you *like* it here,' she snapped. 'Sort it, or I don't care about your pride, or how much you hate him, we're accepting that slug of a property developer's offer!' And she stalked off.

Mack stood looking at the ground, hands on his hips.

'You didn't just buy that today, for this, did you?' I asked.

He shrugged, glancing up. 'I borrowed it off a mate.'

Taking a huge bottle out of the car, he started pouring it into the pressure washer.

'I didn't think you had any mates.'

He wrinkled his brow. 'I thought *you* were my mate.'

'I meant apart from me.' I scuffed one foot against the dirt, then got out my phone and took a bunch of photos while Mack attached a hose to the washer.

'Ready?' he said, holding the gun like a graffiti cowboy.

'Let me do it. It's enough that you set it up.'

He held the gun out of my reach. 'You'd better get changed first. Wouldn't want to ruin your clothes.'

'I'm shooting water at a wall. How am I going to ruin my clothes?'

'I don't know – it should be impossible. But I have an ominous feeling you'll find a way. Call it a hunch.'

And of course, by the time I'd put the bike in the shed, stomped inside, dug out some clothes that I didn't mind getting paint-and-water-splattered, and then swapped them for alternatives that I didn't mind Mack seeing me in, made two cups of tea and come back out again, half the graffiti was gone.

Mack had washed off all the horrible bits, leaving a wall of meaningless pronouns and words like 'next' and 'of'. And, for some reason, that little piece of thoughtfulness, rather than the torrent of threatening abuse all over our houses, made me want to weep.

He took the tea, brow furrowed. 'Why don't you go inside? I'll finish it off. It's nearly all done anyway.'

'No chance.' I wrenched the washer out of his other hand, rather more forcefully than planned, pressing the release button as I jerked it back.

It wasn't me who ended up needing to get changed.

But, hey, at least it was detergent, not paint.

And I didn't stop smiling until every last letter had vanished, which I was half wondering might have been his plan all along.

In fact, the grin didn't leave my face until the estate agent's car pulled up and she, and her hipster clients, got out and started nosying about. I stuck the washer in the shed and went inside, nodding a polite hello as I passed them. Hillary didn't need to worry about me sabotaging her and Mack's attempts to sell the house. The sooner she stopped being my neighbour, the better.

And I still wouldn't have done what I did next, if it hadn't been for what happened the following morning.

33

I'd had another appalling night's sleep, fretting about who had vandalised the cottages. I knew it was personal. And someone local. Who hated me. Or thought it funny to write threats across my house.

That morning, while still feeling about three inches tall, I answered the door to Hillary West, queen of love, romance and utter gorgeousness.

'Hello?' I tugged at my vest top, as if that could hide the fact that I was still wearing my pyjama bottoms at ten in the morning.

'You'll be pleased to hear the viewing was a crapbucket.'

'What?'

'Are you going to let me in? This Northern mizzle ruins my hair.' She stepped in before I could correct her geography, pushing me backwards into my own kitchen. So that was where Mack learnt how to do it.

'Is that my fault too?'

She ignored me, tweaking at her fringe while using her phone as a mirror.

I waited, curious to see how long it would take for the insults to start.

'We have a viewing today at four.' Pausing, she fiddled with her jacket collar. My goodness, if Hillary West looked uncomfortable this was going to be a humdinger.

'Okay.'

We waited a bit longer.

'So, if you wouldn't mind, we'd prefer it if you stayed out of the way.'

'Excuse me?' I would have laughed, had I not been standing there in my faded pyjamas after having three hours' sleep.

'The estate agent indicated you didn't make a very good impression yesterday.'

'I said hello as I walked past. What would have made a better impression? Ignoring them? A hug and a kiss?'

'You were dressed... erratically. And your tracksuit bottoms had wet patches in critical areas.'

'I'd been using a pressure washer!' I snorted. 'Did you see how wet Mack got?'

'Yes, I did see your pathetic attempt at flirting. Pretending you can't control a jet-wash to get a man's attention. It made me nauseous.'

'Is that what this is about?' I asked, no longer laughing. 'You think I'm after your husband?'

'You work it out,' she snarled. 'And, either way, do both of us a favour and back off before making an even bigger fool of yourself.'

'I'm in my own kitchen! How can I back off?' I yelled, as she swept open the door with a flourish.

'And I don't know if this—' she waved one hand up and

down in the direction of my outfit '—is supposed to be lounge wear, but, trust me, it's not.'

She slammed the door before I could think of any retort more advanced than blowing a raspberry while flicking two fingers. So I did both, at the wall.

And then I called Ashley and left a message on her answerphone.

I wasn't proud. But I wasn't ashamed, either. That came later, once Ashley had finally got around to listening to the message.

* * *

Monday morning, Kiko strode up to the school gates like a samurai heroine. I barged my way past the gossip-hunters to give her a hug.

'The adventurer returns!' Sarah crowed. 'You look fantab-ulous, woman!'

'I feel it.' Kiko flung back her head and closed her eyes. 'It was so scary. So tough – so-o-o-o-o tough! – I thought I must have lost my mind. Missing the girls felt like a fish-hook snagged on my ribs the entire trip. I have never known pain and exhaustion like it. And that includes childbirth. For the first two days, anger and frustration and guilt powered me up those slopes. And then I realised, up there with just me and some very intimidating team-mates, a million miles of clear skies and blisters the size of walnuts, I was angry and upset at the wrong person. It was all my fault.'

Sarah started to protest.

'No!' Kiko said, in a voice she must have found in Nepal. 'It was. It is. *I* let my life become this. *I* let myself be this weak, walked-over, wishy-washy excuse of a woman. *I* didn't fight for me or my children when Adam's poor choices stole our precious time with him. I *empowered* him in shirking his responsibility. I *chose* to put everybody first and myself last, like it was the noble thing to do. What a load of drivel! How is neglecting myself, pretending I have no needs, or feelings, or worth outside of what I do for other people, in any way helping my daughters to grow up to value themselves? To expect to be treated honourably in a relationship? I was raising my children to think that women, wives, mothers, are worthless! Or, at least, worth *less*.'

She took a deep breath and smiled. 'Well, I've apologised and promised it won't happen again.'

'You go, girl,' Sarah whispered.

'What did Adam say?' Lucille asked.

'He said he's very happy to have his wife back,' Adam said, pushing through the huddle, Hannah strapped in a sling on his chest. 'And I wasn't talking about the past three weeks.'

'He's taken a sabbatical,' Kiko told me and Sarah later, once the bell had rung for school and the crowd had dispersed. 'Three months off to get our family back on track.'

'And the charity is okay with that?' I asked.

'They're probably grateful not to have him sticking his nose in all the time, trying to do everybody's jobs for them. He managed to get about four days' work done while I was away, and they coped fine. He's got a great team who will relish the challenge.'

She watched him pointing out a robin to Hannah a few metres away.

'I don't know what happened while I was gone. I might never ask. Especially why the living room has a new carpet. Or how the cat's ginger splodge is now on the opposite ear.

But they've survived. Had maybe started to thrive. And I'm guessing you two had something to do with that. So, for all the help I don't want to know about, thanks.'

'You're very welcome.'

If our incredible friend didn't want to know about the pasta bakes dropped off, the lessons in braiding hair, the frantic texts that had, to be fair, dwindled to a trickle, that was fine with us. We were so darn pleased for her we could skip down the street singing 'The Sound of Music'.

So we did.

And when Tezza shouted rude comments from his taxi window we sang even louder.

'I'm done being invisible,' Kiko yelled after him.

'Amen to that, sister.' We laughed. 'Amen to that.'

Once I'd removed the spam, the nonsense and the weirdos, the new Squash Harris post had seventy-four comments. Heart pounding, mouth as dry as Squash's sense of humour, I set my laptop up in the Camerons' kitchen.

'Before I show you this, I need you to remember it was done with your best interests at heart. It was kind of sneaky, but I knew you wouldn't let me if I asked, and—'

'What?' Dawson scowled at me. 'What've you done now?'

'Just keep an open mind, because it's worked out really well.'

He made one of those grunts that reminded me he'd be a teenager in a couple of years, and glared at the table.

'Here.' I tapped my mouse, bringing the Squash Harris page to life.

We sat there for a very long time. The only sounds were

Dawson's occasional mouse clicks and the distant rumble of Hunt and Destroy from the garden. I think I held my breath the whole time.

Eventually, Dawson shut down the computer and sat back. 'A risky move.'

'I *knew* everyone would love it.'

'Not everyone.'

I'd kept the handful of less than awesome comments to prove authenticity.

'There isn't a single piece of art in the world that *everyone* loves. But the fact that some totally objective and unbiased strangers do love it is amazing.'

The hint of a smile twitched at the corner of Dawson's mouth. 'Yeah.'

'So you aren't mad?'

'Are you going to let me take over the site? I need to answer the comments. And do a questions page and news updates. And why did you pick that picture for the home page? It's rubbish. And couldn't you find a decent scanner? The colours are all wrong.'

'Are you going to add some information about the author and illustrator?'

Dawson picked at a fingernail. 'I thought we were trying to get people to *like* the comic, not hate it.'

'Half of Middlebeck Primary already love it. They aren't going to change their minds because it's you. But it might help them get to know you a little better.'

'Loads of authors use a fake name.'

I considered this. 'You're right. It's up to you. We *are* telling your mum and dad, though.'

The back door flew open and a herd of hollering buffalo streamed past. When the dust settled, I said, 'And if your brothers find out, it's going to be almost impossible to keep it secret.'

Dawson frowned.

'But I won't tell them if you don't.'

'Can I have my computer time now, so I can do some stuff on it before dinner?' He glanced at me. 'I mean, what you did was okay, but...'

'Go for it.' I wrote down the login and password. 'If you want help figuring anything out, just ask.'

He skidded off to where the family computer sat in the living room, appearing at the kitchen door again three seconds later. 'And, yeah. Thanks.'

Dawson vanished before I could get a reply past the lump in my throat.

And I realised then, this whole thing was not about getting people to know and like Dawson. It was about helping Dawson like himself.

* * *

I had spent more than a few anxious evenings counting pennies and finding out what I could about rewiring and damp-proofing, poking about in nooks and crannies and cata-strophising about what the council's report would say. One morning, unable to bear the wait any longer, I called the Environmental Health department and asked for Darren Smith.

'Darren who?' the receptionist asked.

After several back and forths and toings and froings, we established that Darren Smith had never worked for the local council, or any neighbouring councils, in any way, shape or form.

'Sorry, duck. Sounds like someone's having a joke.'

I wasn't laughing.

The next morning, I found Jamie back from his latest mission and flipping heart-shaped pancakes in the café.

I explained about the mysterious Darren Smith. Jamie slid one more pancake onto the steaming stack and handed them to Sarah.

'I can think of a few explanations. The most likely one is that he was scoping it out. In which case, he would've been back well before now.'

'He wouldn't have seen anything worth nicking. Apart from my laptop, and every house has one of those. Even the TV is ancient.'

'So maybe he's moved on.'

'And the other explanations?'

'Were you with him the whole time?'

I nodded. 'Yes. And there honestly wasn't anything on show worth taking.' I shook my head. 'He genuinely seemed bothered about the house. Could he have been hoping to get some work out of it? Like, have come from a local building firm?'

'Has anyone contacted you offering to do work?'

'No.'

'Maybe he wants to scare you into a cheap sale.'

That got my attention.

'I'd keep an eye out for anyone making you an offer. And if you want, I can look at your security. Are you sure no keys are missing?'

'Pretty sure.'

I helped myself to a pink cupcake from a plate on the counter-top. That helped, slightly, so I had another one.

'What's your gut telling you?' Jamie asked, working on his next pancake order.

'Well, I know someone who's very keen to buy my house. Although this seems a ridiculously elaborate charade considering what it must be worth. And well beneath a respectable and successful businessman.'

'Are we talking about Fisher?' Jamie looked at me, eyes sharp.

'Yes. Why? What do you know?'

'I know he's neither respectable nor successful these days. I've got a few things on in the next couple of weeks, but leave it with me.'

'Thanks, Jamie. I really appreciate it.'

'One more thing,' Jamie said, as I grabbed a third cake and stuffed in a scrumptious bite of lemony lusciousness.

'Mmmf?'

'Stay watchful, for now. Lock your doors and make sure your phone's charged. Oh, and talk to that bloke next door. It can't hurt to have another pair of eyes on it, and he seems to be looking out for you. And, well. Be careful.'

34

As it turned out, before I got a chance to call in on my neighbour (who I might have been avoiding since my call to Ashley) he messaged me:

What time do we leave for this wedding?

We?

I stared at my screen. *We?*

Was Mack coming with me to the wedding? In all the stress of the past week or so I'd barely had time to think about it beyond trying to find a dress to wear. I'd asked Ellen, but I drowned in her one posh dress that had avoided being chopped up when the triplets decided to make parachutes.

Hesitant to ask Sarah, a good couple of sizes bigger than me, when I mentioned it to Kiko she snorted. 'No chance. You'd be better off wearing your grandmother's old dressing gown than one of my monstrosities. Each and every one of them designed to suit a nothing, on-the-road-to-nowhere

fuddy-duddy, via Blandsville, Frump-land and a 1998 factory
outlet shop.'

'Fair enough.' It looked as though I would be wearing one
of my sister's cast-offs. To her own wedding. And if she made
any comment about it (and really, it was a *when* not an *if*) and
if I felt defensive and stressed (again, *when* not *if*) I might be
forced to make a similar remark relating cast-offs to her
choice of groom. Which would not end well.

I couldn't afford to get arrested again.

I had way too much to do.

On Saturday, I took a lasagne and a load of ironing round
to Frances' farmhouse, only to find the village grapevine had
beaten me to it.

'The bedroom beside the bathroom, look in the
wardrobe. There'll be something that fits. Let me see you in it
before you decide. I'd love to see those glad rags again but my
legs aren't friends with the stairs today.'

I left the lasagne in the oven, and went to find a dress
belonging to an eighty-five-year-old farmer that might fit me.
I thought it went without saying that I was praying I wouldn't.

But I'd forgotten, this particular farmer had travelled the
world, once upon a time. Rubbed shoulders with the rich and
successful. Cherished quality, craftsmanship, excellence.

I swept down the staircase in the first one I tried. A silk
1950s tea-dress. Frances then insisted I try a load more (it
didn't take much persuading, to be honest). We ate our
lasagne dressed like extras from *Downton Abbey*, hair coiffed,
jewellery twinkling, silk gloves getting in the way, the air rich
with memories of fabulous days gone by.

So, when Mack's message buzzed through as we deli-
cately nibbled at our tartes Tatin, feeling more than a little
giddy in my beaded bodice and string of pearls, I replied

like the suave, sophisticated socialite I was masquerading as:

Starts at 11, so leave 6.30.

'Your face has gone an alarming shade of raspberry,' Frances remarked.

'I'm fine,' I said, not sounding at all fine. 'Mack messaged about coming to the wedding.'

'You invited Mack?' Frances looked at me sideways, eyes shining like the silver candlesticks she'd insisted I set out.

'No. He offered. And I *thought* I'd said no.'

'Why on earth would you do that? And sensible chap for overruling you. I'm all for making up one's mind and sticking to it, but why on earth turn down the chance to spend the day with an attractive man with lovely manners?'

'He's married.'

'Excuse me?' Frances' wispy eyebrows shot into her hairline.

'Well, he's been separated for eighteen months. But his wife has been around a bit lately. I think they're working things out.'

'Well, they can't be working things out very well if he's coming to a wedding with *you*. If he considers that appropriate behaviour it might explain why his marriage failed in the first place.'

'No, it's not like that. He offered to come as a friend, when he heard that... well. It's complicated.'

'Hmmm.' Frances was not convinced. Neither was I. But the pull to have Mack with me... Seeing me looking half decent, rather than covered in mud, cobwebs or bobbly old pyjamas, was almost irresistible.

He replied that evening, as I lay in bed mooning at the borrowed dress hanging on the back of my door:

Too early. I've booked a couple of hotel rooms for the night before. If you feel the need to pay me back, we can work it out later. What time can you leave Thursday?

I threw good sense and sound moral judgement out of the window, and replied:

Can be ready 6.

I quickly followed it up:

And thanks, hotel sounds great. I can pay you back in cake or cash, you choose.

Him:

Always cake. What information do I need from that invitation? Hit me with the worst of it.

Me:

Being over twenty-five, it'd be impossible to type all that out without developing thumb blisters. Not a good sister-of-the-bride look. I'll drop it round in the morning.

Him:

Along with a dossier on my fake identity? As a professional agent I expect full background, work history, hobbies, habits, style of

underpants etc. if I'm going to pull this off. Who is Mack Macintyre?? And what is the nature of his relationship with Jenny
Birkenshaw?

Oh, boy. I put my phone down.

I knew, *knew*, this man should not be making me feel like
this. My heart should not be pounding for another woman's
husband. Skin humming. Stomach swooping. I sent one
more message:

Just be yourself (I might get to learn something about you!) And
Jenny is totally happy being FRIENDS with Mack Macintyre. See
you Thursday.

I switched my phone off and picked up a gardening book
I'd salvaged from the Hoard, forcing myself to concentrate on
organic composting techniques until I was too tired to think
any more.

* * *

I was flapping about in my bra, changing my top for the ninth
time in an attempt to achieve that classic 'don't care, but
somehow happen to appear stylish and stunning nonetheless' look, when a jaunty toot from the front of the house
signalled my wingman was ready to go.

Stuffing my head into the original T-shirt I'd chosen three
days ago, I yanked a brush through the cloud of static that
was once my hair, swiped my rucksack off the bed and half
ran, half tripped down the stairs.

I came to an abrupt stop at the kitchen doorway,
pausing to take a big breath before I opened the door and

saw Mack standing in front of me, arms folded, eyes crinkled.

'You're fine.' He grabbed my rucksack and disappeared.

'What the hell am I doing?' I muttered, as the reality of the next three days, pressing down on me for weeks now, grew to suffocating.

'You'll be fine. I'm with you, buddy.' Mack had reappeared.

'Mmmmf.' I didn't tell Mack that him being here was part of the issue.

'We're going to have enormous fun rigorously mocking your preposterous sister and her twazzock life-partner's ludicrous nuptials. We're going to laugh off their scorn, play up to their judgemental pre-conceptions, eat a huge amount of food and drink gallons of pretentious wine at their expense. Plus, I'm dying to see how many of those wedding etiquette rules we can break in the next thirty-six hours.'

As a degree of feeling returned to my arms and legs, Mack took hold of my hand and walked me round to the car.

'In you get.' He opened the door.

'Wait.' I reached one hand up in a 'stop' gesture as he started to move round to the driver's side.

'What? Have you forgotten something?'

'For the record, can I stress, while it's easier if we go with Mack Macintyre for the sake of the seating plan, guest book and whatever other dreadful nonsense has been planned, I'm not asking you to pretend we're something we aren't. I'm so grateful not to be walking into that wedding alone, but I don't think it's okay for a married man to pretend he's with someone else. And I don't care if everyone else there thinks I'm a sad, sorry failure. I'm starting to realise that might not be true. So, who cares what they think?'

Mack winked at me. *Not helpful.* 'Okay. But while we're on the record, I wouldn't do anything that might upset my wife. Even if you cried. Or tripped and lost your glasses again.'

'Okay. Great.' *More helpful, thank you.*

'Great. Let's go. Mack Macintyre's hoping to squeeze in a couple of wee drams before bed.'

Was there anything as bittersweet as driving through the rain at night, cheesy old pop songs crackling in the background, laughing, gently bickering, telling stories, playing Revels roulette, sometimes saying nothing at all, with a lovely man, who made your heart pound whenever he glanced across at you, or barked with amusement, or crinkled up the two lines between his eyebrows as he listened to the story of your life, when that man happened to be married?

I knew I liked Mack. Liked him plus found him attractive. I could work at keeping those two feelings in separate boxes. But in the quiet moments, with the only sound the radio and the swish of windscreen wipers, I became painfully aware that we were huddled side by side in one of the smallest cars ever invented. In the intimacy of the darkness, I didn't feel like friends, or neighbours. I felt like a woman sitting inches apart from a man she was teetering on the edge of falling in love with.

I didn't want the journey to end. I wanted us to get lost in the moors and end up driving all night. Or at least as long as my bladder held out. Honestly? I wanted to stay in that car forever. For the rest of my life to be one long, intimate, funny, tender, heart-wide-open journey with Mack.

After a stop for coffee and fuel (Mack wanted a full tank in case a speedy getaway became necessary), we arrived at the hotel around eleven. Crunching up a long drive to a floodlit courtyard, we pulled to a stop in front of what could only be accurately described as a castle.

'We're staying at the wedding venue?' I asked, my voice a tad strangled, eyes fixed on the turrets towering above us.

Mack shrugged. 'I figured it would be easiest. Is there a problem? The reviews were excellent. Apparently, it's got the best venison in the—'

'Whole of Ayrshire,' I finished.

'You don't sound very happy about that.' He turned to face me.

I pushed my glasses up, rubbed my tired eyes. 'I've stayed here before. Several times. With Richard.'

'Ah.' He peered out through the windscreen. 'Kind of a weird choice for his wedding, then.'

'He likes venison.'

I took a deep breath. 'Mack, I know how much a room here costs. When you said a hotel I was thinking a Travelodge, or a crusty B and B.'

'Well, at the risk of sounding like the infamous blowhard Richard the Richest, I can afford it.'

'Still, though...'

'Still though, I'm shattered, I really want to try a whisky and the deal I got on the rooms is non-refundable so we might as well enjoy it.'

We checked in, and went to the bar for a drink. My nerves too jittery to contemplate alcohol, I sipped on lemonade until Mack asked me to go to bed so he could enjoy his whisky in peace.

'Try to get some sleep. And if you say sorry or thank you again I'm going to abandon you to the golf course. It's going to be fun, remember, breaking the wedding rules, drinking champagne and hunting for Z-list celebrities.'

I nodded and left before my mouth popped open and said the words expanding in my head like an airbag: *Thank you, Mack Macintyre, for everything. Thank you for being you. And thank you for letting me be me. And I'm really, truly, sorry but I LOVE YOU. Goodnight.*

It wasn't a good night. But the next day? Better than I hoped.

35

I didn't attend the pre-reception brunch, held in a private dining room and clearly marked as invitation only. Instead, Mack and I whiled away the morning with tea and mince pies in the lobby, which had been transformed into a Christmas wonderland overnight, along with the rest of the hotel. We sat beside the enormous tree, covered in red and silver bows and topped with a figurine that looked remarkably like Zara, and played 'spot the wedding guest' as tall, slim women in enormous hats glided past accompanied by men in tight suits brushing the fake snow off shiny shoes.

'They all look the same,' Mack mused. 'It's a good job your sister will be in a wedding dress or I might end up congratulating the wrong person. Do you know any of these people?'

'One or two. I've not seen anyone from work yet.'

'Well, I'm guessing *she* won't be at the wedding,' Mack whispered, as a woman in a blue habit and black veil walked past. 'Can't picture Richard or Zara knocking about with nuns.'

'Well, you lose.' I picked up my oversized teacup and attempted to hide behind it as someone else swished past. 'That nun is the bride's mother.'

'Really?' Mack looked delighted. 'Her outfit must break about six different guidelines in the dress code. Wearing a veil to someone else's wedding is one thing. But a *black* veil?'

It would be funny if it weren't true. Zara was either going to flip out, disinvite her own mother or force her into an emergency dress from Jaeger.

'Do you think she'll join in the dancing later? Or, wouldn't it be great if she's got some flash mob, choreographed routine up her sleeve?'

By the time I'd wiped up the tea laugh-snorted out through my nose at that image, Mum had vanished.

'Can you call her?' Mack asked.

'She doesn't own a phone.' I wasn't going to mention anything about the house or the journals until after the ceremony. The risk was too high that it'd send her running again. Or, even worse, crying... that would not go down well. What kind of person made a nun cry? Made her *mum* cry? At a wedding? When it was her *own daughter* getting married?

I could wait a few more hours.

Ten minutes before we were due in the ballroom, I rustled down the stairs in Frances' dove-grey swing dress and the fancy shoes I'd bought myself. With my hair pinned up, new glasses and a simple silver necklace round my neck, I hoped I might look elegant. At the very least I looked tasteful. And, most importantly, I felt like *me*. Not a cheap imitation of my twin. She might not even recognise me. I was fairly hopeful Richard wouldn't, having never looked that closely in the first place.

A man stood up from where he'd been leaning on a pillar wrapped in ivy and tipped his head in acknowledgement.

Wowee – I must have looked even better than I thought. He was, to put it bluntly, gorgeous. After living in Scotland for five years, I now finally got the hype about a man in a kilt. This guy had the whole shebang – white shirt, jacket, sporran, those funny brogues with laces up his ankles. Short dark hair, a Celtic warrior's jawline, he stood there grinning at me, and I felt the blush from my silver shoes right up to the diamond clip in my hair.

Flustered, I wobbled precariously, keeping my eyes down, hand gripping the bannister until I reached the bottom.

The kilt-man was Mack. Hair cut, beard gone. Shoulders back.

He offered the crook of one arm, leaning in and whispering in a fake Scottish burr, 'Aye, you'll do, then.'

'You'll do, yourself,' I said, wondering if my heart was thumping hard enough for him to see it bouncing against the bodice of the dress.

'Well, you know, it's traditional for Macintyre men to don the family tartan at special occasions.'

'That's Macintyre tartan?'

He winked as we joined the queue of guests waiting to enter the ballroom. 'It is now.'

I hadn't been to many weddings, so didn't know if it was normal to have a seating plan for the actual ceremony. I suspected that, short of high-level aristocrats, seating plans didn't get beyond the one side for bride, one for groom. But at least this way I could avoid that sticky question. I knew which one I'd had more conversations with in the past couple of years. And only one of them had, well, done stuff with me I'd rather not think about now. Or ever again.

I swallowed a wave of nausea, tucked my arm more firmly in Mack's and we shuffled to our seats, three rows from the back. A scan of the plan told me Zara's housekeeper, Claudia, and my dad weren't there. I recognised a few names from Dougal and Duff, but unsurprisingly none of the minions I'd hung about with were on the list.

As we sat and waited for things to start, I felt a genuine twinge of pity for my sister. Twenty-eight years old and the only family here were a mum who'd ditched all earthly attachments and responsibilities, including her own children, for a God Zara didn't believe in, and a twin sister she'd treated like dog poo and then wiped off and disposed of accordingly.

None of these women, with their over-the-top air-kisses and five-figure handbags, was a real friend to Zara. They'd be scouring the whole event like starving vultures, gorging on the tiniest flaws and relishing the catty remarks and gossipy criticism. The stupidest thing about competition (and, believe me, every detail of this day was part of the great who's-winning-at-life competition) was that you ended up feeling either superior and isolated, or inferior and therefore jealous. Nobody won. I breathed a deep sigh of relief that, despite my mother's past attempts, I had never even qualified to enter.

I leant to the side slightly, nudging Mack with my arm.

'Is it okay if I say hello to Mum?'

He sat to attention. 'I insist. Let's go.'

'Feel free to stay here and read your programme.' Having not seen Mum since she took her vows, I still wasn't sure quite who I'd be saying hello to.

'No chance. I promised to stick by your side today. We've

barely started and you want me shirking my responsibility? Us Macintyres are made of stronger stuff than that.'

'I know your surname isn't really Macintyre. I made it up, remember?'

His mouth twitched, and I couldn't help wondering how much that bushy beard had previously kept hidden. 'I don't know what you're talking about.'

Rolling my eyes, I led him to my mother.

'Mum, this is my friend Mack. Mack, Isobel.'

Mum nodded her head. 'Call me Sister Claire.'

'I'll try.' Mack smiled. 'But I've got two sisters and that wouldn't necessarily be a compliment.'

'How are you?' I asked Mum – or was I supposed to call her Sister Claire too? 'How long are you staying?'

'I'm very well, thank you. And I'm flying back this evening. I hope we can spend some time together before then.'

Watching her making small talk with Mack, I had to agree that, despite the grey hair and lack of make-up, she did look well. I tried to put a word to what was different about her... and then I realised, I'd never seen her so *still*. She looked peaceful.

Wow. I guessed the whole religious conversion thing was genuine, then. And seemed to have worked.

She suddenly took my hand. 'Jenny. I've missed you so much.'

Um, what?

Thankfully, at that moment Rob Duff, as in *Dougal and*, who thought Richard was an irritating upstart in need of a good kicking (according to his PA, Meg), assumed his role of best man and called the two hundred guests to take their seats.

Richard entered the room being pulled on a sleigh by four groomsmen dressed as elves, as the 'Sleigh Ride' Christmas song jingled in the background, a ludicrously jolly accompaniment to the strenuous job of heaving a sleigh down a white carpet in twenty-three-degree heat while wearing stripy green and white tights.

'This is brilliant.' Mack grinned, settling in to enjoy the spectacle.

I would have answered, but was too busy fighting the panic now twisting itself up and around my head like a musty blanket as my stupid, idiot eyes refused to move off Richard. That swagger. The way he jerked his head when he greeted people. His preposterously fake laugh. I couldn't believe I'd fallen for it. Let him use me.

'I think I'm going to throw up.'

Mack's hand gripped mine, and held on. 'You're fine. I've got you.'

I concentrated on those smooth, warm fingers, let them steady me, like an anchor in the storm of memories, feelings and regrets. And for the next hour, allowing everything to pass in a blur meant I was, just about, fine. Throughout Zara riding in on a donkey, which I assume was some twisted reference to the nativity story, being given away by Ian Dougal (her boss – really?); the carols, the ten bridesmaids, the doves, the first kiss under a bunch of mistletoe. The pretend tears, the genuinely atrocious bride and groom duet of 'Baby It's Cold Outside' and the fake snowstorm as they walked back down the aisle. I held onto that hand, like a life-line to reality, and I listened to Zara pledge herself to the man I'd thought I loved, and I tried hard to wish them well.

We trooped out into the muggy heat for a fir-tree-planting ceremony in the enormous blanket of fake snow, no one asking what the point of planting a tree here, rather than in their own garden, was. Everyone pretending to ignore Zara's choice of language when her husband flicked a clod of dirt onto her dress.

Trooped back inside for photographs in the great hall while those who didn't make the cut drank mulled wine and nibbled endless tiny canapés.

I hid at the back, trying to remember not to look as if I was being strangled by my own awkwardness. Most people ignored me, after their automatic full-body scan classified me as either: INSIGNIFICANT or AVOID! Two women, having given me the once-over, sidled in towards Mack. 'Are you with the bride or groom?' they purred.

'No,' Mack replied, causing blinks of surprise as he looked away, uninterested.

'So why are you here, then?' one of them persisted, squeezing in next to me.

'I'm with Jenny,' Mack said, no less fierce for lack of facial hair.

'Really?' She screwed up her tight face as best she could in sympathy and disbelief. 'And is that a fixed arrangement, for the whole night?' She took a long slurp on her straw. 'Or are you open to a better offer?'

Before Mack could reply, the other woman's hand shot out and clutched her friend. 'Shut. Up!' She gasped. 'Jenny, as in Zara's psychotic sister?' Her eyes jerked between Mack and me. 'Does Zara know you're here? Does *Richard*? Isn't there a restraining order? Are you, like, out on parole, for your sister's wedding? Oh! I get it!' She pointed at me in delight. 'He's, like, her, oh, what's it called? Her guard. Her escort! To stop her doing a runner.'

'She doesn't look like a nutter,' the first one said, eyes

narrowing. When I heard her sneer that word, only Mack's hand on my arm stopped me throwing my drink in her face.

'Oh, don't let her pretty face fool you,' Mack said. 'I'd have warned you not to insult her, but, oops – too late. Make sure you lock your door tonight. And maybe wedge a piece of furniture in front of the window? I mean, I do my best, but these government-issue handcuffs can only do so much. And a man's got to sleep some time. Oh, hang on one second.' He pulled out his phone. 'Could you hold this?' He handed his drink to the first woman before she had time to react. 'I need to take this call. Keep an eye on her for me, would you? I won't be more than five minutes, fifteen, tops.'

And with that, he vanished through the crowd. As did the women a split second later. Although they weren't quite so slick, toppling into a table on the way and causing the heads to fall off a rapidly melting ice-sculpture of the happy couple.

Mack reappeared a minute later. 'Do you want to get out of here? Go for a walk or something?'

Did I?

Old Jenny – absolutely. Why would anyone in my circumstances want to be here, unless it was to cause trouble?

New Jenny? The woman I was trying to be had made a promise to stop running away. From scary woods, falling-down houses, family problems, unnerving nun-mums or her past mistakes.

Yes, I had lost. The man, my job, my home, my pride.

But, honestly? Zara had kind of deserved that punch. And everyone in this room who knew what had happened knew that too. Most of them were probably jealous that I'd got to tear out a chunk of her perfect, pretend hair. And it wasn't as if I hadn't apologised, about forty-seven million times.

No more running. No more hiding. No more excuses. I was here because I'd been invited and I was jolly well staying.

'No.' I shook my head.

And then the photographer ruined it by requesting all family members to gather for the next picture.

Mack's eyes met mine. 'Best get up there, then.'

Hardly. I couldn't breathe, or speak, let alone make my way across a slippery parquet floor in six-inch heels.

The bride's mother appeared and stepped inside a giant snow-globe, the backdrop for all the photographs. Zara mimed for her to remove the black veil but Sister Claire merely smiled.

'Come on, family members,' the photographer called again. I shrivelled up against the wall, and tried to appear like just another statue. My complexion surely more stone-like than human at that point.

A gaggle of people who must have been Richard's family – judging by the swagger and the oversized heads – squeezed into the snow-globe and arranged themselves around him.

'Wait!' Sister Claire said, popping her head out of the side of the globe. 'Jenny's not here. You can't take it yet. JENNY?'

Zara tried to yank Mum back, eyes resembling a couple of those glass balls in museums with blue electricity zapping about inside like lightning. 'What are you talking about?'

'JENNY?' she called again. 'Oh, she must have nipped to the ladies' room.'

'*What are you talking about?* Why would *she* be here?'

'Presumably because she was invited,' Mum said. 'I'm sure your schedule allows a couple of minutes to wait for your own twin to be included in the photographs. You share the same DNA. Were one person once upon a time. You can't get more family than that.'

'She does not share my DNA and we were never one person. We are non-identical twins, Mother. And she was *not* invited to my wedding.'

'Oh, crap,' I breathed.

'It's not too late to sneak out the back and pretend we were never here,' Mack said.

'Well, you did once share this womb, and these breasts!' Sister Claire pointed to indicate which womb, and which breasts, she was referring to, in case anyone wasn't sure.

'You bottle-fed us!' Zara hissed.

'I know you weren't close growing up, but you lived and worked together for six years. Why wouldn't you invite her? I expected her to be a bridesmaid, to be honest.'

'Why wouldn't I invite her?' Zara's voice was bouncing off the baubles hanging from the rafters, all thought of who might hear forgotten. 'Do you recognise this nose, Mother? I'll tell you why there is no reason on this earth that could have persuaded me to invite that jealous, lowlife maniac to my wedding day! Last year, she—'

'I'm here!' I practically screamed, wobbling on my tiptoes and waving my hands about. I don't think either Birkenshaw twin wanted that titbit broadcast across the hall. Richard certainly didn't, judging by the way his eyes were bugging out of their sockets.

He spent the eternity it took me to reach the staircase whispering in his wife's ear, presumably reminding her who else had been invited and was therefore witnessing this scene, and asking if she wanted her wedding day to be remembered for the bride going ballistic.

Which was how I ended up jammed beside Zara, doing everything I could not to cringe under Sister Claire's hand resting on my shoulder, pretending to ignore the frantic gossip zipping up and down the room like a swarm of wasps and trying not to faint from the unbearably stuffy heat caused by cramming into a giant glass ball in the height of summer.

As soon as the photographer had finished, I stumbled off towards the ladies' room, head down, whole body trembling.

Before I reached it, a hand from behind gently pulled me to a stop. Turning, expecting to see Mack, instead I found myself face to face with my ex-boyfriend.

'I'm so glad you came,' he said, voice low.

'I'm not sure Zara would agree.' I looked down at his hand, but he didn't take the hint.

'She'd have regretted it later if you weren't.'

'No. I really don't think she would have. Why would you invite me without telling her?'

He hunched his shoulders. 'I thought it would be a good chance for you to make up. You must miss each other.'

'No. We don't. We didn't exactly get on even before... what happened. There's no making up to do.'

'I wanted to apologise for that.' Richard slid his hand down to my wrist. I yanked it away and tried to avoid gagging. 'How it all happened. I really, really liked you, Jenny. And your sister, she kind of put me in a difficult position. You know what she's like when her mind's set on something. But I never meant to hurt you.'

'Mmm-hmm.'

'I'm glad you came, though.' He twisted up his mouth in what I knew he considered to be his sexiest smile, because he once asked me to rate his smiles in order. *'I've* missed you. And you look amazing.'

'You are kidding me?' I laughed then. The whole situation

was preposterous. I knew Richard was only hoping to keep his ego fully inflated by watching me melt beneath sexy smile number three. 'Thank you for your apology. Duly noted, but really not necessary. You hooking up with Zara was the best thing that ever happened to me. Have a nice life, Richard.'

36

Mack and I decided to give the carol singers with bagpipe accompaniment a miss, instead opting for a pair of huge armchairs at the back of the library, and more tea and crumpets. We did attend dinner, having correctly guessed we'd be at an obscure table at the back, with a few of Zara's lesser acquaintances and the now infamous nun.

'The house is beginning to take shape,' I said to her as we ate our starters. 'I've done loads of work on it. Clearing it out, sprucing up the bits I want to keep.'

'That's very nice. I'm glad you're making a home. But please don't fall into the trap I did and start placing your worth in what you own, not who you are.'

'If I did that, I'd not consider myself worth very much.'

We finished our salmon in silence. I waited for the roast venison to arrive before pressing on.

'What was it like, living there?'

Sister Claire carefully chewed and swallowed. But in her sidelong glance I saw the first real glimpse of my mother since she'd arrived. 'I left, aged seventeen, and never went back. I think that tells you enough.'

'Why?'

She put down her knife and fork and dabbed her mouth with a napkin. Bent her head for a long moment.

'Please, Mum. Why did I never get to meet my grandmother?'

Another minute or two ticked by. While the rest of the table tucked into the Brussels sprouts and chestnut stuffing, chatting, clinking crystal, tipsy hands gesticulating wildly, my mother and I sat in some sort of bubble.

Finally, she gave a slow, determined blink, and turned to me. 'Your grandmother and I did not get on. She was a... difficult woman. Controlling. Rigid. I thought she blamed me for your grandfather leaving. I blamed her for driving him away. And I couldn't forgive her. So instead I spent the next thirty years trying to forget.'

She wiped away the tear running down her cheek. Speechless, I handed her a napkin.

'Thank you.' She blotted her face, took a couple of slow breaths. 'I have made my peace with God, but I can never make peace with her. And I must live with the pain I caused. The unanswered questions.'

She clenched her hands together in a fist on the table. 'Whatever has gone on between you and Zara, please sort it out. Whether we like it or not, family matters.'

'I take your point, Mum. I'll try and talk to her before we go. Maybe not on her wedding night, though.'

I sat back, unable to eat any more. Braced myself.

'I don't want that to happen to us.'

Mum frowned. 'What to happen?'

'I don't want us to end up never seeing each other again. I want to be able to forgive you.'

I picked up my water glass to take a gulp, the contents sloshing as my hand shook.

'Forgive me for what?' Sister Claire had gone. Isobel Meadows, proud socialite, stared back at me.

'Don't you think that the damage caused by your childhood might have affected me and Zara? Mum, I can't ever remember you telling me you love me. Giving me a proper cuddle. When I was ill or upset you mostly told me to grow up and get over it.'

I had more to say, so much more, but the hot pain in my lungs and throat was too much to bear. I pushed back my chair. I couldn't do it. Couldn't handle the rising panic. Then Mack, laughing with the woman on his other side, took my hand in his and gently squeezed it, coaxing me back towards the table.

'Excuse me one moment.' He turned to me, keeping hold of my hand, and bent his head close to mine. 'You've got this,' he whispered, the kindness in his eyes so deep and beautiful it struck my very soul.

After the longest, tensest, most despairing silence of my life, my mother slowly reached out and took my other hand, pulling it up between us on the table.

'You're right. And I'm sorry. I have not been a wonderful mother. I perhaps failed you in more ways than most. But I knew no better. And all I can do now is ask for your forgiveness.' She took a long, juddering breath. 'I love you, Jennifer.' I managed to meet her eyes for maybe a fraction of a second before the pain got too much. 'I love you. With all my heart. Surely you knew that?'

No, Mum, I didn't know that. I would have been surprised to find she loved me with a teensy cranny of her heart.

We sat in frozen silence through dessert, and then the speeches, which I didn't hear a word of, although Mack later assured me that was probably a good thing, and the choreographed first dance to Mariah Carey's 'All I Want for Christmas Is You', interrupted by one of the bridesmaids starting to bop in the corner with her husband, at which point Zara stopped the music, screeched for seven minutes about how it was her day, and no one was going to steal her limelight however jealous they were, then insisted on starting again from the beginning.

'I need to tell you something else,' I managed to croak out, once the Celtic band had got under way. 'Can we go somewhere quieter? Maybe the library?'

And there, I told my mother about the brother she'd never known. More tears spilled over as I tried to explain what I'd learnt about Charlotte from the diaries.

We wept for secrets untold, the brother never mourned – the family that could have been, had Charlotte Meadows got support, spoken up, talked to her daughter, been brave enough to dare to love her. We wept most of all for the bright young girl who became a lonely old woman, unable to let go of a single memory, a scrap of her past, as if surrounding herself with things could replace what she'd lost, those who had abandoned her. Dying as she had lived: alone, unloved, estranged.

And we wept for a family still here, yet utterly broken.

As we sat together on a sofa, my mother leant over and hugged me and, however much I'd pretended I didn't care, it was the hug I'd been waiting for my whole life.

'I'm sorry,' she mumbled over my shoulder, both of us too awkward to meet the other's eyes.

'I know.' I leant my head against hers. 'You did the best you could.'

'That's not good enough.'

'No. It's not. But hearing you acknowledge it helps.'

'Will you come and visit? We have so much more to talk about, and my taxi will be here soon.'

'Come to the convent?'

She pulled away, laughing gently as she wiped her face. 'It's not called that, but yes. I'm in charge of the goats.'

'You hate animals.'

'I used to hate a lot of things I'm learning to love.'

'Okay, I'll try. But it won't be for a while. I've loads to do on the house first. I'll send you the journals, though.'

'Thank you. That would mean a lot to me.'

'And one day, you should come and see the cottage for yourself.'

'Yes. One day, God willing, I'll be ready to go back.'

Mack wandered through not long after that, surreptitiously checking if we'd finally stopped blubbering.

Sister Claire adjusted her habit and frowned at me over the top of her reading glasses. 'Now what are you doing still here? There's a party going on – you can't spend the evening sitting with your mother. Go and dance.'

'I'm not really in the mood. I think I might just—'

'Jennifer, that man has been nothing short of an angel all day. The least you can do is give him a dance.'

'I don't think Mack's into dancing. He's not really the type.' I glanced up as Mack reached our sofa.

'Whatever made you think that?' He peered down his

nose, fake Scottish accent so over the top it was barely comprehensible.

'Oh, I don't know. The grumpiness, the miserly existence and refusal to socialise with anyone, ever? The complete lack of anything resembling fun, or frivolity, or joy in your life?'

By this point, Mack had yanked me off the sofa, through the doorway and onto the dance floor. He pulled me up close to his chest in a classic ballroom hold. 'What are you talking about? I've got *you* in my life, haven't I?' He raised one eyebrow, ever so slightly, tweaked a soft smile, just enough to cause the sides of his mouth to crease, and, honestly, if he'd not been holding me so firmly I might have melted onto the floor right then and there. In my defence, it had been a long, emotionally exhausting day. I'd not slept much and I was probably dehydrated from all that crying.

'Now, shut your wee mooth, stop thinking so damn hard and dance with me, woman.'

So, instead of making a smart remark about his woeful accent, I shut my wee mouth and I danced through the firework display, the arrival of Santa, complete with reindeer, the impromptu Highland Games on the front lawn and the arrival and departure of the three ambulances. I danced until the band strummed its final note.

I shouldn't have been surprised at Mack being an awesome dancer. He seemed to be good at everything. What made my heart sing, and groan, both at the same time was that, in his arms, I didn't seem so bad myself.

I knew it was wrong. Utterly wrong. I could shut my eyes and pretend the state of Mack's marriage was nothing to do with me. We were only dancing, as friends. Mack was helping me through a difficult day. He looked at me like that because he felt concerned. My eyes kept being drawn to his face because I was still getting used to it without the beard. Joking, laughing, nuzzling into his shoulder as he rested his chin on my head didn't count as flirting, did it? And if our hands lingered a microsecond too long once the last dance finished (and they did, believe me, I noticed) it meant nothing. Not to him, anyway.

Someone flicked the main lights on, blinking us back to the harsh glare of reality. Dancing with Mack might be okay. How I felt every time he touched me, looked at me, spoke, stood in the same room, was not. It was time to get a grip on myself. Or, at the very least, go to bed and try to figure out a way to possibly manage to do that.

Mack carried my discarded shoes as he walked me to my door. Kept a careful distance as we rode up in the lift. Checked I still had my room key and dipped his head to say, 'Goodnight, neighbour. Sleep well,' disappearing into the next room before I could pull my wits about me enough to say, 'Goodnight, and thank you for helping what should have been one of the worst nights ever become the best.'

Which was probably a good thing. Who knew what would have popped out on the end of that sentence?

I was torn between wanting to get back home, where Mack had a wife and I had a brain plus a conscience and I didn't love Mack, and wanting this evening to last forever.

37

Breakfast the following morning consisted of strong coffee and a few mouthfuls of porridge, if the creamy, sweet and salty bowlful of heaven we ate could be called porridge. Mack and I spent breakfast talking about everything except what an amazing time we'd had, or how, having hated Christmas my whole life, this year I'd already had two and because of him both of them had been wonderful, or how I'd never laughed so much in one night, or how totally right I'd felt in his arms, or whether he could see the kiss that never happened hovering between us too, and whether that meant we couldn't be friends any more.

'Can you give me a minute?' I said after queuing to check out.

Mack tapped me on the shoulder with the complimentary newspaper. 'Take as long as you need. Should you require Mr Macintyre, he'll be leaning against this pillar looking protectively menacing.'

I rolled my eyes, smothered my smile and did my best to stride confidently yet casually up to Zara, gliding towards the library. It felt as if two massive hands were in my chest, squeezing the life out of each lung. The closer I got, the harder they squeezed.

She ignored my faint, 'Hello,' and, 'Good morning,' forcing me to sort of fling myself in front of her before she reached the library door.

'Oops. Sorry,' I wheezed. She shook her head slightly, eyes on the doorway, lips pursed as if confronted with a hideous reeking troll and not a freshly showered relative. Determined not to be dissuaded, I planted myself firmly in her way. 'I just wanted to say—'

'What the hell do you want?' she snapped, speaking over me. 'It's bad enough you showed up here at all. I'm not interested in anything you might have to say.'

'Mum didn't speak to you?'

'Yes, she spoke to me. And I told her what I'll tell you. I'm. Not. Interested. I gave you a home, a job, a life. For six years I let you wear my clothes. Stood up for you in the office when people moaned about what an irritating wuss you are. Tolerated your weird infatuation with my housekeeper. Which, by the way, was not only embarrassing but totally destroyed any respect she had for my authority. And you maimed and *humiliated* me, in front of Dougal and Duff. Virtually ruined my chance of making partner, which you know full well is the only thing I've ever wanted besides a date on Simon Cowell's yacht. Someone left an application form for *Judge Rinder* on my desk! And now you show up at my WEDDING! Why? Why are you here? Haven't you done enough?'

'I'm here because Richard invited me,' I said. 'And I wanted to see Mum, and to wish you well. You're my sister, whether we like it or not, so I'm here for you, if ever you need someone. Otherwise, I hope you get what you want from life and can finally be happy.'

Zara's nose sneered close to snapping point. 'I will *never* need you,' she said, laughing in disbelief. 'I *won*, Jenny. Slam-dunk. Clean sheet. Anything I wanted or needed from you, I've already taken.'

'A kidney?' I muttered, walking away. 'How to get a hug from our mum? Your first real friend?'

I dozed most of the way home, while the sound of Mack's Proclaimers playlist wafted in and out of hazy dreams. Still half asleep, once I'd stumbled to my door it took a moment longer than it should have to realise it was already open an inch.

'Oh, no.' My stomach lurched. My kitchen, my pretty, precious, tidy kitchen, had been trashed. Jamie's portable oven had gone. Cupboards stood wide open, their plates and bowls and the two vases carefully chosen from the Hoard in pieces on the lino below. The bin lay on its side, contents strewn across the floor. I dropped my bags and ran through to the living room. The old, blocky television had been smashed. The sofa cushions slashed, bookcase tipped over.

The rest of the house was the same. The boxes waiting for the car boot or charity shop emptied, their contents scattered. The small selection of Charlotte's jewellery I'd kept had been taken, as had the old record player and crate of LPs. Mostly, it was the mess that got to me. I shuddered at the thought of grubby fingers pawing through my carefully sorted, cleaned, tidied future. My arm hair bristled as I took in the carnage, vicious damage inflicted on mirrors and curtains, the lovely duvet from Mack shredded, books ripped open. This wasn't someone simply looking for items to flog. This was meant to intimidate, upset and frighten me. If I'd been at all in doubt, my un-stolen laptop sitting on a chair placed in the centre of my bedroom was proof enough. When I flicked it on, the screen went straight to a website selling houses.

Shit.

I blinked, hard, clenched my jaw tight and started scooping the clothes tossed about my bedroom into the laundry basket, anger and horror pumping like lava through my veins. Marching out to take it to the washing machine, it was only then I noticed Diana, and the message rang loud and clear.

Mack found me a few minutes later, a huddled heap at my plastic housemate's feet, scrabbling to piece back together the shards of my shattered courage.

* * *

'*Months* of hard grind,' I said, voice strained. 'I'd worked so hard. It was starting to look okay. Like a home was emerging from the mess and the dirt. I'm not sure I have the energy to start again.'

'That's exactly what they want you to think.' Sarah, grim-faced, poured a rare second glass of wine and handed it to me, slouched on her sofa. 'You can't let them win.'

'Why not?' I said, ignoring the wine. 'Why not take up Fisher's offer of a flat with no electrical problems, or plumbing disasters? Brand-new appliances and freshly - painted walls that probably aren't even mouldy. If they don't win this time, what will they do next?' I thought of

Mannequin Diana, and shivered. Decided on a gulp of wine after all.

'Once Jamie's back, he'll find whoever this is and string them up. Like, literally. He'll find a nice big tree and let them swing. Don't give up, Jenny. Think positive.'

'Urgh. I just don't want to think about it at all any more. How are things with you? Any progress with that guy you liked? What was his username – HeartBaker? Did he finally agree to a date?'

'Yes.' She looked down at her empty plate. 'But I wish he hadn't. He stood me up. Who does that? At least those others turned up. Even if I wished they hadn't.'

'Oh, I'm sorry. Another dud.'

'I dunno.' Sarah shrugged mournfully. 'It was sort of my fault. I pushed him into it, after he'd asked to take things slow. Told him it was now or never. But he could have chosen never – he didn't have to arrange to meet me in Scarlett's and then leave me hanging.'

'That sucks.'

'Yep.'

'So that's it with him?'

Sarah turned pink. 'I'm so pathetic. I messaged him three times last night. And then I got worried, that maybe something had happened. Like he'd had a car crash, or his house burned to the ground with his phone and computer inside. So, this morning I called him.'

'Oh, dear. He answered?'

'Yeah, so unfortunately neither he nor his phone are dead. Or seriously injured.'

'What did he say? What did *you* say?' I shuddered to think.

'Well, the line was really bad so it was a lot of me yelling about what a waster he was, and telling him to go shove his compliments and his promises and his sweet little jokes up his own app. While he crackled and hissed, and said stuff like, "I'm sorry, something came up," and, "Please let me explain," and, "I'll make it up to you." I told him, if he's so keen to make it up to me, why am I the one phoning to see if *he's* all right?'

Sarah opened the freezer and pulled out a giant tub of caramel ice cream. 'So that's it. I am officially over it. This particular story did not have a happy ending.' She scooped out two enormous bowlfuls. 'I mean, if a Zac Efron lookalike happens to start calling into the café and we get chatting, and after a decade or two he doesn't seem like a dud, I *might* have a coffee with him. But I'm done being disappointed.'

I watched her shovel in a mountain of ice cream. 'What about Jamie?'

'Really?' she mumbled, before swallowing her mouthful. 'Are you still going on about that? He's been hanging around in the café for weeks now, and not made a move. So, I'm guessing he's either not interested or not man enough. And we both know there's nothing Jamie's not man enough for.'

I ate my ice cream and said nothing. If Jamie wasn't brave or decisive enough to act on his feelings, maybe he *wasn't* strong enough to take Sarah on.

The next morning, Ashley tumbled into my kitchen. 'I made gingerbread,' she announced, with great significance. 'To cheer you up.'

She placed a plastic tub on my table, keeping hold of a pretty tin decorated with butterflies.

'Thanks, Ashley. That's really kind of you. I could do with a break before I start clearing up the wreckage in the dining room. Do you want tea?'

'Ye-e-e-e-s-s-s,' she replied, eyes darting about. 'But I have this other cake for next door. Seeing as they got burgled, too. They might want to talk things over with a glass of lemonade.'

And then I remembered.

The phone call. Made in a storm cloud of anger and offence, for reasons now seeming petty. Hillary West had made me feel stupid and pathetic and a failure. Feelings that had a lifetime's worth of painful memories associated with them. Feelings I'd been working my backside off to move on from, and thought I had finally succeeded at.

I was impressed Ashley had held off this long. Maybe it wasn't going to be as bad as I feared.

'Mack is a really private guy,' I said. 'I'm sorry, but he's not going to want to talk to you. Or have you help him clear up his three possessions. I can drop the cake round, though. I'm sure he'll appreciate it.'

'Jenny, it's *gingerbread*. It's not for Mack.'

I knew the cake wasn't for Mack, but it was only when she waggled her eyebrows at me that I remembered the Hillary West book, *The Gingerbread House*.

'Right. Let's go, then.' I didn't bother telling her Hillary West might not live up to the imaginary novelist she'd created in her head. Hillary could burst Ashley's bubble herself.

Mack answered the door. Hanging back behind Ashley still didn't stop my stomach flipping over. I couldn't handle his face so exposed, so *there*. He really needed to grow that beard back for his, and my, protection.

Ashley introduced herself, reciting the words like an actress on one of those local adverts for car dealerships. 'Is your wife in, at all? I've made her gingerbread. Not a house –

I mean, I thought that might be a bit much. I didn't want her to think I was weird! Ha! Ha!'

Mack swivelled his eyes to me. A little tiny explosion went off in my chest with a sad whistle. 'No. You can leave the cake here, though. She'll be back at the weekend.'

'Oh. Well.' Ashley's whole body drooped. 'I very much wanted to give it to her myself. I'm such a big fan. Like, about as big a fan as you can get without being sinister. I've written to her dozens of times. But I've never invaded her personal privacy! I've always respected her wish to remain out of the limelight. It's just, well, when Jenny mentioned she lived so amazingly close, I had to come and tell her in person how she has totally, completely, changed my life. I'm only brave enough to be here because of her.' Her voice faded to a mumble. 'I promise I'll leave her alone after that. If she wants to. I mean, if she wanted to go for a drink or bounce any ideas off her biggest fan, of course, I'd be more than willing to—'

'Okay!' Mack said. 'Bring the cake round on Saturday.'

'I just would so love to meet her before she moves. I can't believe she's been this close all this time and now it's nearly too late!'

'I said it's okay.'

'I promise I won't mention her writer's block!'

Mack's face clouded over faster than a hurricane. He shut the door, growling something about gossip and rights to privacy and peace.

While indignantly huffing her way through helping me straighten my dining room, Ashley suddenly sprang bolt upright, her jaw hanging open.

'What?' I glanced outside, in case she'd mistaken the postwoman for a bestselling author.

'I've had the most brilliant idea.'

'What could that possibly be to do with?' I stuck my hands on my hips.

'I'm not going to tell you what it is because you'll only try and talk me out of it. But it's perfect!'

On consideration, I decided I didn't want to know AT ALL.

'Okay, I won't interfere if you promise it isn't illegal or stalkerish and doesn't involve me or my house.'

'It's definitely not illegal and you and your lovely house don't feature in the plan one bit. I promise.'

'And?'

'Oh, phooey,' she puffed. 'It's not stalkerish if you only do it once.'

38

I was flopping about on Saturday morning, half-heartedly looking at paint colours on my phone, when it pinged with an email. Still a rare enough occurrence to warrant my immediate attention – I took a look.

I recognised the Hickleton Press logo straight away, thanks to the Hillary hunt. My first thought was one of panic, wondering what on earth Ashley had dragged me into this time, and whether the second person in under a year had taken out a restraining order against me.

But this was nothing to do with Hillary. I skimmed down, had to go back to the top three times to check I was reading it right.

Hickleton Press loved Squash Harris.

As in, enough to want to include it in their top children's magazine. Enough to make an offer that made my ears pop. Not that the money mattered, but the faith in Squash Harris it implied did. A lot.

I *knew* that comic was bleepin' brilliant.

I called Ellen.

"Ello?'

'Hamish, is that you?'

'Nope.'

'Hamish, it's Jenny. Can I speak to Mummy? Is she there?'

'Not Hamish.'

'Okay... well, whoever it is, please give the phone to Mummy.'

'You have to guess.' I could hear him wriggling with glee.

'Is it... Superman? Batman? Admiral Nelson?'

'No-o-o-o-o!' Hamish squealed.

'Well, then, you have to give me a clue.'

'I once ate a whole camel 'cos I was hungry and then floated down a river and was looking for treasure and there was a big hole in the ground like a giant long slide that went down, down, down to an underground cave with a dragon what breathed ice instead of fire inside and... Oh, Mummy's shouting I have to get my shoes on. Bye, Jenny.'

The phone beeped off.

I'd call round later. It would be nicer to give the great news in person, and Ellen might need help looking for her phone.

I was rereading the email for the ten-thousandth time and musing over how Mack had played down the fact that his 'contacts' who could help with the comic included a wife who wrote bestsellers for a giant publishing company, when two cars pulled up in the clearing. I'd done a sterling job of ignoring the slamming doors and clacking heels the night before, but this time I peeped out to see the estate agent climb out of one car. And then Ashley emerged from the other.

If her grin had been any bigger it would've swallowed the clearing up whole.

My heart sank even as my mouth let out a bark of nervous, guilty laughter. Ashley had been right – it was a cunning plan. Then, as I watched through the window, two more cars screeched up, doors flinging open to let half the members of the book club spill out, followed by what seemed to be an impossible number of small children.

Ellen and her youngest four, Kiko with Lily, balancing Hannah on one hip. Sarah with Edison and Lucille with her eight-year-old son, Toronto. I careened out of the back door and round to the front without even thinking about putting some shoes on first.

The adults were now assembled in front of the bewildered estate agent, while the kids clustered round the bottom of a tree, watching Toronto dangle from one of the branches.

The estate agent was protesting. 'The appointment was made with Naomi Brook. Nobody else is allowed in. It's policy.'

There were nudges and rolled eyes. Naomi Brook was the main character in *The Gingerbread House*.

'We are not letting her loose in that house alone,' Ellen muttered, out of the agent's earshot.

'That can't be true,' Kiko, straightening her newfound backbone, said. 'What if we all want to buy the house together, as a rental property?'

'Then you should have told me in advance. The owners have asked for particular discretion in this case. And I can't possibly allow children inside. I'm sorry.'

By this point, the owners had come to investigate. Hillary pushed her sunglasses up past her perfect fringe, frowning. 'Is there a problem here?'

The estate agent whirled around. 'No!' she simpered. 'It's handled. I've explained that viewings are by named appointments only. The others will have to arrange something for another time. This isn't an open house, after all! Now, Naomi, would you like to come this way?'

Naomi Brook appeared to be frozen to the spot. The only thing indicating she remained alive was her continuously changing complexion, like a lava lamp, fading from white to pink, through to green then back to white again.

Sarah, never one to wait and see what happened when she could instead prod someone into action, did precisely that, with a good hard poke in the ribs. 'Urgh,' Naomi/Ashley groaned, then sucked in an enormous, gasping breath as though she had literally forgotten to breathe for a few minutes.

She stammered. 'I... I love you.'

'Right.' Hillary rolled her eyes. 'Mack, keep an eye on her. And I don't see why everyone can't look round. The kids can stay outside. Julie can watch them. Maybe we'll get a little bidding war going.' She tossed her head at the estate agent. 'If you'd been doing your job properly, you'd have thought of that. Now, are you showing them or do you need me to do that too?'

'Wait,' Mack said, sounding more than a little resigned.

'What?' Hillary snapped.

'Who's Julie?' Kiko asked. 'I'm not leaving my baby with a stranger.'

'I think that would be me,' I said. 'Julie, Jenny... same difference.'

'These people don't want to buy the house.' Mack sighed.

'Shut up, Mack.' Hillary spoke through gritted teeth. 'They haven't looked at it yet.'

'They're Jenny's friends.'

'Who's Jenny?'

'Julie.'

'For the record, I'm more of an acquaintance,' Lucille chipped in.

'Is this true?' Hillary whirled on me. 'Is this another one of your attempts to sabotage my house sale? You've got a bloody nerve.'

'How would this sabotage the house sale?' I asked, hackles rising.

'Because once this genuine buyer saw all these feral children rampaging about—' a fair enough description, as illustrated by the triplets now charging past brandishing sticks, while Toronto waddled after them lugging a boulder '—they'd obviously not want to move here.'

'The truth is, we're a book club,' Ashley said, sufficiently recovered to form a sentence. 'And we all absolutely love your novels. I personally have read every one over twelve times. You are such an inspiration, and we are honoured to have you living locally, even if only for a short while. I've written to your agent so many times inviting you to the book club. It would mean everything, if you could come. Just pop in for a few minutes. We meet in The Common Café, so you can walk it if the weather's good...'

'You like my books?' Hillary asked, in disbelief. '*You* like my books?'

'I love them,' Ashley squeaked. 'We all do.'

'Ahem.' Lucille coughed. 'No offence, but some of us prefer deeper literary themes. Preferably something that isn't anti-feminist.'

'What?' Hillary looked like a ventriloquist's dummy, her round head swinging from Ashley to Lucille and back. 'Deeper literary themes? Anti-feminist? Are you joking? I've won the Camberley Literary Award for Feminist Literature.

One of the judges was French! Right. I've had enough. Which one of you is...' she leaned in and read the estate agent's folder '... Naomi Brook? *You* can view the house. You book-club people can leave. Now. And take these children with you.'

Ashley was gobsmacked for the second time in fifteen minutes. 'Naomi Brook,' she echoed, slowly and clearly.

'Yes. That's what I said. Where is she?'

'She doesn't know,' Ashley said. 'She doesn't recognise the name. It's not her.'

Having reached the same conclusion, the others now turned to me. It was a useful distraction, seeing as Lucille looked set to gouge Hillary's eyes out.

I screwed up my face, bit the side of my cheek so hard I left a bruise. Eventually managed to come up with something. 'I guess there's more than one Hillary West living in Sherwood Forest?'

It was then I saw Mack, eyes wide open, an expression of utter horror on his face.

'It's okay,' I blabbered. 'Just a case of mistaken identity. I sent a form off to the DVLA to see who owned the car, back when you were being all cryptic and mysterious. And when I saw it was Hillary West, I put two and two together and made... ninety-two.'

'But this Hillary West is an author too,' Sarah said. 'She's won an award. There can't be two authors called Hillary West from round here, surely?'

'Number one,' Hillary ground out, 'I'm not from "round here". I hate it here, which is why I'm trying to sell this chuffing house, so I can finally move on with my life. And, two.' She sucked in a deep breath. 'I am not Hillary West. I'm Sienna Stracken. Author of the prize-winning literary classic

The Wheel of Woman. I do *not* write romance-by-numbers drivel.'

'Oh, my life,' Lucille shouted. 'Can I just say, I'm your biggest fan!'

Ashley burst into tears, letting out a sound an elephant might make if someone trod on its trunk.

'So, was it an actual wheel or not?' Sarah asked, before Ellen gave her a shove. 'Yeah, now's probably not the time. Forget I asked.'

'But if you're not Hillary West, who is?' Kiko asked. 'I thought the only other person living here was Mack.'

We all looked at Mack. If Charlotte Meadows had hoarded a sculpture entitled 'Angriest Man in the World', it now stood here on the scrubby grass.

'You are flippin' kidding me,' Sarah murmured. Ashley wiped her nose on her blue spotty mac and peered closer.

Ellen appeared to be the only one of us capable of rational speech, given that Lucille was now off to one side gushing over Sienna Stracken. 'You're her? Hillary West?' she asked, in the same gentle voice she used to coax Billy down from the roof of the greenhouse.

Mack furrowed his eyebrows until they almost became a moustache. Crossed his arms then stuck them on his hips. 'No. And yes.'

Hah! Ellen's gentle voice was irresistible.

'Hillary West is a pen-name?'

'No.'

'But you are her?'

'This could be bigger news than we thought,' Sarah said, glancing at me.

'I'm him,' Mack replied, emphatically.

'But how can you be him, when she's a she, and how can you be Hillary West, when you're Mack?' Ashley wailed.

Good question. Twin ribbons of hurt and foolishness tangled themselves round my internal organs.

'My name is Hillary Mackenzie West. When your name makes people automatically assume you're the opposite gender, it's not unusual to go by your middle name. However, my publisher decided that if readers happened to assume I was a woman, that would sell more books.'

I uttered a noise, something like a strangled snort. Mack's eyes flickered over in my direction. His gaze caught mine, and we froze there. I couldn't tell if he felt mad at me for blabbing to Ashley, forcing him to reveal himself, or regretful for covering up something so momentous when I'd shared my worst secrets.

He shook his head, narrowing one eye slightly.

Okay, then. Mad it was.

The estate agent cleared her throat and summoned up a cracked smile. 'Um, is there anyone who actually wants to view the house today? Naomi? No? Right, I'll leave you to make your own way back. Mr and Mrs West, I'll see you at your four o'clock viewing.' She started marching over to her car, taking a sudden swerve in Mack's direction, and prattling, 'I love your books! *The Way It Was* got me through my darkest days, after I lost Horatio. I mean, I know losing a terrapin isn't quite the same as losing your husband, but the way Helena managed to keep going, well!' She sucked in a breath. 'Anyway. I'll see you at four.'

'Ms Johnson?' Mack said in a tone that sent every bird in the forest flapping for cover.

'Um. Yes?' She paused, key fob pointed at the car.

'Can you please vet the rest of the day's appointments to

ensure they are serious buyers? And make sure they know
we're prepared to negotiate on price if it means a quick sale.
Failing that, give Fisher a call. Tell him I've changed my
mind.'

Mack stalked off out of sight. I stood there, limbs like
concrete, listening to the pounding of blood in my ears.

'Jenny, look, I did brought you this,' Jonno said, hands
extended. 'To make you feel happy.'

'Thanks, Jonno. You're awesome.' I attempted a wobbly
smile.

'Do you love it?' he asked. 'Here, you can keep it.'

'Yes. I love it because you gave it to me,' I said, picking it
up. 'And, ooh!' I pantomimed surprise. 'It did make me feel
happier, you're right!'

I wasn't lying, either. Amazing what an eight-inch dead
slug could do for a girl's mood.

Ellen dragged me back to her house, where we kept going
over and over things, until the only possible distraction was a
mass game of Hunt and Destroy.

'This game is a cruel parody of real-life events,' I whispered to Ellen, both of us pressed underneath her car on the
driveway. 'The Hillary hunt has destroyed things with my
best friend.'

Ellen rolled her eyes over to me, while managing to keep
her head completely still. 'He just needs time. He knows you
didn't mean to out him.'

We waited while two pairs of trainers, one wellington
boot and a flipper flapped past, accompanied by loud
shushing and giggles.

'He's realised I tried to out his wife.' I shuddered. 'He
probably thinks she's right, and I am trying to sabotage the
house move.'

'Were you?' Ellen asked, in that gentle, tell-me-everything voice again.

'No!' I retorted, as loud as was possible in the middle of Hunt and Destroy.

'But perhaps you were trying to sabotage something else?'

'What are you saying?'

'It would be understandable if your feelings had slipped over from friendship into attraction, Jenny. Especially with him being separated when you met. If you developed feelings for a man you thought was single, it's hard to wind those back in again.'

'My feelings have not slipped over! I don't find Mack attractive!'

'Oh, come off it. Everyone finds Mack attractive. The difference is whether you act on those feelings. If they've grown into more than "well, yes, he's yummy but looks aren't everything and, more to the point, he's legally married, end of, move on", into "I can't stop thinking about him. I do stupid things that end up hurting people because my head is so full of him there's no room left for rational thought" then you need to do something about it.'

'Like what?' I asked, terrified she was right, and I'd called Ashley in a subconscious attempt to force who I'd thought was Hillary into behaving in a way that made Mack not want to be with her any more and stay with me instead.

'Move? Or let him move. Seriously, you can't mess with someone's marriage. If they're really making another go of it, you must respect that and keep the hell away.'

'I do respect that. I hate myself for having these feelings. And you don't have to worry. Mack isn't interested in me anyway.'

'Jenny, he went to a stranger's nightmare wedding just to make you feel better.'

'He didn't do anything to indicate he has feelings.'

'Apart from drive you several hundred miles and back, spend the whole time looking out for you, dance with you all night and pay for the whole thing.'

'He was being a friend.'

'Really? Does a friend need to shave off his beard in order to—?'

'POW POW POW POW POW!'

To my huge relief, we were destroyed.

And honestly, if Ellen was even partway right, and my stupid, evil emotions had snuck up and taken control of my rational, moral brain, I might find a way to destroy myself with more than a potato gun.

39

I woke before dawn the next day, wretched and exhausted, unable to eat or go back to sleep. And this, despite the joy of showing Dawson the Hickleton Press email, everyone decamping to a celebratory meal at Scarlett's, and umpteen texts from Sarah and Kiko reassuring me it wasn't that big a deal. I was sick and tired of myself.

The black was hovering, just out of sight at the corner of my vision. It gleefully gobbled up my self-hatred, my doubt, my guilt. And it grew.

I dragged myself through the next couple of weeks, on the one hand glad the Mini had gone, and Mack with it, preventing me from messing things up any more. I hoped he'd gone because the black kept reminding me I deserved to feel terrible. To have lost him. And it was getting louder. Harder to ignore.

But on the other hand, I now lived alone in the forest with the criminals who were trying to force me out still prowling around. I didn't want to think about what their next step would be. I was seriously rattled, flinching at every creak and bang, back to cycling the long way home, locking the door and praying Jamie would soon be free for his very own game of Hunt and Destroy.

I drifted through the motions with the kids. School had finished for the summer, so Will only needed me when prepping timetables or otherwise getting ready for the next school year. I used every last drop of energy on taking care of them, listening, playing, helping, encouraging. Dawson showed me his new Squash Harris character, a woman who lived in the woods and had special powers to take damaged things and make them beautiful and useful again. 'She's the Bester. Because she sees the best deep down and knows how to bring it out. She does it for houses, look.' He flipped the page over. 'And for people, too. She always has brilliant advice to turn bad situations into good ones.'

'She sounds incredible. I love her hair, and her amazing blue eyes. I could do with a bit of advice from the Bester right now.'

'Duh, Jenny!' Dawson goggled at me. 'You'd better look in a mirror, then!'

I buried my head in his hair instead, managing an eight-second hug before he prised himself away.

'Jenny?' he said, as I made to go home that Thursday, looking forward to some peace so keenly I could taste it.

'Yes?' I slipped into my trainers while he hovered on the stairs.

'I'm glad Mum picked you as our childminder. I'm going to miss you when we go on holiday.'

The chunk of my heart not yet submerged in black squeezed. 'Me too.' I winked at him, for want of anything better to say. 'Now go and sort that messy room out before Dad comes home.'

'On second thoughts...'

The day of Lucille's Tough Muck, I strolled to Frances' farm-house across golden fields ripe for harvest, the beaming August sun chasing back the shadows.

'I'll have some of that, please,' I mumbled, as I pushed through the wheat sheaves, not really sure who I was asking. I stopped, briefly, at the farm gate and closed my eyes, feeling the warmth of the glow penetrate my eyelids. Sucked in a deep, deep breath of gentle air and a soft breath of peace kissed my frazzled brow, my knotted jaw. Hope.

'Jenny?'

I opened my eyes to find Frances, leaning heavily on her stick, a few metres away. 'Are you all right?'

I nodded. 'Yes.' And for a brief moment, I truly meant it.

'You look worse,' Frances announced, as we started off towards the Tough Muck location, high in the hills of the Peak District.

'I could say the same to you,' I retorted, with a smile.

'My body, maybe. But look at my eyes. Not while you're driving, please. My soul is strong. Yours is sinking.'

I pretended to concentrate on a tight junction, wary of scraping the sides of the truck.

'Why is your soul flailing, Jenny?'

Could I ignore this until she fell asleep? I guessed not. And there wasn't much point arguing with her, either.

'Probably several reasons.' I sighed. 'Where do you want to start?'

'At the beginning? I always find things less confusing that way.'

'We've only got an hour and a half.'

'Talk quickly, then. Cut straight to the chase.'

'I'm not sleeping very well, since the burglary. And feeling jumpy. I can't decide whether to sell the house, which feels a bit like running away. But isn't running away the most sensible option sometimes? So, instead of starting to redecorate, getting an electrician in and all the other million jobs that need doing whether I'm staying or going, I'm hovering in this limbo of inactivity and indecision.'

'Hmm.' Frances looked dubious.

'I really don't like myself right now.'

'Ah, that's more like it.' Frances perked up at this, which I felt was a rather inappropriate response. But, hey, she could get away with it.

'Why not?'

'I'm making bad choices about how I spend my time, getting nothing done, avoiding making a decision.'

'No. That's not it.'

I spent a mile deciding whether to be annoyed or not.

'Try again,' Frances said.

I thought about it. Not why. I knew why. I thought about whether to tell Frances. 'I'm angry at myself for doing a stupid, selfish thing and hurting a friend. They've moved away, so I don't even know if they forgive me, I can't do anything to make it up to them, and I miss them so much it makes me ill. Which means I feel even worse, because I have no right to miss them like this. I'm a horrible person. And fighting this guilt, trying to ignore the hurt, I feel like I'm going mad.'

'Go on.'

'That terrifies me, because I've only just begun feeling like a person I can live with. I can physically feel it, a black shadow wrapping itself around my heart, my brain, my lungs. Everywhere. Like something off *Doctor Who*. And I'm trying to fight it off, but it's exhausting. I'm so tired. And even now I have amazing friends for the first time ever, I'm still so lonely because the shadow is cutting me off from everything. So, yeah, I hate myself right now.'

Frances handed me a lace handkerchief.

'You need to forgive yourself,' she said quietly. 'Whether Mack forgives you or not is meaningless if you can't forgive yourself. That will help you vanquish the shadows.'

Ur, I didn't remember mentioning Mack...

'But I don't deserve forgiveness,' I said, my voice breaking. 'I did an awful thing, and am still feeling wrong things about Mack. Which makes me think wrong things. How do I stop that? I'm the worst type of person. I hate people like this. I don't want to forgive a person like that.'

'If Sarah told you she'd discovered her HeartBaker friend was married, and she was therefore trying to erase her feelings for him, which she felt dreadful about, but was struggling to do so, would you hate her for it?'

I sighed. 'No.'

'What would you say to her?'

I shrugged. 'I'd probably give her a big hug and tell her that as long as she stayed away from him from now on, she'd be okay.'

'There you are, then.'

'But if I forgive myself, isn't that saying it's all right, what I did?'

Frances laughed. 'No, it is not. It is saying you choose grace, anyway. If what you did is all right, there's no need for forgiveness.'

'I hadn't thought of it like that.' I let that thought wash over me, like a warm sea.

'Precisely.'

* * *

We were the last to arrive. Or so we thought. While we were examining the course map with Sarah, Kiko, Ashley and Ellen in the car park, hoping to find a good spot to cheer Lucille on, a filthy, dented black Jeep pulled up beside Frances' truck.

The Jamie who clambered out looked, if possible, worse than his car. He looked as if he'd already done the Tough Muck. Twice. He had a ripped T-shirt, combat trousers coated with crusting black slime, a bloody bandage over one ear and so many bruises and scrapes we couldn't tell where the tattoos ended and the dirt began.

'Been on holiday, Jamie?' Sarah asked, but the joke couldn't hide her concern.

'Something like that.' He nodded, throwing her a look so intense I'm surprised she didn't burst into flames. 'I hoped to be back in time to clean up, but, well, these bad guys have no consideration for my schedule. Is that a changing room?'

He grabbed a bag from the boot of his car, returning seconds later clean, the bandage replaced with a neat plaster, and wearing running shorts and a fresh T-shirt.

Jamie looked exactly as anyone would have predicted underneath his shirts and jeans. I nudged Sarah, who glanced at me, a smile tweaking at the corner of her mouth to match mine. 'Shut up.'

'Right, Frances. Shall we get going?' Jamie asked.

'We're going here.' Kiko searched the map again. 'The Assassinator.'

'Well, we'll see you there, then, won't we?' Frances crowed, taking off her long coat to reveal a pair of tracksuit bottoms and a fleece. 'We'll give you a wave.'

'What?' Ellen frowned as Frances handed her the coat. 'Aren't you waiting with us?'

'Sitting around watching other people have the time of their life? I don't think so!' she exclaimed, tugging on her hat. 'Come on, if we hurry we can get a good spot near the front of the pack.'

'What on earth are you doing?' Kiko shrieked.

I had a glorious feeling we already knew the answer to that.

'We're conquering the Tough Muck,' Jamie said. 'Hopefully raising some money while we're at it.'

As they reached the mass of runners, Jamie bent down and sort of flipped and lifted Frances onto his back. She let go of his shoulders long enough to send us a queenly wave over the other competitors' heads.

'That woman,' Ellen huffed, wiping her eyes. 'Incorrigible.'

'I hope I'm brave enough to be where she is at her age,' Kiko said.

'I wouldn't mind being there at any age,' Sarah breathed, before turning a shocking shade of red and clasping one hand to her mouth. 'I meant, in the race. Not *there* there. Being bold and not caring what anybody thinks. I did! Honestly! Oh, shut up.'

We laughed all the way to the Assassinator viewing point.

An hour, a flask of tea and a giant flapjack later, we watched the first competitors plop out of a huge pipe and land in a pit of mud. Squelching across to the other side, they then scaled a ten-foot wall using a rope, before carrying on to the next obstacle.

Jamie was one of the first out of the pipe, immediately followed by Frances, who scrabbled onto his back again. He waded to the rope, and pulled himself up and over the wall. With a grown woman on his back.

'Is he ninth at the moment?' Sarah asked, evidently finding it difficult to speak with her mouth hanging so far open.

'Yes.' I nodded.

'If he ran by himself, he'd be first.' Ashley absent-mindedly took another bite of her coconut cookie.

Sarah wrinkled her forehead. 'What kind of man sacrifices the glory of first place to make a crazy woman's dream happen? After rushing here already half beaten-up and looking like he's not slept in days.'

'A man unbothered by his ego,' I answered.

'A *real* man,' Ellen said, looking hard at Sarah. 'With no trace of dud in him.'

'Imagine a man like that.' I couldn't help smirking. 'Good-looking, with a successful business, who also made time for books, cooking, that sort of thing.'

'Likes kids...' Kiko added in a dreamy voice.

'All right, I get it,' Sarah said, loudly. 'A man like that would be perfect. Okay? But not if he didn't like me. Jamie knows I'm looking for a relationship. He clearly isn't feeling it.'

'Lucille!' Kiko shouted, and we raced to the front of the fence, screaming and hollering as she sploshed through the mud.

'How are you doing?' Ellen yelled.

Lucille looked up, gasping. 'I think I might just lie down and sleep in this lovely mud for a bit.'

'Don't you dare!' we hollered back. 'Think of Chris, Toronto and Summer waiting for you at the finish line. Think of the struggle of women everywhere, for thousands of years, fighting against men saying, "You can't do it, just lie down and have a rest, little lady." You didn't lie down and sleep in the middle of your forty-seven-hour labour, did you?'

'I lied,' Lucille cried. 'It was only thirty hours. The first time I went to hospital it was false contractions.'

'Well, you bloody well get up that wall anyway!' Sarah screamed. 'You show 'em, Lucille, all the mums at school who think you're stroppy and snobby and take the mick out of you for going to that phoney college!'

'What?' Lucille froze mid-stride. The man behind bumped into her, sending her headlong into the mud. What emerged a few seconds later was a beast. Teeth bared, arms pumping, Lucille thrashed her way to the wall, grabbed that rope and launched herself over.

'Well, we know what motivates Lucille, then,' Kiko said.

'We'd better get to the finish line.' Ellen headed off with Kiko and Ashley.

'Ahem,' I coughed in Sarah's ear. She jumped so hard she nearly tumbled over the fence into the mud pit. 'Thinking about anything, or should I say one, in particular?'

'Shut up.'

From our vantage point near the finish line, we could see the last obstacle, 'Log It or Lose It'. A spinning log, stretching across a mud pit. The only way out of the pit was swimming through a pitch-black tunnel of freezing cold water. Several runners didn't even bother with the log, plunging straight into the mud and through the tunnel. Most who tried fell at least once, usually more. But we had faith in Jamie. At least, the figure encrusted in mud from head to toe with a woman on his back, powering over the top of the hill and towards the final straight, who we hoped was Jamie.

As they approached Log It or Lose It, Frances slithered off his back, the only competitor still mud-free from the shoulders up; Jamie must have done something spectacular to get her this far with her head above water.

They appeared to be having a brief argument, Frances folding her arms and Jamie eventually shaking his head before turning his back on her and sprinting over the log, carrying on until he crossed the line in sixteenth place. Not that anybody was there to congratulate him. The eyes of every spectator were locked on the old woman tucking a loose strand of hair behind her ears before hurling herself onto the log.

She nearly made it, too, but halfway across she slipped and went in. The crowd went berserk, hollering and cheering and whistling as she staggered upright, thigh deep in the mud.

Holding her hands above her head in a dripping thumbs-up, Frances ploughed on towards the tunnel. The cheers faded as she disappeared inside and every single person seemed to be holding their breath.

'It's ten metres,' Ashley muttered. 'Can she even swim any more? She's going to drown. Or freeze. Or else her heart will give out. Shittlesticks, Frances. What the hell were you thinking?'

'What the hell was Jamie thinking, more like?' Sarah sobbed. 'We all know Frances is bats, but Jamie should know better. How could he abandon her right at the end?'

It felt like forever. The crowd began to fidget and mutter.

Three more competitors came charging down the hill and across the logs.

'How long until someone goes in to get her out?' Kiko asked. 'They must have rules. Did the race officials even see her go in?'

I grabbed onto Sarah, our hands trembling together.

Still we waited. How long had it been? Five minutes? Six? It felt like ten times that long.

'Jamie,' Ellen breathed as he jogged back towards the tunnel exit, crouching down to look inside. A tiny hand poked out of the rim of the tunnel and batted his away.

The people around us began to buzz as another hand joined it, soon followed by an arm.

'The tunnel's deep,' someone said. 'You have to pull yourself up as well as out.'

My heart was jammed somewhere in my windpipe. We clung to each other, praying for our friend.

'Jamie's there, it's fine,' Sarah repeated over and over. 'He'll not let anything happen to her.'

Frances was dying. Her own cells were turning on her, wreaking destruction and chaos. She had appeared so frail in recent weeks, as though a fit of coughing could shatter her into pieces. But we had underestimated quite how a stubborn mind, unshakable spirit and three decades of hauling haybales, sledgehammering fence posts and dealing with unruly cows could overrule a disease, telling it, 'No, you can't, and don't you dare.'

Like Lazarus from the tomb, Frances groped and fumbled and would not quit until she lay in a brown muddy heap on solid ground.

'He's *got* to carry her now,' Kiko said.

Or not, apparently. Jamie bent down, one hand on

Frances' back, hopefully checking she was still breathing, then waited another endless three minutes until she hauled herself first onto all fours, and then upright.

'Come on, Jamie,' Ellen urged. 'At least take the woman's arm. Hold her hand.'

But no. Jamie walked with Frances, didn't take his eyes off her, but didn't offer so much as a finger as she hobbled, shuffled, dragged and carried the proud body that had taken her through a lifetime of challenges and adventures over the finish line, Lucille careening past a few seconds later.

I was too darn relieved to be crying. But I might have been the only one who wasn't.

We hurried over, wrapping Frances in a blanket along with so many hugs she grew irritated and ordered us to stop. 'Well, I *would* say I told you so.' She smirked. 'But it isn't very gracious.'

'Frances, you nearly gave us a stroke,' Ashley cried.

'Well, you should have more faith, then.'

'Is that it, now?' Ellen asked. 'Are you finally done with all these challenges?'

Frances tried to pull up a corner of the blanket to wipe a streak of mud off her cheek, but her arm couldn't quite manage it. Ellen gently patted her face clean with a tissue, taking hold of Frances' hand when she'd finished.

Frances closed her eyes. 'Yes. Just one adventure left. The big one I've been waiting for. I'm ready.'

40

With Frances safely in bed, I hurried back through the woods to the Common, where the rest of the club were enjoying a post-Muck celebration.

Sarah dragged me into the kitchen the second I arrived. 'I don't know what to do. I'm totally freaking out. I can't even *look* at him. How did I never clock how hot he was before?'

'Maybe it was the shorts?'

'No! Not his looks! Him carrying Frances round that course was about the sexiest thing I've ever seen.' Her eyes grew round. 'He's lovely!'

'There's no need to look so horrified about it.'

'But I feel really we-e-e-eird.' She buried her head on my shoulder. 'We're friends now. What if I say something stupid and ruin it?'

'I genuinely think that's impossible.'

'What if I go on a date with Jamie and then HeartBaker comes back with a brilliant explanation and I have to choose between them?'

'Who would you choose?'

She groaned. 'I dunno.'

'Well, you need to decide. Jamie deserves better than you dating him with one eye on your inbox.'

'ARGH!' She picked up a wooden spoon and threw it across the kitchen where it clattered into a tower of saucepans. Three seconds later Jamie burst in.

'Everything okay?'

Sarah gaped. They both turned red in sync, which looked so cute it was ridiculous.

'Um, actually, Sarah, I wanted to talk to you.' Jamie stuck his hands in his jean pockets. I would have sidled out but he was blocking the doorway.

'Ungh?' she mumbled.

'It's about HeartBaker.' I'd seen Jamie pretty sheepish more than once over the past few months. Today he looked at risk of being roasted and gobbled down with mint sauce.

'What?' Sarah grabbed the counter behind her. 'You didn't hunt him down, did you? Is that why he stood me up? Have you done something to him? And all this time I thought he was a selfish, lying slime-ball.'

'No!' Jamie looked horrified. 'I don't know what you think it is I do, but I don't hurt people. Well, unless strictly necessary to avoid other people being hurt... Anyway, no! And he'd *tried* to get in touch with you. He was mostly in areas with no signal. Underground. Out at sea. Places like that. When he left, there was no time to explain and he thought he'd be able to let you know later on, but things kicked off a lot quicker than planned, he was kind of... ambushed. And he'd have walked away, left someone else to deal with it, put you above his work but there was a kid. A boy. And he thought, if this was Edison, Sarah would want him to get her boy back. *HeartBaker* would do anything to get him back. And if he walked away from that, just to find a phone signal so he could call and cancel a date, or explain why he didn't turn up, he wouldn't be good enough for you anyway.'

'Urrr, just to be clear, we are talking about *you* here, aren't we?' Sarah asked.

Jamie took a breath so deep I thought his T-shirt would burst open.

'You are HeartBaker.'

He nodded.

'Okay. I will have many, many questions about that later, and you'd better have some damn good answers. For now, get over here and kiss me.'

If it had been possible to squeeze myself into one of the cupboards, believe me, I would have. Instead, trapped behind both Sarah and Jamie, who I was fairly sure were oblivious to my presence in the kitchen, I opted for wedging myself into the corner of the room. Yes, it would have been tactful to turn my head to the wall, but I'm ashamed to say I peeped, as Jamie took three strides over to Sarah, gently cradled her head in his hands and looked in her eyes for a full minute, before slowly, so slowly I nearly shouted, 'Oh, for goodness' sake, get on with it!', he pressed his lips to hers.

* * *

I spent the next few weeks working hard at forgiving myself for what was, in the grand scheme of things, hardly worth having a nervous breakdown over. Talking it through with my friends helped. Getting my mind off my own problems and onto other things helped too. Watching Sarah trying to play down how increasingly potty she was about Jamie was delightful. Kiko and Adam took the girls to Japan, and started a weekly date night. She was considering going back to work part-time, once she'd figured out what she wanted to do.

'Nothing in an office.' She shuddered as we gathered round a picnic bench on the Common on the last weekend of the holidays. She winced as Lily let out an ear-piercing scream in response to Edison and Jonno waving their muddy sticks too close to her face. 'Or with children.'

'There's a healthcare assistant's job going in the maternity ward,' Ellen said, after instructing the boys to play somewhere else.

Kiko took a sip of coffee. 'I'd quite like to be a taxi-driver.'

'A *what*?' Sarah goggled. 'Ferrying drunks home from town at all hours of the morning? Have you lost the plot?'

'I wouldn't mind making sure people got home safely. I'm used to having hardly any sleep. But, I was thinking more of providing an alternative to Tezza,' Kiko said. 'Now the bus services are being cut again there must be plenty of older people needing help with their shopping. Tourists who'd pay good money to access the local attractions accompanied by fascinating facts about the forest. Service with a smile, for a change.'

'Tezza would be so furious,' Ellen said.

'Do it,' Sarah added, grinning.

'I'm looking into it. But Adam's back to work in a few weeks, so I'll need to find some child-care. If only I knew someone amazing at looking after kids. Someone local, flexible, gorgeous...'

'Maddie would be over the moon to have more girls in the house,' Ellen said, looking at me. 'And you could get a lot more decorating done with the extra income.'

'I could,' I mused. 'Except, I'm considering my own career change. I love looking after your kids. And that job has saved my life in more ways than one. I hate to leave you in the lurch, but I've been wondering about whether I could hack it as a teaching assistant.'

'Yes!' Sarah said, banging her mug down on the table. 'Yes, you could. I'd pay you myself to assist teaching Edison.'

Ellen beamed. 'Talk to Will about it. He'd love to help.'

* * *

A fortnight into the new term, after stuffing three filthy PE kits in the washing machine, texting Dawson to say that, yes, he could stay at Lily's house for tea, and agreeing that, yes, the triplets could build a teddy cannon as long as no teddies were hurt in the process, I answered a sharp rap at the door.

'Grandpa!' the boys whispered, before promptly disappearing upstairs.

Great. I'd heard nothing, from either Jamie or Brenda, about the possible culprit behind the intimidation tactics at the house, and with no further incidents I'd finally managed to stop jumping at every creak or bang. But I hadn't been able to shake my suspicions about Fisher.

'Ellen won't be back for an hour,' I said.

'That's not a problem,' he replied, slithering past me into the hallway and dumping his briefcase at the bottom of the stairs. 'I can wait.'

Not a problem for whom? I chuntered to myself, following him into the kitchen.

'I'll have a coffee,' he said, sitting down at the table.

'Grandpa, you have to say please or Jenny won't let you have one,' a lion growled as it crawled into the room. ''S rude not to.'

'Oh, I'm sure Grandpa just forgot.' I flicked on the coffee machine.

'Because old people forget things,' the lion rumbled, stalking round the table. 'It's cos more cells in their brains are getting dead every day.'

'Um, I don't think that's quite how it is.' I handed Fisher his coffee, pouring another one for myself, half wishing I could add a splosh of something to ease my nerves.

'I heard your neighbour has moved on.' He shook his head, smiling. 'Things go from bad to worse out there in the woods for you. One disaster after another.'

I gave the lion now clinging to my ankle a pat on the head. 'I'd hardly call Mack not being around a disaster.' A horrible thought crashed into my head. 'Have you bought his house?'

'Why?' Fisher sat up then, nearly spilling his coffee. 'Is it back on the market?'

It was my turn to be surprised. 'Was it ever off the market?' *What?* Had Mack changed his mind and decided not to sell? What did that mean?

Fisher sat back in his chair. 'So, what about you? Still determined to hang onto that money-pit? I hope you've had it rewired. A primary cause of domestic fires, dodgy wiring. We wouldn't want a tragedy, now, would we?'

Before I managed to work out whether I'd been threatened, a loud roar erupted from the top of the stairs followed by what sounded like several elbows, knees and heads crashing down to the bottom.

By the time order had been restored, Fisher had scooped up his briefcase and gone. The unpleasant disturbance in the atmosphere, however, lingered. I went to rejoin Hamish,

Jonno and the lion, now nursing their bruises in front of a DVD.

'Can I have Gummy?' Jonno asked, face peeping out of a blanket.

'Where is he?' I asked, scanning the living room.

'We shooted him out of the cannon.'

I trotted upstairs, poking my head in on Maddie to remind her it was homework time, before bracing myself to enter the pit of mess the triplets called their bedroom. Searching through the dressing-up clothes and piles of stuffed animals, I eventually spotted a pair of bunny ears under the bunk bed. As I got onto my hands and knees to reach it, my eyes landed on a thin green plastic folder. Thinking it looked more like something belonging in Will's filing cabinet than a little boy's bedroom, I pulled it out and flicked it open.

Gummy forgotten, I sat back against the bed and started to read.

41

When Ellen arrived home a few minutes later I briefly filled her in on the day's events and cycled home as fast as my shaking legs could pedal me.

Unable to even think about eating, I studied the folder again. I was desperate to knock on Mack's door and show this to him. If he wasn't selling the house, this affected him too.

Should I call? Send a text?

I needed to know what to do, but there was no way I could talk to my other friends about it.

After work next morning, bleary-eyed, head pounding, I washed down some painkillers with a swig of scalding tea and spent the day on my laptop, researching Fisher's company and recent land acquisitions, then searching images of him at local events and press releases, trying to spot him with the phoney inspector.

By three-thirty, the headache had been replaced with information so red-hot I needed oven gloves to scratch my forehead. I was still deciding what to do when Will arrived home.

'Jenny! I've brought some leaflets and things you'll find useful. And Ellen said you might be interested in work experience? Don't worry about dinner – there's pizza in the freezer.'

Over the next hour Will patiently answered my questions, talked to me about different options for becoming a teaching assistant and, most important of all, poured encouragement and optimism all over my decision. Will was a crazily busy man. On top of running a school and being a husband and father of five children, he'd found the time to dig out all this information for me.

And I'd spent the day searching for incriminating evidence against his father-in-law.

I had to tell him, before my guts twisted up to the point of no return.

'I found a folder in the boys' room yesterday. Fisher had left his briefcase on the stairs, and Hamish admitted taking the folder to see if it was a treasure map. He wasn't completely wrong. It actually contains plans to build a giant leisure complex in the forest.'

Will leant back on the sofa. 'Yeah, he had this idea a few years ago to convert the campsite by Hatherstone Hall – by Scarlett's – into an upmarket eco-holiday village thing. Ellen's sister, Erica, was going to run it. But he needed some Hall land, and they weren't interested in selling.'

'These plans were for the area to the west and south of the Common.'

Will frowned. 'I remember that land going up for sale a year or so ago. But nothing ever happened so I guess we all forgot about it.'

'Fisher bought it.'

'To build a holiday village? Wouldn't he have to apply for

planning permission? Have a consultation with the parish council or something?'

'The main problem is access. According to the folder, he can't submit a proposal until he has a way to get people in and out. The Common is protected land, so that's a no-go, and the northern boundary is all Frances' farmland, no public roads. South and west, there's the river and the nature reserve.'

'Looks like he's made a bad business decision, then. No wonder he's been so grumpy lately.'

'There is one solution.'

Will waited, realising we were about to get to the point.

'He could use the private road leading up to my cottage, and build the entrance to the resort there.'

'How would that work?'

'Ownership of the road is tied up with the cottages. And there are clauses preventing it being used as access for a business, so even if Mack and I didn't mind visitors driving up and down all hours, even if he didn't have to route the road through my garden, bulldozing my shed and cutting through a public footpath, *even if* we didn't mind eco-lodges and a restaurant, a pool and spa, staff buildings and a shopping complex being built right on our doorstep, *if* we wanted to agree to all this in return for generous compensation, we simply couldn't.

'But the thing is, if *someone else* bought the houses, and those clauses were to mysteriously disappear, given that no one else is likely to know about or protest against them, well, who knows?'

Will digested this for a couple of minutes. 'There'd be way too many objections and issues for a development that big here.'

'The folder has a list of people, or businesses and organisations, likely to object. Along with how Fisher plans to persuade them, if necessary. I have to say it does also have a very compelling case about the boost to the local economy and jobs market, the fact that the whole development would be eco-friendly, carbon neutral, offset by some very generous donations in the right places.'

'I always knew he was a toad.' Will shook his head. Helped himself to a biscuit.

'I was on the list.'

'What?' Will looked up. 'Of course – he has to buy your cottage before he can even get started. *And* Mack's.'

Hands numb, I opened the folder to the list of names. Next to *Jenny Birkenshaw,* in neat black font, someone had typed 'money – should buy off at reasonable price. Building regs, red tape, intimidation. Fire?'

Below it was the name *Mackenzie West.* Beside his name, underlined, it said, 'WIFE'.

The front door slammed. Ellen was home. I wiped clammy hands on my jeans. Six months ago, I would have run at this point. But my time with the Camerons had taught me that they did things differently. 'I'll check on the kids, put the pizzas in the oven.'

I forced down half a slice of pizza while the kids chattered to their dad about the teddy cannon, Dawson's newfound interest in manga, thanks to a certain girl at art club, and the latest research findings in astrobiology. Mummy was tired and needed a rest, so had permission to skip dinner.

Mummy looked even worse than I felt.

'Don't!' She pointed at me, uncurling herself from the armchair in the tiny study. 'Don't you dare cry. If you set me off I'll not be able to do this.'

I sank into the spinny office chair. 'Do what?'

She rolled her eyes up to the ceiling. 'Speak to Brenda.'

'You're calling the police?' The tears, jostling at my eyelids, evaporated.

'It's the right thing to do.' Will came in, carrying three mugs of coffee.

'Are you talking to your dad first?' I asked.

Ellen shook her head. 'It'll only give him time to figure out a way to wriggle out of it. If he's broken the law, paid people to vandalise your house and smash up your stuff and... and frighten you and hurt you, if he is really planning to set your house on fire...' She shook her head again, harder this time, as her voice gave way.

Will sat on the edge of the chair and took her hand. 'We don't think this is the first time he's crossed a line to get what he wants. It's the first time we've been sure, and it's far worse than anything we suspected, but, well, we can't turn a blind eye to this.'

'I don't want to!' Ellen cried. 'I always knew he could be ruthless and mean. But *this*? This is monstrous. No wonder Mum left. This is probably why she barely contacts us, because she's all tangled up in his mess and doesn't know what to do about it.'

In the end, Ellen only got as far as arranging to see Brenda in the morning. She drove me home afterwards as steadily as if it were her driving test.

'I'm *so* sorry,' I said as we arrived at the front of my house.

Ellen turned off the engine. 'You'd better not be apologising for my father running a campaign of terror against you.'

'I'm not. I'm expressing my sorrow that it happened. I can't imagine how hard this must be.'

She wiped a strand of hair off her forehead. 'Like I said, I'm not massively surprised. But, yeah, it's still horrible. And I know the next few days, probably months, maybe years, are going to be horrible too. I can't even *think* about how I'm going to tell my sister. And if he ends up going to prison... how do I explain that to the kids?'

'I can't imagine he'll go to prison.' My voice squeaked in alarm. 'He didn't hurt anybody.'

'Maybe not physically.' Ellen looked at me pointedly. 'And who knows what else he's done on that list of grubby threats? Is it any better if you've paid someone else to commit your crimes?'

She sighed. 'Either way, we'd better try and get a good night's sleep before the volcano blows. I won't be going in tomorrow, so you can take the day off.'

'You'll keep me posted?'

'Of course.' She leant over and kissed me on the cheek. 'If you need anything. And by need anything, I really mean if you get scared, or sad, and want to talk, call me. Don't worry if it's the middle of the night. Most likely I'll be awake.'

I whispered it again: 'I am so sorry.'

'Me too. Now get inside before Will starts to worry we've gone to tackle Dad ourselves, Squash Harris style.'

I didn't call Ellen that night, when the fear and worry crept inside my head to dance with the darkness.

I didn't call my friend when I choked on the self-pity. Self-pity, and anger, at once again being the victim, a mere irritant to be trampled underfoot while others strode onwards to success.

I called a different number. Three times, hitting the end call button as soon as the phone started ringing.

I turned my face to the wall, and imagined him there,

lying parallel to me, only a layer of brick and plaster between us, and I talked at the non-existent Mack until my throat grew hoarse, the streaks on my cheeks dried up, my eyes closed, and I passed over into blessed nothingness.

* * *

It didn't take long for the scandal to break. Three days after Ellen and I, and a whole load of other people, spoke to the police, Charlotte Meadows' jewellery, Jamie's oven and the old record player appeared in my living room. Having been working on teaching assistant applications in my kitchen at the time, rather than feeling spooked by the impressively quick and impossibly quiet delivery, I tapped off a quick message to Jamie saying thanks.

Later, I found out he'd discovered them in Tezza's garage. For some reason, Tezza never reported Jamie breaking in. But I did hear he had nightmares for months afterwards.

And, according to Sarah, the mystery of the Beast of Middlebeck was now solved, thanks to Jamie's undisclosed interrogation techniques. I seethed at the knowledge that I'd actually paid the Beast of Middlebeck to use his taxi service, in order to avoid encountering that very same beast. Thinking about him coming face to face with Jamie at crazy-o'clock helped, as did the fact that he'd been so easily dissuaded from repeating the performance after Brenda had made it clear she was keeping an eye on things. Knowing that no one in the village would be using Tezza's taxi ever again helped more.

In the midst of this whirlwind, caring for extra-excitable and anxious children four days a week, volunteering with the formidable Year Fives of Middlebeck Primary, stripping wallpaper, bartering with electricians and plumbers, coaxing soup into my agonisingly frail friend – in the midst of all this, like a pathetic, pointless soundtrack on a loop in the background, my heart ached for Mack.

I repeatedly beat myself over the head with the truth that Mack being gone was a good thing. He was not mine to miss, or want, or love. Obviously the best thing was for him to go and enjoy his life with his wife, and leave me to get over it.

I even let Sarah and Kiko sign me up on the Lovelife! dating app, spending a couple of half-hearted evenings flicking through profiles looking for men with eyes like hot chocolate and furrowed brows.

But how did you stop loving the person you loved, when, as far as you knew, they were still lovely?

I learnt there were good days, when the ache was nothing but a faint buzzing in the background. And other, not quite as good days, when it felt as if a lung were missing.

On a particularly not-so-good day at the end of October, I sent him a text:

Hi Mack. I hope you and Sienna are doing well. I have a dry-rot specialist coming on Friday. He asked if okay to check out your side too. Is it? Does someone have a key to let him in? Maybe the estate agent? Best wishes, Jenny

I pressed *send*, pressed the other hand to my galloping heart, closed my eyes and counted to ten and strolled, fake-it-till-you-make-it casual, into the kitchen to find some empty calories to distract me.

Right on time to see the genuine Hillary Mackenzie West wiping his feet on my welcome mat.

42

We stared at each other for what seemed like a long time but nowhere near enough. Drops of rain meandered down the side of his face and hair. He wore his old jacket. New jeans. No beard.

I twiddled my perfectly adjusted glasses. Hoped he couldn't tell that my skin was sparking like a poked bonfire, my throat swollen with all the jokes and the questions and the stories I'd whispered at the wall, longing to finally reach the man they were meant for.

'Hi,' he said, pushing his hands into his pockets.

'Hi.'

'I got your message,' he said, still holding my gaze like an eyeball magnet.

'Quick response,' I managed to squeeze out.

'Yeah, I was on my way round anyway. To let you know I'm back.'

'You're back.' *Wow, well deduced, Jenny.*

'Yeah, and I'll be in working – writing – on Friday, so, the dry-rot guy can call in whenever.'

'Thanks.'

'Right. Well. I've got unpacking to do, so—'

'I was about to make tea. If you want one,' I gabbled, while my conscience shook its head in disapproval, wagging a finger at me.

'That'd be great,' Mack said, before I had a chance to take it back.

'And Sienna, would she like one? Is she... here?'

Mack frowned, finally taking one hand out of his pocket and wiping the remains of the rain from his hair and face. 'No.'

'Oh.' I poked at my glasses again. Still perfectly positioned. Tried to mentally will the excess blood to retreat from my face and neck.

Mack filled the kettle. Lifted two mugs from the dresser and plopped a teabag in each one.

Then he stood facing the counter for a few seconds before turning to look at me.

'Sienna is no longer my wife.'

I nearly choked on my own tonsils. Which, it turned out, sounded a lot like a giraffe retching. Mack poured the hot water, dunked the teabags and dropped them in the bin. Sploshed in some milk and pulled out a chair for me to sit on.

I was now recovered.

'That seems fast. I thought divorces took time.'

Mack sat opposite me. 'She started the process over a year ago.'

I frowned. 'But she invited you to London.'

He grimaced. 'She invited me to reveal up close and personal how irredeemably over our marriage was. And, spending time with her and her swanky new bloke, seeing the woman she's chosen to become, for the first time I thought that was probably for the best. The weekend visits were to supervise the house sale. She didn't trust me to squeeze out maximum profit.'

'I'm sorry.' And in that moment, I really was. 'I know it's not what you wanted.'

It was Mack's turn to flush. 'Well. It had become harder not to want that. Which may be why I held on longer than I should. The guilt of being offered an easy way out. I didn't want to break our vows, but I realised she'd already destroyed them. I watched Sienna with this smarmy fool and knew she'd never loved me. Not really. I'd probably have tried again, anyway, if she'd asked. Found a way to make it work. But I discovered in London that we didn't even like each other any more. So, out of respect I agreed to sell the house, so she could make a clean break.'

'Wow.' *Wow. WOW! Information overload... systems in danger of overheating... Mack does not love or even like Sienna...*

'Why didn't you *tell* me?' I knew this wasn't about me, or even about us, but, really, had all the jumbled emotions of the past few months – the guilt, the embarrassment, confusion and hurt – been for nothing?

Mack looked down, his face blank.

'All this time I thought you were back with her. Then you disappear, and I assume you've moved in together, and you hate me for blowing your cover. I blamed myself for forcing you away.'

'Why would you think you forced me away?'

'Uh, because you didn't even say goodbye?' I was nearly shouting now.

Mack looked at me, dark eyes serious. 'I'm genuinely

sorry about that. Really, I should have said goodbye. But right then, I *was* angry. About a lot of things. Mainly what a total failure I'd become. And I guess some of that got turned on you. I've been a lousy friend.'

'Mack, we *aren't* friends! Friends don't spend all that time with each other and not share the biggest things going on in their life. That whole Ashley thing would never have happened if you'd trusted me enough to tell me who you were. Let alone what you were going through. You didn't have to tell me, it's none of my business, but don't then pretend we're friends.'

'I'm sorry.' He ran one hand over his head, agitated. His hair was shorter. It suited him, drew attention to his eyes. Not that I noticed or cared, of course.

'I feel like a complete idiot.' I sounded like one too, raspy and overwrought.

Mack took a deep breath. 'I didn't tell you because I needed time. To process, and work through it. To grieve for my marriage. To start to heal.'

'This is what I'm talking about! Friends help each other through these things. You've seen me at my worst, in a dozen different messed-up, humiliating situations. Friends are honest. They don't hide what's really going on.'

'That is *not* what I was doing.' Mack's voice was calm, but his eyes were blazing. 'I didn't tell you, because I didn't trust—'

'You didn't trust me!' I cried. 'That's the whole point!'

'I didn't tell you because I didn't trust *myself*!' He stood up, the chair scraping across the floor with a howl.

'What the hell is that supposed to mean?' I asked, the words vibrating through the tension in the kitchen.

'I was a wreck, Jenny. I didn't want to hurt you. To start something I couldn't handle. It was easier to hide how I felt, let you think I was married. It gave me time to figure out whether the feelings were real. I care about you too much to risk making you my rebound.'

I was so pathetic that even as my rage swirled my heart skipped at the news that Mack had feelings for me, whatever they might be.

'Right, and you needed to pretend you're with her, to prevent us "starting something"? Possibly a tad presumptuous, considering how many times I've stated I'm not interested in a relationship right now. Never mind a relationship with you.'

Mack reared back as if I'd slapped him. 'Right.' He scowled. 'I must have imagined it.'

'I will not have another man make a fool out of me. You did this to avoid hurting me? Well, newsflash: I've been hurting since you left.'

I shook my head, the anger leaking out of me like a popped balloon, leaving only a mountain of sadness. I closed my eyes. 'I think you'd better go now, please.'

When I opened them again, he'd gone.

* * *

The following evening, I sprawled on Sarah's sofa, stuffing crostini into my mouth and waiting to hear her verdict.

'You need to bake him another cake,' she pronounced.

I sat up, nearly choking on a chunk of feta cheese. 'What?'

'A good one. Maybe dinner, too.'

'What are you talking about?' I asked. 'He lied about

being married, then disappeared without saying goodbye, leaving me thinking he never wanted to speak to me again.'

'And he admitted he was a total mess. Not thinking straight. And he didn't know that you'd been harbouring all these lust-ridden, guilty feelings.'

'Ur, he seemed pretty confident in how I felt.'

'Maybe when you get used to keeping massive secrets, it kind of becomes a habit. Like his armour. After being hurt and rejected by Sienna, he spent all that time alone, lost in his own thoughts. Yeah, he should have told you, but he thought he was doing the honourable thing by not doing that.' She pointed a piece of bread at me. 'The question is, do you want to be friends with Mack again? Or more than friends? In which case you need to firstly forgive him, then secondly tell him how you feel and what you want.'

'I don't know what I want.'

'Well, duck, you'd best figure that out, then, hadn't you?'

* * *

Bones rattling, I stood on the doorstep and racked my brain for a way to apologise. But when he opened the door, Mack jumped straight in with, 'I'm sorry.'

'I'm sorrier.'

That made him smile. 'Peace-offering?'

'White chocolate and raspberry brownies.'

'You'd better come in.'

In the end, we sat outside in the autumn sunshine, watching the squirrels scamper after nuts as we sipped coffee and eased back into each other's company with neutral topics like the progress on the house. Eventually, emboldened by laughter and the warmth of good conversation, I tested things a little further.

'If you weren't with Sienna, where have you been all this time?'

Mack thought for a minute, running a hand over his missing beard. 'I thought I couldn't write any more because I'd realised love was a load of crap that brought nothing but pain and disappointment, and that people can't be trusted. So, I went home.'

'You went home?' Goodness, my witty repartee knew no bounds this morning.

'To my parents. Whom I love. And who have always loved me, unconditionally. And I let them love me, in all the best ways. I watched them love each other. I visited my sisters and their kids, ate chips and threw a Frisbee and had tickle fights. I remembered what love was. And I started writing.'

'That's so great.' It was so great I hardly even cared that it was his family who'd reminded him what love was, not the weird woman next door.

'And once I'd started, well, I couldn't stop. So, I finally had something worth sending to my publisher. And they liked it. Enough for me to buy out Sienna's half of the house. Which means I'm back. For the first time in nearly six years. I'm back.'

'Return of the Mack.' I toasted him with the dregs of my coffee. 'Welcome home.'

He smiled so hard, it reached every corner of his face.

'Right, well. I've a deadline to meet. And this time I actually mean it. I'd best get back to work. It's really good to see you, Jenny.'

'You too.'

Cue gigantic, enormously awkward pause. *You too? Snap out of it, woman and find something to say!*

'Don't forget to let the rot guy in on Friday. No grumpy "get orf my land, I'm busy writing my next bestseller and the creative flow cannot be disturbed".'

'Yeah, yeah. And in the meantime I'll be listening out for your next disaster.'

43

What with one thing and another, it was soon December, and the book club Christmas party. Although, with the challenges now complete, we would be reverting to being a boring old temper-fizzing, insult hurling, food-throwing book club.

My third Christmas of the year was looking to be the best yet. I had joined the Camerons on their annual trip to fetch a tree straight from the forest, smothering it in gluey, glittery stars and recycled paper chains. I had clapped until my hands were sore at their church nativity, giving an extra cheer for the three mini-warrior angels despite their inability to resist performing an unscripted fight scene. I had helped write dozens of Christmas cards for Maddie's class postbox, and dropped off a nervous but excited Dawson at his school Christmas disco. I had also joined Ellen in distributing food hampers and gift boxes for vulnerable families and those with no family to speak of whatsoever. It meant more than I could say that, by some miracle, my Christmas would be spent with a family like this one.

Frances was in hospital, due to what she called 'pesky

stomach mischief', and what we called three days of uncontrollable vomiting. To Edison's delight, Florence moved into The Common Café, where the attentions of a small boy would hopefully ease the pain of missing her owner.

'Must be getting a little crowded upstairs,' Lucille remarked, as we lounged on the café's sofas, clustered around the crackling fire, red and white Scandi-style bunting hung along the mantelpiece. 'First Jamie, now a dog.'

Jamie levelled his gaze at her, no less serious even when topped off with a pair of antlers. 'On the rare occasions I make it upstairs, we all fit in just fine.'

'You've not moved in, then?'

'Not until we're married.'

'You're getting married?' Ashley blurted, nearly toppling backwards out of her chair into the bushy tree, which had been covered in baubles made out of miniature Christmas jumpers.

'First I've heard of it,' Sarah said, standing frozen stiff with a tray of mulled wine.

Jamie shrugged. 'I told you, I'm not staying over without Edison knowing it's permanent.'

'I thought the answer to that was that you didn't stay over.' The glasses on the tray rattled. 'Is this a proposal? Because you could've picked a better time, like when I'm not wearing a snowman apron and I've had time to get my roots done.'

Jamie calmly took the tray from her and placed it on the table. He'd come a long way since the Tough Muck. 'I'm not proposing now. But when I do, I won't give a crap what you're wearing or what your hair's like. And I'll be doing it with your son present, not a load of gawkers. Okay?'

He waited, ever patient, while Sarah summoned up the ability to reply. 'Okay.'

'Hurry up, Jamie.' Ashley took a glass, the ends of her tinsel hairband dangling dangerously close to the winter-spice candle centrepiece. 'You don't want to keep a woman waiting too long.'

'It's been four months!' Sarah blustered, fooling no one.

'Well, moving on from Jamie and Sarah's personal business,' Ellen said, 'we have a book-club timetable to plan.'

'Here we go.' Jamie grimaced, grabbing a handful of nuts.

'And before *that*,' Ellen replied, ignoring him, 'I have a letter to read. From our absent member.' She unfolded the letter, cleared her throat, and read:

"I wanted to say this in person, but the despicable cancer has been up to its tricks again. However, Ellen has promised to write this down and read it to you later, so listen up:

Thank you.

Thank you for what you have done, and how you have done it.

Thank you for not treating me like a doddery old woman but a friend who still has a functioning brain, albeit a little foggier than before.

Thank you for listening as you wiped my face and laughing as you helped me balance on the loo.

Thank you for still telling me your troubles, and your silly little stories while warming my soup and dabbing cream on my sores. The ups and downs of your days may seem small in comparison to mine. But they are not. They are light in a ferociously vast darkness.

You have all been a light to me. Your kindness. Your time. Your respect.

I am not afraid of dying, as you know. But I have at times been terribly afraid of what it may entail.

I am a little less afraid of that now. Because God has sent me an army of angels.

I hope you have all learnt something these past few months. Something important. About yourselves. About each other. About what matters.

This is what I have learnt: my adventures were fun. Exciting. But fun and excitement is fleeting. What lasts, what matters, are the people you get to share your adventures with, talk and laugh about them with. The people who will remind you of the beautiful moments when your bones are screaming and your throat is raw and you are so tired and frustrated and blooming well peed-off you can't bear another second in your own body. The people who can turn the light on. It is the people we love – and, if you haven't figured it out, I love you all like the children I never had.

I hope you keep sharing your stories, and learning from them. I hope you remember this year, and your batty old friend, when you are eighty-five and life can seem more of a burden than a gift. This is nearly the end of my story – this chapter at least. Thank you for being part of it. Now, you can get on with arguing which book you'll be reading next. What a relief Hillary West has writer's block so you won't have to listen to Ashley whinging on about reading his for a good long while. And please don't forget to give Florence a piece of cake. Two pieces – she can have mine.

May all your days be merry and bright,

Frances."'

Florence poked her nose above the tablecloth at the mention of her name, tongue out expectantly.

'Cinnamon or pumpkin spice?' Sarah rubbed her silken ears. 'One of each? Go on, then, if your mistress says so.'

We opened our cheap, cheerful and downright cheesy secret Santa gifts, ate and talked, laughed and sang along to 'White Christmas', hoping our old friend wasn't too uncomfortable or lonely, even as we went through our diaries and promised to do what we could to help her last days be merry and bright, too.

Around nine o'clock, Ellen made another attempt to get us back onto books.

'Ashley, are you quite all right?' she asked, a snippet of irritation creeping in as Ashley, increasingly fidgety and distracted, twisted to peer out of the bunting-covered window for the tenth time in a minute.

'Yes. I just thought... I'm... no. Actually, I wanted to... no. No. It's nothing. Please, carry on.' She shuffled her chair back, and stuck on an expectant smile.

'Right. If everybody's ready, I've no idea where we are with the rota, so—'

'Yes!' Ashley shouted, having been unable to resist one last peek. 'Yes. Thank goodness. I thought he'd stood me up.'

'You have a *date*?' Lucille sniggered. 'And you invited him *here*?'

That had better not be her date, I thought in a rush of startling aggressiveness, as he opened the café door with a blast of icy air and stepped in, stomping his boots on the mat.

Ashley let out a stream of high-pitched giggles, her Santa earrings swinging. 'Of course it's not a date.' She pressed a hand to her flushing chest. 'It's the completion of my challenge. Finding Hillary West was only the first bit. If you remember, getting her – *him* – along to the book club was the end goal.'

'How could we forget?' Lucille muttered, but she winked at Ashley as she did.

Kiko got up and dragged a chair over as our guest author joined us, greeted by Ashley flapping about as he unwrapped his scarf and tugged off a chunky bobble hat.

'I'm so glad you came!' she squawked.

'Glad to be here.' He didn't especially look it. 'Sorry I'm late. I tend to get submerged when I'm reaching the end of a book and lose all track of time.'

I'd seen him a few more times since his return, but so fleetingly it was nearly as bad as him not being here. When our paths had crossed – in the café morning-coffee queue, my advance apologies for noisy workmen, another bonfire, and one evening when he'd ended up staying for a curry – Mack had been friendly, but definitely nice-neighbourly, not I-think-about-you-all-the-time friendly. We'd talked about the cottage, Dawson's comics, family, the whole Fisher situation. But then he would check his watch and make his excuses, too soon. Way too soon. I'd begun to hate that book and its stupid deadline, his greedy, selfish publisher. I was more jealous of that book than I had been about Sienna.

There had been a couple of moments, when the conversation had fallen silent, or our eyes had met across the picnic table in the twilight. Ending up squashed together in the crowd watching the Christmas lights being turned on at the village green. The morning someone had knocked into me in the café and he'd flung one arm around my waist, grabbing the coffee-cup.

Okay, there had been quite a few moments. On my side. But I kept remembering Richard, and how I'd scooped up every smouldering glance, fallen for every last-minute request, been so utterly, completely wrong when it had come to love, lust and plain old lechery. The messages Mack and I exchanged every few days felt intimate to me, like the kind of conversation a couple would have. But they weren't that different from the texts I exchanged with Kiko, or Sarah. I had no idea where the lines were drawn. And I wasn't about to risk losing my friend again.

So, when Mack took a seat, nodded a hello to everyone, then crinkled his eyes at me, I hadn't the foggiest what that meant, beyond it making my heart sprout wings and do a loop around the Christmas tree. I hoped nobody had noticed, but, from the smirks and the raised eyebrows, I might have been kidding myself.

Ashley rambled a welcome. I didn't hear a word of it. Glancing at Mack, I found him looking straight at me. Embarrassed to be caught glancing, even though he was the one staring, I gulped down some water, praying I wasn't getting sweat patches on my top. Despite the freezing temperatures outside, it seemed to be growing hotter and hotter by the fire.

There was a subdued round of applause, and Mack cleared his throat.

'Ashley asked if I'd tell you about my new book. I don't want to give too much away, and at this point anything's liable to change, but I can tell you it's my favourite yet.'

'Is it set in Sherwood Forest?' Ashley asked.

'Yes.'

'And?'

'And...' Mack grew quiet. I risked a peek and found him gazing at the star-shaped lights twinkling amongst the bunting. He picked up his phone and fiddled with it, put it down again. Looked at me quickly, then back at his phone. 'It's different from the others, because it's written from a male point of view.'

'Tell us about this male,' Ashley breathed.

'Well, he's a bit of a chump, to be honest. He's made a monumental mistake, and instead of taking it on the chin, dealing with it, he's decided the best response is to wimp out on life, and hide away feeling sorry for himself. He justifies it by saying this way he won't mess up again, and won't get hurt. And, importantly, he won't hurt anyone else. He's spending every day in a mindless grey funk and wondering why he can't work any more – he's a songwriter, by the way. And then, one day, this woman turns up.'

I didn't have to move my eyes off the table to know every single person swivelled their head towards me.

Was it possible for a human woman to roast in her own hormones?

'And she's the opposite of him in every way – life has thrown her the biggest dungball, and she just pushes it off, dusts herself down and fights back with all this energy and bravado and determination. And she grabs this guy by the scruff of his neck and drags him out of his cave, back into the world.'

You have got to be kidding me.

I cannot breathe.

I managed to suck in one final, strangled breath. It turned out final breaths sounded like a hippopotamus hugging a windy warthog.

'Anyway.' Mack let out a shaky laugh. 'You'll have to read it to find out more.'

'Oh, we can't wait, can we?' Ashley said. 'It sounds simply incredible. Now, questions. I'll go first. Where did you get your inspiration from for this story, and was it you and Jenny?'

Excuse me? I opened my mouth to protest. Then I remembered I was desperate to hear the answer, so I shoved one of Jamie's mini mince pies in instead.

'Maybe, in parts. She is an inspiring person to know.' He coughed. 'Also, my parents. The Neil Diamond songs they play while cooking dinner. My sisters' families. The reintroduction of beavers into the UK. A conversation I overheard in the queue to buy a newspaper. And, as always, everyone I've ever met, and everywhere I've ever been, somehow mashing together inside my imagination and eventually congealing into something vaguely coherent. For starters.'

'Is it a love story?' Sarah asked.

Those naughty women. I begged a sinkhole to appear and swallow me up right there. While at the same time my ears nearly strained off the sides of my head.

'Yes. Falling in love with life again, mostly.'

'Mostly, but not completely?' Ashley needled.

'Put it this way. I don't think my regular readers will be disappointed. And that's all I'm saying. You really have to wait and read it.'

The conversation moved on as Mack answered more questions. I assumed they were about his other books, or his career in general. I'd given up listening, due to the more pressing issue of struggling to breathe. That, and my own wild thoughts careening about my head waving their hands about and screaming, '*Mack thinks I'm an inspirational person to know. That has to be a good thing, right? Can you inspire someone in a* bad *way? She inspired me to write a book about avoiding a disastrous rebound relationship with an annoying neighbour. HOW DO I INSPIRE YOU, MACK?*'

'Right, well, if there's no more questions, I'd best get back,' I vaguely heard Mack say, as if from the end of a very long tunnel.

Mack stood, his features in silhouette as he hovered on the edge of the glow cast from the candles. Tension crackled. Nobody moved or spoke.

Which seemed a little rude, considering he'd interrupted crafting his latest blockbuster to come and visit a village book club, and now nobody even offered a thank you, good luck or please come again when the book is finished.

Lucille sneezed, swiftly muttering, 'Damn, I'm so sorry,' as she fumbled for a tissue.

Kiko thrust a napkin at her. 'Shh!'

Mack rubbed a hand over his messy hair before carefully putting his hat on. He cleared his throat. Twisted his body round to look at the door, turned back.

'Can I walk you home?' he asked.

'I think he means you, Jenny,' Ellen stage-whispered, leaning closer. 'It would make sense, you being neighbours.'

I scrabbled my wits together, took the deepest breath I could, and jabbered out a sort of 'yes'.

So while the others finally offered appropriately enthusiastic goodbyes, I shrugged into my coat and hat, patting to check my keys and phone hadn't miraculously climbed out of the pocket, and we set off into the frosty night.

Walking. With Mack. In the dark.

Oh, boy.

44

As we entered the black of the forest, I slipped on a patch of ice. Mack, without breaking stride, took hold of my hand.

The feel of his hand wrapped around mine. Warm, assured, still a perfect fit. Gooey, tingling loveliness ran down my arm like honey and settled in my stomach.

Halfway home, he still hadn't spoken. Part of me didn't care, didn't care whether he felt me quaking. Wasn't bothered if he'd only taken my hand to stop me tripping, and had spent the rest of the time wondering how to extricate it without seeming rude. I could have kept on walking like that for hours, in and out of the moonlight, feet crunching on the frozen leaves in time with each another, the night deliciously chill against the throbbing heat beneath my skin, carrying the scent of pine trees.

But the other, possibly wiser, certainly bolder part of me had to get some answers. Like, what the heck was going on, for starters.

And when, as we reached the clearing behind our houses, the first few flakes of snow began to fall, softly twirling in the glow of the fairy lights I'd hung in every window, I took that as a sign.

Bursting with impatience and frustration and an unbearable mixture of fear and hope, I stopped beside the picnic bench.

Mack turned to face me, still holding onto my hand, his face silver in the moonlight, a snowflake settling on his eyelashes.

'You wrote a book about me.' I paused, corrected myself. 'About us.'

'No.'

Oh. Okay, then. Slightly embarrassing. Should we pretend this never happened?

'I wrote a book about two entirely fictional characters.' Mack looked away, as if searching for the words, then bent his head towards me once he'd found them. 'But I thought about you, about us, whether there could ever be an us, how it would happen, what I would say and how you would look when I said it, the whole time.'

'Oh.'

'Yeah. Oh.'

'So how did you imagine it would happen?'

He grimaced. 'Not like this.'

As I struggled to reply, he tugged on my hand. 'In my head, you looked pleased. Had that smile that makes my heart keel over. Not... anxious and uncertain and like I've just invited you to come and see the collection of human bones in my cellar.'

'I don't know what's happening here.' I did feel anxious, and uncertain, and suddenly very small.

Mack sat on the bench, gently pulling me down beside him. I could feel the heat of his body through the thick jacket he wore, my own body shivering involuntarily in response.

'You're freezing. Shall we go inside?'

I shook my head. Being out here in the dark made it easier. It felt safer, somehow, to do this half hidden in shadows. Mack unwrapped his scarf and wound it around my neck, frowning slightly as he adjusted my hat. When his hand skimmed the skin below my ears, I thought the air in my lungs froze.

He took a deep breath. 'What's happening is that, while I can write love scenes where strong, kind, sexily amusing men find the perfect words to tell a woman they've fallen for them, I'm discovering the reality is very different. Possibly because I'm not that strong, and probably not that kind, sexy or amusing. So, I guess what's happening is I'm messing this up.'

'I think you're *very* sexy,' I blurted out, to my horror. *Nice one, Jenny. Good choice. Much better than telling him he's kind, or strong, or amusing.*

Mack went completely still.

'Perhaps you'd like to have another go?' I offered, deciding we were way beyond nerves or embarrassment now.

'Okay... um... Jenny, being with you... it makes me feel like... Christmas every day?' His eyes widened in shock at the sheer horror of what he'd said, before we both burst out laughing as I punched his jacket.

'That is not a compliment! I hate Christmas, remember?'

He shook his head, cringing. 'This is why I have an editor.'

'You're telling me!'

'You just called me very sexy! I was... rendered insensible.' He slowly reached up and brushed a snowflake off my cheekbone with his knuckles. 'Okay. Last try. Come on, Mack, get it together! Right: Jenny. In the past few months I've realised some things about love, other than that I didn't know what I was talking about. I realised love is the person who knows you at your worst, while hoping for the best. It's wanting to know everything, but having all the time in the world to find that out.

'It's who you want to call when the roof leaks, destroying your office, or you write the first paragraph in months you feel proud of. It's dancing all night and, instead of hating it, it's the best night of your life, because being with them makes everything better. It's believing that maybe you can risk it all on one person again, because they are completely worth it. It's like waking up after years asleep and finding life isn't so hideous after all. It's breathtakingly beautiful if you know where to look. Who to look at.' He stopped, pulled a wonky smile. 'Any better?'

'That depends.'

His smile became an awkward laugh. 'Can you give me a hint? 'Cos I don't think I've got anything else.'

'Just to be completely clear, you are talking about me?'

He bent his head closer until I could see nothing but those molten eyes.

'I'm *always* talking about you. *Thinking* about you. Spending a ludicrous amount of money on an authentic Macintyre kilt in some warped attempt to impress you. Waiting for you.' He paused, swallowed, his voice no more than a breath. 'Loving you.'

I kept my eyes firmly fixed on his as I reached deep into every nerve, trying to summon up the composure to reply as my head spun and heart stuttered.

'I lied. I don't hate Christmas any more.'

He watched me, the hint of a smile on his lips.

'The two Christmases I've had this year were both just about perfect.' I dropped to a whisper. 'Because I spent them with you.'

The smile burst into a grin. 'Spend this Christmas with me and I promise you won't hate that one either.'

Mack placed one of his hands either side of my face. They were freezing against my flushed cheeks, but when he lent closer and pressed his lips against mine, I really didn't care.

'Well?'

'Yes, I'll spend another Christmas with you.'

We were both grinning so hard now we could barely manage to kiss again. But, hey, where there was a will there was a way.

'And the Christmas after that.'

'Yes.'

Another kiss.

'And the one after that?'

'Yes.'

This time, I ducked my head back before he could kiss me. 'Maybe we can continue this conversation inside, before we end up freezing to the bench and buried in snow?'

'That's a good idea. I've got a lot of Christmases I want to ask you about.'

I unlocked the cottage door, stamped the snow off my boots and shrugged out of my coat in the welcoming warmth. As I turned to face him, Mack wrapped me up in his arms, and I was home.

ACKNOWLEDGMENTS

This has been my first book working with an agent, and I owe huge thanks to Kiran Kataria, for not only seeing the book's potential, but for fantastic support and wise counsel which has transformed the process into a team effort. I'm also tremendously grateful to have been invited to join the Boldwood team, and have been boldwood-ed over by their enthusiasm and encouragement. Particular thanks to Sarah Ritherdon for her insightful editing.

Squash Harris was the main character in a series of books my daughter wrote in her early teens – thanks for the loan, Ciara, I hope Squash did you proud.

It's been a long road between books this time, and would have been a much harder one without the unfailing support of so many people: Jo, Pearl, Vicky and the Free Range Chicks' unfailing enthusiasm has been priceless. As has that of the Kings' church – I'm so blessed to call you my family. A particular mention to Julia Childerhouse – thank you for laughing with me, listening to me and loving me so well.

To everyone who has asked me when the next book is out,

written a review or got in touch to say you enjoyed the last one – it means the world, and makes all the difference. Thank you.

As always, much love to the Robbins' family for cheering me on and teaching me the importance of laughter (especially directed at myself). Ciara, Joseph, Dominic – seeing your stories unfold is my greatest joy. And George, being with you for the past 23 years has not been like Christmas every day... but whatever each day has been like, you've made it so much better.

MORE FROM BETH MORAN

We hope you enjoyed reading *Christmas Every Day*. If you did, please leave a review.

If you'd like to gift a copy, this book is also available as a ebook, digital audio download and audiobook CD.

Sign up to Beth Moran's mailing list for news, competitions and updates on future books.

http://bit.ly/BethMoranNewsletter

ABOUT THE AUTHOR

Beth Moran is the author of three previous books, including *Making Marion*. She regularly features on BBC Radio Nottingham and is a trustee of the national women's network Free Range Chicks. She lives on the outskirts of Sherwood Forest.

Visit Beth's website: https://www.bethmoran.org/

Follow Beth on social media:

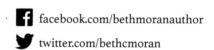

facebook.com/bethmoranauthor

twitter.com/bethcmoran

ABOUT BOLDWOOD BOOKS

Boldwood Books is a fiction publishing company seeking out the best stories from around the world.

Find out more at www.boldwoodbooks.com

Sign up to the Book and Tonic newsletter for news, offers and competitions from Boldwood Books!

http://www.bit.ly/bookandtonic

We'd love to hear from you, follow us on social media:

 facebook.com/BookandTonic

twitter.com/BoldwoodBooks

 instagram.com/BookandTonic